UNSHACKLED

THE SANDSTONE TRILOGY, BOOK 2

MICHAEL BEASHEL

UNSHAKLED

Michael Beashel

ISBN: 979 8 6913624 53

Publishing and Marketing Consultant: Lama Jabr
Website: https://xanapublishingandmarketing.com
Sydney, Australia

Cover by Mark Thacker, Big Cat Design
Front cover photograph: Getty Images

THE SANDSTONE TRILOGY

Three novels, *Unbound Justice*, *Unshackled* and *Succession*, span 37 years of Sydney life in the second half of the nineteenth century. They follow the fortunes of John Leary, who in 1850 leaves his rural home in Ireland and sails as an assisted immigrant to New South Wales.

His trade is carpentry but his ambition is boundless. By hard work, talent and opportunism he manages to create his own construction company, never ceasing the struggle to become the biggest and the best. The building industry becomes a metaphor for his chosen city, with its mixture of squalor and grandeur, of corruption and high ideals.

The Sandstone Trilogy is a historical drama with a rich cast of compelling characters. It is also a family saga, in which love, revenge and tragedy all come to influence the Learys' destiny.

'The author must have an intimate knowledge of the construction industry, considering the richness of the material and his passion for the subject.'

Robin Fleming
Acres Australia

THE CHARACTERS

The Leary Family
John Leary
Clarissa Leary (nÈe McGuire) John's wife

The McGuire Family
David McGuire, Clarissa's father
Christine McGuire, Clarissa's mother

The Connaire Family
Sean Connaire
Veronica (Vonnie) Connaire, Sean's wife

The Forde Family
Maureen Forde (nÈe Leary), John's sister
Liam Forde, Maureen's husband
Michael Forde, their son
Irene Mary Forde, their daughter

The Blacketts
Beth Blackett, (nÈe O'Hare)
Henry Blackett, her husband

The O'Hare Family
Jim O'Hare, Beth's father
Anne O'Hare, Beth's mother
Olivia and Sarah, Beth's sisters

Gerry Gleeson
John's and Maureen's uncle

Businessmen, Bankers and Bureaucrats

Brian Atkins
Gregory Blunt
Andrew Brown
Robert Clancy
James Finlayson
Rupert Jenkins
Malcolm Robinson
Harry Shelby
Bill Thomas
Damien Wexton

Leary's Employees

Frank Cartwright, chief estimator
Sean Connaire, general foreman
Jack Johnson, purchasing manager
Bob Jones, bricklayer foreman
Ed Larkin, carpenter foreman
Dan Reynolds, accountant
Barry Watson, foreman

CONTENTS

CHAPTER ONE

AT A DINNER PARTY IN A TOORAK MANSION, JOHN LEARY WAS watching his wife, Clarissa, as she chatted to their host. He couldn't help admiring her courage in being in public in her condition. It was like her to do that: she was fearless and independent. Two days out from their homeward journey to Sydney, after a six-week visit to Melbourne, her changed figure was just noticeable. A slight puffiness below her cobalt blue eyes was the only change to her clear features, but nausea had been her constant companion.

They had married in Sydney in February 1853 and the last two years had flown by in a blur of wedded bliss. It was while they were on this visit to Melbourne that Clarissa had told him she was expecting a child, and they were both excited at the prospect of their firstborn. A doctor in Collins Street had confirmed her pregnancy, and now they were looking forward to telling loved ones at home their news.

John Leary was doing well in the colony of New South Wales. After much hard work, he'd become a shareholder in an expanding construction business. His twenty-three-year-old wife was the key to his success, with her wealthy father, David McGuire, financing the company and holding the major share. During the last two years the company had grown to be a respected contractor for the building of warehouses, factories and mansions. But John wanted to be independent, not to be reliant on anyone. To do that he needed to be in a position to finance himself. But first he needed to build up his funds so he could extend the firm further and then he would show the world that John Leary could achieve success without needing Clarissa's father's money.

His first years as a struggling building worker haunted him like an unwelcome dream, reminding him that, but for luck, he'd still be pinching pennies—and also that his luck could change in a heartbeat, returning him to that time.

The dinner party came to an end. The hosts Timothy Paterson and his wife Jane were saying goodbye to their guests in their foyer. Clarissa seemed distracted. She turned to John and said, 'Dear, I've left my bracelet on the dinner table. I'll go back and get it.'

'Don't trouble yourself,' he said, helping her on with her coat, 'I'll go.'

John made his way back through the house and retrieved the bracelet from the dining table. He placed it in his pocket and was making his return when he overheard two women in conversation. Through a partly opened door he recognised one of the women as the sister of their host. He continued walking but stopped when he heard his name mentioned.

'No, it's not *his* money, dear. It's Mr McGuire's.'

'Really?'

'Indeed, it's his funds in the business, John Leary was penniless when he came to New South Wales. He'd still be a carpenter without McGuire. No, the man was lucky marrying into money.'

John's blood went cold. His shock morphed into irritation. The woman was right, and that's what galled him. He wasn't his own man. He continued on through the house, struggling to get himself under control. At the front door, Timothy Paterson was holding Clarissa's hand and smiling at her.

'He's just run an errand for me, Mr Paterson,' she was saying.

'Ah! Here he is,' Mrs Paterson said, looking at John.

Clarissa turned to John with the same smile, which changed just a little when she saw his face. Seeing her smile fade a little, John pushed his irritation aside.

'Mr Paterson has kindly arranged a cab for us, dear,' she said.

John extended his hand, which was gripped by his host. 'Thank you for a wonderful evening.'

'Our pleasure, Mr Leary,' Paterson said. 'Please write to us next time you're both in Melbourne. We'd very much enjoy seeing you again. Give my regards again to Mr McGuire.'

John kept his face animated, but his irritation remained at the mention of his father-in-law. 'Thank you,' he said, 'we shall.'

Mrs Paterson took hold of Clarissa's hand and said in a low voice, 'And all our best wishes for your forthcoming baby.'

'Thank you, Mrs Paterson,' Clarissa smiled. 'You are too kind.'

John took Clarissa's elbow and escorted her out into the late July chill to the waiting cab. He was still thinking about the comments he'd overheard in the house.

'Are you all right, dear?' she asked.

He wouldn't let his mood spoil an otherwise wonderful evening. 'Yes,' he said, smiling at her. 'I'm all right. Just feeling a bit off. It might have been the oysters I ate.'

She smiled. 'You did have a few.'

'Indeed, I did!'

The dusk enveloped the Sydney-bound steam clipper and Clarissa glanced at the other first-class passengers on the deck reserved for those fortunate enough to pay the fare. She turned to John. 'Does this remind you of our voyage out?'

John smiled. 'It does.' Five years earlier he'd come to the colony as a twenty-year-old assisted Irish migrant. He was a trained carpenter and had emigrated with the ambition to become a master builder—not an unreasonable dream in the rapidly growing colony of New South Wales. Clarissa and her mother had been on the same ship, though they were travelling as paid passengers. There had been an instant attraction between John and Clarissa, which over the months of the journey had developed into a strong bond.

John put his arm around her and said, 'I know the first thing you'll do when we get home.'

She smiled and stretched up to push aside a lock of hair that cloaked his blue eyes. 'And what's that?'

He smiled down at her, 'Tell your mother about the baby.'

'She will be overjoyed!' she said, leaning her head against his chest. At five-feet-four she was almost a foot shorter than him. She placed a hand on her stomach and John felt her tense.

'What's wrong?' he said.

'Just a cramp. Oh, I can't wait till it's born.'

'Nor can I, but for now, I'm keen to see Sean and find out how the jobs are going.'

'They'll be all right,' Clarissa said. She shivered. 'Come, let's go below.'

In their cabin later, as Clarissa slept beside him, John stared into the darkness, worrying about the business. He thought of the company as his, but in truth he was only one of three shareholders. His father-in-law, David McGuire, had changed the shareholding in his favour in June the previous year, so that John owned 40 per cent of the company, his good friend and general foreman Sean Connaire held 9 per cent and Clarissa's father held the remaining 51 per cent. Though McGuire wasn't a builder, he held the power and was a cautious man who took minimum risks. John wanted Leary's Contracting to be the biggest and the best and he couldn't do that if David McGuire hobbled him.

In the bowels of a three-storey warehouse in Clarence Street, Sean Connaire sweated in the late afternoon Sydney haze. 'Jesus,' he said, 'the day's warm, it is.'

'Mate, especially for July,' the carpenter foreman replied. 'I'm drier than a Baptist. The first beer at Cochranes won't touch the sides.'

'That it won't, Jack. But if you're comin' down to the pub with me tonight, then shake a leg.'

'All right, boss, all right, keep your shirt on.'

Sean felt he was in the midst of chaos. His job foreman was ill and Sean had stepped in to run the site. The job had to be finished by Christmas. Carpenters, lined four in a row, were nailing like fury, keeping up the pace to lay the boards to the first-floor framing. Masons above them were yelling for more mud, and the walls were under way. Their client, Finlayson's, hadn't paid them for the last month's work and Sean, as a part owner, should have done something about it. Finlayson's had given him a barrowful of excuses why they hadn't paid for the work carried out, and he'd heard they were having money troubles. Sean wasn't a businessman, he was a carpenter and a damned good one. A small private company always needed cash, John had said.

'Jack, keep these chippies under control,' Sean said. 'I'll check the brickies.'

'Right, Sean.'

Sean climbed the ladder to the scaffolding above where labourers were mixing mud and filling buckets to serve the six brick-layers who were laying the common bricks to the outside walls up to the roof. Sean eyed the vertical mortared joints between the bricks, the perpends. 'Keep them aligned. I'll check on them tomorrow.'

One heavyweight bricklayer wiped the sweat from his forehead and pointed his trowel at his work. 'I don't lay my bricks any other way, Mr Connaire.' He grinned and said, 'I'll even give you a plumb bob and you can line them up yourself. You know my work.'

'I do, Dan. Just keep up the quality, like on Cochranes.' Sean scanned their work area with a keen eye. 'Don't overload those planks. No more bricks there.' A labourer nodded and speared his shovel into the mix to turn more mud, its odour pungent.

Cochranes in Day Street—that's where Sean had met John Leary, who'd been the supervising foreman on that pub. Leary was ambitious. Sean had never met such an impatient and restless tradesman. He seemed to be driven by a demon to get ahead. Not content to learn and make good his trade as a master carpenter, the man wanted to get on the next rung and, once that was achieved, up to the next. Which was why John wanted to control his own company.

Satisfied the brickwork was in order, Sean shimmied down two ladders and stepped around the trenches, scanning the earthenware. Thirty feet of clay pipes, their collars packed with cement, lay in the excavated sandstone under a string line. He closed one eye and checked the alignment. Good. 'When are the pans coming again, Harry?'

The plumber stood up, his hands caked in fresh mud. 'The day after tomorrow, with the basins.'

'Those toilets have to be finished this week.'

'That they will be, boss.'

'The council inspector?' Sean said. 'When's he coming?'

'Tomorrow morning.'

'Good, I'll be here with you to meet him.' Sean continued his site inspection, making sure all was shipshape.

The captain raised his glass to his passenger, 'Mr Leary, tomorrow is the end of our trip. I hope it has been pleasant.'

'It has, thank you, Captain. My wife and I have admired your seamanship and enjoyed your company.' John looked out the port-hole at the sunset, its glow reflected against the swell. 'When do you think we'll dock?'

'At first light, you should be able to spot the entrance to the harbour. We'll tie up about two hours later.'

Clarissa stood up. 'Captain, if you don't mind, my husband and I will say goodnight.' John also stood up, keeping his head bent to avoid the low ceiling. They made their goodbyes to the other dinner guests and went below to their cabin.

Clarissa was paler than usual.

John took her hand. 'Are you feeling all right?'

'Yes,' she said and smiled.

He kissed her. 'Good. If you don't mind I'll go topside, and have a final smoke.'

'Don't you want to read? Some poetry might set you at ease.'

'Byron can wait,' he said, smiling. 'I'll be along shortly.'

Up on the aft section of the deck, he looked out on the sea wake and the phosphorescence shimmering behind him. Things were going well on the home front, he had a loving wife whom he adored, a baby on the way and their future was bright. He was eager to get back to work and he wondered how Sean had managed while he was away. Thinking of work reminded him of those comments he'd overheard at that Paterson dinner party. They still irritated him. He flung his cigar butt into the Tasman Sea and returned to the cabin. Tomorrow couldn't come soon enough.

At ten o'clock the next morning, the clipper took the tension on its mooring lines at Albion Wharf, Darling Harbour and the familiar smell of Sydney—its smoke and tanneries, dung and dust— returned. Two crew members extended the gangplank and John and Clarissa waited to disembark.

'There they are!' she said.

David McGuire and his wife Christine waved to them from the wharf. David was a tall, slim, good-looking man in his fifties. Christine had a trim figure and pleasant features but, John noted, wore her usual wary expression.

Once in the carriage, Christine looked down at her daughter's figure, raising an eyebrow as she looked up at her face.

Clarissa responded, laughing. 'Yes, Mother, I'm expecting.'

David's face lit up and he shook his head. 'A baby!'

'Yes Father, and it'll be born around the end of the year.'

David took Clarissa's hands and squeezed them. 'That's wonderful news. Wonderful.'

'Congratulations to you both,' Christine said. 'It's God's blessed gift and we rejoice in that.'

Christine's eyes glistened and John was glad. 'Thank you, Christine,' he said.

'Not at all, son-in-law, not at all.'

'I'm still unwell most mornings, Mother.'

'That will pass, my dear. We'll talk all about it when we get home. So, how was your sojourn?'

'John spent two weeks looking at wire suppliers, including ... Patersons, dear?'

'Yes,' John said. He'd almost forgotten the business connection, only remembering the dinner party. 'Timothy Paterson,' he said. 'I'll talk to you about it later, David.'

'But we had some restful times,' Clarissa continued, 'between the theatre, parties and sightseeing.'

'Excellent,' David said. 'A grandchild! How grand is that.'

On their way home, John glimpsed familiar sights and sounds as the carriage bumped and swung along the toll road down to Woolloomooloo.

'I know Point Piper's a bit of a journey from town,' David said, 'but I wouldn't change it. Just to get away from the smoke and smell and to be on the waterfront with the bush behind is a blessing.'

After the midday meal, John and David moved to the study. As he admired the views over Blackburn Cove, John thought about how their company had come to be formed in this very space, which, like the rest of the house, he had built.

'It's good to have you back, John.'

John nodded and smiled. 'Thank you.' He'd missed their banter about business and the dynamics of Sydney's explosive growth. And he'd missed David, too, who'd been a surrogate father to him since he'd come to the colony. That's what troubled him. John liked the man, very much, but he couldn't separate the fact that David still had control of Leary's.

'So, how is wire selling down there?' David asked. McGuire Wire made and sold fencing wire and it was a profitable business.

'All suppliers, including Patersons, have their hands full just meeting demand in Victoria. None showed any interest north of the Murray River.'

'Good. Then New South Wales will still be ours to fence. The trip's been worthwhile.' David handed him a file. 'Read that before you get to work tomorrow. It'll bring you up to date.'

'Could you just give me a summary now?'

David paused. 'We're still having material supply problems. Timber and bricks.'

'The whole industry is suffering,' John said, 'not just us. So what's changed?'

'Because we're still a young company, suppliers are bypassing us even more. The majority of the goods are going to the bigger builders.'

'They always did.'

'It's got worse, John.'

'What? In six weeks?'

'Indeed. We're being delayed and have to make up time when we finally get deliveries. That adds to our costs.'

'What about early payment, or payment on delivery?'

David waved his hand in dismissal. 'I started that a week after you left, but no change so far.'

'We have to get more work,' John said. 'More jobs will get us better attention from the suppliers.'

'Granted. But more jobs will demand more workmen.'

'The situation is improving. There are more available tradesmen than there were a year ago.'

David smiled. 'Agreed, and our cash flow has improved, overall. Finlaysons are a slow payer though.'

'How's Clarence Street going?' John asked.

David pointed to the file. 'Sean's report is in there. It's on schedule but there's a money issue. I'll let you follow that up. With you being away, I've neglected my other business. Never mind, you're back now, and you can get us more work, too.'

John opened his file and started to read. He was back in the fray, doing what he loved.

Clarissa and her mother were discussing the important forthcoming event.

'Did you know you were expecting before your trip?'

'I thought I was, Mother, but I had to be sure before telling you.'

'Well, we've got you here now and can look after you—and more importantly our grandchild.' Her eyes glistened. 'I still can't believe it!' She clasped Clarissa's hands and squeezed. 'I did so wish for you to have a baby. Ever since your marriage, I've prayed for it.'

'I have too and now it's here. I'm happy, so happy. A little boy—'

'Or a girl.'

'Or a girl.' Clarissa smiled.

Christine took the silver teapot and poured two cups, giving one to her daughter. 'When in December is the baby due?'

'The doctor in Melbourne confirmed it would be around the end.'

'There's not a moment to lose. One of the bedrooms upstairs must be changed to a nursery, things to buy—my goodness.'

Clarissa smiled again. Knowing her mother's penchant for organising things, she herself would have to take the lead, otherwise Christine would plan everything down to the last detail. And yet, there was something nice in that, she thought, looking at her mother, whose eyes were shining with excitement. She would let her help, let her choose some nursery items, at least. 'There's a lot to do,' she said, 'and I've got my own thoughts about arranging upstairs. It'll only be temporary. John's got plans for a new house for us—not far from here.' Christine's face registered surprise and Clarissa chastised herself for her lack of tact.

'That's nice, but land is getting expensive, and he may not be able to afford—'

'I know,' Clarissa said, fighting off a sudden bout of nausea. 'We're in your loving care. Let's just get things ready for the baby. John and I have time to worry about the rest.'

Her mother put her teacup on the tray, nodded and smiled. 'Yes, of course.'

Clarissa knew John was keen to move into their own home as soon as possible, but she hoped it wouldn't be until after the birth of their child. Giving birth seemed frightening but at least her mother would be with her, which gave Clarissa some comfort. And this baby would be her mother's first grandchild: she would welcome her new role and give the baby all the love she had.

In his George Street office, John looked at his desk calendar. He shook his head. Here it was the middle of September. He'd been in Melbourne for six weeks and had been back in the saddle six weeks, yet the time had flashed by. The new lease for their premises lay on his desk. He checked and found two documents missing, appendices on the list of fixtures and fittings.

'Mrs Dawes,' he called out to his secretary.

'Yes, Mr Leary,' she said.

'Come in here.'

She came in with pad and pencil.

John held up the lease to her. 'Where are the appendices? They should be with the lease.'

'I have them. They were——'

'I need them now.'

Mrs Dawes was in her forties and highly competent but John was angry. He sensed that she knew why. It had to do with money, rent and control. 'Bring them to me,' he said.

'But Mr Leary, you asked me to check on two things for you. That's why I had those documents.'

'You should have done them by now.'

'I'm sorry. I still need to get——'

'What? Get what?'

He saw that she was surprised by his bullying manner. He'd never treated her like that before, but he couldn't help himself.

'The final Leary's stores list,' she said. 'You asked me to be accurate. You said——'

'Yes, yes, very well. Just bring me what you have. That'll do for now. Come on, I don't want to be kept waiting.'

'Yes, sir.'

She returned with the two documents and placed them on his desk. He said nothing, picked them up and watched her leave. He knew he shouldn't have spoken to her the way he did, but he didn't have time to worry about that now. He'd sort it out with her later. For now, he had to concentrate on the lease.

He was in two minds about renewing it. The rent demanded was 10 per cent higher and he really should look for a cheaper place, but it suited him to be located in town near his jobs. Their building consisted of two floors: an open area for work desks, a kitchen and meeting room on the ground floor, and three offices on the first floor for himself, the accountant and chief estimator. There was a yard at the back that stored construction equipment, four shelves of scaffolding and some machinery. Collecting his lease papers, he'd decided to renew it.

Four of Leary's five projects, including a factory in Newtown that they'd just won, were on schedule and to budget, but Clarence Street was a problem. Finlayson's hadn't paid for work done in July and John was ready to stop work and lodge a notice under the contract. Looking down at the letter on his desk, he was satisfied with its contents. It would cost them wages for the down time, but enough was enough. The client had to pay for the work contracted. He'd told Sean the previous day that he should get things ready to stop work and make the site safe, in case the client's cheque was not received in two days' time.

He looked up and saw that it was dark outside; the time had flown by again. He got his jacket and hat from his cupboard and headed out the door of his office. 'Goodnight, Mrs Dawes,' he said and added a note of reconciliation. 'Enjoy your evening.'

She seemed pleased at his change in mood. 'Thank you, Mr Leary. Oh, before you go, Frank wants a word.'

'Right,' John said and he stepped into the office adjoining the accountant's where Frank, his chief estimator, worked. Frank looked up from his desk as John walked in.

'Will you be in the office in the morning? I have to go over this Annandale tender with you. The Branstons job.'

'I can do it first thing. Seven?'

'Good. Thanks boss.'

John departed his office buoyed by the prospect of maybe adding another job to his business and better, more cash flow to pay for his now increased rent.

Two people were waiting for the accident to happen—the watcher on the Leary's Clarence Street site and the one who'd paid the watcher. The watcher stared up at the worker on the plank thirty feet away. It must happen soon, the watcher thought, cramped among the new timber. It has to. Beads of perspiration stood out on his forehead, some sliding down to drop on his leather apron. *I cut the underside of the plank. I fixed it so the whole thing will go, wall and all.*

The worker stopped and raised his head. He stacked another brick. The plank groaned, the worker paused and the watcher grinned.

Sean left his site hut, feeling angry, and looked around. He had two days to stop work and get the site closed up for what he guessed would be more than a week. He hated doing that. Time would be wasted in getting the trades demobbed and off site and then if they were successful, in trying to get going again to full swing.

There was action everywhere; they were at the peak of the site's schedule. *Bloody client! They wouldn't pay what they owed in forty-eight hours! It's a bastard.* Sean climbed one ladder, then another to the top floor with its completed timber joists. He had a quick look around and, satisfied, went back to the ground floor and made his way to the entrance of the warehouse where two carpenters were securing timber jambs to frame the main opening. Sean watched them work. 'Make sure that opening's square,' he said. 'It's fourteen feet neat, not a sixteenth of an inch either way. I don't want any complaint from the joiners when they come to measure up for the doors.'

One carpenter put down his drill and wiped his forehead. 'Thinking like you, boss. I've had the tape—'

A roar filled Sean's ears, followed by a scream. *God, what was that? It sounded like . . . no, couldn't be, not a collapse . . . no, not on his site!*

He looked up and a dust cloud stung his eyes. The haze cleared to show a jumbled heap of brickwork, scaffolding and timber which a second ago had been a large part of the second-floor superstructure. He saw a man covered in debris lying at the bottom of the twisted mess, shining in fresh spattered blood, one arm at a grotesque angle. Sean's stomach heaved and he leaned against the nearest wall. The two carpenters attacked the debris to get their trapped mate out. Sean looked above them, worried about the rest of the structure. One side of an unsupported second-floor wall wavered in the air. He yelled, 'Look out, get out of the way!' The teetering wall seemed to hesitate, then fell in an accelerating arc and the two chippies disappeared under it. Sean staggered. *Sweet Jesus.*

Then silence filled the site. Wind gusts blew the dust away, leaving behind the ferrous smell of blood. Men stood transfixed as if caught in a dream, quiet as a cemetery.

Sean's heart was pumping as though it would burst through his skin. Sweat broke out on him. Then a speck smarted his eye and jolted him as Ed Larkin arrived by his side. The workmen were dazed. They looked to him for direction. One glance told him that not much more would fall yet, but they didn't have much time to get things to rights.

'Jack,' Sean said. 'Go to the city hospital and get an ambulance back here, then go to the office and tell Mr Leary what's happened. Harry, you and the others clear this, but not until a team secures the roof.' The joint, where the walls had once been, looked like a snapped tree after a storm. 'The other walls want bracin', and no one leaves till I tell 'em. We'll want lanterns for tonight, ropes and grub. Team foremen get cracking.'

Things happened fast. The men seemed glad he'd taken action. It was ugly work, pulling debris from bodies, not knowing where to start. Hard men, men who'd fight in a pub and break skin at the drop of a hat were like babies playing at blocks, all fingers and toes, not knowing where to start. One twenty-stone man let out a sigh as he covered a body with a tarp. Others were gentle in handling the remains of their dead workmates.

Sean's heartbeat returned to normal. *This was bad, real bad.* He shook his head as he fought his nausea. Death meant the police, the press and his partners all demanding answers.

On the floor above Sean, the watcher nodded. It had worked better than he'd wished. He was annoyed about the deaths but glad about the destruction.

A carpenter, near him, stared at him and yelled. 'Don't just stand there, lend a hand!'

The watcher nodded again. His job done.

It took John ten minutes to rush to Clarence Street from his George Street office, oblivious to other pedestrians, carriages and coaches passing by. The horror of three deaths. Nausea rose in him, burning and tearing.

'Watch out, mate.'

John leaned back as a loaded dray missed him by inches. He coughed as the dust engulfed him and the driver's curses faded. That would have solved his problems—his troubles gone in one blow of a wagon's wheel. His pulse returned to normal as he breathed long and hard, several times. Determination surged in him, just for a heartbeat, but it was there.

Think. Think, he told himself. *What to do first?* Nothing came to mind and he concentrated on what was in front of him. Ironically, this area had seen his first successes. Even today there was building activity everywhere and shops along George Street still sold gold fossicking paraphernalia: woollen shirts, picks, shovels, tents, pots and canvas. John remembered the first strike in 1851, and how with tradesmen in short supply, a lot of them hotfooting it to the lure of the yellow metal, opportunity had resulted in promotion for him. That time seemed an eternity ago now as he came onto the scene of the accident.

A small crowd had gathered at the site's entrance and John forced his way through and stopped. The collapse was worse than he'd imagined. The ambulance had arrived. A blood-stained tarp caught his eye. Underneath it were the bodies of three Leary's workers. John's legs felt weak. He saw Sean and waved him to come over. He led him to a quiet corner. 'What happened?'

he asked.

Sean shook his head, his face haggard 'It just collapsed. The whole top back wall just fell.'

'How?'

'I don't know, John.'

'Was it braced?'

'Yes.' Sean wiped his face. 'One died in the fall and two others copped it trying to dig him out.'

Workers were busy with ropes and timbers and John could see that Sean had made good progress on securing the structure. 'Dear God Almighty! Who were they?'

'Spiers, Hughes and Cronin.'

John knew them. 'Have you called the police?'

'They're on their way.' As the ambulance workers passed him with their terrible loads, Sean crossed himself and John did the same.

John looked at Sean. 'Do you need anything?'

'Just the cause of all this,' his partner said.

'Get it, Sean, and get it quickly.'

The site was quiet now. The flickers from the hurricane lamps made the workmen's shadows dance in the darkness and Sean's nose tweaked at the smell of destruction. Workmen were superstitious, like sailors, but stoic about death. Most of the men took things in their stride: many of them had seen their siblings pass away and their own fathers die young. Sean turned to the policeman and said. 'I don't know how the accident happened, it was in front of me and I . . . then it happened.'

The police sergeant scratched his head and turned to his subordinate. 'Take good notes. Mark the date, the eighteenth of September. We'll need a statement from anyone who saw anything.' The sergeant turned to Sean. 'Mr Connaire, do you have a list of your workers? I'll be needing that.'

'I do, but I'm sure none of them were responsible for this,' Sean said, waving his arm at the debris 'It must've been the materials.' He sighed. 'I just don't know.'

The police sergeant glanced at him and said nothing.

Sean looked down. He was sure that faulty materials—the mortar most likely—had probably caused the disaster and if so, the responsibility was his. He had no time to waste. He'd grill the bricklayer and his labourers first. It was lousy timing, what with the client not paying, the workmen screaming for their wages, and now this.

The police report wouldn't make good reading and the *Herald* newspaper would be here tomorrow with their journalists crawling all over his site. He had a lot of work to do, and a big problem to solve.

The watcher waited in the passage behind the Hero of Waterloo Hotel. A southerly gust rattled the iron sheeting near him, making him jump. He shrank further into the shadows as a well-dressed man came up beside him.

'So, it worked?' he said.

The watcher nodded. 'It did.'

Ten crisp one-pound bank notes couldn't disguise a large knob on the man's left hand.

The watcher palmed the money and said, 'Pity about the men killed 'cause I'd got to know one of them.'

'Killed?' The gentleman hissed, leaning menacingly towards him.

'Yeah, pity.'

The man stared at him for a long time. 'I told you. A disruption, slow the site, something small ... not that!' He shook with anger and closed his eyes. 'Tell me about it. Tell me everything.'

The worker shrugged. 'He wasn't a bad bloke. The partly-cut plank worked a treat and with the loosened scaffolding and dodgy lime that I swapped for the good stuff, yeah, better than I'd hoped.'

The well-dressed man's eyes widened. 'That's horrific, man. What have you done?'

'You wanted action.'

'Good God almighty! This is a disaster.' He paused. 'But it's done now. Get the hell out of Sydney. Word will get around quicker than a new gold strike.' Digging a hand into the pocket of his tailored jacket, he gave more money to the watcher. 'You'd better lie low for now. Don't go back to your lodgings. Make sure you're on the next boat to Melbourne tomorrow. And stay there. Stay there for the next twelve months.'

The watcher nodded and left. The well-dressed man grimaced. *Jesus wept! I only wanted to slow Leary down. The police will be all over this like flies on shit.*

Sean's site looked like a rubbish pit. A clutch of thrown-together timbers braced the remnants of the warehouse's upper side walls. Everything was a hotchpotch. Sean seethed.

During the previous twenty-four hours he and the architect had sweated to find the reason for the collapse. Sean was as sure as he could be that it was caused by a dodgy mortar mix, and he was even surer it was deliberate. The architect had gone over the specifications, worried that perhaps he'd left out something basic, but he'd found everything was in order. And that made sense, otherwise the rest of the walls would be suspect too, and they weren't. Sean had interrogated Bob Jones, the bricklaying foreman, who'd told him he could vouch for all of his labourers, except one who'd only signed on a week ago and had now disappeared. Could the missing labourer be the key?

Sean had also been helping the police with their enquiries, taking samples of mortar and selected debris away for checking, and he'd given them a list of the workmen on the site. Hunger pains gripped him; he couldn't remember when he'd last eaten. It was now late in the afternoon and the insurance investigator stood by his side. The man was good at his job and had made a thorough examination of the site.

Sean scratched his head. 'You know,' he said to the investigator, 'I haven't seen anything like this in all me years of building.'

'Perhaps, Mr Connaire. However, as you may or may not know, the contribution of negligence to the cause of the accident will be taken into consideration in any final recommendation of payment. Indeed, the final payment may be reduced if your company has been found to be negligent.'

Sean kicked the ground in anger and looked up as John Leary walked towards them, his face solemn.

Leary looked at the insurance man. 'How long to complete the investigation?'

The man placed his pencil in his jacket and closed his compendium. 'Matter of fact, I'm just finishing up. I take it, Mr Leary, that you're aware of the circumstances of the accident?'

John nodded and glanced at Sean, who hadn't had anything further to tell his boss from their last meeting. Now was crunch time. His senior partner and the insurance man stood either side of him like two bookends crushing the guilt from him.

'Leary's Contracting Ltd,' John said, 'is experienced. This sort of incident isn't typical. Indeed, it's a first.'

'That may be,' the investigator said, 'but your construction company is just over two years old, and this is the largest job it's built and for which it is insured.'

'It is a new company,' John agreed, 'but we, myself and my partners, Mr Connaire here and my father-in-law Mr McGuire, seek the AMP's payment of the total cost of reconstruction of this warehouse. Anything less than that will be regarded by us as a breach of the policy and I will seek to remedy such shortfall, if any, within the due processes of the law.'

The investigator adjusted his tie. 'It's my job, Mr Leary, to obtain the details of the accident and damage caused, and to make my recommendation. It will be up to the AMP partners to assess the amount of compensation. May I bid you both good day. You'll receive formal correspondence in due course.'

With that he stomped over a mound of broken bricks and left the site.

Sean watched the investigator's retreating back before he turned and spoke to John. 'Thanks for them words. I didn't tell the investigator everything. I think it was the—'

'Sean,' John said, his voice harsh, 'the shed.'

John collected his thoughts as he headed to the shed. Sean was the boss here, the one in charge. He should have seen it coming. The accident could've been avoided. Was Sean back on the drink? With each step towards the shed, John was becoming angrier. Yes, Sean had stumbled. He had wanted more responsibility and more say. Maybe this job was too big for him? Maybe he had let things happen, closed his eyes to sloppy work? Missed things.

John ducked inside the shed. 'Close the door,' he said to Sean. He grabbed a chair, leaned on it and looked around. All the drawings were in order, the schedules of work all marked up and the paperwork filed. John felt himself shaking. His face muscles were tight. 'I want an explanation,' he said.

Sean scratched his head and scowled.

John was losing patience. 'What happened, Sean?'

'I can't make it out. I think I've found the answer, but I'm trying to find the person. I think it was the brickie's labourer, a bloke called Miller.'

'You *think* you know,' John said. 'Either you know or you don't. Which is it?'

Two vertical creases appeared above Sean's nose. 'Don't come the heavy with me, John.'

'Why not?'

Sean's chest heaved. 'Now, come on. I did everything right, everything.' He banged the table. 'It just happened.'

'But deaths, Sean, bloody deaths, for Christ's sake! On *your* watch.' He let go of the chair, clenched his fists then unclenched them, then grabbed a roll of plans and flung them in the corner. 'Bloody hell!'

Sean turned to the window and looked out. 'It's been hell, mate. I haven't slept. The wife's worried. The kids are strangers to me. They're scared of me.' He looked at John and said in a quiet voice, 'Me, their own father who loves them more than life.'

John wasn't to be put off by Sean's sorrow. 'I want answers. You didn't see anything?'

'Nothin'. It was busy, it was. Men crowding the site like a pub at opening time. But I knew what was going on, in every corner.'

'You're sure?'

'I'm sure, John. I had good help. The boys kept watch about safety. They—'

'But it's your job to supervise, to run this site.'

'I did supervise.' Sean looked hard at him. 'What are you saying? You blaming me? Do ya think I'd let three men die? Do you?'

John's fists clenched again. 'You're the boss here. It's your responsibility. Yes, you're to blame.'

Sean's shoulders sagged. 'I know. That's why I can't sleep.'

'You haven't been back on the booze, have you?'

'No! Haven't touched it. *I haven't touched it.* How could you ask that?'

Sean was an alcoholic and his lapses had been fewer these last two years.

'I'm your boss,' John said. 'It's my right. Three men dead, Sean. Three men.'

Sean's face was haggard and for the first time John realised what he was going through. Sean, his best and only general foreman, was good at his job and the safety of his site and of his men was always his top priority. More, Sean was a stickler for quality and knew his materials and the skill of his workers. There had to be another cause.

'I'm a good general foreman,' Sean said. 'I know everything that happens on my site . . .'

'Not everything,' John said with emphasis.

Sean blinked. 'I've thought about nothing but them dead men and their . . . families every second.'

'Yeah, well, that's not going to help them.' John sighed. 'David had a visit from Finlayson this morning. Haven't seen him in a month of Sundays and in walks our client as bold as brass and would you believe it, he's threatening legal action.'

'What the hell. He's the one who owes us heaps. Hasn't paid us in ages. I think—'

John held up his hand. 'That's what we're up against. He's all bluster but he's not the one I'm worried about. It's what he says to others. Our reputation will suffer.'

John tapped Sean's chest. 'Get the answers. I want facts. I want to know what happened and who to hold responsible. That's your job. You've got a week and I want you to prove to me that you don't deserve sacking.' John pushed past him and left the shed.

Bloody great. Sean sat down, hung his head in his hands. Instead of being supportive, John had turned on him, blamed him. He didn't deserve that.

Then the shed door opened. It was Bob Jones, the bricklaying foreman.

'Boss, I've found something. Come with me.'

Sean was about to get John back but decided against it. It was his site and he was the one to solve this. He joined Bob and they climbed the scaffold and went to a rear side wall, which was half demolished by the accident. The foreman stopped at a section of wall. With little effort he pulled out an exposed brick and pointed to the remaining brickwork.

'See, Sean,' Bob said, 'it's the mortar mix for sure. The rest of the brickwork is useless and would have fallen anyway. It was the labourer that I put on—he was the one who did the mix.'

'Miller?'

'The same. We can't find him and the address he gave us wasn't right.'

Sean took the brick from the foreman and looked at it. Bob Jones knew bricks and mortar like a mother knows her children. The brick shouldn't have come out so easily from the wall. The mortar had not stuck to it. Sean threw the brick to the ground and swore. 'Bob, you'll have to get me that man. Bring him before me so I can throttle him in front of his workmates. Then, if he's in a fit state to walk and talk, I'll take him to the nearest police station and have the greatest pleasure in seeing him charged and watch him hang.'

Bob Jones smiled and nodded. 'Aye Sean, 'tis a good idea. But there's one thing wrong with it.'

'And what's that?'

'Miller won't be in any fit state for you to see him once I've finished with him.'

Sean nodded. 'Just catch the bastard.'

John entered his in-laws' house that night, went to the lounge room and found Clarissa seated on the sofa. 'How are you, dear?' he said.

'Good evening, John,' a voice said from behind him.

Turning around, John saw his mother-in-law coming into the room. 'And good evening to you, Christine. How was the Orphans' Event?'

'It went off very well, thank you.'

'And did you get many admiring glances on your new hat?'

Christine seemed pleased. 'I did.'

'Good.' His mother-in-law was in a very good mood.

'I'm so looking forward to having a grandchild,' she said. 'It won't be long now.'

'No, it won't. We can't wait for the birth either.' He took Clarissa's hand. 'How is your nausea? Have you eaten anything?'

Clarissa cringed as if the thought of food would make her

vomit. 'Nothing. I couldn't stand to eat anything. How are things at work? Is Sean managing on Clarence Street?'

He wouldn't tell them about the accident just yet. 'He is.'

'Are you sure? You look a bit strained.'

'I'm all right,' he said. 'There's a lot to do but nothing you have to worry about.'

Clarissa nodded twice but her worry lines remained. John sensed she didn't believe him. 'Can I get you something to drink?' he said.

'I'd like a lime and bitters drink, please, with some of that crushed ice. It seems the only thing to settle me these days.'

John stirred her drink and poured himself a Jameson's whiskey. David arrived and they went in to dinner.

After the meal, Clarissa and Christine repaired to the drawing room. Clarissa poured herself a glass of water from a pitcher and noticed the daily newspaper. Putting down the glass, she took the paper over to the lounge and started to read.

There wasn't much happening in Sydney town, and she turned to the world news section of the paper. There was still war in the Crimea, and it looked as though England had the upper hand. Flicking through the pages, she came to the society news. She smiled, then frowned as she read on. 'Mother, do you remember a girl called Beth O'Hare? You know the girl John introduced us to at church in the early days, before we were married?'

Christine paused with needle and thread. 'O'Hare? Yes, I think so. A bar girl? Is that the one?'

'That's her. It says here that she's just come back from her honeymoon.' Clarissa read on. 'Her husband Henry Blackett is a leading horse breaker.'

'A horse breaker? Are you sure? That doesn't sound like that young lady we met.'

'I hope she's as happy in her marriage as John and I are,' Clarissa said. Yawning, she stood up and said she thought she'd go to bed. Her mother wished her goodnight. As she headed to the stairs, she saw John coming out of the study; his lips were set firm, his jaw muscles tight.

'Coming to bed, dear?' she asked.

A smile replaced his frown. 'I'll be up in a while. I'm just going outside to have a cigar.'

'Perhaps some reading after that?' she said.

But John hadn't heard her. As she trudged up the stairway, she thought, there's something troubling him. *I know it.*

At the end of the following week, John came to the Clarence Street site and grimaced. The repair work to the walls stood out, with the new brickwork and its drying mortar stark against the old. The average punter couldn't tell the difference but to those in the know, it was a renovation job. The job was now back to where it was when they issued the notice to Finlayson's, but there'd be no more work on the site until they paid up.

The police report had confirmed Sean's suspicion that the wall had been sabotaged by faulty mortar and they'd also discovered a plank that had given way because it was sawn on the underside. It found that the deaths of the three men were grounds for murder charges against the missing labourer, whom the police were seeking. The motive was unknown.

This was little comfort for John. If it was sabotage, why? All his suppliers seemed reliable and he owed none of them money. Leary's wasn't a big builder, yet, so it was threatening no one. It was all strange—more so, worrying. And what he was particularly unhappy about were the headlines in the *Sydney Morning Herald* for two successive days after the accident, painting a poor picture of the company's lack of safety.

Sean came up to him and pointed to the repair work. 'It's looking better,' he said. Sean seemed to want John to acknowledge the fact.

'It is Sean, and you've done a good job in the time.'

'Yeah, well, it doesn't make the loss any better.'

'No, but I owe you an apology. I was too quick to judge.'

Sean nodded. 'I'll take that. Now, let me show you how I'm going to get back on schedule once Finlayson's pay up.'

~

David entered John's office at eleven that morning. 'What's the latest situation?' David asked.

John sighed. 'It's sabotage. We've had the architects, police, the press and the insurance investigators all over the site—'

'Sabotage,' David said. 'Why?'

'I don't know. A disagreement between men on site perhaps? But to go to this length of destruction . . .' He shook his head. 'I just don't know. By the way, Finlayson's are threatening to pull out. They've cited our contract, where if there's an accident and loss of life, and the police are called, then . . .'

'Then what?'

'They can rescind the contract, David, and sue for damages with no costs to themselves.'

'And does that apply if it's sabotage?'

'Probably not. Finlayson's could be in an awkward position in that case.'

'You don't suppose that with their money problems,' David said, 'they'd have resorted to this?' It was a possibility, John thought. 'Then there's AMP,' David continued, 'whom we haven't heard from yet.'

'And Branstons have given notice that they won't accept our tender on that Annandale site.'

'It's not good, John. I just don't know why somebody would do this. I can only assume it has to do with some commercial disagreement. Or it's just plain jealousy.'

John nodded. 'Two clients are worried about us, as well.'

'Who?' David asked.

'The Anglicans on the church and Alan Wallace on the Surry Hills warehouse. They want an explanation about Clarence Street and a copy of the police report.' John slammed his fist on the desk, making David start. 'Well I'm damned if Leary's is going to suffer for this. I'll find out who did it.'

David met his look. 'Of course. We'll get through this. I'll try to calm our clients and at the same time try and get some money for the workmen's families. Come around later to my office.'

On the exposed Waverley headland, the wind blew steady and always would, but these men beneath him would not feel the breeze, never again enjoy the coolness of it on their cheeks on a summer's day or smile at their children or laugh at some joke. John bent down and placed a single rose on each of the three graves. He stood up and made the sign of the cross. The silence of the early morning shrouded him and he felt a kinship with them. But there was anger, too.

'I'll not rest until I find the man or men who killed you. I owe you that at the very least. You put your trust in Leary's and we let you down.' John's throat tightened. 'I will do anything—legal or otherwise—to get justice for you.'

CHAPTER TWO

GERRY GLEESON PLACED HIS CHISEL AND MALLET ON THE PLANK beneath him and grimaced at the click of his middle-aged knees as he eased his six-foot-three-inch frame upright. Shaking the dust from his greying, copper-coloured hair, he wiped his hands on the shirt stretched taut over his middle. *Christ, he must give this game away.* He called out to his assistant, 'Smoko! After that we've two more courses to do before knock-off.'

They climbed down the scaffold ladders from the third-storey Sussex Street warehouse. On the ground, his assistant organised the billy while Gerry opened his boarding house-prepared meal to the October morning sunshine. They ate in silence for five minutes, then Gerry threw his tea leaves onto the rubbish pile. 'Bad news what happened at Clarence Street t'other week. I knew two of the men who died.'

'Did you,' asked his fair-haired assistant. 'Where from?'

'One of them worked in Pyrmont, where we quarried the yellow block.'

'Ah, the block. That's the best sandstone, not like the stuff we got here, eh Gerry.'

'Too true, too true. This stuff's average. The block cuts like cheese in a straight grain, not like this sod, which shears too much. But yeah, I did know the fellows and I'm sorry for them. There's talk of the accident in town. Some say it was no accident, it was plain bloody murder.'

'Murder?'

'Gut feeling is all, walls don't collapse that easy.' Gerry pushed himself up. 'Come on, back to work. Where're the others? Liven them up.'

Back on the scaffolding Gerry knelt and selected an oblong block of sandstone. He saw the grain, picked up his tools and went to work. The right force of steel on steel was enough to transform the rough cube into a block ready to lay. As he continued to work the sandstone, the past paid him a visit. His life had changed in 1828, when back in County Cork, a man he'd been close to was murdered in the course of a robbery. Gerry had had nothing to do with it but the police had had a different story, and the judge had handed down his verdict—transportation for life.

Gerry was a stonemason and his trade was needed in New South Wales. He'd worked hard with the convict gangs, building bridges and culverts north of Wiseman's Ferry along a section of the Great North Road, until his overseer, a surveyor, had spotted his talents. He had made Gerry a trusty and prepared him for his ticket-of-leave. That gave him hope to get himself out of his canary rags and above the level of convict humanity.

'Need more mortar up here!' Gerry yelled to the team on the ground. His assistant grabbed the windlass rope and pulled up the bucket of fresh mud. Looking down at the rising load, Gerry remembered those gangs. His overseer had taken the time to teach him, to show him technical books and how they could help him in his trade. While the convicts slept and ate, Gerry had laboured beside the light and stink of a pannikin lamp, straining his eyes to learn new words and their meanings. His overseer had been patient and had helped Gerry as much as he could. When he'd got his ticket-of-leave Gerry had written to his sister in Ireland about his better circumstances. He had received no return letters. He had also changed his name from Riordan. New country, new start, new name. It was a pity, though, that he'd lost touch with that overseer.

Gerry had read about the Clarence Street accident and its builder John Leary in the *Herald*. His elder sister Maeve had married a Leary. Maeve . . . Maeve. Gerry remembered her at the Cork dock when the transport had sailed. She wasn't going to let shame stop her saying goodbye to her brother, a convicted murderer. And yet she'd never answered his letters. Gerry shook his head; Leary was a common name in Ireland. But somehow he felt there was a connection. He couldn't put his finger on it but the name kept calling him, as though his forebears' superstitious natures were telling him something was there for him to dig into.

Reaching for another lump of stone, he decided to find out a bit more about John Leary, just to be on the safe side of his superstition. It's probably nothing, he thought.

David McGuire looked out at the passing parade on George Street and focused on the boy selling newspapers: a simple job. He wanted something to distract him from the anger he felt. He looked back at the man sitting opposite him at the meeting room table. 'I'll put you on notice, sir,' David said. 'Leary's Contracting will not accept the insurance company's assessment of the damage. It's a grossly undervalued offer.' David leaned forward and placed both hands on the table. 'We've done our assessment of reinstatement, loss of profit, and loss of a client,' he caught the eye of the man, 'and our costs are significantly higher than your assessment.'

The investigator picked up his satchel, placed the papers inside and clasped it. 'You're entitled, sir, to quantify the damage as you see fit.' He stood up. 'AMP's offer is full and final. I bid you good day, Mr McGuire.'

David had had enough. 'You're not interested in seeing our figures?'

'That's not our responsibility. If you're not satisfied by this offer you are free of course to reply—'

'You leave me no choice then. I will be replying! I will be briefing counsel this afternoon.'

The man nodded and left the room. David was in the right and he knew he had a case, but it would be bloody difficult proving it. It was one thing to have right on your side, but it was quite another to make an insurance company understand real costs.

John came in and sat down opposite him. He had a file in his hands. 'Was that AMP?' he said.

'They've dug in on what they'll pay and it's not enough.' David glanced at his correspondence and handed John a piece of paper. 'That's another letter from a potential client. It's not good reading.' He watched as John read the contents.

'Shite. If this keeps going, we'll soon be out of business. Have you written, told them it wasn't our fault?'

'I have, John. But we have no evidence. It happened, and it's our responsibility.

What about other jobs?'

'There are a few. There's this one, a large one, I think we could get. It's for Blunt's. We have to win it . . . at any cost.'

David frowned. 'What do you mean, "any cost"?'

'We have to win it, cleverly or otherwise. Whatever it takes.' John tapped the file on his lap. 'It's all here, the measures, pricing and suppliers' quotes.'

'Then there's this insurance claim,' David said. 'We're going to fight this. I'm briefing solicitors this afternoon—'

'Solicitors! David, that'll cost us a fortune.'

'I'm prepared to pay. It's a matter of principle, I've read the policy. AMP must pay for any cost, and I repeat *any* cost that's incurred. That includes the cost of restoration, the cost for delays in rebuilding and any other costs including subsequent losses due to the sabotage. A letter from our solicitors will be sufficient to make them pay the claim in full.'

'Maybe, and that's good of you. But please keep the costs low. You've told me that owners can't keep putting funds into a business indefinitely. There must be a time to say enough's enough.'

'Let me be the judge of how much money I'll put into Leary's.'

His father-in-law was calling the shots again. This rankled with John, more than ever, but the company needed David's money. Unlike John, David had little love of construction, so there was a risk that he might consider selling Leary's if the business ever got too bad. John would have to make sure that never happened.

'How much cash have we got?' John asked.

'Enough to last a month.'

John hadn't realised cash was that tight. 'Just to the end of October? That'll go quickly.'

'The rest of our projects are paying their way. Correct?'

'The Enmore church, the Surry Hills warehouse, the Glebe town house and the new factory at Newtown are all in front.'

'So it's just Clarence Street.'

'And what it needs to get it going again,' John said, 'until we resolve this insurance mess.'

'There's some good news,' David said. 'James Finlayson's coming to the party. He acknowledged the sabotage was beyond our control. Our notice hit home, how they'd breached their agreement in not paying for June and July's work. I'm collecting a cheque from them this afternoon for those two months' cost of construction.'

John closed his eyes for a moment. 'That's something. But what are we going to do if our existing customers start to delay payments because they think we're dodgy? Or worse, we get no future work because of this mess?'

'That's why we need this new job you've got. Winning that will hopefully settle them and we can put all this behind us. So get cracking, grab that file and win us our next job. In the meantime, I want you to do an audit of the five sites and their foremen, including Clarence Street. We want to be assured of their safety. And if need be, make improvements.'

'I certainly will. There's one thing I'd like to do.'

'What's that?'

'I want to use an investigator and get him on the trail of this labourer, Miller. I want to know why someone did this.'

'Very well. But don't spend long on it. There are other things to do.'

~

Gerry Gleeson was sitting at a table in Skinners Family Hotel. It was a popular corner pub, as its main doors fronted the intersection of Hunter and George Streets. He took a swig of his beer and looked at his companion. 'Well, that's a good drop after a full day's labour,' he said, as he put his glass on the table. He wiped his mouth. 'How's work, Rupert?'

'Not bad,' his companion said.

A short man with red hair, Rupert Jenkins was a builder with whom Gerry had worked on projects where skilled stonemasonry was wanted. Gerry knew him to be tough but fair. He hadn't seen him for a few years and it was good to talk about old times.

Rupert went on, 'You know, it's odd, Gerry, the older I get, the softer I get. I'm not as tough as I used to be.'

Gerry smiled. 'Too true, too true. It's just old age.'

'Still take you on.'

'You and whose army?'

Jenkins smiled now. 'No, but I want to give it away. I was doing all right for a time and could have got a lot bigger.'

'What happened?' Gerry said pulling himself upright and pointing to the glasses. 'Same again?'

'Aye,' Jenkins said as he brushed a fly away from his mouth. 'Put my faith too much on one man. He was going to make me big, but these things happen.'

'Think about that. Won't be long.'

Gerry came back with the beers and placed them down. 'What was the man's name?'

'What?'

'The man, Rupert. Just what you said. Come on, don't go daft on me. Who was he?'

Jenkins nodded and put his drink down. 'John Leary.'

Gerry stopped his beer in mid-air. 'John Leary. You mean the builder John Leary? The one from Leary's Contracting?'

'The same.'

Well, there's a turn up. I see the accident in the paper, and then two days later, here at the pub the name comes up. Gerry's superstitious nature came to the fore. Fate was drawing him towards the young builder.

Jenkins prodded him. 'What's up?'

'Hmm?'

'You've gone quiet. Do you know Leary?'

'No,' Gerry said, 'but tell me about him.'

'A young man, tall, very tall, like you. Probably mid-twenties, a scar over his left eye.'

'From fighting?'

'Don't know, but he's Irish.'

'County?'

'Leinster, I'd back. He started with me as a chippy and ended up a foreman looking after a few sites.'

'Know anything about his history?'

'Little of his family, but he has a sister here, Maureen, a nice woman, about five years older than him. He was the best worker I ever had. I thought we could do great things together. He even offered to buy a share of my business but I refused him. And I lost him. Went off to start on his own. Married into money.'

'Did he? Well, I should be able to find out something about him.'

'Why?' Jenkins said.

Gerry looked at his empty glass. 'Always pays to know the builders.'

Jenkins finished his beer and put out his hand. 'I've got to go, mate. Still got a business to run. Let me know when you've finished Sussex Street. There's always room on my team for a skilled stone-mason foreman. Even one with a big head.'

'Get away with you,' Gerry said as he gripped his friend's hand. 'I come to Skinners now and then so we'll probably run into each other.'

'We might.'

Gerry sat back. John Leary had a sister named Maureen! Maureen was the name of Maeve's eldest child. He had to fill in the gaps, find out more about this man Leary.

~

John put his pencil down on his office desk. He'd gone over his figures and he was square with the costings for the Blunt tender, but nothing stood out that would give them a leg up. Even allowing for no profit, discounting suppliers' prices and with the skinniest over-heads covered, it would still be a tight price.

David played by the rules. He always had, but John knew it was now anybody's game. The sabotage had happened. Someone was responsible and men had been killed. Without David's money funding Clarence Street and paying the costs of defending their name, they'd be in trouble. John prickled with irritation. John wasn't getting free of his debts; rather he felt David's bonds binding him closer. The memory of the dinner-party talk he'd heard in Toorak only seemed to fan his anger.

They had to win the Blunt tender. Could he do it? An idea came to him. It would be risky, but the company's survival demanded it. Leary's had no cash reserve. It relied on each client paying its way on each project. This was happening but not on Clarence Street. If one or two other clients delayed payments because of doubts about Leary's worksite safety, then they'd be in deep strife. So he had to act.

Not all business happened above board. Yes, he had to do it. He had to win this job any way he could. If that meant being unethical, then so be it. A bribe.

Forget their new home. There'd be no cash splurged from Leary's until they had solid income. Clarissa would understand and be patient. John looked at his calculations and scribbled new figures. Bribing Blunt meant compromising his integrity, but he never again wanted to experience the fear he'd felt just after the sabotage. And there was the matter of justice. He'd vowed to the three dead Leary's workers that he'd do right by them, and he couldn't do that if he was a pauper with all he'd strived for over the last two years wiped out. He had to do it so Leary's would survive and be stronger. Nothing like this accident would ever happen to him again. And more importantly, he wanted to be the topmost contractor, demonstrating to the detractors and the doubters his ability to succeed. The people in Toorak, Glebe and other places would soon discover that he wasn't indulging himself and spending his father-in-law's wealth, but earning his own wealth by his own hand. He was going to prove to them all that he wasn't just any builder, but the best builder in Sydney.

With this new resolve he felt calm. Blunt had a few problems and John was going to 'buy' this job. How? Grabbing a pen he wrote a note to Damien Wexton, the private investigator he'd used to help him nail his sister's rapist. On the eve of his departure from Dublin, John's sister Maureen had been raped and John had later found out that the culprit was in the colony. Getting justice for Maureen had become more urgent once John had learned that Maureen was emigrating to New South Wales with her husband and child. John had dealt with the rapist in his own way and Maureen was now safe in Sydney with her family.

John arranged to meet Wexton at Skinners Hotel at the end of the week. He wanted him to find out everything about this missing labourer.

'Your parents aren't joining us, Clarissa?' Maureen asked, as she and her husband sat down to dinner at Point Piper with Clarissa and John.

'They're dining with the McCreadies tonight. They asked me to pass on their love.'

John was thinking of his meeting with Blunt and how best to plan his approach, but Liam, his brother-in-law, broke his concentration. 'John, it's strange to think that you spent all that time in Melbourne, and didn't see the Town Hall in Geelong. It's nearly completed. It's an architectural masterpiece that I'm sure you would have appreciated.'

'Perhaps I was remiss, but there were other things to see. How are things with you?'

Liam fiddled with his serviette ring. 'Fair to middling. The end-of-year exams are coming up and one of my students is struggling with his classics. But he excels in woodwork. He'd make a good carpenter. That reminds me, any repercussions from the site accident?'

'A few clients got skittish,' John said, 'and the insurance company was slow on the uptake. It was no accident, Liam.'

Maureen said, 'It was a terrible loss of life. I'd like to hear more about it, other than what the *Herald* has said.'

'So it was definitely sabotage?' Liam said.

'We're sure it was,' John said, 'and we have the evidence. The police are involved.'

Clarissa patted her face with her handkerchief. 'Why would anyone want to do such a horrible thing?'

John refilled his glass from the whiskey bottle. 'I aim to find out.' He looked at Clarissa's wide eyes.

'And Sean? How is he taking it?' she said.

'Like us all, my dear, pretty hard. I've taken steps to help the police get the culprit. I want to know why.'

Towards the end of the evening, Maureen noticed that Clarissa did not seem well. She stood up and said that it was time she and Liam left.

'It's been lovely seeing you,' Clarissa said. 'Maybe tomorrow or the next day, I'll feel better. I want to see Michael, too. It's been too long. What sort of an aunty you must think me.'

'You're a good one.' Maureen hugged her. 'Please don't make yourself a stranger. Come around to Surry Hills, whenever you wish.'

The New South Wales Government had issued a notice to Gerry Gleeson that one of his stonemasons needed to confirm his standing as an immigrant. Gerry wanted things put to rights: his man was a skilled worker and he wanted to keep him.

He met the official and soon had the problem sorted. After filling out the requisite forms and paying a small fee, he got to keep his mason. As he was about to leave the building, a thought struck him. 'Is there someone here who could tell me about passenger lists and about who's come to the colony in the last few years?'

'I don't do that,' the man said, 'but if you go to the second floor, to the records section, they'll be able to help you.'

'Thank you.'

After searching for half an hour Gerry discovered that a John Leary had come to New South Wales in October of 1850. There was a list of Leary's next of kin, including his father Richard and his mother Maeve, whose maiden name had been Riordan. Gerry was taken aback by seeing his own surname, the one he had relinquished to become Gleeson.

John Leary *must* be the son of his sister Maeve! Well, well, Gerry thought, a relative in the colony. So John Leary was his nephew, younger brother to his niece Maureen ... But Gerry didn't want to see them right away. He didn't know why, but he needed to think about it.

Gregory Blunt ran his business from a warehouse at the wharf end of Market Street. It was three doors down from a similar warehouse John had extended two years before for the McCreadies, who were wool merchants. Blunt had called for tenders for a new and bigger warehouse to be situated next door, on a cleared site that he owned.

'Mr John Leary to see you, Mr Blunt,' a middle-aged clerk said, as he led John into the office.

John's prospective client, seated at his desk, had broad shoulders, a beer-barrel chest and thick black hair atop a face with prominent features.

'Thank you for seeing me, Mr Blunt. I know you're a busy man. I'm here about the Leary's tender.'

Blunt's eyebrows came together like a hedgerow. 'I don't think I can help you, Mr Leary. My architects are the ones you want to speak to; they have all the technical details and so forth.'

John sat down, uninvited, on a chair opposite the man. Blunt appeared surprised. 'It's not the technical details I came to talk about, but how much I want to win his job.'

Blunt looked at him in silence for what seemed a long time. He pursed his lips. 'Go on.'

John felt the leather of the seat warming under him. 'What I mean to say is, I'm prepared to offer the lowest price.'

'That's what I expect my contractors to submit. The lowest price normally wins any tender. Is there any other way?'

Here goes. 'Mr Blunt, I understand from my investigations that you have a problem with a supplier.'

'A supplier? I don't follow. All my suppliers are sound.'

'What about Johnsons?' John said. 'I know they're holding goods from you until you pay them.'

Blunt pounded the desk. 'They're bloody thieves! They agreed to be paid *after* they delivered the supplies I ordered from them. That's what they said. I've issued notices to force them.'

'But that will take time and you can't wait. That's what I know.' John wouldn't cower under Blunt's stare.

'You're well informed, Mr Leary.'

'If I can get Johnsons to give you the goods—'

'I won't pay before I get them, I tell you.'

John understood Blunt's pickle. He'd once had the same problem with a supplier and knew a way to get out of it. 'What if I can get you the goods without you paying up front? I would expect a favourable recommendation on the approval of my tender.'

Blunt leaned forward. John felt the tension spreading on him like a creeper. He had to hold his line just a little longer.

'Are you offering me a bribe?' Blunt said.

John charged ahead. 'I wouldn't call it a bribe. I solve the problem for you and you can solve a problem for me. I'll go one better. When I put my tender in, if it's not the lowest price but meets all other requirements, then I'm prepared to equal the lowest price you get.'

Blunt nodded. 'I see what you're offering. But tell me ... why are you going to this trouble? I've done my checks on Leary's, on the architect's recommendation. I've found everything above board. In fact you'd be the preferred tenderer.'

John baulked. Had he overplayed his hand? But he still hadn't won the job. He wanted certainty. 'So you haven't heard of the accident? I thought you would have checked that out.'

'I saw the report, and I made my own inquiries on the suspected sabotage, which satisfied me. So again, why this offer?'

John stood up and placed both his hands on Blunt's desk. 'Let's just say that I want to guarantee I win this project for my own reasons.'

Blunt paused but kept John's look. 'Leary, I've heard your offer and it's still a bribe. Now get out.'

John was shocked. 'What's that mean?'

Blunt stood up. 'You heard me. You've just lost a job. Pity, because you stacked up, from what I've heard. Close the door on the way out.' He sat back down and opened a file on his desk.

John wouldn't move. He was desperate. 'Mr Blunt?'

Blunt looked up. 'Are you still here? I said—'

'I want this project.'

'I'll get someone else. It's not difficult.' Blunt stood up again and came up to him. 'Now, I asked you to leave. You're a big lump. I'll get a few scratches but I'll still add another scar or two to that face of yours.'

John sat down and Blunt made to grab him. 'Wait,' John said with his hand out. 'Give me five minutes. That's all.'

Blunt stopped in mid-stride. 'Why should I do that?'

'Just five minutes.'

Blunt sat on the edge of his desk with his arms folded. 'All right, five minutes.'

'I withdraw the bribe and I apologise,' John decided he had nothing to lose. 'The sabotage has affected our reputation and I have to get this job to win it back.'

Blunt sniffed. 'You've got four minutes.'

'Mr Blunt, I can still give you what you want.'

'Pay Johnsons, you mean?'

'No. That's your problem but I can help there. We know the owner and—'

'You've got three and a half minutes. If you can solve Johnsons, I'm in debt to you. Where's the difference in that from the bribe?'

John nodded. 'I can arrange a meeting and strategy, that's all. After that, you're on your own.'

Blunt said nothing. No more minutes mentioned. Maybe there was hope. 'Go on.'

John took a deep breath and offered an alternative plan that he'd considered as a last resort. 'I'm prepared to open my books to you on all the costs for your new warehouse construction, materials, labour, machinery hire and supervision.'

Blunt sat down as there was a knock at his office door. 'Come in.'

'Your next meeting is about to start, sir,' the clerk said popping his head in the door opening. Blunt nodded, looking at John. 'Tell them I'll be with them shortly. I'm just about finished here.' John felt his stomach grip with tension, his prospects slipping away. The clerk withdrew. 'You've still got a minute, Leary.'

'You'll see all the costs for the project. I'll build it for no profit.'

'But—'

'No profit and I'll give you a guarantee that the cost will not be varied.' He hadn't thought that bit through. Think. Think, he told himself. Then it came to him. 'I'll get three quotes for everything. You'll know exactly what your building will cost.'

Blunt pursed his lips. 'Everything? Steel? Timber?'

'Yes.'

'And I can say who I want you to call quotes from?' Blunt said. 'Not just your favourite suppliers?'

'Yes, Mr Blunt.'

'Even the small orders?'

John saw a glimmer of light. Blunt understood what was being offered. John went on the attack. 'All right, say we limit calling quotations to items above fifty pounds.' This was it. John thought.

'Drummond!' Blunt yelled.

The clerk reappeared. 'Tell Mr Thompson to go to our regular,' Blunt said. 'I'll join him in half an hour. My shout.'

'Yes, sir.'

'Now, Mr Leary ... why would you want to do a job like this and not get a reward for your risk? That's not business.'

'It's not, but I can afford to have one project built at cost. I need the turnover. I need our current clients to see that we are a reliable builder.'

'I don't know.'

'Mr Blunt, you must have a budget for this new warehouse. No businessman would start without one.'

'I do, but you won't know it.'

'Fair enough but I'll ask this,' John said. 'If I get my suggestions agreed by the architect on changes in the design that will save you money, then I'd want a share of that saving.'

'What if no savings can be made?'

'Then I don't get a quid. But I've got some ideas.'

'Such as?' Blunt said.

For the first time, John smiled. 'That's what we'll talk about once you agree.'

Blunt looked at him for a moment. 'I'm not yet convinced but I'm leaning your way. Let's work out a few more details.'

Thirty minutes later John left the office. He'd done it. No fancy words or best prices here. John had convinced Blunt that Leary's would build it at cost, saving Blunt the builder's profit. There was no signed contract yet but John had received Blunt's handshake and had recommended two items that would save Blunt money and gain Leary's 50 per cent of that saving. One was an alternative roof sheeting that David McGuire's company could supply, which was cheaper but equal in quality to the architect's specified product, while the other was the large entrance double doors, which John and Sean could make themselves.

The confrontation had ended and it wasn't everything, but it was a start. Blunt's project was a big one and it would show their current and potential clients that they were a trusted builder. They would get precious money from the client. Leary's could then delay the payment of that cash to suppliers and tradesman until they'd made a fuss. John had got Blunt's assurance that the terms of their agreement would remain between them.

Now, all he had to do was to meet Wexton and find out about this bloody missing labourer. If Wexton dragged Miller here to this vestibule right now, John would quite easily thrash him to within an inch of his life and walk away with a clear conscience.

On a hot night, nine days into October, a breeze wafted through Cochrane's in Day Street, the two-storey hotel John had built when working with his old boss, Rupert Jenkins. Jenkins's name reminded John of the letter he'd received that day. He had a few moments before his investigator was due and he brought out the letter from his pocket and read it again, still intrigued by its contents. It was from a man called Gerry Gleeson, a stonemason who had worked with Rupert Jenkins. In his letter, Gleeson wrote that he thought he and John might be related.

Gleeson wrote that he was born in Leinster and his surname before he changed it was Riordan. He had had a sister named Maeve, to whom he was very close, and she had come to farewell him when he'd been transported to New South Wales in 1828. He'd changed his surname to Gleeson when he got his ticket-of-leave. From what he knew so far about John, he thought John's mother might be his sister Maeve, which would make John his nephew. In his letter, he suggested that they meet.

John was quite excited by this letter. John's mother's name was indeed Maeve, and her maiden name had been Riordan. She had told John that her favourite brother Gerry had been transported to New South Wales in 1828, two years before John was born, but that no one had heard from him again.

John had tried to find his uncle's whereabouts when he'd first come to the colony in 1850, but despite his best efforts, he could find no trace of him. The change of name would certainly explain that. Reading the letter a second time, John had a thought. *Was this man really who he said he was? Or did this have something to do with the sabotage? Could Gleeson be a threat?* John had decided he would ask Wexton to check Gleeson out before agreeing to meet him.

Looking up from his letter, John saw that his visitor had arrived. As Damien Wexton came towards him, John stood up. The investigator was ten years older than him and had a stocky build and sharp eyes. It had just been under four years since John had used him to track down his sister's attacker.

'Mr Wexton,' John gripped his hand, 'we meet again. Please sit down. If I remember, you don't drink grog, so there's a juice for you. It's new, a Raspberry Shrub, made with berries, vinegar, sugar and water.'

'Sounds good. Thank you Mr Leary,' Wexton said as he sat down.

'Have you got plenty on?'

'I keep busy. But I can fit you in,' Wexton said, taking his notebook out of his coat pocket.

Fit him in? Investigation work must be well paid, John thought. 'We had an accident on one of our sites a while back.'

'I saw something in the *Herald*. How are you coping?'

'Struggling. Three men are dead.' John folded his arms. 'I want to find the culprit, because I think it was deliberate.'

The investigator sipped his drink. 'This is good. Tell me, why do you think it was deliberate?'

'We've tracked the cause to a faulty mortar mix and a suspect plank. It's sabotage, I'm sure. Once we've got that man, we can unearth the motive.'

'What do you want me to do?'

'The bricklayer's labourer who made the bad mix is a man called Miller.' John pulled a sheet of paper from his pocket. 'Here're some facts, including the name of the constable who did the investigation.'

'Thank you.' Wexton placed it in his notebook. 'I'll get the police report and start. The trail's probably cold but I'll check other sites, and the Labour Office. If it's murder, it's likely he's done a bunk, so I'll go to the shipping agents.'

'Good idea,' John said.

'Do the police have a description of him?'

'Yes, a good one.' John leaned forward. 'Mr Wexton, this is important. If I can find this man, I might be able to find out why he did this. I'm sure he didn't act alone. Oh, and I have another matter that shouldn't cause you too much trouble. Could you check out a stonemason named Gerry Gleeson? He claims to be my uncle and he sounds good on paper, but I'd like to be sure before I meet him.' John gave him a copy of Gleeson's letter, then stood up and stuck out his hand, 'Write to me in a fortnight and tell me how you're going with both matters. I'll fix your expenses.'

Wexton drained his glass, and put Gleeson's letter in his notebook, then put that back in his coat pocket. Shaking John's hand, he said, 'Gleeson should be easy, the labourer not so. Don't get your hopes up on that one.'

'I have faith in you,' John said.

David McGuire walked up the stairs to his office at McGuire Wire in Sussex Street, a happy man. His solicitors, Wilson and Company, had reviewed the insurance contract and had agreed with him that he had a case against the insurers. They'd also confirmed that the offer from the insurance company was inadequate. Further to his meeting with Wilsons, they'd sent a letter of demand to the AMP that if it didn't agree to meet the full cost of the accident, including compensation to Leary's, by 5 November, then Wilson's would issue writs against it for costs and damages.

David was a relieved man for the first time in weeks. John had told him that the Blunt tender for the Market Street warehouse was just about won. He opened the door to his office, sat down and started a worry-free day at McGuire Wire.

John accepted the contracts from Gregory Blunt in Blunt's office. He leafed through his copy and noted the 10 per cent deposit to be paid to Leary's as an advance payment. That deposit would have to meet actual audited costs for the warehouse construction but it would help him because they'd have Blunt's cash first, before they were obliged to pay any monies to workers or suppliers. How they timed their payments to others could then be stretched out. All in order and he entered the date—15 October 1855—and signed both copies just below Blunt's own name. He then shook hands with his new client. 'Well, that's it,' he said. 'I'll be around tomorrow to collect the latest plans.'

'I'll let you and the architects sort that out,' Blunt said. 'But I want this building up and running as fast as possible. October next year at the latest.'

'Don't worry.'

Blunt grunted. 'I won't. That's your problem from now on, but I'll hold Leary's Contracting personally responsible for any overruns to the budget or time delays.'

John felt relief on leaving Blunt's office. On his way down the stairs, he recognised a small, red-headed man. 'Mr Jenkins. It's grand to see you.'

Rupert Jenkins's face lit up with pleasure. 'John. John it is. How are you?'

'I'm well thank you, and yourself?'

'Can't complain,' he said, smiling, 'no one would listen. And your good wife, Clarissa?'

'In a delicate condition, Mr Jenkins.'

'Congratulations! Wonderful.'

John was chuffed to be telling people about the pregnancy. 'Why are you here? To see Mr Blunt?'

'I am, but from your happy face I fear that that you've got good news on this one. I thought mine was the lowest price, or close to the lowest price, so, you've got it, right?'

'We have, Mr Jenkins. Have you got time for a drink?'

'Let me see Mr Blunt and I'll be right with you. I've got a feeling I won't be long.'

John stepped into the Market Street sunshine amongst the smells and sounds of horses and wagons. The colony's transport relied on animals, but something would soon revolutionise that. The steam train was going to be the biggest thing since the invention of the wheel. He'd read about some of the impressive canal systems in England, but the railways would be a big improvement on that. A tap on his arm interrupted his thoughts.

It was Rupert Jenkins. 'Well, I knew I wouldn't be too long. He wouldn't tell me who'd won the job, but I guessed.' Jenkins grinned. 'Still want that beer?'

'Does a diamond sparkle?'

'Then let's go.'

They walked up Market Street and turned right into Sussex Street.

Jenkins was struggling to keep up with John's strides and John slowed down, respecting his friend's age. Jenkins had given John his first job in the colony and he would always be grateful to him for that.

'So, how are things going?' John asked as they turned into Day Street.

'Not bad, not bad. But since you left us, I seem to have reached a milestone in my life. I'm thinking of calling it a day, especially now, after losing this last tender.'

They arrived at Cochrane's and walked in. It was mid-afternoon and quiet.

'Well, John, do you remember?' Jenkins said. 'It was here that you told me about your plans to have a go on your own.'

'I remember.'

'Hey, it was sad about that accident you had.'

John's good feeling took a hit. 'It wasn't an accident, it was sabotage.'

Jenkins looked horrified. 'Dear God, I hope you find the culprit.'

'So do we.'

John looked around at the pub he and Jenkins had built, and a thought distracted him from the deaths. He'd read an article recently that said to build a company quickly you could buy a share in your competitor's business or purchase it entirely. John's long-term plan to build Leary's slowly had been changed by the sabotage. Now he had to move fast. He wondered if he could make an offer to Mr Jenkins now. It was a bullish move, but there was no time like the present. 'You said you'd like to get out of the building game?'

Jenkins took a swig of his beer and nodded, 'Yes, I've had enough. If I sell now, I'll get a pretty penny for my effort.'

This could work. John had to discuss it with David, and money to purchase would be hard to find, but he had an instinct about this. 'And are you planning to sell?'

Jenkins looked sharply at him. 'Are you interested in buying?' He smiled. 'I knocked you back the last time you asked.'

That had been three years ago and John had only wanted a share at that time. 'And what about now?' he asked.

'Maybe.'

'You have a good name around town, Mr Jenkins.'

'Now, don't feed me bulldust.'

John grinned. 'And with your contacts and Leary's, I think we would do well. Very well indeed.'

The little man looked at him and paused before speaking, 'This is big stuff. Get me another beer and we'll talk about it.'

John stood up. 'I suppose you've got a value on your business?'

'I may have. I may have. Now, get them drinks.'

By the end of the next half hour, John had agreed a purchase price for Jenkins's business. For one thousand pounds, which he thought reasonable, he could get a storage yard, construction plant and gear and, better yet, Jenkins's ongoing contracts. Now, all he had to do was convince David McGuire that it was good business.

When he got back to the office, a report from Wexton about Gerry Gleeson was waiting for him. *That was quick.* Wexton said that confirming Gleeson's story had not been difficult—it was all on the records. Wexton had tracked down the name of the overseer of the convict gang who'd helped Gleeson get his ticket-of-leave, and the various builders he had done work for. Gleeson was highly regarded for his skill and his honesty.

Gerry Gleeson finished work, returned to his boarding house in Elizabeth Street and collected his mail from his landlady: just one letter. He was hungry and looking forward to dinner. Surrounding him were other lodgers waiting for the landlady to put the meal on the table. One was reading the paper, one tapped tobacco from his pipe and two others were arguing over the price of gold. Gerry might have been alone for all the interest they showed in him. But he didn't mind. He was his own man and had his own income. Stonemasonry earned him his wages, which he put towards his board and moderate drinking, but thrift and spare living had enabled him to gain a separate income from wise investment in wool, stocks and bonds. Property he eschewed. He was content to be looked after by others, and his history in the convict road gangs had made him comfortable in groups like his fellow boarders in the dining room.

Finding out that John Leary was his nephew had unsettled him. Should he still try to meet him or not? He looked down and opened the letter he held. It was from the young man himself, saying he and Mrs Leary would be delighted to meet with him on 18 October at seven in the evening for dinner at their Point Piper home. *Well, that's something. Point Piper, eh?* Gerry had imagined that the Learys would live in town or Glebe.

He was both curious and excited. After dinner tonight, he'd reply and accept their invitation. What would his nephew think of his criminal past, he wondered?

He picked up a newspaper and an article caught his eye. Mr Thomas Mitchell, the former Surveyor-General, had died in his Sydney home. Mitchell had been the champion of the Great North Road on which Gerry had laboured all those years ago.

The landlady slipped a hot plate under his nose and the onion sauce distracted him. Putting down the paper, he took up his knife and fork and eagerly tucked into the hot stew.

John looked through the window from David's office to the floor below. The Darling Harbour warehouse was much bigger than the Sussex Street one, as it needed to accommodate the stacks of corrugated iron and tall rolls of fencing.

'Just four weeks ago,' David said, 'a major incident nearly crippled us and here you are rattling on about buying a business.'

John smiled and turned to face his father-in-law. John was about to say that he'd already struck an agreement with Jenkins but decided to wait. He would like to convince his father-in-law first. 'You're right. It does seem like bad timing, but we have to act and grow. Being bigger is going to protect us, make us less of a target.'

David looked surprised. 'A target? A target for what?'

'Look, I'm not sure, but we know we've been the victims of sabotage. And why? I think someone sees us as a threat.'

'That's drawing a long bow, isn't it?' David said. 'There's plenty of work around. And after all, you've no proof who did it.'

'I don't, not yet, but look, Jenkins is a good builder with a good reputation. For a thousand pounds, it's a great buy. We—'

David shook his head. 'It may be a good buy, but how can we raise the money? We've got no reserve, we're on probation with the bank. No, it's not on, no way.' David joined him at the window and pointed to his stock. 'That's what matters to me,' he said. 'These and wool broking.'

John struggled to control his anger and resentment. He needed David to agree to the purchase of Jenkins's building company, plus he was dependent on him for raising funds. But he must learn to play a long game if he was to get his independence. He regained control of his feelings. 'I take your point. At present I run Leary's and you deal with the things you know. But David, we're a small company and the sabotage has put us halfway into the ground. We have to get bigger to survive.'

David shook his head. 'No. Going into more debt is risky. I don't like it.'

'I know you don't.' If only John had the money, the things he could do with it . . . 'Jenkins's company is sound.'

David sighed. 'You might be right.'

'I am.'

'Don't push me. I still have the final say in this company.'

Yes, you do, unfortunately.

David continued. 'I think Jenkins is solid, and I know the man's reputation. What I can't understand is your insistence on growing the company so quickly.'

John sat down. 'I just want to protect what we've got. Buying Jenkins's company would help do that.'

'Well, I'm not convinced.'

John wouldn't give up. 'Can you get more money from the bank? I know it will mean extending the mortgage on your businesses, but can you do that?'

'Yes, but I won't.'

John baulked at David's firm set lips and hard eyes. He'd seen that look before when David had dug his heels in. 'Why not?'

'Just what I've told you. Listen to me, and listen well. I'll not borrow now to buy more companies.' His face hardened further. 'It's too much exposure.' David waved a hand in the air. 'But, I'll think about it.'

'But—'

'You're sure that Jenkins's business will help Leary's grow?' David said.

John thought before answering. Sure, Jenkins was a good builder, but what of his debts, and did he have any claims against him? A bit more money paid for the right information would be money well spent. 'I am, but I'll do some more checking.'

'Good, now leave me to get on with running my other businesses.'

The mid-October sun was setting in the west and shimmering across Blackburn Cove.

'It's not yet seven, dear,' Clarissa said from her chair in the drawing room. 'Your uncle will come. Please sit down.'

John was about to turn back from the window when a cab

appeared in front of his house. Moving the curtain a little aside John was curious to see what his uncle looked like. The man who alighted seemed to be in his forties. He was tall like John but thick-set, the build of a stonemason. His smile was warm as he paid off the cab. His jacket was not tailored like a gentleman's but it had an acceptable weave to match his pressed trousers and his shirt was good quality and clean. John suddenly recalled that his uncle had been a convicted murderer. He found that hard to believe, watching him walk confidently to the gate and from there up to the front door. John said to Clarissa, 'He's here, dear.'

John opened the front door himself and looked at the sunburned but kind face of his uncle, whose blue eyes twinkled. His uncle took off his hat and smoothed down his grey-streaked, russet-coloured hair. 'Mr John Leary?' he said in a lilt that reminded John of home.

'Yes it is. Mr Gleeson?'

'That's myself.'

'Please, come in. Come in.'

'Thank you.'

John escorted Gerry into the foyer and Clarissa came out to meet them. 'This is my wife, Clarissa, Mr Gleeson.'

'I'm very pleased to meet any of John's family,' Clarissa said giving Gerry a warm and welcoming smile.

Gerry noticed Clarissa's pregnancy. 'How do you do, Mrs Leary, and if I may, you have my congratulations.'

'Thank you and please call me Clarissa.'

Gerry seemed to relax a bit more, smiled and nodded. 'Then you both must call me Uncle,' he said. ''Tis a lovely house you have, Mr . . . John,' he said looking around.

'Thank you, Uncle. Please come through to the drawing room. Would you like a drink?'

'Jameson's if you've got one, thank you, John,' Gerry said as he sat on a lounge chair.

John brought them their drinks and then sat down beside Clarissa on the sofa. They all just looked at each other for some time until Gerry spoke.

'There's so much to talk about.'

There was, John agreed. His family in Kildare hadn't spoken much about his uncle and when they had it was in whispers, and briefly. 'You work in Sydney?'

'I do. Have for many years, since I came off the gangs, I used to do a lot of work for Rupert Jenkins, who I understand is a good friend of yours too."

'He is indeed,' John said. 'He gave me my start in the colony.'

'Do you have family here?' Clarissa enquired.

'Other than you, you mean?' Gerry said his eyes twinkling. 'I'm afraid not, I'm a bachelor.'

Stella, their maid, stood at the entrance to the drawing room. 'Dinner is ready, ma'am.'

'Thank you, Stella,' Clarissa said.

'Come, Uncle,' John said. 'Let us eat.'

Over the three-course meal, they talked with ease about Cork, Kildare, their journeys to New South Wales, Maureen and her family, and the Clarence Street sabotage. Gerry didn't seem self-conscious about his convict past, but spoke with an honesty that John found refreshing. He reminded John of his mother and he found himself warming to the man.

Gerry finished his pudding. 'That was a grand meal, thank you, John.'

'The first of one of many, Uncle,' Clarissa said. 'It's been wonderful meeting you. Why don't you and John return to the drawing room?' She took hold of his hand. 'Please excuse me. It's been a long day and I tire easily these days so I shall say goodnight. I look forward to seeing you again soon.'

Gerry took both of her hands in his. 'I'd like that too. Thank you again, Clarissa and goodnight.'

In the drawing room, John poured ports for both of them and the two men sat down.

'Maeve must have been thankful at least,' Gerry said, 'that I was exonerated.'

This was news to John. Their family had heard nothing from New South Wales over the years. 'Exonerated?'

'Aye. The law eventually found the real culprit who'd killed my friend in Cork. I received a conditional pardon. Didn't Maeve get to know?'

'No,' John said, 'not that I know of.'

Gerry frowned. 'Odd, that. I was told by the authorities that she would be informed.'

John sipped his drink. He found it odd, too, that Gerry hadn't tried to contact his sister since 1828. 'You gave the authorities her address?'

'Her old address, in Leinster. The one I wrote to myself.' His face grew sad. 'But I never got a reply.'

John said, 'Your letters must have gone astray somehow! I'll give you my parents' correct address and you can write and tell them all your news.'

'That'll be grand,' Gerry said, brightening. 'Your father-in-law, now, he must be a generous man, to support you in your ventures?'

John's sense of well-being faded. Again he was reminded of his obligations to David McGuire.

Gerry must have sensed John's mood change. 'No? You told me he's helped you.' Gerry paused and smiled. 'You want to be in charge, that's it?'

It was a comment that flew with the speed of a miss-hit nail and it struck home. John coloured and forced a smile and a reply. 'David's the major shareholder,' he said, 'and he's entitled to the most profits. We work well together.'

Gerry seemed to be puzzled by John's answer. He proffered his empty glass to John. 'Please?'

John was glad to be able to turn away from his uncle's gaze and refill their glasses. For some reason, Gerry Gleeson had a sense of John's insecurity and had made the comment to see John's reaction. It was time to change the subject.

He sat back down with new drinks. 'So, how are you finding the prices of labour?'

Gerry paused and replied. 'Quality is average and clients are getting poor service on all counts, especially in my trade.'

John agreed. For the next hour they talked about the industry they loved and John soon forgot about David McGuire.

As John saw Gerry to his cab, he said they must arrange another dinner, so he could meet Maureen and her family.

'Oh that would be grand. I'd love to see Maureen again. I was very fond of her when she was a little girl,' Gerry said. 'And to think she has children of her own now . . .'

As Gerry's cab headed back to town, John retreated to the drawing room to have one last drink. He'd liked his uncle: he was not easy to fool and John had nothing but admiration for how he had overcome his convict past and made a life for himself in the colony. He especially liked that Gerry loved the building industry as much as he did. But it was more than that, Gerry was a link to home, to his mother, in particular, and he suddenly realised how much he missed her. He wrote to her when he could, but he wished she could see for herself what a success he had made of his life in New South Wales.

In the cab, Gerry felt lighter than he had in years. It had been a pleasant evening. John and Clarissa were 'blood' and they were good people. He looked forward to getting to know them better, and Maureen and her family too. Family: for so long he'd been on his own, and now in a matter of days he was the family elder. He determined that he would live up to that role, particularly for John. Maybe he could use his connections in the industry to try to find out a bit more about who caused the accident in Clarence Street. Have a chat to that site's bricklaying foreman, whom he knew. Yeah, he could do that.

Clarissa was in her bedroom, getting ready for bed. She'd liked John's uncle. He seemed a nice man, a man of good character. It was early days but she hoped that Gerry might be able to support John and provide a much-needed family connection, and perhaps help John deal with the deaths of his workmen. She knew they were weighing heavily on him.

Her nausea had disappeared during the last three days and her baby's movements had subsided. Other than a mild pain in her back she felt good. She slipped off her shift and massaged the underside of her tender breasts, feeling immediate relief. She examined herself in her bedroom's full-length mirror. Her hand slipped over her huge belly with its prominent navel. The pregnancy had thickened her hair and her skin glowed. Her mouth was acceptable she thought, but not her nose, it was too thin. *Oh well, I can't have everything.*

Over the past four weeks since the site accident, John hadn't touched her. She suspected it was due to his anxiety but also she had been so unwell. Lately, though, he seemed better. Now, the thought of him undressed in the next room, perhaps naked, filled her with desire.

John walked in from his dressing-room. A throb of pleasure, not felt for many months, tremored through her.

She didn't move but caught his look in the mirror, his eyes fixed on her bottom. Her excitement intensified and she turned and faced him. She took a step towards him and ran her hands over his shoulders and chest that his new French nightshirt showed off so well.

John looked down at her.

Clarissa smiled and took his hand.

He held it for a moment and she thought he might not want her but then he brought her hand to his mouth and kissed it. She led him to the bedside and with impatience helped him off with his nightshirt. 'Lie down. On your back.'

Arranging herself above and facing away from him seemed natural and yet she couldn't see him. But it felt more than good and she gave herself over to pleasure.

John's heartbeat slowed as Clarissa settled on her side next to him. Her breathing quietened and she was soon asleep. Clarissa had *wanted* him. Her eyes had been glowing, unblinking; she had that look he'd remembered. She had been unwell for so long that he'd got used to her not being interested in sex. And work had been so demanding that by the time he went to bed he was exhausted: even if Clarissa had been up for it, he wasn't sure that he would have been. Perhaps meeting his uncle had raised her spirits. He suddenly realised that his own spirits had been strengthened by meeting his uncle. They would build on this first meeting. He sensed that he'd have to talk straight to his uncle in all things. Gerry seemed to have an uncanny way of understanding what made John tick and getting to the truth. He was like John's mother in that respect; he could never put anything over her.

Clarissa stirred. She had taken him by surprise tonight, reminding him that the passionate woman he had married was still there. It had been good, he had to admit, and he had missed it. They used to talk a lot in bed and he missed that too. There was a lot to catch up on but where would he begin? Would she understand how hurtful those comments he overheard in Melbourne were? He didn't think so; she'd tell him to ignore them, those people didn't matter. Clarissa led a privileged life; she could walk in anywhere and be accepted, and she had no understanding that it was different for John. He wanted to be accepted for his own hard work, not be dismissed because he had married her and because his business was funded by her father. Just thinking about it caused him to grind his teeth. He had to find a way to free his company from David's control.

The walls and ceiling of the Newcastle coach house seemed to be all too constricting. John was impatient to get away from here and be home. The coach back to Sydney was having a last-minute repair done to it and John wanted to vent his spleen. Four other passengers clustered near him were deep in conversation and the constant buzz of chatter was irritating him. The coach driver came into view.

'When are we leaving?' John demanded.

'Mr Leary, we're nearly ready to get going. We just wanted to make sure the replacement part would make the journey back. We shan't be too much longer. We—'

'*We* should have been away an hour ago. This is a poor show and I'll make my complaint in writing to your superiors.'

'I'm sorry again, Mr Leary.'

'Well, don't waste any more time speaking with me. Get back to it.'

The driver scurried off and John sat back down on his bench, fuming.

One hour later, John was waving away the dust that had puffed into the window of the coach. It was the middle of November and it had taken him a week to find out about timber in the lower Hunter. There were ten millers felling the great cedar trees to the northwest of the town, but the difficulty was in obtaining a regular supply due to the demand for quality timber. Hardwood was adequate for structural timbers—the bearers, joists and other heavy beams—but for joinery, architraves, skirting and the like, cedar was the only choice. It had been difficult getting the facts on sawmills; the millers were as secretive as Freemasons. But he had come away satisfied.

David had relented and agreed to buy Jenkins out, and the bank had, with conditions, extended the mortgage on the wire and fencing businesses. Due diligence had found Jenkins's company to be sound with few debts, and John had two clients who wanted speculative terrace houses built in Woolloomooloo. These houses did not have to be built to the highest quality. Clients paid a fixed price for each terrace and John was determined to build them for less than Jenkins had and pocket the change.

There was more good news. The insurance company had met the full cost of the sabotage.

On the other hand, Wexton had found out little about the missing bricklayer's labourer. The investigator had got a sniff of a trail at the wharves where a man fitting Miller's description had booked passage to Melbourne. John agreed to Wexton's suggestion that he should find out more in Melbourne, but was conscious of the money being spent in pursuing this man. He cursed the labourer.

Ignoring the other coach passengers, John concentrated on developing his plans for his timber supply and its transport to Sydney. Controlling this cost would be the challenge, winning David over to the scheme another. Yet again he wished he could be independent of his father-in-law. Given his own financial situation, that seemed unlikely.

But what if David would sell his majority Leary's share to somebody John could control? Far-fetched, he agreed, but this would leave David to run his own businesses and set John up as the true *owner* of Leary's Contracting. That would silence the gossip in Toorak as well. He smiled and caught the eye of an ageing matron sitting opposite. She blushed and looked away.

He'd be known all over Sydney as the core of Leary's, not just the kept son-in-law of a wealthy man. He would build a secure future for Clarissa and their new baby, a big solid company, a great company! Yes, he had to find a friendly buyer to take out David's share. That he couldn't do in this coach, but he could read. He brought out Coleridge and soon was immersed in his poetry.

Gerry Gleeson scanned the Clarence Street warehouse site. The three-storey building looked like it was nearing completion. Carpenters, fearless at heights and tethered to nothing, were noisily nailing the rafters to the ridge board. Scaffolding was just about removed and a load of roofing iron was being delivered. Plumbers' and plasterers' heads were down and the site was humming. All looked good. Stacks of lime, cement and sand were not placed at random but in set positions—all materials that Gerry was familiar with.

The sight of it reminded him of a cathedral in Cork where he had been helping to build a new altar. The altar had had a pair of gold inlaid tabernacle doors, but those doors had been stolen. Not by Gerry, but he had got the blame. Conviction for the theft was sufficient to transport him but he was also convicted of the murder of his best friend and alleged accomplice.

Crime or rather criminals plagued their family, it seemed. Two weeks ago when he'd been reacquainted with Maureen she'd told him about her rape in 1850, a shocking bit of work. And now on this very site—murder. Gerry was determined to do all he could to help John find the culprit.

Lost in thought, he didn't hear the man's question.

'Can I help you there?'

Gerry turned and faced a wiry, dark-haired man in his early thirties. 'Just taking a look. Mr Leary's your boss, isn't he?'

The man placed his boot on a newly-laid step and watched Gerry. 'He is. What's it to you now?'

'My name's Gerry Gleeson. And you must be Sean Connaire?'

'I am,' Sean said, smiling broadly, 'and I'm happy to meet John's uncle. He told me all about you. What can I do for you, Mr Gleeson?'

Gerry felt his firm handshake returned. 'Gerry, please Mr Connaire. John spoke highly of you, and told me you are friends as well as partners. I like to look at sites and how they're run. You probably know I'm a stonemason by trade. Tell me something, if you can. John told me about the sabotage and I'd like to know how he's coping. Do you think it's affecting him?'

Sean paused and it seemed to Gerry that John's partner was considering what to say. 'It's like this, Gerry, he's knocked about pretty bad. He takes things personal-like and he's had history of dealing with bad men.' Gerry remembered what Maureen had told him about John's pursuit of his attacker. 'He's not been himself,' Sean continued, 'that's all I can say. But he's a straight man, doesn't take any shite about building and pays a fair day's wage for a fair day's work. Anything else you want to know?'

Gerry leaned against the wall, hot now from the mid--November sun. 'I want to help him, Sean. I want to get the man or men who did this. Can you tell me all you know? You were here when it happened.'

Sean bowed his head and his lips formed into a straight line. When he looked back at Gerry his face was grim. 'In a way I wished I hadn't been. I've got some time before my next inspection. Come to the site office and I'll tell you all I know.'

Jack Johnson was waiting for John Leary in the yard area of McGuire Wire's Darling Harbour business. Jack tried to control his irritation from escalating to anger. To distract himself from thinking about his employer he thought of the new suit he'd pick up from the tailor on Saturday morning—a beauty that had cost him three weeks' wages—but John Leary returned to his mind again. He was due to meet him in five minutes.

For the past three months, Leary had run the Clarence Street site hard, and Ed Larkin and Sean Connaire had taken the brunt of it. Sean had told him that Leary left his house before dawn and arrived at his George Street office before the sites opened. His boss would then work ten to twelve hours, either in the office or supervising on sites. He was a lot different from the John Leary that Johnson had first met and grown to admire, and to whom he owed his job. Leary had employed him when he'd left the Royal Navy. Johnson had admired his employer's honesty, respect for others and fair-minded nature, but that had all changed and the deaths on the Clarence Street site were the cause, of that he was sure. All the men on the Clarence Street site felt the same as he did.

Leary's Contracting now had four commercial projects under construction, plus a church, one Georgian-style mansion and three sets of terrace houses, employing nine foremen, including Sean as general foreman. Jack Johnson had been promoted from clerk to Purchasing Manager. He didn't hear John walk up behind him and jumped when he spoke.

'Come on Jack, let's have a look around.'

'As I reminded you last week,' Jack said as he accompanied his boss, 'we have too much stock here for the Blunt job. I know you want an inventory of cement and hardwood but both suppliers are screaming to be paid.' John appeared not to be listening. 'Did you hear me? I don't wish to—'

'Jack, I heard. We've too much stock. So what, I need it all.'

'Mr McGuire only agreed to give us part of his yard until the end of November. That's in ten days' time.'

'You let me worry about my father-in-law,' John said, stopping and facing him. Johnson noticed the fine lines around his eyes that hadn't been there before his Melbourne trip. 'As a matter of fact, I'm thinking of buying a brick company and maybe a timber company soon.'

Johnson was dumbstruck, but John started walking again.

'What's that?' Johnson said. '*One* would cost a mint, but both! Where are you going to get the money?' Johnson felt the anger pulse through him. He didn't care. He was a manager and had the right to ask and he was ready for an argument.

John stopped and walked back to him. 'All I hear is whining. Let me worry about the money. You just get this stock to Blunt's site. By the end of the week, I don't want to see anything here that should be on site. So clear it out and clear it out quickly.'

Johnson's breathing quickened; he wouldn't be put aside. 'And what will I tell the suppliers? They're gunning for you now to pay for this stuff. They'll not wait forever.'

John shook his head. 'I'll pay them when I pay them. I want to keep the cash as long as I can. Blunt's job is a tight job. If the merchants yell at you, tell them to piss off.'

'I'll tell them,' Johnson said, 'but that won't settle this. It'll just make it worse. John, you want brains here and you used to have them.'

'I've still got them. Someone has to around here.'

Johnson went for broke. 'You can't bring them back, John. They're dead, but life goes on. You have to, too.'

Leary grabbed Jack by his coat's lapels and pulled him close. 'How dare you!' His eyes were wide, his mouth grim. 'They did their jobs and did them well. Just do your job and get those suppliers off my back.' He let go of him. 'Jesus, Jack, have some balls and bloody use them. You want to stay here? You want this job? Clear this lot now and get rid of those creditors or you'll draw wages as a yard man tomorrow.'

Johnson counted to five. That was a threat but he needed his job. 'Right.'

John smiled. 'That's a good lad, Jack, good lad.'

Johnson shook his head as John walked away. *Stubborn bastard!*
Shut up and saw wood, he thought. That's what he had to do. Just
say nothing and keep his head down. But for how long he could do
that was the question.

John went to bed that night feeling somewhat relieved. Cash was
flowing into the company again and Clarence Street was paying its
way. Clarissa looked asleep. There hadn't been a repeat of her offer
to make love and he hadn't expected an invitation, as the baby was
due in a month.

He pulled the covers up, the movement waking Clarissa, who
struggled to sit up. Rubbing her eyes, she said, 'I want to speak with
you. There's seldom time these days.' Her tone wasn't warm.

'What about?'

'Us.'

Women always seemed to want to talk at the oddest times.
'Can't it wait till tomorrow?'

'No.'

'Right then, speak to me.'

'I feel like there's a distance between us.'

'How so?' he said, smiling. 'I'm right beside you.'

'That's not amusing. I mean we've not talked properly for ages.
I know I've been ill and you've been busy at work, but I'm better
now and I want us to be as close as we used to be, especially as our
baby is almost here. I want you to talk to me, tell me what's going on
with you. You've not been the same since those men died at the
Clarence Street site. You're preoccupied, distant.'

'I'm not distant. I'm just working hard ... for our future. We
have to set ourselves up. We need the money to stand on our own
two feet, not be reliant on your father and his money—'

'You go on about that. You didn't worry about Father's money
in the past,' she said, drawing a dressing gown over her shoulders.
'Why the concern now?'

The words overheard at the Toorak dinner party echoed in his head. 'I've always been concerned about the money and being beholden to your father. We live in this house rent-free, and it's not right.'

Her reply was sharp, 'It's not right?' There was a pause then she sighed. 'Forget your pride John … please. You see me now—the baby's due at any time and you want us to move? What's wrong with you? I don't know you lately. I understand you want to build the company but it's become an obsession. It seems that's all you care about, and you've changed. You're brusque with me, the servants, everyone. What is going on? I really would like you to talk to me about this.'

'You would, would you?'

'I'm your wife. I love you and I'm worried about you. What's caused you to change? I think about the wonderful times just after we were married.'

'Making money isn't easy, Clarissa. This isn't one of your Dublin tea parties.'

'Sarcasm as well. See, that's exactly what I'm talking about.' She pressed his arm. 'I know you're working hard, but what's the problem?'

'I told you. I have to get ahead. That's hard to do. Now go to sleep.' John's neck muscles tightened. These questions. He was sick of questions. Everyone wanted answers to questions—foremen, suppliers, clients. All pecked at him like a crow on a bone. He was tired of it, and now his wife. But her pleading look softened his anger.

'John, please, what *is* wrong?'

'It's what everyone's talking about. Your father's financial hold on Leary's.'

Clarissa frowned. 'Everyone?'

He knew that he'd exaggerated, but that's how he felt it and he was glad that it was now stated. 'Even in Melbourne they talk about it.'

'We've been to Melbourne once. What did you hear there?'

'It was nothing, dear. Go to sleep.'

'No, John. What you may have heard in Melbourne or elsewhere was just gossip. It's only words. Dear me, father will give you control eventually. Why this mad rush to get it? You'll have it. Just be patient.'

Her words were firm and sensible. He was still angry but he knew that was petulance. 'I'm still me, but words can still sting.'

She smiled. 'They can but they won't kill you, dear. Ignore them. Now, please share your problems with me. Don't cut me out. You still love me, don't you? I have to know.'

He took her in his arms. 'I do, Clarissa.'

She looked up at him for some time. 'And I you. I'm glad we had this talk. Sleep well, my love,' she said kissing him before lying back on her pillow.

He did love her, but their conversation confirmed that Clarissa didn't understand why he needed to be in control of Leary's and his family's destiny. It might have been gossip but for John there was an uncomfortable truth in the words he overhead. His pride was wounded and the only way he could salve that was to break free of David and his money. He lay there in the dark, calculating how much money he'd need. It was too much. Finding someone who could purchase David's share was his only option, but despite his efforts he hadn't been able to come up with anyone.

CHAPTER THREE

'WELL,' DAVID SAID AS HE AND JOHN RELAXED IN DAVID'S STUDY, 'it's the twentieth of November and the company is stable. Not out of the woods, but we're in better shape than we were. Those terrace house contracts are profitable.'

'I'll build anything,' John said, 'even another development job.'

'Like Riley Street?' David said and John nodded. 'But that's not your bailiwick, John. Taking risk on buying land, and selling the damned things once built is a headache, surely.'

'Granted, David, and I'd only do another one if all the risks are known. The land has to be the right price, the building design kept simple and the houses easy to sell when the time is right.' He paused. 'But, it has to make money.'

David nodded. 'On another subject—'

'What is it? Not more trouble, I hope?'

'On the contrary,' David said and smiled, 'it's good news, or it could be. You remember Peter Smith?'

John lit a cigar. 'Yes, why?'

'The Smiths. They had the house three doors from us, number seventy-nine, that one with the large verandas and the high pinnacles.'

'Of course. The man passed away in September, didn't he?'

'Sadly, yes. If you recall, Smith built it with the receipts from a big strike in Ballarat and he spared nothing to build it. Well, he got himself into difficulty, lost a fortune and his wife has to sell it, quickly and privately. She's going back to England in ten days to avoid the scandal. She's desperate and it's on the market for five hundred pounds.'

John whistled. 'That's a steal for Wolseley Road. Sounds like land value alone.'

'I suggest you make an offer. I know it's not exactly what you want but it's here in Point Piper, close to us.'

It was worth considering, John felt. 'But the money. It's such a lot of money.'

'I haven't mortgaged this house for any of my businesses.' David looked at him. 'I'm prepared to do that and buy it for you both.'

John's pleasure at this sudden and generous offer became tinged with irritation. By the terms of his marriage to Clarissa, any home that David bought for them would be in David's name for a period of ten years. After that, the title would go to John. But at least they'd have their own home. 'I don't know what to say,' he said. 'It's a wonderful surprise, and I know Clarissa will be happy. How can we ever repay you?'

'It comes with a condition.'

'In addition to you holding the title for ten years?'

David paused. 'When I first met you, that's what I decided, but that may well change.'

'For the better?'

David smiled. 'For you and Clarissa, yes. But let's see how things go for a while.'

Was David softening towards him, John wondered? If he was, John was glad of it. Despite his desire to be free of his financial control, John admired and respected David a great deal.

'But, as I said there's another condition,' David said.

'And what's that?'

'It's a minor one. You've been different since July. The sabotage has had an effect, sure, but I think it's more than that.'

'I don't follow you,' John said tapping his cigar. 'I haven't changed.'

David nodded. 'You have.'

The clock ticked in the silence between them. 'I'm the same now as I was before, but if you feel I've changed then, how?'

'John, I'm your father-in-law and I feel . . . well, I'm fond of you. You must know that. What I see isn't good. It's your manner, your attitude and your behaviour to my daughter.'

'What do you mean?'

'It's your distance from her. As if she was a stranger to you. And then there's Sean: you still haven't set things to rights about the sabotage.'

'I've apologised to him.'

'So he told me, yes, but he sees a change in you as well. I'm telling you this so you can start to correct it.'

John felt under attack, but he smiled. 'Now come on, I'm not that bad. Sure, Clarence Street has knocked me and yes, I'm keen to build the business, but what you see before you is the same John Leary.'

David sighed and raised his eyebrows. 'I won't argue with you, just hear me out. You need to get out of this funk. Things here are back to normal and Sean and I can manage for a while. I want you to take a rest and go to Bathurst, to the family property.'

'Why?'

'For a rest John, a rest. Clear your head. And if you get bored, there's plenty to do up there that should keep you on the tools. I've done a list of tasks.'

'But Clarissa? The child's nearly due.'

David put his hand up, his palm facing John. 'It'll only be a week. You'll be back in time.'

It might be good to get away from Sydney. 'All right,' John said and smiled.

'Spend some time there and come back your old self.'

'I don't think I need to get away but if it means a new house, sure I'll do it.'

'Good,' David said and placed his hand on John's shoulder. 'Let's hope it puts you in a better frame of mind.'

~

In her room, Beth Blackett poured some water from the jug into the bowl and freshened up. The china was acceptable and her room in the Bathurst Inn comfortable and cool. In the afternoon, she'd been reading an article about horse breeds and thinking about her husband, Henry. That morning they had talked about buying brood mares and had differed over the price that a Sofala breeder had wanted. Henry was in Sofala now, trying to buy stock.

After putting the finishing touches to her toilette, she left her room and headed to the dining room. On the way, she wondered how her husband was getting on. They'd not been married a year and he was a fair and generous man on the whole. He hadn't required intimacy all that often, though, and wasn't the sort of man to force himself on her. But Beth needed physical love often and she wondered if that was proper. Some of the girls whom she'd worked with in pubs were tarts, giving themselves freely and without concern. Beth didn't consider herself a tart: she'd not been with a man before Henry, although she had come close with one. It was she who had to take the lead when she felt the need, but she always made sure that it seemed to Henry as if he'd made the move. It often shocked her that she fantasised about another man while making love to her husband.

When she entered the dining room she noticed a man reading the newspaper in the lounge area. She knew him at once: John Leary.

John had travelled to *Clontarf*, the McGuire family property just outside of Bathurst, and within half a day of arriving had been bored. Gathering his tools he then spent three days repairing a storage shed with new timber framing and iron sheeting. Today, after a hot bath, he'd headed to town for supplies for the property overseer. Having secured his stores in the wagon he'd looked forward to a Jameson's and a good meal. The Bathurst Inn was the best in the area for cleanliness and food.

He relaxed in the lounge conversing with a guest, then picked up a newspaper and began to read. As he turned a page he glanced up and saw her: a petite, well-dressed, full-figured woman standing nearby. Her dark hair was gathered under a smart brown bonnet that matched the colour of her eyes. 'Beth,' he said.

She smiled. 'It's nice to see you, John. How are you?'

He stood up, pleased to see her. 'What are you doing in Bathurst?' He shook his head. 'I can't believe it.'

'My husband and I are here to buy horses. Henry's still at Sofala but he's due here any time.' She paused and looked down at the newspaper near John, her eyes widening as she noted the article. 'I've just come back from Ballarat. Father's grave is there. He was killed at Eureka a year ago.'

'Oh,' John said glancing at the paper. 'I was just reading the article on the anniversary. I'm very sorry.'

'Thank you.' Beth recovered and scrutinised him. 'There are so many things to speak about, like Clarissa and your family. Are you staying in town?'

'On a property five miles north. David McGuire—'

'Your father-in-law?'

John nodded. 'He wanted me to come here and have a break. There's always work to be done and that's what I've been doing.'

'And how is Clarissa?'

'She is expecting—any week now.' *God, he'd forgotten how good-looking Beth was.*

'Congratulations,' she said.

'Thank you.'

'If you have time this evening, I'd like you to join Henry and me for dinner. We'd welcome your company.'

'That's kind of you, Beth. I heard you were married. Congratulations to you as well.'

Beth paused for a moment, then said, 'Thank you.'

He hadn't seen her for three years and in that time she had become more attractive and her speech more refined. She must be twenty-two now. Yes, she would be. The thrust of her chin, balancing her sensual mouth, was as he remembered. He'd met her when she had been a barmaid and had rescued him from a drunken binge. Their friendship had continued even when he had been courting Clarissa. His pulse quickened.

She blushed under his gaze. 'So, will you join us?' she said. 'Henry and I have a table reserved.'

No, he didn't think so. After all she was a former love and he wasn't in the mood to share her with any man, even her husband. 'I'm sorry. I have other duties this evening. Maybe——'

A hotel employee came up to them. 'Excuse me, Mrs Blackett. I have a message for you.'

'Thank you.' Beth took the note and read it as the man left. 'It's from Henry. He's going to be late.' She smiled at him. 'A pity you can't make it. The dinner invitation is still open.'

'I was going to check my supplies,' he lied. 'But that can wait. I'd be delighted, thank you.' John had a sudden urge to hold her as he had many years ago.

At the table, sitting opposite John and catching up on each other's news, Beth felt a stirring of her old feelings for him. She'd often regretted that she had never given herself to him in the time they were together, before he married Clarissa.

'Your mother and sisters,' John said, 'are they in good health?'

'They are, thank you. Mother's life is easier now and the girls are growing.'

John grinned. 'Not still keen on tackling me on sight?'

She smiled with him. 'I think they're past that stage.' Her smile faded. 'It's Father I miss.'

'If it doesn't hurt too much, please tell me about his passing.'

'I was sad for months after it happened, of course, and it's still painful. Father was with a group of diggers demonstrating against the licence tax. When they were asked to disperse they refused to do so, and the constabulary opened fire. His licence was found on him. He had been shot in the chest.' Beth's eyes glistened. 'He was murdered by the police.' She brought a hanky to her eyes as their meals arrived. She managed to pull herself together after the waiter left. 'The way he died still has an effect on me.'

'He was your father and it was a brutal way to go. Please don't think me rude, but tell me about Henry. Is he a good man?'

Beth nodded and closed her eyes for an instant. She understood that he was trying to distract her and was glad for that. 'He's a good man, John. I met him in Sydney, in the pub. Do you remember the Royal in Woolloomooloo? The one where I first met you?'

Those times returned to him in a flash of happiness. 'I remember.'

'I told you I wanted to get out of that hotel,' she said. 'Well, I did.'

John was enjoying his food, but Beth toyed with her dinner. She was still upset and she was conscious of the other dining patrons who now surrounded them.

She took a sip of water to calm herself. 'Henry came in one day and ordered a drink. You know how much I love horses. Well, Henry's a horse breaker. He came to the hotel on a few more occasions and, after a while, we struck up a friendship.'

'A friendship which turned into something more,' John said.

'Yes. We had something in common.'

'It seems so.' John's gaze was steady, unsettling her. 'You got what you wanted, a good husband who shared your love of horses.'

'Well, Clarissa had you wrapped around her little finger from the start.'

He smiled at her description. Her eyes locked onto his again and saw in them a look she knew. He covered one of her hands with his. She responded with her own and squeezed. 'I'm glad I found you.' She looked at her half-eaten dinner. 'I hate waste. I still do, despite my better life.' She sighed. 'Visiting Father's grave and remembering how he died has distressed me more than—'

Her eyes moistened and filled as he pressed her hand again.

'You must have been very close to him,' John said.

She shook her head and took a handkerchief to her tears. 'He did well at the goldfields. The miners called his strike a golden hole. He was more successful than we had thought, especially towards the end. He left us a fortune. You're looking at a wealthy woman,' Beth said. *And a woman who needs your touch!*

This is impossible, Beth thought, mentally shaking herself. She wished that Henry would walk in here now and break this spell. The connection she felt with John was so strong. John seemed to know what she was thinking, and this unnerved her even more, especially as her fingers had been twirling a button on her blouse. 'So, how is married life?' she asked.

'It's certainly different. Clarissa is expecting, as I told you.'

A vision of Clarissa's swollen figure with John's baby inside came to her. All the more painful given that her own attempts at having a child hadn't been successful. Pushing those thoughts aside, she asked, 'When is the baby due?'

'Pretty soon. She's had a difficult time, been sick throughout the pregnancy.'

'I'm sorry to hear that.' She took her hand away. Again, her eyes filled with tears.

A middle-aged man approached their table and looked at both of them in turn. 'Beth,' he said. 'Is anything wrong? I'm sorry to be so late.'

'Henry, no, I'm all right. It's just that I was telling John about Father. Henry, this is Mr John Leary. He's staying in the area. He's an old friend. We met in the lounge tonight and we've been chatting about old times over dinner.'

Henry hesitated, then put his hand out. John stood up and shook hands with Beth's husband, who said, 'Are you in Bathurst for business or pleasure?'

'A bit of both, Mr Blackett,' John said and he looked down at his now empty plate. 'In fact, I've had rather a long day so I'll bid you both goodnight.'

'If you insist,' Blackett said with politeness.

'Thank you for being so understanding about Father, Mr Leary,' Beth said. 'Will we see you tomorrow?'

'I'll be off at first light, back to the property. After that I'll be doing some exploring of the area, then return to Sydney.'

'I hope Mrs Leary is well,' Beth said, 'and your baby is born healthy and happy.'

'It's been a pleasure to meet one of my wife's friends, Mr Leary,' Blackett said. 'Perhaps we'll see you in Sydney some time.'

'I hope so,' John said.

Beth looked at John as he left the room and decided she definitely would see him again.

On the way back to Sydney on the coach, John found himself thinking of Beth. He was still attracted to her. But she was a married woman. And he was a married man, soon to be a father. It was not to be thought of. He turned his thoughts to wondering how Clarissa was faring.

The baby would be due within the next fortnight, or so the doctor had said. John was looking forward to getting back home. He'd been restless the past two days as he explored the country on his horse. At times he'd thought about the Clarence Street murderer and how he wished that he could be caught. The fact that Miller was running around free weighed on him. He'd even had a dream where he was choking the bastard, watching the man's life slip away under his pressing fingers, only to wake in a sweat to the stillness of the night and its blazing stars.

Someday he'd find that labourer and perhaps the man behind him who was the real mongrel. His uncle had offered help and would keep his eye out. For that John was thankful. He was reminded of his own search to track down his sister's rapist. The man had slipped away before he could be brought before the court, but not before John had given him a severe beating. John closed his eyes. He knew he would do the same to Miller and his master, if he got his hands on them.

The crack of the driver's whip startled him and he wondered whether he should meet Beth again in Sydney, even if she had Henry with her. Clarissa would take a dim view of a past relationship being continued. Better to forget about his former friend.

Christine McGuire sat on the veranda outside Clarissa's bedroom, fanning her face as the late afternoon sun blazed down on their Point Piper home. 'John seems in a better frame of mind since his return,' she said to her daughter.

'He is, Mother. He's a better man than you give him credit for.'

Blackburn Cove and the headland opposite shimmered in the haze. It was just like her mother to continue to be sceptical of John, the husband Christine had never wanted for her. Turning to the table between them she poured another glass of iced lemonade for her mother, who took a sip before speaking.

'Time will tell,' Christine said, 'but he's still not right. Ever since your holiday in Melbourne he's been a different person: angry, bitter and rude. Let's hope Mr Gleeson, who seems an upright man, can restore John's equanimity. Perhaps it was that accident, but could there be anything that you've done to upset him?'

Clarissa shook her head and opened two more buttons on her strained blouse. Christine could see that there was pain in her daughter's eyes. 'Are you all right?'

'I'm managing. It's just ... the baby is pressing and it's taking my breath.' Clarissa struggled to adjust the cushion behind her and Christine got up to help her.

For the next hour, as they chatted about baby names and expectations, the sun descended, its orange orb making the trees on the headland stand out in relief, their branches wafting to the warm northwesterly wind.

Stella, Clarissa's maid, arrived to take away the drinks, and Christine stood up. 'Don't be too long out here, dear,' she said.

'I won't.' After a few minutes Clarissa rose and walked with difficulty through the French windows, closing them behind her. Pain flashed as her baby kicked and she smiled. Oh, I wish John could have felt that, it had a male's brutish force. She thought of the baby inside her: *I wish it would come and end this discomfort.* Did all mothers feel this way? Surely she wasn't the only one suffering like this.

Another sharp movement jabbed her right at the base of her

womb. She sucked her breath in. That was like nothing she'd ever felt before. Only gripping the table edge helped her through the pain, her knuckles turning white from the effort. As she stood there, a warm dampness spread between her legs. Doubling over in agony, she felt herself falling and called out, 'Mother, come quickly. I need you!'

Clarissa opened her eyes to darkness, and perspiration covered her forehead. She felt so odd and so sore. It was as though she'd been kicked in the stomach, and her skin was tender and torn. Yes, she'd given birth to a baby boy. In between periods of consciousness, she'd heard the midwife's garbled words describing the infant.

Features came into focus and she wanted a drink. It wasn't her bedroom; it had the scent of a guest room's mustiness.

'I'm here, dear,' John said.

She reached and clasped his hand as he sat on the bed. 'We have a son,' she said.

He smiled with her. 'We have, my darling. It was a little early but he's well.'

More pain shot through her as she reached for a glass of water.

'Here, let me do that,' John said, handing the glass to her.

She pushed herself up with a grimace and drank. Her parched throat sucked up the liquid like a sponge.

Christine entered the room followed by Stella. 'How are you feeling, dear?' her mother asked.

'Evening, ma'am,' Stella said, 'I hope you're not in too much pain. I have something for you to eat.'

'Thank you, Stella. I am hungry.'

'You gave us some trouble after you collapsed,' her mother said, 'and the midwife took her time getting here, but all has ended well.' Her mother clasped her hands as though she was going to sing. 'A big boy, about ten pounds. Another Leary but he's got your looks and he will have the McGuire breeding, that's for sure.' Clarissa looked at John and he rolled his eyes back at her. 'But he's healthy,'

Christine continued, 'and will need feeding soon, so better get yourself prepared.'

Clarissa's breasts ached. Her son was now dependent on her. 'Mother, could you tell the midwife I'll be ready in ten minutes. I'll have something to eat first.'

'I shall, my dear,' her mother replied and left the room.

Downstairs in the drawing room, Christine found David pacing the floor.

'How is she?' he said. 'Is she sleeping? Has she drunk anything?'

'She's had a glass of water and is eating something now,' Christine replied. 'She's through the worst of it.'

'I'm glad that everything seems all right. I've seen the infant.' David's eyes filled with tears. 'Oh what a little beauty. The size of him! He's going to be as big and as broad as his father, you'll see. I can't wait to pick him up and play with him.'

Christine smiled. 'Well, be patient for a few days, until he gets a little bigger.'

David smiled with her. 'I suppose you're right.'

'Now, on another matter,' Christine said, 'you're going to buy the Smith house for them, aren't you?' David seemed a bit put out at this change of subject but nodded. 'I'd like to remind you,' she said, 'of our agreement before Clarissa was married, that you were to buy a house in your name only.'

'Yes, yes, I know. But I may have second thoughts.' David looked upstairs. 'Come, if we must talk about this now, let's use my study.'

'Very well.'

After he'd closed the study door, David turned to his wife, 'I remember the agreement.'

'I don't trust him. I'm sorry David, but that's how I feel. My instincts haven't changed and indeed his behaviour recently would seem to confirm that my original convictions were correct.'

'Because of the sabotage business?' David waved his arm in dismissal. 'Anyone would be affected by that. Good God, Christine, men were killed.'

'I know and that was very sad. But it's the other things I've heard. The way he wants to grow the company, indeed the pace of that. It all points to a blind ambition that needs money and lots of it. He'll ruin our daughter in the long run if he gets his hands on our assets.'

'I think you're being overdramatic. Let me worry about the business. He's only been back two days but he seems in a better frame of mind. He just needed a holiday.'

'A holiday for that man won't change his motivation. He'll do anything to build his business and use anybody's money to do it,' Christine nodded. 'There, I've said it and if you don't like it . . . then that's that.'

David sighed. 'I'll consider your view, although I don't agree that the lad's like you say. Let's just concentrate on Clarissa and her baby for the time being.'

Upstairs, John removed the tray from Clarissa's bed and placed it on the chest of drawers.

'Darling, hold me,' she said. 'I'm so happy.'

He came to her, hugged her and kissed her and she snuggled into him.

He broke away. 'The baby will be here any moment. I'd better go.'

'No stay, please,' she said.

'Are you sure?' He smiled, 'I'd like to.'

'Good.'

There was a knock on the door and the midwife brought the baby in and approached the bed.

'Let my husband hold him, please.'

John stood up and reached for his son. His eyes glistened and Clarissa soon had tears in her eyes as she watched her husband with his son.

'That's right, sir,' the midwife said. 'You've got your hands just right.'

'It's so incredible,' John said looking down at the bundle he held. 'A son. He's heavy.'

'I'm glad you were here,' Clarissa said.

'Yes, we hadn't expected him to be here so soon,' John said.

'There was not much I could do about that, I'm afraid.'

John shook his head, still looking at the infant. 'No, the little man wanted to be born. See! He smiled! It'll be Richard, yes? After my father?'

'I think that would be nice, my love.' She pressed his hand.

'Mrs Leary,' the midwife said, 'I have to get you ready. If your husband could leave us.'

'I'm going,' John said, smiling as he handed her the baby.

∾

Gerry Gleeson scowled as he looked at the *Sydney Morning Herald* on his landlady's dining-room table. 'Damned Englishmen. Why don't they just get out of the Crimea?'

In October, just two months past, the British and French fleets had fired on Russian forts on the Dnieper River, with little loss to their ships. 'That's a turn-up after the Light Brigade's disaster of a year ago,' he said.

'What are you muttering about?' his eating companion asked.

'The British ironclad floating batteries attacking the Russians.'

'Good. I hope all ships will be built like that. Splinters from timber ships are a bastard of a way to die.'

'We'll not have that language at my dinner table,' their landlady said. 'I'll remind you to keep civil tongues when you're in my company.'

'Sorry, ma'am,' they muttered together.

Gerry was about to fold the newspaper when he glanced at the births and deaths section—always something of interest there. The name Leary jumped out at him and he read on. *So a little Leary has been born, eh? Richard Leary. Well, there you go.* They'd named him after his grandfather. Gleeson smiled. He'd send John and Clarissa a congratulatory note. Maybe Richard Leary in time would accept that his great-uncle, though once branded a criminal, wasn't a bad man.

∾

Brian Atkins, Worshipful Master of Sydney's Number Two Lodge and the youngest son of a Gloucestershire peer, sat in his armchair in his mansion in St John's Road, Glebe. He was reading the Tenders Section in the 6 February edition of the *Sydney Morning Herald*. Leary's Contracting was advertising for suppliers to provide materials for a tender they'd won to build a warehouse in Balmain. Leary, that bog-bred papist!

Atkins had inherited his father's brown eyes; wavy brown hair, now tinted with grey; fair complexion and Lord Percy's hatred of Catholics. Cromwell was his hero. Leary was tainted with the Fitzgerald dynasty through his wife Clarissa, who was related to them. The Fitzgerald dynasty of Kildare had become the effective rulers of Ireland in the 15th century. Lord Percy's ancestors had been killed by Catholics in Portadown during Cromwell's occupation of that cursed island. Over the last two hundred years Atkins's family had maintained control of their Irish lands, but the Catholics continued to fight against them, most recently in the July 1848 rebellion. His father's view was that the only good Catholic was one chained to a plough or dead under the peat. It was a view strongly held in every fibre of Brian Atkins's five feet, eight-inch frame.

Atkins, an intelligent man, had watched his oldest brother prepare to inherit the title, while at the same time glorying in the victories and medals collected by his other brother, a Guards' Colonel. Brian, the youngest, was packed off to New South Wales at the age of twenty-nine with his inheritance and the hope that he would make a good life there. He arrived in 1840 and was disappointed to find that there was no permanent meeting place for their Number Two Lodge. The brothers had to contend with worshipping in designated dwellings. At one such meeting, he'd overhead a comment about a forthcoming wool clip and was able to turn his modest inheritance into a small fortune.

Though making money was no part of his aristocratic breeding, he discovered that he had a talent for developing properties for sale or rent, and his fortune continued to grow. As this was the Antipodes, he felt he could not be condemned for turning a quid in such a manner, and soldiered on. It became his passion. He used two main contractors to do his work: Shelby Contractors and Thomas Constructions. Be it a warehouse for lease, a gentleman's residence or a terrace of houses for sale, he relished the challenge of getting the right deal as much as he had riding to hounds.

He'd kept tabs on John Leary. In October 1854 Atkins had been going to purchase a site in Riley Street in town, get Shelby or Thomas to erect terraces on it, and then sell each terrace to individual buyers. Atkins would have made a tidy profit from the sale of each house. But Leary had come on the scene through David McGuire, who'd known the owner of the site.

Leary, the insufferable hedgerow nationalist, had convinced the site's owner not to sell his land to a developer like Atkins. Atkins, or someone like him, Leary had said, would get a development profit from packaging up the whole process. Why pay a developer *his* profit when the original owner could make money from develop-ing the site himself? Leary would build terraces at a fixed price for the site's owner on the owner's land; Leary would make a profit on building the terraces, and the owner would have newly-built terraces he could lease for a steady future income. Or he could sell each or all of them at a future date. Damned cheek! That was the first time that Atkins had lost out on a deal. And Leary was creating his own market and not relying on architects and clients bringing him projects to build or to tender on.

Developers were developers. They took the risk in buying land, financing it, providing it with services and utilities, building the warehouse, house or terrace and looking for buyers. Builders such as John Leary should stick to just *building* and not meddle in the business of developers. But it had got worse. In January one year past, Atkins had seen a good site in Glebe and wanted to purchase it, build a house on it of sterling proportions and sell it to his gentleman Freemason friend at a tidy profit for himself. Again John Leary had got between Atkins and his profit-making plans. Leary had convinced Atkins's friend to buy the land himself and then John Leary and his company would build him a house of equal quality. All for a sum a lot less than that Atkins had quoted to his gentleman friend for house and land. Atkins had to do something to stop Leary undercutting him and destroying his business.

Sydney needed only three big builders: Shelby, Thomas and the Maxton Brothers. There was no room for upstarts to challenge that cartel or—God forbid—take business from developers. Let Leary fossick around the smaller jobs and leave the large and prestigious ones to the top three. Upstarts, especially Kildare scum, upset the balance, the order of things, and they should be discouraged. Strongly.

Atkins got up from his breakfast table and placed the newspaper on the sideboard.

John hung up his hat and paused in the lobby. *Bede Hall*, the former Smith house in Wolseley Road, was well-planned and well-built, with drawing rooms, a dining room, kitchen and study on the ground floor and a handsome staircase to the first-floor bedrooms and bathrooms. It was the end of the first week in March and they'd been in the house for two months.

He was happy with the house but not with its ownership. David would hold its title for ten years. This separated it from the assets of Leary's Contracting, which meant that David didn't trust him—and rightly, because John would have mortgaged the house to raise funds. But now he couldn't. He felt he was going backwards. But then he remembered that just before he'd gone to Bathurst, David had said he was considering changing his mind about that time period. He should follow up with him about that.

In the drawing room Clarissa was sitting next to the window studying a document. 'Good evening, darling,' he said. 'What's that you're reading?'

Clarissa smiled at him. 'Good evening, dear. It's a report from McGuire Wire. I think my father could do a better deal on this new type of wire press just available from England.' Clarissa had helped her father in his business when she'd first come to the colony, but her marriage and pregnancy had kept her away from it. Now she wanted to become involved again. However, with her newborn son, that might prove impossible.

John walked to the sideboard and poured himself a Jamesons. Clarissa continued to read and he sat on a lounge chair enjoying his drink. He thought about the time he spent at the office and the hours required to run the many sites, even with Jack Johnson's increasing assistance.

He had to know everything about construction. Not just the building side, but also the connecting processes and risks; how to plan for shortfalls in supplies, how to lessen the double handling of materials and the sequence of work on his sites. Control was everything. The Surry Hills warehouse had been completed on time a week ago and there were still five projects, including a row of ten terrace houses in Darlinghurst, in various stages of construction. He wanted to expand again. He took personal responsibility for every brick and every piece of timber that went into a new terrace house, warehouse or church.

Clarissa looked up from her reading and caught him looking at her. Putting down her paperwork, she stood up and walked towards him. She looked inviting. They had restarted their intimacy and he knew it was the reason for his calmness.

'Would you like another drink?' she said.

'Yes, thanks. Is there any mail?'

'Yes, I'll get Stella to bring it in'

She was handing John his drink when Stella came in with five letters spread on a silver platter. John took his whiskey and sat down to read while Stella lit the gas sconces. The first four envelopes were about business but the last one looked a bit the worse for wear and it bore a Dublin postmark. Something from home, he hoped.

He took out the letter, read the first paragraph and paused. Words formed, their meaning registering, but a part of him blocked acceptance. He read the first paragraph again and bit by bit its contents sank in. The letter was from his eldest brother, Kieran. 'Clarissa, it's bad news. My mother has died.'

Clarissa put down her report and went to him. She placed a hand on his forearm and looked at the letter. 'Oh no! How? When?'

John shook his head and dropped the letter. Trembling, he raised his hand to his forehead. 'She died in her sleep after a short illness in December. My father was too grief-stricken to put pen to paper.'

Clarissa held him. 'I'm so sorry.' After a moment, he made his way to the window and looked out into the March dusk. 'I'm glad she didn't suffer. She had a good life, but I'll miss her.' He leaned against the windowsill and cleared his throat. 'I can imagine what Da is going through after a lifetime together. They were happy, if you can measure happiness by the feeling of contentment you had when you were with them.'

Clarissa stood beside him. 'Come and sit down darling, please. This is dreadful news. It's unfortunate you're so far away. You'll want to tell Maureen and Gerry.'

'Yes,' he said, trying to clear his head to think. 'Please get word to both of them to come here as soon as they can. I'll just go upstairs for a bit, if you don't mind, and wait for them.'

'Of course, darling. I'll inform Mother and Father too.'

He walked from the drawing room, his legs feeling weak. Closing the bedroom door, he sat on a chair near the window and looked at the view. The brightness of the light contrasted to the softer glow of the Irish sunsets of his memory. Images of his mother came to him. She might have been far away but she was always in his heart. He'd carried a nail box full of guilt when he remembered that she'd wanted him to stay in Ireland and train as an architect. If he'd stayed he could've seen her often but would that have stopped her passing? No. She was gone but her soul lived on. She'd never seen her grandson nor seen her favourite brother again but he sensed her spirit was near. John's sorrow deepened and he gave way to his tears.

On a Friday, a week before Easter, John's grief was getting easier to carry. It had been a long, dark eight days since he'd received the news of his mother's death, during which time he, Maureen and

Gerry had attended a Mass said for her soul at St Mary's. Now, looking for a distraction he scanned the work on his desk and realised that he had to do something about organising his time better. The smell of his newly-painted office was pungent and he should've waited one more day before returning to it.

On a pile of correspondence was a letter from Harrison's, a timber business in Melbourne that was for sale. Harrison was keen to sell but John wasn't interested. The difficulties in transportation and control far outweighed any possibilities for profits. There was enough timber here in New South Wales, especially from the Cooks River area and the Hunter.

Jack Johnson walked into his office. 'Can I see you?'

'I'm busy, Jack. Can't it wait?'

Jack had changed. These past six months had put grey streaks in his hair and added flesh under his eyes. John wondered why. He was paying Johnson a high salary to keep him and he was an important part of Leary's Contracting.

Sean came in and Jack nodded to him. John wondered why Sean had come in now. Was it something to do with Johnson?

'No, it can't wait,' Jack said. 'It's about the payroll. I need another two clerks to help me. With the number of employees we've now got, I'm working late nights. Last week I made two mistakes.'

Sean leaned against the window sill. 'The ordering's falling behind too, John. Jack needs a hand.'

'I don't think so,' John said. 'Work smarter, Jack, not longer. No extra staff.'

Jack folded his arms. 'Why not?'

'Why not? Jack, get to bed earlier and get some rest. That'll make you work better. Now, off you go. I'm busy.' Jack glanced at Sean.

'No use getting Sean to fight for you,' John said. 'My mind's made up.'

'Well, you've been warned,' Jack said and left the office.

'And what's your problem, Sean?' John asked.

'Why did you do that?' Sean asked. 'We can afford another clerk or two. I've seen Jack. He's been here at sparrow fart and till late—'

'I've made my decision. Now, what do you want?'

'What's got you worked up?' Sean said.

John sighed and sat back. 'I don't know, I don't. Maybe the smell in here. Maybe it's losing my Ma.'

'It's a big thing, John. We all prepare for it but when it hits us, we still reel.'

'Yeah.' Sean was looking at him sympathetically but John wanted none of it. He was angry and Jack had triggered it off. Why? He knew Jack was struggling doing his job but John was suspicious of his purchasing manager's motives. John sensed Jack had it in for him and would take any opportunity to make mischief. But then why would he? Perhaps John was over worrying,

'Any news on Miller?' Sean said.

John was relieved to think about something else. 'Nothing yet, mate. It's a bloody mystery but one I'll solve. I have to,' John said. 'So, what do you want?'

'Training. I've thought about what we talked about last week. We have to get our sub-foremen ready to take on a site.'

'As general foreman, that's your job.'

'It is, but we need leadership. Our foremen have to know there are men under them who are gunning for their jobs and for mine in time. I want our sub-foremen to see where hard work and ambition can get them. You've ploughed that field. We want them to be hungry, that's how you build a good business.'

John nodded. 'You're onto something, because we are going to get bigger. It's best to use the men we've got, not employ others. Any ideas?'

'The sub-foremen need to see you in action,' Sean said. 'You come to sites but they've got to see you in here and how the whole company works. They'll still be responsible to their foreman but this will give them great training.'

'Right,' John said and thought for a bit. 'From next Monday morning, starting at eight in here, I want you and Johnson, Reynolds, Frank Cartwright and the five sub-foremen for a weekly one-hour meeting. The agenda will be simple: the next week's work, program, suppliers and new building ideas.'

'Good. Now about Jack. I've worked up the cost. We can manage it.'

John's irritation returned. 'You think he needs those men?'

'I do.' Sean was adamant.

And he was probably right, John thought. 'Very well, but make sure Jack keeps them busy.'

'He will. That's it for me. How is the little fellow?'

John smiled for the first time in many days. 'Growing and noisy, but he's chipper.'

'Say hello to Clarissa for me. You and her should come over some time. I'll invite Gerry as well.'

'Thank you, Sean. Now, I've really got to get on with it.'

'I'm gone.'

Sean left and John thought about the business. There were three top contractors in Sydney whose members were rich and influential, and it would be difficult jumping over them. They were a cartel, each protecting the other. It didn't matter how good Leary's Contracting was, how quickly they built, and to what quality, it could never be in the top tier without doing something different. He had to find a way to crack that club.

At the Hero of Waterloo hotel, Colleen Anderson was cleaning the last few glasses, inspecting each one as she did. It was quiet for Easter Monday and it would be a good time to replace half the old glasses with new ones. There was only one punter, a working man, leaning on the bar with his back turned to her, a full glass beside him. Bob the barman was wiping over the beer taps.

A well-dressed gentleman walked up to the bar. By his look, Colleen guessed a drink wasn't on his mind, as his eyes were fixed on the worker. As he placed both hands on the bar, she noticed a lump near the gentleman's left thumb.

The working man picked up his drink and nodded to the gentleman. 'Evening.'

'Come with me,' the gentleman said in a well-educated voice. They walked over to a far table.

'I'll get the new glasses now, Bob,' Colleen said. She went into the nearby storeroom and closed the door. She grabbed a set of steps, took them over to the shelves at the back where the new glasses were boxed, and climbed up to get them. There was an opened highlight window above another locked door near her. She heard chairs scraping in the bar area adjacent to the storeroom.

'What the hell are you doing here?' a man said. 'I told you not to come back.' He sounded like the gentleman, but she wasn't sure and she kept still.

'I need money,' the other man said.

'I gave you money. Someone will recognise you. I should've thrown your note away and not come.'

'But you didn't, did you?'

'No, I didn't,' the gentleman said. 'What do you want anyway?'

'Money, like I said. Otherwise I'll write to the police about Clarence Street . . . the accident.' Colleen's shoe slipped on the step tread but she managed not to fall. She was now interested. 'I will,' the man continued. 'I'll say you done it. All them building workers dead. Now . . . what's it worth to keep me gob shut?'

Colleen shivered.

'How much?' the gentleman said.

'Fifty quid.'

Another pause.

'I won't pay it.'

'Then I'm out of here.'

'Wait,' the gentleman replied in a harsh whisper, 'I haven't got that with me,' 'I'll get it, but that's the last. You try to see me again to get more money and I'll make sure it's the last sight you see.'

'I'll be here tomorrow night,' the other man said.

'No, not here. At Skinners, the day after tomorrow, seven p.m. Now get out.'

She heard a chair scrape and Colleen climbed back down, went to the storeroom door and pushed it open a tad. The man she'd heard demand the money was the worker. He slipped out the pub's door. Footsteps sounded near her and she hid herself from view but saw the suited arm of the gentleman as he walked past her and up to the bar.

'A Scotch whisky,' the gentleman said.

Damp with perspiration, she leaned back. Accident? What accident? The blackmailer, and that's what he was, she was sure, could be a building worker. Cocky. What would her friend Doreen say? She remembered Doreen's brother was in the building game. And Doreen worked at Skinners.

When were the two men going to meet? The day after tomorrow, Wednesday, they'd said. Colleen waited till the gentleman left and went to the bar. 'Let's lock up, Bob.'

'Right you are.'

Colleen was eager to talk to her friend at Skinners.

'That's right, Doreen, tomorrow tonight.'

'But Colleen, would you know him again?' Doreen said as she wiped over the mirror at the back of the Skinners bar.

Colleen's brow wrinkled. 'I'd know them both anywhere.'

'Well, are you goin' to come here tomorrow night?'

Colleen moved sideways as a customer leaned on the bar.

'Pint of Bass, please, Miss Little, when you're ready,' the man said.

'Doreen, please, Mr Gleeson. I've told you to call me that. How's work been today?'

'Same as usual,' Gleeson replied. 'Why? Know someone who wants a job?'

Doreen grinned as she put the beer on the bar. 'Not me.' Doreen smiled at him and turned to Colleen. 'Mr Gleeson might know about those men,' she said to Colleen.

'What men?' Gerry asked after draining half his glass.

'My friend here,' she said nodding at Colleen, 'overheard something strange. She thinks it's about building—'

'Mr Gleeson, it's all confusin' but I overheard a bloke talking

about Clarence Street, a site, I think, yes, and an accident. Yes ...
that's it.'

Gerry Gleeson held his glass in space and turned to Doreen's
friend. 'Miss?'

'Anderson. But call me Colleen.'

'I'd like to hear what you have to say. Now let's go over to a table
and you can tell me everything.'

On Wednesday night, Gerry Gleeson, Bob Jones and Sean
Connaire were sitting in an unlit area in Skinners Hotel, where they
had a good view of the bar. *You can be lucky sometimes,* Gerry thought.
He knew Bob, the Clarence Street bricklaying foreman, and had
chatted with him previously about the sabotage that caused the
deaths of three of the workers. Gerry had gone to Bob's house the
night after hearing what Colleen had to say about the conversation
at the Hero on the Monday night. Bob had wanted to tell John
Leary but Gerry had cautioned him not to. It might all be just a
ruse, or Colleen Anderson had misheard the two men, and he didn't
want to get John all riled up for nothing. But he agreed they should
tell Sean and the police.

The two men had then gone to the police, who organised to
have their men outside Skinners, ready to move in when Gerry gave
the word. Now, the three of them were waiting and watching, but it
was nearly closing time. Colleen had said that the suspicious pair
were to have met at seven. It was long past that.

Colleen was at a nearby table, also in semi-darkness. The others
watched as a man came in and went to the bar.

Gerry poked Bob Jones, who was rubbing his eyes. 'Is that Jim
Miller, Bob?'

'Aye, that's him! I'd know the bastard anywhere. Come on.'

Bob and Sean stood up but Gerry pulled them down. 'Let's wait
to see if his mark turns up, then we'll get them both.'

'But he might leave,' Sean said.

He might too, Gerry thought. 'Just a bit more time.'

Jones nodded.

They waited another ten minutes until the staff were locking up. Still the gentleman hadn't shown. Their quarry put his drink down and headed for the door.

'Quick,' Gerry said, 'let's go. Sean, you stay here in case he doubles back.' They headed outside to Hunter Street. Gerry refocused his eyes in the street's darkness and by the gas street lamp saw the man twelve feet ahead. 'Come on, Bob,' he said.

They quickly walked up and pounced on the labourer.

'Jim, back in town?' Jones asked.

Miller's eyes widened as he tried to shake them off. His fear gave him away and Gerry knew they'd got their man.

'Not so fast,' Gerry said, tightening his grip. 'Get the police, quick.'

'Is this the man you employed, sir?' A sergeant appeared beside them with another policeman.

'It is,' Jones said.

'You're quite sure?'

'Oh yes, I'm very sure.'

'Very well.' The sergeant slapped irons on the man. 'James Miller, I'm arresting you for the murder of the three men at Clarence Street.'

'I didn't do it,' the labourer said, his voice quivering. 'You've got nothin' on me.'

The police manhandled the offender into the back of a wagon and locked the door. John will be relieved to hear we've got the murderer, thought Gerry.

'I'll need you both to give me your statements,' the sergeant said touching his helmet. 'We'll send for you.'

Next door to Skinners, a man in a well-cut suit sank further into the shadows of Hunter Street. He placed a sharp-edged knife back into the sheath underneath his jacket. Well, that was a turn-up. The police had just made his job easier. He was glad he hadn't needed to move in and kill Miller as he'd walked by. Murder was a filthy and conscience-troubling business. However, he knew the blackmail wasn't going to end and he desperately needed to silence the man. He smiled. No one would believe the labourer's story. No one. But then, there was still a risk he'd be unmasked.

～

John sat near his drawing room fire on a late March evening. 'I can't believe it. Grabbed, just like that, having a beer at the pub. Now we may find out why he killed those men.'

David nodded. 'It probably won't come out till the trial but it's good news. And even better that your uncle had a hand in it,' John agreed. 'Should you write to that investigator?' David said. 'He may not have seen the paper.'

'He would've seen it,' John said as he refilled his glass, 'but a good idea.' He'd tell Wexton, but he wanted him to continue his digging. He wanted information on the arrested man's connections.

'You spoke last week about the Australia Club,' David said. 'Why the interest?'

John sipped his port. He had learned that the directors of the two largest contractors were members of that Club. 'I want to meet Shelby and Thomas.'

'Why?'

'It's good business to understand your competitors. Who knows, they could help us, perhaps even do partnerships with us.'

David blew his smoke at the fireplace. 'Partnerships? That seems risky.'

'Not if you set up the contracts properly. Two contractors building a project in association. It has benefits. Both make a quid out of it.'

David nodded. 'If you say so. But let me have the final say on whom you choose.'

'Of course,' John said. *God, help me find a way to be free of the man.*

'I have to go to the Club on the thirtieth of April to meet a new client,' David said. 'Come with me then and I'll introduce you to them, if they are there.'

'Thank you,' John said.

There was little time to spare in his busy days, but he'd managed to find information on his top-notch competitors. Visiting pubs was the best way. Once, John had accompanied Gerry, who knew a wide circle of tradesmen. Workers talked to him about their bosses, who the bricklayers were, what material was going to site, the top performing workers and other details. John made notes later at night, compiling useful details.

It had surprised him that the three top builders, Thomas, Shelby and Maxton had problems too—instances of shoddy work, suppliers who let them down and clients who didn't pay on time—just as he'd experienced. Putting his port down, John looked up to see David looking at him.

'I must say,' David said, 'since Christmas you seem to be your old self—just about.'

John smiled. He didn't feel any different, but if David believed that, then he'd not upset him. John wanted his independence but he would not treat David shabbily. 'Perhaps little Richard is the reason.'

David stood, 'Whatever the reason, it's good. Now, it's late and I'm tired. I'll say goodnight.'

John saw his father-in-law out, then returned to his study to consider his next project. Through a leading firm of architects, the Sydney Council had advertised for tenders for a memorial hall to be built in Park Street. Leary's had three weeks to prepare and lodge their tender. He badly wanted the exposure that this monumental building project would give the company. Everyone would know who built the memorial hall, and it would lift Leary's up to the top level, in competition with the big three.

Nearly four weeks after he'd submitted his bid, a clerk led John into a Council anteroom and pointed to a table with four chairs on each side of it. 'Please take a seat, Mr Leary. Mr Clancy will be with you shortly.'

The clerk left and closed the door after him. John didn't sit down but paced the room. It was encouraging that the Council wanted to talk to him. The tender he'd submitted must have been attractive. Since 1842, the Sydney Council had operated from sub-standard accommodation here in the George Street Market Building. There was talk of a new building to be built on the site of the old graveyard, bounded by George, Druitt and Kent Streets, but it was still in the planning stages, and not even the architects had been briefed. Building over a graveyard would be interesting. Did they leave the bodies there or remove them? He checked his watch. Clancy was running late and John's

irritation rose.

The door opened and Robert Clancy walked in, clasping a folder of papers. He was tall. His stud collar seemed two sizes too large for his neck and his waistcoat and jacket clothed a man in need of a good feed.

'Good morning, Mr Leary. Thank you for coming in.'

'Mr Clancy, it is a pleasure.'

'There are aspects of your tender I'd like to discuss. Unfortunately, my two colleagues aren't here, and as you know, with any public tender I cannot interview you alone.' Clancy smiled, showing teeth that needed attention. 'But this is not a formal tender meeting, so we will be just discussing things in general with a list of queries we want your reply to. Please sit down.'

John sat and retrieved his tender documents from his case.

Clancy sat opposite him and cleared his throat. 'The committee's recommendation is that you are the preferred tenderer for the Park Street Memorial Hall and that, subject to your company meeting some minor requirements, Leary's will be recommended to the Aldermen as the preferred contractor. The Council will ratify that at their meeting, in just over a week, on the fifth of May.'

John exhaled in relief and excitement. 'That's very encouraging news, Mr Clancy,' he said. 'What do you want from me?'

Clancy looked at his notes and tapped a finger on the table. 'This Memorial Hall, Mr Leary, will take months to construct.

It has a prominent position in Park Street.'

'An excellent location, I agree.'

Clancy stopped tapping. 'Your company is not a big builder, but the exposure you'll get from the company signs you'll put in front of the building will be worth much to your company in the form of

additional work, new jobs and such, and profit. Am I right?'

John concentrated on Clancy's outline reflected on the polished timber table. 'Yes, it's possible, but I'm a little confused. What are these requirements you want satisfied?'

Clancy got up from the table, went to the window and looked out onto the street. 'Your company will benefit from this site and I think that benefit should be shared.'

Shared? John was surprised. Why would a public servant be interested in how much money John would make from exposure? The Council was only interested in getting a quality project built to its architect's specifications and finished on time. The man's comment was odd. Suddenly, John realised what was going on. Clancy wanted money in *his* pocket. 'Shared?' John said. 'You mean income we may get from exposure, as you say, should be shared with others? But how do you measure that income?'

Clancy smiled and spread his arms. 'I'm a public servant, Mr Leary. You're more experienced in the world of commerce. No, what I'm saying is that any additional income should be given to a charity, a charity which the Sydney Council supports.'

'I'm sorry, but you haven't told me how you measure this added income? Surely this would be the case for any contractor building this project?'

Clancy sat back down and looked irritated, 'I'm not making myself clear,' he said. 'Let's not discuss it further.' Clancy busied himself with his file and John waited. But what if there were no other matters that Clancy wanted solved? Was this why Clancy was seeing him alone? John felt his conscience challenged but he fought it and won. It was worth the risk and he decided to push and tempt the sparely built man.

'Forgive me, Mr Clancy, but how much is your annual salary?'

Clancy looked hard at him and paused. 'It's a matter of public record. One hundred and eighty pounds a year, Mr Leary. Why? Is that of interest to you?'

'It is because—and I've taken the liberty to check—I don't know how someone with your experience and responsibility can be paid such a lowly sum.'

Clancy's eyebrows came together. 'It's the standard salary. I can get no more. It's difficult, but I try to supplement my wages with other income.'

'Is that permitted?' John asked.

'As long as that other income doesn't have a conflict of interest with this place.'

'But is your total income enough to live off?'

Clancy shook his head. 'It's not.'

'You still have to have additional money to buy the things you want?' John said, and decided to flatter the man. 'You're a man of intelligence with a family, no doubt, who wants the nice things life has to offer.'

Clancy's eyes expanded and he seemed to be closely listening to what John was saying. John plunged in. 'How much money a year would you consider to be *acceptable* to live on, say for the next three years?' Clancy paused again and John worried that he'd overplayed his hand.

'For the next three years? I would've thought two hundred and forty pounds a year would keep a man and his family well looked after.'

A 30 per cent increase. Handsome, John mused. 'That would be a fair salary, too. Now Mr Clancy, do we have an understanding?' Clancy said nothing and John filled the silence. 'That is to say, if your salary were two hundred and forty pounds a year, you'd be happy to walk by the Memorial Hall building construction site and see a Leary's Contracting sign outside it, would you not?'

Clancy smiled. 'Mr Leary. I think if my salary was what you said, I would be very proud to walk by such a site.'

John exhaled. 'Very well.' He drew out a sheet of paper and

wrote on it. 'Here is a post-office box number. I request that you take this home and let me know by return mail of your personal banking details and I'll take care of the rest. Is there any other question you care to ask me? Any other minor detail you want us to clear up?'

Clancy tapped the table again. He seemed relieved. 'Yes.' He opened his file and withdrew a paper. 'I'd like your written response to these by close of business tomorrow night. I'm anticipating your answers to most of them. If you want to look at them now, you may wish to comment.' John took the sheet and glanced down the list. They were non-essential inquiries about John and his company, mainly financial, which he could answer with ease. He suspected that Clancy had used this meeting as a subterfuge to seek out John's commitment to paying him a bribe. There was a chance that he would have won the Hall project without a bribe, but now he *had* it. Well, the meeting had a good result. 'Subject to your satisfactory response to these questions,' Clancy said, 'I will be recommending to the other committee members, of which I am the chairman, that Leary's Contracting will be awarded the new contract in Park Street for the Memorial Hall.'

John shook Robert Clancy's sweaty hand and couldn't release it quickly enough. On his way out he thought about what he'd just done. He'd bribed a council official, so what? It was done all the time and the cost of Clancy's *fee* could be disguised as something else and written off on the job. If that took him to the next stage for Leary's Contracting, then so be it. He felt good about it. But should he feel good? He'd compromised his character again, hadn't he? The noises on George Street distracted him and he shrugged off his scruples, again. The Memorial Hall job would get him closer to independence from David.

John was finishing getting dressed for his attendance at the Australia Club and was struggling with the gold stud of his collar.

'One of these days,' Clarissa said, 'women will be allowed into such clubs. I managed Father's businesses, probably better than most men. I should be permitted to grace their hallowed halls.'

John smiled at his wife's outburst. 'God forbid. It's a club for men only. That's just how it is.'

'What do you talk about there? Horses, gambling—women, perhaps?'

'The only reason I'm going there is to try and meet Shelby and Thomas. I have to find out what makes them tick and how much profit they're making.'

Clarissa helped him with his collar. 'So it's really business then? Why this interest in your competitors? I'd have thought you'd have enough on your plate dealing with your large staff and all the jobs you've got on.'

John grinned as Clarissa's deft fingers did their magic. 'Never miss a chance to know your enemies.'

Clarissa rested her hands on his chest. 'Enemies? They've done nothing to you.'

He had slipped up in saying that. Since the sabotage he'd viewed almost every stranger who touched his life in some way as a danger. 'You wouldn't understand. They see how I'm growing, don't worry. They see Leary's as a threat to them. No, I'll always keep an eye on them.' He ran a finger down her cheek.

Clarissa nodded and picked a loose cotton thread from his jacket. 'How do you know that they are against you, for sure, I mean?'

'I'm not sure.'

'There's plenty of building going on,' she quipped. 'Everyone can share.'

John was a little surprised about Clarissa's naiveté, especially given how commercially astute she'd been, working in her father's companies. Perhaps she was trying to get him to tell her his real feelings and doubts. 'That's nirvana,' he said. 'Your father wouldn't be that gracious to a new entrant selling fencing wire.'

She smiled. 'Maybe you're right, but do you feel threatened by Shelby and Thomas, my love?'

John frowned. She *was* prodding him and he became defensive. 'I haven't met them yet, so how can I be threatened?'

'But you did call them your enemies. What made you say that?'

Clarissa was looking at him with a keen interest. Clearly she knew his weaknesses and his insecurity. Yet *she* was no obstacle to him and he loved her.

'Not all businesses are cut-throat,' she said calmly. 'Not all men are—'

'Let's leave it, please. I'm to meet your father at his house at six and it's nearly that now.'

Clarissa was about to say something more but seemed to think better of it. She turned and went into his dressing room. Coming out, she held a silk handkerchief, which she placed in his jacket. 'Now, go and have a good night, and don't come home too drunk.'

John and David entered the Australia Club, a large house in Macquarie Street that had been bequeathed by a wool baron. The foyer, about forty feet square, served as the club's reception and cloakroom. They walked up to the first floor where men in suits puffed cigars and drank single malts. It was Wednesday evening on the last day of April.

'We're in luck,' David said. 'I see Shelby. He's over there by the bar, talking with someone, another brother Freemason, I'll bet. Let's start with him.'

John was apprehensive as they crossed the room towards the contractor. Was this the man who'd caused the sabotage? David had said that Shelby was a Freemason. They were known to not like Catholics. Shelby's companion smiled and left him. The contractor's height surprised John. For a man running one of the top building companies in Sydney, he wasn't impressive. His chest came just above the bar, which was unfortunate because it dwarfed him further, but his cuff links twinkled and his suit was well cut.

David put out his hand. 'Ah, Shelby, how is life treating you?'

'McGuire, it's good to see you. It must be what, six months?'

'Just about. I'd like to introduce you to my son-in-law, John Leary. John, meet Harry Shelby.'

John put out his hand and Shelby tilted his head.

'Leary? Are you in the building game?'

'Aye. I've got a few jobs . . . around the place.'

Shelby smiled. 'If you're the same Leary I've heard about, then you're making a name for yourself.'

John was right. Shelby had noticed his work.

'You won the Memorial Hall job,' Shelby continued. 'Well done.' The council hadn't yet decided that, John thought. Maybe the man was testing him.

'We haven't been told about it,' John said.

'I've got a man in the know. You've got it.' Shelby paused. 'And there was some other stuff, wasn't there? An accident?' John's jaws tightened and Shelby held his gaze then smiled again. 'But that could've happened to anyone. Wouldn't worry about it.'

John smiled also, though he was on edge. 'I'm not worried about it. Got the man who caused it.'

'Care for another drink, Shelby?' David asked.

'I'll have a straight scotch, thank you. Yes, I saw that in the paper. Any idea why, Mr Leary?'

'John? A drink?' David said.

'Jameson's with a splash, thanks. No, I don't, Mr Shelby. Some-one's behind it. Murder's a big risk if the man just had a grudge.'

'But you don't know?' Shelby inquired.

'No.' John decided to change the subject. He didn't have any evidence that Shelby was connected with the sabotage, just suspi-cion. 'So, how have you found the market lately?'

Shelby took the whisky from David. 'This year is better. There's work around, as you know. In fact, I've had to knock some back. There are good government jobs coming out—one down at the new terminus in George Street.'

'With the railways?' John said, looking surprised. 'I thought all that work was tied up?'

'Are you staying for dinner?' David asked. 'Would you care to join us?'

'Thank you, McGuire. I'd like to.'

'Then let's go to the dining room.'

Over dinner they discussed the economy and how the railway was opening up opportunities.

Shelby looked over John's shoulder and smiled. 'Thomas!' he called out, standing up.

This was further good luck and timing. John looked at the man Shelby had addressed. Thomas was overweight and his dinner suit was tight on him.

'Thomas,' Shelby said. 'I want you to meet David McGuire and his son-in-law, John Leary. Gentlemen, Bill Thomas.'

John and David stood up and shook hands with Bill Thomas. 'You're welcome to join us,' David said.

'Thank you. Leary, now that name's familiar.' Thomas said. 'You're a builder ain't you, Mr Leary? Seen ya name around town.'

John nodded. 'Yes, Mr Thomas, but we're not in your league.'

Thomas dropped his big frame into a chair, grabbed a waiter and ordered a drink. His red face and manner were testimony to an afternoon on the grog. 'We all got to start somewhere. I broke my back for a miserable bastard. The mongrel's gone to hell, as far as I know and good riddance to him.'

John smiled.

They discussed business throughout the meal and at the end of the dinner, when the port and cigars came out, David excused himself for his appointment. Thomas looked as though he was about to fall asleep, but Shelby and John talked for half an hour until Shelby suddenly said. 'I'll be frank with you, Mr Leary, I've kept my eye on you. You've got a touch in winning jobs and building them right.' He reached into his pocket and removed a silver case. He withdrew a card and gave it to John. 'Let's keep in touch. Now, if you'll excuse me I have a family function to go to. So, until next time.'

John had been wary of Shelby all evening, but he decided to show politeness. 'It's been a pleasure meeting you, Mr Shelby.'

As he and Selby were shaking hands, a man passed their table.

'Evening, Atkins,' Shelby said. John turned to the stranger. 'Mr

Leary, I'd like to introduce you to a friend of mine, Mr Brian Atkins. Atkins, John Leary.'

Atkins smiled at John as if he knew him and John racked his memory as he accepted Atkins's hand, but nothing clicked. 'Mr Leary, I'm pleased to meet you.' His accent was educated, John thought.

'Tell me,' Shelby said, 'are you staying long?'

'I was just leaving,' Atkins said and grinned. 'But it's good to see you again.'

'I'll accompany you on the way out then.'

'Excellent,' Atkins said. 'Evening, Mr Leary.'

Thomas was snoring away and John sat back down and thought about the two builders. Shelby seemed clever, but John was suspicious of his compliments. Maybe John *was* a threat to him, maybe Shelby wanted to stop him for good.

'Well, time to go home?'

John looked up to see David standing beside him. 'I'm ready if you are.'

David smiled at the snoring Thomas. 'Let him sleep. I'd need one of your cranes to get him out of that chair.'

They walked out into the cool autumn air, where David's carriage stood waiting.

John sat back in its warmth. 'You don't think that Shelby or Thomas could have anything to do with the sabotage?'

David brought the folds of his overcoat close around him. 'Why do you say that?'

'Well, we're a competitor and we're growing.'

'Maybe ... but that's stretching things. Thomas is a simple fellow and Shelby's well-connected *and* wealthy. He would have no reason to stoop to murder. No. Believe me, that labourer acted alone, you wait and see.' David pulled his gloves on and paused. 'Did you agree to meet Shelby again?'

'I did.' John remained silent, mulling things over, until the carriage was back at Point Piper. If it had been Shelby who'd paid Miller, then why? And if it wasn't Shelby, then who had?

Brian Atkins rested his eyes on the blaze of his dining-room fire. The purity of flame, he mused—it could consume most evil things. John Leary was evil by race and corroded by his Papist views. It had been three days since Brian had first been close to the man and he believed that he'd been in the presence of low life. It had taken him all his breeding just to shake hands with Leary.

'Mr Atkins,' a female voice broke his reverie. 'You seem lost in thought.'

Atkins looked into the blue eyes of Miss Elizabeth Higgins. She was slim, of blemish-free complexion and full breasted. Her father, the banker Thomas Higgins, was seated by her side. Bill Thomas and Harry Shelby were also at the table. 'How rude of me, Miss Higgins. I was thinking about the Petersham land purchase. My apologies, I'm ignoring my guests.'

'We'll talk more on that on Monday, Atkins,' Thomas Higgins said, 'but now I'd like your opinion on this wine consignment I'm considering. It's a claret but its nose has something different . . .'

Atkins let him ramble on while he looked at Elizabeth. She smiled at him and looked down coyly. They'd been seeing each other these last six months and the friendship was developing, but not as fast as he'd expected. He wanted to marry her, but she'd been guarded with her affections. Just the other week she had confided to him the reason why. Her heart had been broken some three years previously when she'd fallen in love with a wealthy businessman, a William Baxterhouse. That romance had been cut short when the man fell from grace, both financially and with the law, and had disappeared. Atkins sympathized, he was not troubled by this information and resolved to increase his campaign to win her.

'So what do you think, Atkins?' Higgins said. 'Is it worth the money? I can get three dozen sent immediately.'

Atkins concentrated. Higgins knew his wine and would not buy rubbish or just pay any price because a drop was popular. Atkins replied, 'It's worth it. I may buy some too.'

'Good,' Higgins said and sipped more of his Bordeaux.

'Scotch whisky is more my line, Mr Higgins,' Harry Shelby said. 'Single malts.'

'That's the drop,' Bill Thomas agreed. 'Atkins, that lamb was delicious.'

'Thank you, Bill,' Atkins said. He glanced at the clock and at his dinner guests, all Freemasons, except for Elizabeth, of course. The other two men at his table were the Gadens. Privately wealthy from wool and mining, brothers James and Brian dabbled in construction through their company, Maxton Constructions. They were also Atkins's third contractor of choice.

Atkins considered it now a good time to sow some seeds against the upstart Irish contractor. Higgins had been the one to provide information on Leary and it wasn't complimentary. The banker told him of Leary's effrontery in approaching Higgins at the Bank of New South Wales some years ago, demanding funds for Leary to start his own business! The nerve of the young man, Higgins had spluttered. That was all music to Atkins's ears. 'Gentlemen and young lady,' he nodded to Elizabeth, 'you are all known to each other and you all respect each other,' nods and smiles all around, 'but you do compete for my projects, and other clients like me who have work for you.'

'True,' James Gaden said, looking at his two building competitors, 'but the work is shared around. So, I for one am not complaining.'

'Me either,' Thomas said, his speech now slurred.

Harry Shelby just looked at Atkins and smiled.

Good, Atkins thought. 'While not resorting to poor form and talking business in the presence of such a charming young lady, I'm curious to know your opinions on the rise of the developer–builder.'

'An odd term,' Thomas said.

'A builder,' Atkins explained, 'who doesn't just build, but does what I do. Buys the land and packages up the whole deal.'

'Are there many of those in Sydney?' Elizabeth asked.

'No, thank the Lord,' Atkins said. 'But there are a few and the numbers are increasing.'

'Can you name one?' James Gaden asked.

'John Leary,' Atkins said.

Thomas laughed. 'Leary! He's just a builder. Blood-blistered fingers and sawdust-covered arms. Met him the other night; so did you, Shelby. He seemed all right. What's your beef, Atkins?'

'More wine and spirits for our guests, Albert, please,' Atkins gestured to his servant. Atkins eyed each man in turn. 'Leary and his ilk are nibbling at my business, my friends. He won't take it all, but believe me he'll become voracious.' He smiled, happy to know he'd put Leary's name out there. 'But, enough of this issue. Please let's all retire to the drawing room and a game of charades.'

'Excellent,' Elizabeth said.

Atkins noted the forced smiles on his male guests. They had to play, just as they had to bid on his work. It was all part of the game.

John rested his binoculars on a table outside his tent. In the final hours of sunshine of Saturday 3 May, the seventh and last race at the Homebush Race Carnival was about to start. Up until now, John had broken even.

The average punters, all keen to make a quid, pressed the rail of the racetrack, jammed against it like bees on a comb. John picked out a few toffs dressed in their best finery, but unable to hide their rawness. These were the lucky ones, the ones who'd struck rich gold seams. They didn't care whether they won or lost, it was all part of the game.

Further back from the rail the crowd was more orderly—the clerks, the merchants' assistants and government workers who could afford to play with a few bob from their wages. Then, on a rise, came the twenty tents of the Jockey Club—of which David McGuire's was one—with better seating and access to fine food and drink. In one of those tents sat Bill Thomas and another man. He was unsighted for a moment, but then John saw it was the man he had met at the Australia Club: Brian Atkins.

A waiter offered John champagne and he looked at his clients splashing out their cash for the next race. There was Robert Clancy from the Sydney Council, James Finlayson, Alan Wallace, Gregory Blunt and others who were new clients. John was getting used to entertaining them. He'd invited his uncle to come but Gerry had work to do.

Laughter from a nearby tent distracted him. He looked at the source of the gaiety and received a pleasant surprise. There, dressed in a red silk dress and matching bonnet, with a wide smile on her face, was Beth Blackett. Her husband was sitting beside her.

As the horses were being settled at the starting gate, Henry got up and left the tent. Beth watched him leave and looking around saw John, waved and smiled. John returned her wave and turned to his guests. 'Gentlemen, I have to pay my respects to a friend. I shan't be too long. Will you excuse me?' He wound his way through the crowd shaking hands with people he knew. He went into Beth's enclosure and she looked up, smiling.

'John. It's grand to see you,' she said. 'Are you here for the day?'

'I am,' John pointed to his tent. 'I'm with people over there.'

Beth's guests stopped talking and looked at their visitor. Beth smiled at them. 'Gentlemen, I'd like to introduce you to a friend of mine, Mr John Leary.'

John shook their hands, though Beth's presence made him forget their names and occupations. Her eyes held his and she said, 'Here, have some champagne and sit by me in Henry's chair. You've just missed him. He's gone to see the new colts we're racing.' She clucked. 'They'll have to be a long-term thing, because I've done my money cold, I have. I hope Henry will do better.'

John smiled and sat beside her. 'It's nice to see you under more cheerful circumstances.'

'That was a sad anniversary,' she said.

They both jerked at the bang of the starting pistol and before long felt the pounding of the beating hooves reverberating through the ground.

They watched the race, entranced. 'Isn't it exciting?' Beth said. 'The way they run, their big chests thrust forward, such beautiful animals. I love them so.' The lead changed a few times in the final one hundred yards until the favourite won. Beth took out a silk handkerchief and patted her brow.

'I had some sad news as well,' John said. 'My mother passed away late last year.'

'I'm sorry to hear that. Did she go peacefully?'

'She did.'

Beth placed a hand on his arm. 'It still must've shocked you.'

'Yes, it did, but there is some good news. I've met a relative of mine, an uncle who's been here for some time.'

'Wonderful.'

John wouldn't mention Gerry's convict past. Even though Beth came from the working classes he felt that as a rich woman now, she may have a poor view of that and then of himself. 'Anyway,' he said, 'it's too nice a day to be sad. Tell me about you.'

Beth's guests were starting to leave. 'Excuse me, just for a moment,' she said. She thanked the men for coming. John admired the ease and confidence she now had with society people. After seeing the last one off, she sat back down with him. 'What would you like to know?' she asked.

He smiled. 'How rich you are.'

'Mr Leary, how rude of you!' But she smiled with him. 'I have a more than comfortable income. Henry's helped me, and after buying land and sires, plus a new house in Sydney, I still have money to invest.' She squeezed his arm. 'I was thinking you might have some thoughts on how that could be best used.'

Her touch had thrilled him, just as it had in Bathurst. He tried to focus on answering the question. 'Well, there are the various stocks available. I hear the railways are very good, even allowing—'

She leaned closer to him, her lips parted, her eyes animated. 'We don't have to talk about it today. Perhaps in town—soon—at a convenient place?' Putting her hand in her bag she withdrew a card and slid it over to him. He grasped it.

John was about to reply when he heard his name called.

'Mr Leary, isn't it?'

'Mr Blackett,' John stood up and put his hand out. 'Did you do any good?'

'Did my money cold, cold. Our colts are going to be pricey if they don't start winning. Beth, my dear, we should go. We have the Simpsons for dinner. Well Mr Leary, nice to meet you again.'

When Henry and Beth had gone, John fingered her card in his pocket and smiled. She wanted to see him again. There was still something between them. Like the old days. But was it? No. He was married and he loved Clarissa.

CHAPTER FOUR

At Point Piper on a bleak, autumn Saturday afternoon, Christine McGuire poured another cup of tea for Lady Anne Dalkeith. The Dalkeiths were pastoralists. He'd been a currency lad and was now a knight bachelor and friend of the Wentworths. Christine envied that clique, which was powerful enough not to let in outsiders. Even after five years of trying, she hadn't been accepted. For the last hour, the two of them shared stories of grandchildren, and charities with which they were mutually involved. Conscious of the time left, Christine was keen to hear the latest news. 'So, how is the situation in Scone? Is the station still well-managed?'

Lady Dalkeith sniffed. 'This weather. Excuse me again, my dear, for one moment. I have a bit of a cold.' She reached over to her purse, extracted a handkerchief and addressed her nose. 'Sir Harry is coping quite well with the new staff, and wool's achieving high prices, the stock likewise. That reminds me. I attended the races last Saturday to present the winner for the charity event, and I saw your son-in-law entertaining some guests. I knew one or two of them, Blackett was there, too. His horses aren't doing well, but time will tell.'

'My son-in-law has to go to the races,' Christine said. 'The company's expanding so he must keep up his entertainment of clients.'

'No doubt. You know, Mrs McGuire, I'm not one to gossip but there was a woman in conversation with your son-in-law, in a very intimate way. It was Blackett's wife.'

Christine's face flushed in irritation. 'John knows her well, Lady Dalkeith.'

Her friend dabbed at her nose again. 'Look here, it's not for me to say.'

'About what?'

'Well, from what I could see, and I was no more than thirty feet away, their conversation was animated, as though they'd known each other a long time and, as you confirm, that probably explains it. All innocent, no doubt. But it's not advisable for married people, who are not married to each other, to act that way in public.'

Christine nodded. 'Thank you, but, as I said, I see no seriousness in what you've told me.'

'Perhaps—oh my goodness,' Lady Dalkeith said as the hall clock struck the hour, 'is that four? I must be going. Could you please call for my coachman?'

'Of course.'

Accompanying her guest to the front door, Christine's skin prickled with embarrassment. She remembered saying goodbye and something about seeing her friend next month. Back in the drawing room, behind locked doors, she composed herself. John and Clarissa seemed close again now. She was sure John's conversation with a past friend was all that Lady Dalkeith had seen. Nothing more.

John tapped his pencil on the table at the completion of the Monday morning staff meeting. With him were his chief estimator, Frank Cartwright; Dan Reynolds, his accountant; Sean Connaire and Jack Johnson. Four sub-foremen were waiting outside ready to be called into the meeting.

Two foremen were not up to scratch. One was working on Blunt's warehouse and the other on the Woolloomooloo terraces. Sean had recommended their sacking and John had agreed. There were plenty of applicants wanting an opportunity to join Leary's or to be promoted from within. 'All right, that's it,' John said placing his pencil down. 'Dan will review the wages. From now, the twelfth of May, all foremen will be paid the same. Only those who have shown merit will get extra pay. I have a list of them here.'

'Can I see it, John?' Sean said. John handed the paper to him and Sean read it. 'Young Harkins is not on this list. He's a good lad, John. He's—'

'He's not working to his peak. I'll not have shirkers.'

'That's a bit hard,' Sean replied. 'His mum's been sick and his Dad's having trouble with the drink.'

Trust Sean to be sympathetic with a drunk, John thought. 'No, he'll not get more money. Is that clear?' Sean said nothing but his lips firmed in a straight line. 'All right, Sean, get the men in here.'

John waited until the four sub-foremen were seated. He grinned at their faces. 'Opportunity knocks, fellas. I want performance and that matters—not just how long you've been on one of my sites.' He wanted to drive them and drive them hard. His turnover was good, he was making a name for himself, and he'd started talking with Bill Thomas about a major railway related contract. 'Mr Connaire here will outline your day's training with the other managers. Please give them all your attention.'

As he turned to leave, John said, 'Just one thing, Sean, we've got the footings ready on the Memorial Hall job, so why aren't we pouring concrete?'

'It's Mr Clancy,' Sean said. 'Always keeps sticking his nose in everywhere. Holding us up.'

'You'd expect that wouldn't you?' John replied. 'He does work for the Council, after all.'

'Aye, but he's making himself a nuisance. Is there nothing you could say to him? I mean, just to get him clear of us?'

John had to keep Clancy on side. 'I'll speak with him.'

'Good'.

John headed to his office. He now employed one hundred and fifty men, in all trades, and their labourers, on six sites, two of which would finish within three months. He needed more work. The Bank of New South Wales was giving him all the money he wanted and his clients paid what they owed before time; some even complained to David McGuire that they would get reminder notes from John on the day before their invoices were due to be paid. John didn't care. Every penny counted.

He walked to his office window overlooking George Street. In the last three years the town had become busier. Horses and drays straining with the booming wool clip made their way to the docks, where hundreds of men were loading and unloading ships. The wealthiest colonials were making money. The Macarthurs and the Wentworths led the pack, but there were others the next level down who were also making money; people who'd invited John and Clarissa into their ranks. He looked at his watch. It was time to meet Beth.

John took a cab at Victoria Park and walked inside its entrance gates. Just the fact of meeting her alone was indiscreet and he felt guilty. They could have met, no, *should* have met in public but she had suggested her carriage. And he had to see her. She wanted advice on where to put her funds and he had ideas on that. That was the only reason, he said to himself, but he had to admit he was still attracted to her and that worried him. Not so much that he was attracted but what that could lead to. He determined that he would talk only about business, be polite then move on.

Underneath a shady tree he spotted a carriage. Its window was down and Beth beckoned him. He opened the door, got in and sat beside her.

'Hello,' she said. 'Thank you for meeting me.'

She looked radiant. 'Hello, Beth.'

Her eyes held his then she looked at his mouth. It seemed she was going to kiss him. *This isn't a good start.* She opened the roof hatch. 'Rogers, please head to Circular Quay by George Street.'

Closing the hatch she turned to him, 'I've got your company for a while.' She smiled, 'Now, down to business. I told you at the races, at Homebush, that I had some money to invest. Do you have some ideas where?'

John concentrated. 'English investment is pouring in at the moment, especially in the railways. Bonds, maybe in the same area.'

Beth turned and pulled the curtain partly across the carriage window and her blouse stretched taut across her bosom.

He fought to focus on investment and its cold hard dimensions rather than her closeness and sensuality. Funds . . . Beth had plenty. Learys. Yes, there might be a way. Now was the time. 'Your money. Does Henry have to approve where you invest?'

'It's my money. No.'

Here it is. 'Would you invest in Learys?'

She grinned. 'Why not? If there's any stock for sale, I'd buy it.'

John couldn't believe his luck. Here in this carriage he may be able to secure his independence. To be free, to be his own man, to not have to put up with people's comments about David's funding of his business. But this seemed too easy. He owned 40 per cent of the company, Sean held a 9 per cent share and Clarissa's father held the remaining 51 percent. John wanted Beth to buy David's share, but it was a large slice.

She was looking at him. 'Well? Have you stock to sell?'

'I do, but it's owned by my father-in-law.'

'What's his share?'

'Fifty-one per cent,' he said.

'He's the major shareholder.'

'He is.'

'Would he sell?' she asked.

That was the rub. 'I believe I could convince him to sell at the right price. He just wants to run his own businesses, not worry about Leary's. Additionally, the extra funds would be ideal at the moment.'

'But, would he sell to me? That might be too much to accept. Clarissa knows me.'

She was right. 'If I can get him to sell, I'd say you were a silent partner.'

'Would he accept that?'

'I don't know, but I'll try.'

She pressed his forearm. 'Please, do that.'

John had an added thought: with Beth as a shareholder he would see her more often. But was that a good idea?

'If you're worried about the offer, John,' she said, 'it would be to an independent valuer's opinion.'

'Of course.'

'And I'd want a good return.'

'Two per cent higher than a bond rate do you?'

She smiled again. 'More than adequate.'

Beth moved closer, or he felt she had, and he was fighting to stop himself from kissing her. *What are you thinking, man!* 'I'd value your investment,' he said, trying to get himself to act like an accountant, 'but I would want something from you as well as your money.' Beth's breathing quickened. 'What I mean is, I'd want your assurance that you wouldn't interfere with Leary's in any way.'

She nodded, as if she knew the hidden ambiguity in his request. 'I understand and yes, I'd agree to that. I'm only interested in getting a return better than the banks, and I see you as a good risk. I'll put it all in writing to reassure you, if you wish.' She traced her finger across his knuckles. That was forward of her and John knew that she was pushing him to show more affection. No, he wouldn't. She seemed to read his reticence. 'Come,' she said, 'I'll drop you off somewhere convenient.'

She was giving him a way out and he chastised himself for his cowardice. He should have been the one to make the move, to break off from this charged attraction—not her. All this time her thigh had been against his and he knew he had to leave. Now. He looked out of the window as the carriage passed Central Station. 'I'll get out here, if you don't mind.'

She seemed put out, but recovered quickly. 'Of course, though I'm a little disappointed we didn't have more time together. But we will meet again. I want to know if Mr McGuire will sell. Till then, John.'

She kissed his cheek, which he accepted as an innocent gesture from an old friend. He alighted and the carriage moved away. John touched his face. It was all wrong, he knew, but he looked forward to seeing her again, and it wasn't just because she had the money to buy David.

∾

John was both excited and anxious. Sitting in his own study after dinner he'd broached the share purchase with David, but his father-in-law wanted to know more about it.

'Why the big secret, John?'

'It's no secret. The buyer is trustworthy, is not in the building game, has the cash and the offer is reasonable. You should take it.' John held down David's stare, not intimidated as he would have been before his marriage.

'You think so? You'll then be fully responsible for the activities and reputation of the company.' David clipped a cigar and lit it. 'So, who's the buyer?'

'Their solicitor says it's somebody you may know. I have his word that the buyer will remain anonymous. It's not a competitor, and I have that in writing and due diligence says the cash is good.'

'I don't know. It's the major share.' David blew smoke towards the ceiling. 'I'll make it easy for you. I'll sell, if you tell me the buyer's name.' John steadied his hand lighting his own cigar, his mind blank. 'John, come on. Why won't you tell me? A name for a share. It's simple.' John scrambled to think of a story. He was so close to getting control of Leary's.

'What's wrong?' David said. 'Is there a problem?'

John smiled, 'No, no problem. It's just the terms. The solicitor says that the buyer has to remain confidential.'

David didn't blink and neither did John. David gestured to him. 'You would sell just over half of Leary's to a stranger? You?'

'On the basis of the offer, yes, I'd accept.'

'And you believe that?' David said.

'I do.'

'You surprise me. You really do.'

'David, I'll have it in writing that the new major shareholder will have no control of the business.'

'That's generous. I have a full say now. Why not this new man?'

John stopped himself from smiling at David's presumption. 'Well, they don't want it. There's certain basic reporting we have to give them but that is modest. Also, there is a requirement for profits. If we don't deliver on those, they want us to buy back their share for what they paid.'

'And you are content with that?'

'We'll make profits, David, believe me. Now, will you sell?' Here it was: his future lay in David's reply.

David nodded. 'It'll be on your head. I'll accept the offer on one proviso.'

John's excitement waned a little. 'And what's that?'

'After my death, the silent partner will be named.'

'Why?'

David smiled. 'It's a little thing only, quirky if you will. Do you agree?'

It was a small risk and he'd take it. 'Very well.'

'Good. The added capital will be a blessing.' David finished his whiskey. 'I'm still curious about the buyer, but now, if you don't mind, I'll go and say goodnight to Clarissa, then head home. It's been a long day and I know you'll want to spend some time with Richard. I'll see myself out.'

John lowered his glass to the table, concentrating on the movement to mask the excitement pouring through him. 'Thank you for that. I'll make the arrangements with the lawyers to draw up the papers.'

Clarissa had just got Richard to sleep. As she turned the gaslight down, she took one final look over the cot and her heart filled with love. She worried that John wasn't seeing enough of his five-month-old son. She saw the baby's changes daily, but John was missing out on the subtle phases of growth. It was a shame, really. Closing the door, she bumped into her father.

'I was just coming to say goodnight to you before going,' he said.

'Have you got just ten minutes?'

Her father's head tilted to one side. 'Of course, my dear.'

'If you're tired we can—'

'No, let's go to the drawing room. At dinner you seemed preoccupied. Is anything the matter?'

'No, but I'd like to be doing something.' She threaded her arm through his and they went down the stairs and met John coming up. 'Richard's asleep, dear,' she said. 'Just creep in . . . quietly. He's a caution to get back down.'

John grinned. 'Very good. Goodnight, David.'

'Goodnight.'

She and her father continued down the stairs to the drawing room, where they sat down.

'So,' David said, 'what's all this about doing something? Isn't the baby a handful enough?'

Clarissa smoothed her dress. 'It doesn't seem so long ago when you first asked me to help you in your businesses.'

David sat back on the chair. 'No, it doesn't. But that was then. I needed you; you were unmarried and had plenty of time. Now, you're a mother with responsibilities to your family.'

'I know. But I have time on my hands and I would like something to do, perhaps to help you again, somehow.'

Her father looked at her unblinking. She'd seen it many times, when David was observing a new client or reviewing a report. It was a look she understood. The lips in a firm line with tight jaw muscles, used like a shield to protect his thoughts, a poker face. She loved him and she decided to continue pleading her case before he replied.

'Don't get me wrong,' she said. 'I love Richard and would do anything for him, but Cook and Stella do most of the work, and I'm not the sort who can attend too many charity functions, you know that.'

'You were never one for society, even though your mother tried many times to force you. So, if I know my daughter, you've got something in mind, hmm?'

'I understand you'd like to sell your Leary's Contracting share.'

117

David smiled. 'As a matter of fact, I just agreed to do that with John.'

Her eyes rounded. 'Your whole fifty-one per cent?'

'Indeed.'

That was startling news; she'd get the details from John later. For now her father was more important and what he'd just said might help her cause. 'In which case, you'll be able to devote all your attention to your businesses, of which you know I have experience and understanding.'

David pursed his lips. 'So, you'd like to help me there again, would you? But you couldn't be "on call", as they now say. There must be a limit to your time, surely?'

She'd thought about this. 'I could work for you, between the hours of say ten in the morning and three in the afternoon. That way, I can see Richard in the morning when he wakes up, and be with him in the afternoon. Would that time of any benefit to you?'

David stood up. 'Any time would suit me. McGuire Wire might be best. It's closer to town than Superior Sheeting.' She'd guessed as much; Petersham, where Superior Sheeting was, would be a hike. 'You know our work. It wouldn't take you long to pick up the traces. Very well, it's the twelfth of May. Give me two days to think it over and we'll talk again at the end of the week. But you must clear it with John.'

Clarissa came up to him. 'Thank you, Father. You don't know what this means to me, to be busy again.'

David smiled and kissed her cheek. 'Just speak with John and get his agreement. Believe me, it'll be better in the long run.'

Later, upstairs, Clarissa sat at her dressing table brushing her hair. 'Do you know the mystery man who's buying Father's share?'

John took off his dressing gown. 'No, dear, I don't. It's confidential. The buyer's lawyers have been acting on his behalf.'

'Well, you'll have to know sooner or later because the shareholder will want to be on the board. And tell me, why sell to a stranger who could take Leary's anywhere? Father had the major share but at least you knew him and trusted him.'

It was a good point, he conceded. John lifted the bed covers and got into bed. 'The new buyer has agreed not to have a seat on the board or be involved in any part of the business. I demanded it.'

'That's unusual,' she said. 'Surely someone owning fifty-one per cent of the company would want a big say?'

John raised his hands. 'I did a good deal. No board representation. The new buyer is a silent shareholder. Satisfied?'

She frowned and wondered why he was irritated, but left it and got into bed and settled herself. 'Goodnight,' she said.

'Goodnight,' he replied and turned away from her. His excitement in getting control of his company was now gone and he knew why.

There was no way Clarissa would accept Beth as the majority Leary shareholder, so he couldn't risk telling her. Clarissa knew of his interest in Beth in the past and that would be the overriding reason why she would reject her. He wasn't in love with Beth, but from her attentions to him in the carriage, he knew that he could make love to her—but at what horrendous cost to the trust in his marriage and the hurt he'd give his beloved! Even thinking about Beth in that way was deceitful.

Could he be honest with Clarissa, nonetheless? Tell her that Beth wouldn't be seen with him in private at any time, secure Clarissa's trust and assure her of his love for her? That's what he should have done, but he hadn't, and that was why he was now angry with himself. The real problem was David. Even if John told Clarissa about Beth and she accepted John's assurance that he would keep the new majority shareholder at arm's length, she would tell her father who that shareholder was—and John would risk losing the only way he could get control of the company.

'John?' Clarissa said.

'Yes?'

She put an arm around him and pressed herself against him.

He wasn't in the mood. 'I want to sleep,' he said.

She said nothing for a moment, then threaded her hand down from his stomach and clasped him. Suddenly, Beth came into his mind; her thigh pressing his in the carriage today and the way her fingers had caressed him. But he pushed those thoughts away. The woman who was touching him now, whose scent was familiar, whose skin was warm and whose mouth would be on his, was his beloved. He turned to Clarissa and kissed her and she responded eagerly.

Clarissa was wide awake. She smiled at John's deep breathing. Men were lucky to drift off to sleep after making love. For her, it always seemed to make her more alert. Some of her friends wouldn't dare talk about the intimate details of their relationship with their husbands, but she wished they did so she could understand some things better. She was surprised John wasn't in a more celebratory mood when they'd got into bed; after all he was about to get what he'd wanted for a long time—control of Learys. Still, he had been responsive when she took the initiative and their lovemaking had been as good as ever.

She sighed as sleepiness still hadn't come and she realised she'd forgotten to talk to John about her going back to work. She knew he wouldn't oppose it; he had been full of admiration for her when she helped her father run his businesses when she'd first come to the colony. Thinking of that time, her thoughts turned to the previous week's gathering at Maureen's. There had been talk of a group of women forming themselves into an association to advance their rights, basing it on a growing but still underground movement in England. The society matrons were stridently opposed, seeing such activities as totally unfeminine. Clarissa had different ideas. Helping her father had been a radical thing to do and it had attracted support from women from all walks of life; many had written to her and had encouraged her to continue to push the boundaries for women.

During the next hour, she watched the moonlight move across her bedroom veranda. She fell asleep with the thoughts of helping her father.

Beth Blackett loved autumn in Sydney, especially mid-May: the tawny leaves, the freshness and the softer sunshine as it came through the awning slats on her first-floor veranda. Her sister Olivia was humming a song in the adjoining room. She was at that awkward age just before puberty, and Beth noticed that lately her moods could change in an instant. 'Olivia, come here, love, and let me braid your hair. Has cook given you anything for afternoon tea?'

'No, she hasn't and I'm hungry.'

Beth smiled. 'Well you'd better eat something, otherwise you'll be too skinny for St Nicholas at Christmas. He won't give presents to skinny little girls.'

Olivia came onto the veranda and pouted. 'That's ages away,' she said. 'And I'm not a little girl. I'm nearly twelve.'

'In September. Now fetch me the hairbrush and the combs, please. We've still got some time before you start demolishing your food.'

Olivia ran away giggling, leaving Beth to sit and enjoy the sun. The front door opened and closed: the girls' governess leaving after another day. Thank goodness for her. Both her sisters had been lazy without supervision, but were now absorbed in their letters.

Beth's mother lived with them in their large house in Glebe. There was plenty of room; they had the luxury of two bathrooms and everyone had their own bedroom. Her mother's days as a servant were over and she was comforted by her deceased husband's wealth. Beth smiled as her mother's footsteps came towards her.

'Where's that rascal Livvy! I know she's here somewhere. Caught her with her hand in the lolly jar.' She stopped on the veranda. 'Oh, it's you, dear. Taking in the afternoon sun?'

'You'll find her here soon,' Beth said. 'I want to braid her hair. I've got about ten minutes before Henry comes home.'

Anne O'Hare's smile faded and she clasped her hands together. Beth sensed her mother wanted to have a serious discussion. She was about to say something when her mother spoke. 'I keep saying it's none of my business, but I'm worried about you. We have spoken before about Henry not treating you civilly. Why just the other day—'

'I know Henry's difficult. But he's basically a good man.'

'I know he is, dear, but he's direct and he belittles you in front of your sisters and our guests, which upsets me. It really does.'

Beth squeezed her mother's elbow, feeling the strength there from years of service. Her mother's eyes moistened.

Olivia came running through the opened French windows, with her smaller sister at her tail. 'Beth, Beth, Sarah's been pulling my hair. She's been hurting me.'

'No I haven't. I haven't. She's just a big bully,' retorted her grim-faced sibling.

'There, there girls,' Beth said, 'let's deport ourselves properly before the master comes home. Olivia, I'll do your hair. Sarah, pick up your sister's book there and read me the first page.'

Their meal that evening followed the usual ritual. The family ate in the formal dining room with Henry at the head of the table and Beth at the other end. Olivia and Sarah sat together on one side with Beth's mother opposite them.

Henry didn't speak much, concentrating instead on his dinner, at times glaring at Olivia or Sarah whenever they fidgeted. They could only glance at him before dropping their eyes to continue eating. Beth compared him to John Leary and she blushed. She didn't want to bring her napkin up for fear she'd alert them all to the gesture and the vivid colour of her face. She recalled her time with John at Homebush, as pleasant an afternoon as she'd had for a long time. Then there was the time in her carriage in Victoria Park. Good gracious! She'd acted like a dollymop, the way she'd pressed against him and touched him. And what if he'd responded? Part of her wanted him to and that part shamed her. She knew she wouldn't have resisted him. As a Mass-going Catholic, the thought that she would so easily commit adultery was unsettling. Her conscience had been an unwanted and persistent companion since that day.

Life was secure and acceptable with her husband and she should be satisfied with that. There were working-class women she knew who were treated badly by their husbands. Henry didn't hit her, thank God, and if he ever did she thought she could deal with him.

Getting the better of punch-throwing drunks had been a weekly job at the Royal Hotel when she'd worked there.

Lately Beth had grown tired of being the one who instigated their intimate times, not to mention the effort of making it seem that it had been Henry's idea. She would have preferred that Henry took the initiative and also that he took it more often. Henry seemed to regard their love making as his duty, though she did manage to get him to be attentive to her needs.

As Henry swallowed the last slice of his lamb, he glanced up at her. She lowered her eyes to her plate, fearing he could read her thoughts. 'How was business today?' she asked him.

'Passable, passable. I've got to go to the bush tomorrow and look at more livestock.'

'That'll be good,' she said. *I should be giving more thought to horses and their availability and not think about John and when we may next meet. I'm a married woman with responsibilities, after all.*

Sunlight bathed the Park Street building site. Building progress had picked up and there was a pace to the work.

Sean skipped between the footings like a gymnast, confident of where he stepped. There was a huddle of workers near the site shed, one of whom was a big man, a good foot taller than his group. He seemed familiar. Of course, Gerry Gleeson.

Gerry was scrutinising the blocks of sandstone that Sean had ordered. He ran his thumb down the arris of one and nodded. Sean grunted. *It looks like the big man approves.* He smiled at the stonemason. 'So, it's all right, Gerry, is it?' Sean said.

'It is, Sean, it is. You wanted me to come on the fourteenth of May and here I am.' Gerry gestured towards four men who stood with him. 'And this is my team.'

'Glad to have you and your men aboard. Well, you best get cracking. The day's half over.'

'Too true, too true, Sean. It's barely quarter past seven but there's no time like the present to start.' He looked down at the foot-ings. 'Were these poured yesterday?'

'Aye.'

'That's a week late. We can't lay stone till the concrete's hardened.' Sean was also irritated by the setback. Gerry sensed Sean's embarrass-ment. 'But there's sorting of the blocks and stacking we can do.'

'Good,' Sean said, 'then I'll leave you to it.' Sean left them and went into his site shed to look at his plans, which was the first thing he did at the start of each day.

Stonemasonry was the main trade on this site, as the hall's external walls would be solid sandstone, fifteen feet high. He knew Gerry would deliver a first-class job and, being part of John's family, he could be relied on.

In the drawing room at Point Piper, Clarissa was helping her sister-in-law as she tried to corral young Michael between pieces of furni-ture. He was being particularly boisterous, unlike his three-year-old sister, Irene, who was helping Clarissa's cook in the kitchen. Maureen lunged one more time and Michael giggled and then yelled as his mother grabbed him.

'Got you, you monkey,' Maureen laughed. 'Thought you'd get away from me, didn't you?'

Michael giggled again. His eyes darted around looking for an escape route and he tried to bolt again. But Maureen gripped him. 'Maybe Auntie Clarissa will get you a lolly, if you're a good boy.'

'I've got a big, red, teddy-bear lolly for you,' Clarissa said. 'Would you like that?'

'Yes please, Auntie,' the boy replied.

Clarissa smiled at her nephew. 'Well, if you're good and you sit still, then I'll bring Richard to join you. Then you can have your treat.'

Michael smiled triumphantly at this and Maureen knew he was up to mischief.

'Now, Michael,' Maureen said, putting him on the settee, 'you're a big boy for five——'

'I am!'

'And you could hurt your cousin if you're too rough.'

Clarissa fetched Richard and sat him next to her nephew. He stuck his fat legs out and as he looked around, he stretched his head so far back he fell over, causing both Maureen and Clarissa to laugh fondly at him.

'Here, let me help you up,' Clarissa said, as she pushed Richard upright.

'Tell me Clarissa, how's John?' Maureen asked. 'It's the end of June and Liam and I haven't seen him for ages.'

Clarissa held Richard as he bounced up and down on Michael's lap. His red face seemed to show he thought it a great treat. 'He's busy. But he's spending some time with the baby, for which I am grateful.'

Richard leaned forward and pressed his finger into Michael's eye. Michael shoved him aside and Richard slipped from her grasp and fell to the floor. Clarissa scooped him up and his mouth gaped open. Two seconds later the yell came, then a torrent of tears. Clarissa held Richard as Stella walked into the room.

'Ma'am, should I take the child now? I think he's due for his supper.'

'Thank you, Stella,' Clarissa said. 'Make sure he eats everything.'

'I shall, ma'am.'

Clarissa watched them go and then looked at her sister-in-law. 'I'll tell you something, Maureen, John's been different for some time now.'

'In what way?'

'I don't know. I can't quite put my finger on it. Maybe it's the responsibility of marriage——'

Maureen smiled. 'I don't think so. He loves you dearly.'

'For the first year or so he doted on me, then that waned.'

'It happens. It's not all love and kisses.'

'I know, but this last year he's been absorbed in building the business to the exclusion of everything else, including his family.'

'Do I get my lolly now?' Michael piped up, still rubbing his eye.

Clarissa stood up. 'I'll get it.'

As Clarissa got the treat, Maureen wondered if Clarissa was just getting used to normal married life. John loved her so, but he loved his business too, and was ambitious.

Clarissa walked back into the room. 'Here you are, dear. Now suck it and make it last.'

Michael pressed the lolly with his fat hands. 'Thank you, Auntie.' Hearing his polite response to Clarissa, Maureen's chest swelled with love for her boy.

Returning to their conversation about John, Maureen said, 'I'm sure that incident on site and those deaths must have affected him.'

'I think they still do. He's preoccupied much of the time. Work is all he seems to care about.' Clarissa shook her head. 'It might be just me.' She gave a wan smile. 'We're all right, I guess.'

Maureen hoped so. There was a closer relationship now between herself and Clarissa and she wondered if was the time to tell her about something in Maureen's past that had affected both her and John. It had happened six years ago and Maureen still thought about it; not quite as often, and thank God the nightmares had faded. But it would be something she'd take to her grave. She decided she would tell Clarissa. 'Do you remember when you mentioned to me, some years ago, that John seemed to have a problem with a man called William Baxterhouse?'

Clarissa frowned at Maureen and then nodded. 'Yes, and you also had a problem with him. John told me at the time that the man had done something to you.'

Maureen looked at Michael sucking hard on his treat. Beside him was a set of blocks that Liam had made for him. John had supplied the timber and had cut them out and Liam had painted them in bright colours, with numbers and letters on them. By playing with them, Michael was learning his alphabet and his numbers. Maureen thought that was very clever of Liam.

'I was attacked by that man before I came to New South Wales,' she said in a quiet voice, so as not to attract Michael's attention. 'He was my landlord.'

Clarissa's face showed concern. 'I'm so sorry.' Clarissa put out her arms to Maureen, who made room for her sister-in-law on the settee and held her hands.

'It was an assault, and it was bad. In fact, I was raped.'

'Oh my God, that's . . . awful, awful.'

Maureen squeezed Clarissa's hands harder. 'It was.'

'Did the police do anything? Please tell me what happened.'

Maureen took a deep breath and closed her eyes for a moment. When she opened them, she concentrated on a vase of flowers and tried not to let the memory of that hellish time in her bedroom in Dublin stop her from continuing.

After Clarissa heard everything, she dropped her head and shivered. 'He disappeared?'

'Yes, he came to New South Wales—'

'I met the man, once or twice,' Clarissa said, putting her arm around Maureen. 'Now I have an entirely different view of him. Surely Liam would've done something?'

'He thought we should leave it to the police, but as you know Baxterhouse escaped before he could be brought to trial. What you don't know is that before he escaped, John confronted the rapist and gave him a real beating. John's been carrying his anger over what Baxterhouse did to me for some time. He feels he can't tell anybody about it. This could be why he's acting so strangely. It may be he feels guilty that the rapist got away.'

Clarissa paused. 'After all this time? I don't know. Why now, and why didn't he tell me? Maybe it's time I spoke to him about it.'

Maureen hesitated. The rape was in the past. Should she leave it there? 'It might be, and then maybe it isn't. You know about it now and I'm glad I've told you, because I felt you needed to know, woman to woman, if you know what I mean. You have to be the judge of when you talk to John about it.'

'Dear Maureen, this is a horrid thing for you to have had to bear for all these years. I wish John had told me. There were many times in the past, before we were married, when he'd often appear distant and I'd see either concern or anger on his face. I knew something serious was troubling him. I do want to speak to him about it at some point.' Clarissa took Maureen hands again. 'When did you tell Liam?'

'Liam has known from the beginning and has been very understanding. I was fearful that his affection for me was only pity and not love, but he loves me for who I am, and always has, for which I am very grateful.'

'That's wonderful. Let's keep it between ourselves for now. I'll let you know when I've spoken to John.' She shrugged. 'Who knows? It may change things.'

A drop of sweat slipped down John's back as the early morning sun glinted through the trees bordering the Randwick park. It was the middle of July and there was dew on the grass but it was humid, which was unseasonal, or was it just his anticipation of the meeting? To be sensible and risk averse, all contact with Beth should have been by correspondence, but by being here now, he knew he'd crossed a line.

He smiled at his colt's whinny, as it tried to talk to the other horses in the big stable, not thirty feet away.

'That's a fine colt you've got there, John.' He turned to see Beth standing, watching him. She was dressed in tight-fitting trousers, riding hat and riding jacket, accentuating her full figure. Her smile shone from her face and John's pulse halted just for a moment, and he found himself smiling as well.

'He is that. Cost me a pretty penny, but he's worth it.' He gestured to the nearby buildings. 'Not a fraction of the cost of the horseflesh you've got in there, but I wouldn't trade him for anything.'

He dismounted and joined Beth on the walk to the stables, where he tethered his horse.

'Let's go in here,' Beth said, stopping near an opened half-glazed door. She removed her hat, shook her hair free and went into the room. It was a working office where paperwork and saddlery dwelt side-by-side. 'Thank you for coming to Randwick so early,' she said. 'It's probably the only time we can see each other, given the circumstances.'

John scuffed the floorboards with his boots, sending up a puff of dust. He shouldn't be seeing her alone and, looking at her now, he knew the reason. Her closeness, her scent and her smile were pulling him towards her. He should not have come. It would be best to be brief and to go.

'I've kept your purchase of Leary's quiet, Beth, as we agreed. David wasn't suspicious. All the forms are signed and I have your written agreements on acting as a shareholder only. Is there anything else you wanted to speak about?'

She stood near him, fidgeting, and he sensed her awkwardness. He suspected she wanted to talk to him about something else, as her note to him had indicated.

Beth touched a kettle on the shelf. 'How about a cup of tea?'

'That'd be grand,' John said.

Going to the iron stove, Beth lit the gas flame, filled the kettle from the sink and put it on the stove.

John sat down on a chair and stretched his legs out. 'You know the last time you made a cup of tea for me? It was in your kitchen in Woolloomooloo. Do you remember?'

She turned around. 'I do. I had to scratch for every penny to feed my sisters and my mum.'

'How are the fiery little villains?'

Beth smiled. 'They miss the time when John the giant used to clod around their backyard.' She sighed in exasperation. 'But they're quite the young ladies now. They're a bit more concerned about how they look, although they're not quite at the stage of being interested in boys.'

Rummaging in the cupboards she brought out a teapot and put into it a couple of spoonfuls of tea. She pulled two mugs from the shelf and turned to him. 'I see a lot of men in this business but Henry doesn't trust me. He hasn't said anything but I feel it. But,

I'm going to see you as often as I want to.' She looked at him as if she expected an answer.

John was pleased to hear this but it made him nervous as well. 'You're not worried about Henry? You're supposed to obey him and be a dutiful wife.'

She looked at him for some time. 'I've thought a lot about us, since I saw you again in Bathurst. I think our friendship is strong. Indeed, I think it's stronger. Do you agree?'

John did. But what was going on between them was more than friendship.

Beth brought the cups over and as he took them, their fingers touched. It was only for a fraction but the sensation was like the jolt he sometimes got from touching certain fabrics. She turned and whipped the steaming kettle off the flame and filled the teapot.

'Clarissa is a good woman,' she said, 'and I don't wish to hurt her. But I want to see you, John, and I want to keep seeing you. There. I've said it.' Beth turned away from him and her shoulders slumped. He sensed she'd made a declaration and wanted his reply.

She'd made it clear she wanted him, and that thrilled and flattered him. She was making it easy for him—but think of all that he was risking! His marriage, Clarissa and their little boy. He couldn't do this to them. He stood up and went to Beth, stopping a foot away. 'I should only see you on social occasions and when business requires it.'

Beth whipped around and stared at him. Her eyes were wide with surprise and her mouth opened, showing a slip of pink tongue. She was about to speak as he put his hand up. He told himself to be strong. Walk away now. Beth's eyes were on his lips and her chest rose and fell. 'But I want to see more of you as well,' he said.

Her eyes glowed. 'Really?'

'Yes, but we can't be alone together.'

She was surprised, then seemed to understand. 'Don't you trust us?'

No, John thought. Is she wanting me to be strong for the both of us? Stop it now before it goes any further?

'No, not alone,' he said and he meant it.

Beth moved away. 'You're right. We're only inviting trouble if we see each other this way. Then,' she forced a smile, 'it's goodbye.'

Her eyes held his and this was the time to go. It was going to be hard to say, but he had to. 'Yes.'

'Right.' She smiled. Her lips were quivering. 'Don't I get a kiss? We are friends.'

He kissed her cheek, her skin warm and smooth. Her hands touched his and he stood back. 'Goodbye, Beth.'

There were tears in her eyes and John hugged her, holding her head on his chest. She put her arms on his shoulders and he gave in, bent and kissed her mouth. She broke away. 'John, I love you. I always have.'

'Hush, don't talk.' John kissed her again, her hands glided down his back and held him. He found the softness of her breasts as he tried to open her blouse.

She broke away, her face flushed. 'Wait,' she said to his surprised face. She opened the door and went outside. There was still time for him to leave. Now, he should go.

'Jack, Jack,' Beth said. 'Are you there?'

'Yes, missus,' came the reply.

'Who's here at the moment?'

'Just me, missus. The rest of the gang won't be here till one o'clock. They're all out trainin'.'

'Good. Run an errand for me. I want you to go to town and get something. It's a set of account books. You know the place in George Street?'

'Yes, missus, I do.'

'Well, go there now and then from there go and see if Mr Henry wants a hand at Redfern. Bring me back the books this afternoon.'

'Very good, missus.'

Coming back into the office, Beth closed the door and pulled down its blind. Her face felt hot and she turned and faced John. Feeling behind her, she locked the door. Her eyes held his as she came towards him, taking off her jacket and unbuttoning her blouse. John seemed shocked and she began to feel self-conscious, then he began pulling off his clothes and she felt better.

131

He was down to his undershirt and trousers when he saw that she was naked. His eyes widened, making her want him more. They would make love and maybe they could make a baby. That risk didn't daunt her; in fact it made her want him even more. She came to him and welcomed his lips as if she wanted his force, his need. His hands passed over her back, and he gripped her buttocks.

Beth stood back and released his belt buckle and John discarded his pants, picked her up and placed her on the table and kissed her again. She lay back and her thighs pressed against him. His eyes closed and she knew he was lost to her. She clung to him, absorbing him, raising her enjoyment and his, until they were both satisfied.

His panting slowed and she lay still, her arms at her side. Her head turned and the vein at her throat pulsed. Her breasts were tender from his attentions, their nipples still hard. A drop of sweat darted down her middle and she shivered as it found her navel. *Well, they'd done it now and there'd be consequences*, but she pushed those thoughts away.

He moved a hair that had stuck to her face.

She looked up at him, then closed her eyes. The rusty spring of the chair squeaked as he sank onto it. Beth leaned up on her elbows and looked at him. 'I don't want you to think I do this all the time.'

John smiled as he put on his shirt. He had nothing else on. 'I know that. I know you. We have something, Beth. We talk the same language and come from similar worlds. You have no faces, fronts or finery, just Beth—and I like that.'

She got up, winced and looked down. 'Goodness.'

His fingers reached out and joined hers as they travelled over the marks on her breasts. 'Sorry,' he said and smiled.

His touch aroused her again. 'I don't mind. Do you love me John? Or is that too much to hear?'

John shrugged. 'I love your honesty and directness. You wanted this and you got it.'

Beth frowned. 'And you didn't? I saw your look at the races and in the carriage. My God, we could've done it both days. I wanted to.' She looked away. 'But I shouldn't have.'

John nodded. 'I know.'

She should end this right now. They had weakened and if it stopped today then that would be one act, a deceitful, trust--breaking act to be sure but they could live with it. Seeing him looking at her, she knew that she couldn't end it now. 'So, when can I see you?' she asked as she picked up the teapot.

'Can we drink our tea this time?' John smiled as Beth ruffled his hair. He became serious. 'Should we? Think of Clarissa and Henry.'

'I want to see you.'

He looked at her for a long time and she worried that he didn't want to see her again. After all, he'd got from her what she'd always kept from him.

'We can meet whenever you like,' he said.

Thank God, she thought.

'Maybe we should have a place to go,' he said. 'Somewhere where no one can trouble us. I'll send a message to you here at the stable.'

Beth nodded and sat on his knee and hugged him. 'How is it with Clarissa, or shouldn't I ask?'

'No, it's all right. She's a good woman and a fine mother. Ever since we came back from Melbourne, things have been different between us.'

'What do you mean?'

'I don't know.'

'Could it be your baby?'

John snapped his head towards her. 'I don't understand.'

Beth got up and sipped her tea. 'You've never been a father before.'

He smiled. 'I haven't, but it's grand.'

'So is it the murders? Those three deaths. Do you think it changed you?'

'That was dreadful but . . . no. I'm still the same.'

'Are you?'

'I don't know. Am I? Would I have been keen to grow the business in spite of the deaths? I think I would have. Leary's has to grow. It has to be bigger to be stronger.'

'It sounds like it's under siege.'

'In a way it is. It's a very competitive business.' He drank some of his tea. 'It's about work. I've got a devil in me, Beth, a devil. He's pushing me to get my company strong and I'm singing to his tune. I'll stop at nothing to do that, and use anybody to help me.'

She smiled and stroked his chin. 'Even me?'

'Even you.' He looked at her, his eyes darting over her thighs, belly and breasts. It was as if he was still inside her and her desire flared again, but something stopped her reaching for him again. It was only a gesture but it gave her false hope that even if they had to meet again, she could always refuse to see him. He reached down for his trousers and Beth wanted to stay his hand, but she didn't. She let him get dressed, as did she. 'Write to me, John,' she said.

He opened the door and looked back at her and smiled. 'I will.'

Henry Blackett looked up from his desk in his Redfern office. 'I've got nothing for you here, Jack,' he said. 'You been running a message for the missus?'

Jack nodded. Henry trusted this Aboriginal man. He'd been with him for many years and he could turn his hand to anything.

'Yes, Mr Henry. Missus asked me to get some account books for her at the clerk shop. Got them here and was about to take 'em back to her when I remember she asked me if you wanted anything.'

'No, Jack I'm all right. Tell me, who was there with the missus when you left this morning?'

'Like I said boss, just me. Hang on a moment, that's right. There was this big young bloke speaking with her.'

Henry's stared hard at Jack. 'Big young bloke? What did he look like?'

Jack scratched his grizzled head and pursed his lips. 'Can't tell you that boss, just got a glimpse of him.'

Henry nodded. There were plenty of big young blokes always hanging around the stable. Could be anybody, he thought, and then another thought struck. John Leary was a big young bloke. No,

Henry thought, it wouldn't be him. 'All right Jack, off to the missus with you and no stopping in the pub on the way. Got it?'

Jack flashed a one-tooth smile and was off.

In the mid-morning coolness, John rode back to town, trying to think about the meeting regarding the Balmain warehouse that afternoon, but all he could think about was Beth. Their lovemaking had been intense. Here he was making plans for further -dalliances as if he were planning the start of a new site. He should feel guilty, distressed at least that he'd been unfaithful, and he should not be seeing Beth Blackett alone again. But for some reason he didn't want to keep away from her and that worried him. And it should, he thought. Clarissa was a good woman and his wife. He enjoyed their intimate times together, but his morning's interlude with Beth had been lovemaking of a completely different kind. Also, with Beth, he'd been able to give free rein to his inner doubts and worries. He didn't want to give that up just now. She was one of the few people who knew more about him and his life than anyone else in the colony, even his sister Maureen.

But, he still knew that all of it was wrong.

During dinner that same evening, John was attentive and interested in Clarissa's day. He might have been overly so, perhaps trying to compensate her for what had happened that morning in Randwick. Of course, that was impossible, the damage was done—but he could at least limit it to that one time. Clarissa delighted in having his undivided attention, and it had been a very pleasant evening so far.

She got up from the table as Stella came to clear the dishes, 'Come to the drawing room, dear,' she said. 'It's warmer. We're still only in mid-July and I thought I'd never say it, but I'm looking forward to summer.'

As they settled themselves in front of the fire, Clarissa smiled at him. 'I'd like to talk about me going back to work.' She looked somewhat apprehensive as she waited for his reply, which she probably suspected would be negative.

'What, with the baby and all? You're too occupied, surely.'

'With the help of Stella and cook,' she said, 'I can manage those things, dear, and I'd really like to use my skills and experience and help Father.'

'He'd consider it extraordinary as well. He mightn't let you.'

She smiled. 'He's all right with it as long as you are.'

He should refuse her. Their baby and the household were her responsibilities, nothing else. Yet her eyes were guarded and he felt that he should agree to what she wanted. Another gesture, he knew, to lighten his guilt. 'All right, if you think you can manage it all.'

She reached over and squeezed his hands. 'Do you really mean it?'

'I do,' he said. She was pleased and he was glad.

'Thank you, dear, thank you.' She got up from her seat and kissed him. He accepted it with alacrity.

He loved her so, and the impact at what he'd done to her was starting to affect him. Whenever she looked at him now, with those trusting eyes of hers, he felt dreadful. He must not see Beth again.

Clarissa sat on the settee next to him. 'I can work only limited hours,' she was saying, her voice excited, 'but I'm overjoyed to be going back. I can start on the first of August.'

'You'll do well, I'm sure.'

'Thank you, dear. Now on a more serious note, I had Maureen and Michael over two weeks ago.'

'Yes, you told me,' he said.

'But not everything, my darling. Maureen told me about something that happened to her which I didn't know, something from her past.'

'Go on,' he said.

'She told me what happened to her in Dublin. The attack.'

His eyes expanded. 'She told you? Everything?'

'All of it. She was violated, and only a woman knows how much pain that would be. Why didn't you tell me, John?'

He stared at the open fire. Well, it was finally out in the open.

'Dear, I was so struck by you at first, your money and all that. I don't know. I felt threatened by telling you.'

'Threatened. How?'

It all came back to him then, in a dark horrible flash. The hospital, Maureen's injuries and, worse, the fear on her face that night. 'Your composure,' he said, 'your confidence and your background. That what's I feared.'

'But dear, I would've understood. I could've helped you. You carried that cross before we were married and there were times when I had doubts that we'd last.'

He looked at her and believed her. 'My sister was raped and she's accepted it. It happened so long ago. The culprit—'

'Came to New South Wales,' she said. 'I met him with you after Mass one Sunday.'

He looked at the fire again and remembered the first time he'd seen his sister's rapist in Sydney, outside St Mary's. Clarissa had been astute enough to notice his shock at that time. 'I confronted him,' he said. 'We fought, and he escaped.' John ran a hand through his hair and looked at her. 'It took me months to accept that I couldn't do anything about his crime. But I have, so dear, please put it out of your mind. My sister has.'

'Don't you ever wonder what became of him?' she asked.

He did at times and would have liked to see him behind bars. 'We fought and he escaped. You can ask Sean about it if you like— he was there.'

'Sean?' Clarissa was surprised. 'He knew about this? Did he know about the rape?'

'Yes.'

'So, it seems everybody knew,' she said. 'Except your wife.'

'Not everybody.' He took her hand again. 'Dear, it was wrong of me not to tell you, especially after we'd married. Can you forgive me?'

She returned the pressure on his hand. 'Of course, dear, but no more secrets, all right?'

He couldn't look at her but kept his voice relaxed. He was now hiding a more unworthy act. 'No more secrets.'

Her eyes were watchful but she smiled. 'Good. Now I'll see to Richard. Thank you for our talk, I've enjoyed the evening very much.' She kissed him again. 'If you've got work in the study,' she said stroking his cheek, 'don't be too late to bed.' Her eyes were mischievous now. 'I'll not wait all night.'

'I won't dally,' he promised, smiling back at her.

CHAPTER FIVE

GERRY GLEESON KNEW IT WASN'T THE TIME TO BE THINKING ABOUT
Mrs Brophy. True, it was 17 August, and two days past it had been
the feast of another great lady, Mary and her Assumption. The altar
boy's tinkling bells at St Patrick's Church Hill rang Mrs Brophy
from his mind. He genuflected and went down the aisle to receive
communion. He'd laid stone in this church's footings and walls and
the surrounds were as familiar and dear to him as if they were his
own clothes.

The faithful file made steady progress, and despite his efforts to
think of something else, his neighbour came back into his thoughts.
Loneliness had been affecting him more of late and he liked the
idea of having a woman friend, someone he could get close to. But
his shyness had got in the way. His landlady had told him the name
of the handsome widow of about forty years who lived next door to
his boarding house. The home she owned was always neat as a pin,
the brass door knocker so polished that it seemed to wink at him as
he walked past. He wondered if that was a sign, maybe a signal for
him to get to know the house's occupant. Sure enough, one morning
she was outside watering her plants. He'd said good morning and
she returned his greeting before shyly looking away.

He'd then made a point of speaking to Mrs Brophy whenever he saw her, small stuff, nothing complicated, but he couldn't seem to take the acquaintance further. Next week he would build up the courage to do so. Yes . . . next week, he would.

After he'd received the sacred host he returned to his pew with bowed head and made his commitment to God for another week, knowing that temptation would see him stumble. But that was for another week. The pew squeaked as he sat his rump down. For the first time he scanned his immediate worshippers. Among the usual folk, he noticed Rupert Jenkins, who'd attended this Mass a few times. After the blessing, Gerry trailed the small builder to the exit. 'How's it going?' he asked when he caught up with him.

'Good day, Gerry, not bad mate, not bad.'

People coming out of the church crowded them, forcing them to separate. Outside, winter's blast hit and Gerry quickly did up his jacket. Looking around, he saw Jenkins standing in the lee of a sandstone wall talking to John and Clarissa. Gerry walked towards them. A fortnight past he'd been in their company for a picnic and in a week's time he'd have dinner at their place. It was nice, after all these years, to have relatives with whom he could spend some time.

'Good morning to you both,' he said to the Learys and nodded again to Jenkins.

'Good morning to you, Uncle,' Clarissa said and smiled. 'How are you?'

That smile could light a darkened room, Gerry thought. 'I'm as well as I can be thank you, dear. Now, how is Richard? On the mend?'

'He's feeling better, Uncle, thank you,' John said, doing up his jacket.

'Has the lad been poorly?' Jenkins said.

'A cold only, Mr Jenkins,' Clarissa replied. 'He'll get through it.'

Jenkins nodded and put out his hand to Gerry. 'And I'll get one too if I stand here too long. I'll bid you all, good day,' he said and he took his hat off to Clarissa.

'I'd better be off also,' said Gerry.

'Goodbye, Mr Jenkins and you too Uncle,' John said. 'We'll look forward to seeing you next week.'

Gerry waved to them and left.

~

In his office the following Monday morning, John was going through his mail. Picking up the first envelope on his desk, he opened it. Inside was a rental agreement from a landlord who owed John a favour. The contract described a set of rooms in Elizabeth Street that John could lease for a modest amount.

This could be a place where he and Beth could be alone. No, he would write back and decline the offer, that's what he should do. But remembering that passionate morning at Randwick, he knew he would sign the contract. It was more than a line he'd crossed now, so, on his head be it.

'Mr Leary, sorry I'm late,' Frank Cartwright said. His chief estimator sat down opposite John.

John pushed his conscience and the contract aside as Dan Reynolds, his accountant, came in, too, and sat beside the chief estimator.

'Let's have it, Frank,' John said.

'We don't need to put in such a low price for the Marrickville job, Mr Leary. We should increase our profit percentage.'

'Just give me two per cent of the build cost to cover our overheads, Frank. I won't quote high for this client. He's a friend.'

'All well and good, Mr Leary but your *friend* quoted us top price on that batch of cement he supplied on the Hall job.'

'Is that right?'

'I can show you.'

John smiled. 'Then, let's return the favour. We're in business after all. Add a profit of ten per cent.'

Frank Cartwright smiled and nodded. 'Done.'

'And you, Dan?'

'Just one thing. We're ahead on cash on all seven projects,' the accountant said, 'except two. Those clients need prompting, Mr Leary.'

'Who? Not the Council or the terraces?'

'No. Balmain and Osgood's on the Newtown site.'

'I'm seeing Brian Osgood today,' John said. 'He's normally pretty good. Draft a letter for me to sign for Balmain. Is that it?'

'That's it,' both men said together, then headed back to their offices.

Leary's was now on a par with contractors Harry Shelby and Bill Thomas, but there was one firm ahead of him—Maxtons. He'd tried hard to find the principals. Their managers were well known, but the shareholders hid among other directorships and were cross-linked with the pastoralists. Those shareholders he had to find.

Gerry Gleeson was nervous; he'd rather have faced a gang of louts in a dark alley with one hand tied behind his back. His palms were perspiring and it was nearing the end of Mass in St Mary's. She was there, as he'd thought she might be. The priest made his final blessing and Mrs Brophy left her pew, genuflected and came towards him down the aisle. Every step closer to him made him more self-conscious. When she got alongside him, she smiled and kept walking. Now was the time.

As he left the church, the late August chill infiltrated his knees and his hands causing them to throb painfully. She was already ten feet in front of him and he hurried to catch her. 'Mrs Brophy?'

She turned to him and stopped. 'How do you do?'

Gerry was stumped for words and said the first thing that came to mind, 'I'm not bad, thank you kindly, and yourself?'

'The same. Are you on your way home?'

'I am.'

'Then if you don't think it too forward of me, I'm going that way as well and I'd like you to join me.'

Gerry smiled. 'You're not too forward, Mrs Brophy, and yes, I'd like to accompany you.'

'Let's go then and to make things easier, I'd like to know your name.'

'It's Gerry, Gerry Gleeson.'

'How do you do, Mr Gleeson?'

They set off across College Street and into Hyde Park, keeping silent during that time. Mrs Brophy was the first to speak. 'I've seen you with a bag of tools on your way to work. Are you a tradesman?'

'I'm a stonemason.'

'An honest trade,' she said and smiled. 'Do you have a job you are working on?'

'The Memorial Hall job in Park Street.'

'A grand project. You must be skilful.'

'I get by, thank you.' He was starting to feel less self-conscious. She seemed intelligent, and interested in what he was doing, and that made him happy. For the rest of the way home they talked about the cost of living, world events, of which she was happily well informed, and the sermon that morning. He was disappointed at finding himself outside her house, so engrossed had he been in their conversation. He didn't want to leave anything to chance. 'If you're going to Mass next Sunday, Mrs Brophy, I'd like to accompany you, if that's all right with you.'

She opened her front gate, closed it and looked at him. 'Ten o'clock Mass, then? I'll be waiting here for you at a quarter to the hour.'

Gerry tipped his hat and smiled at her. 'I'll look forward to that. Good morning Mrs Brophy.'

'And to you, Mr Gleeson.'

After the same Mass, Christine McGuire was sitting with her husband in their carriage as it left St Mary's. She coughed as dust found its way into the window. She pulled out a handkerchief, patted her face and turned to David. 'It was an interesting sermon this morning.'

'Most appropriate,' David replied, 'considering the sudden

upsurge of gold madness. Things have been reasonably quiet for the last six months, but all of a sudden, the fever's struck again. Just like five years ago. Father Hogan was adamant, only evil comes from gold. That reminds me. Did you give him the donation?'

She nodded. 'He was quite excited at the amount.' She looked out the window as the carriage made its way down William Street towards home. 'David, I know it's the Sabbath, but I have to say it.'

'What's on your mind?'

She turned to him to get his full attention. 'Clarissa is working for you again. Are you sure that's appropriate? After all, she's married, with a baby.'

David's neck muscles tensed. She'd expected an argument and had prepared herself for one.

'She just started three weeks ago,' he said, 'and it's on a limited basis, a few hours a week.'

'Only a few? I don't think so. Last week I didn't see her at all.'

He shook his head. 'She's not working a full working week, only some of it. If you haven't seen her, she's probably busy doing other things, but she's not been working for me all the time. Let's get that quite clear.'

She matched his stare for four seconds, before he turned to look out the window. 'I see you support her,' Christine said, 'but understand that I'm dead against it. It's extremely unladylike and that's what Clarissa is, a lady. She's a married woman and she should behave like one. And she's got a child. She should be giving her attentions to her husband.' Christine felt bold enough to give David the other barrel: 'Lady Dalkeith told me that John's been seeing a girl he used to know.'

David's head jerked back to look at Christine. 'What's that?'

She was walking a dangerous line, peddling gossip, but she was determined to dent David's trust in John. 'I'm not suggesting anything. All I'm saying is that John is showing poor judgement in being seen publicly with a former attractive acquaintance. Clarissa doesn't know and I shall keep it from her. But David, it is only one more piece of proof about John's other side.'

'What other side? John seeing another woman? When? How many times?'

'Please don't interrogate me. He has been seen once. Lady—'

'By you?'

'No.'

'So it's once and then only seen by a third party. Really, Christine. It's your dislike for the lad that has not changed since you've known him.'

She said nothing and for the remainder of the journey both stayed silent.

When the carriage arrived at Point Piper, David alighted and helped her down. His arm was trembling. It must be the argument that's unsettled him, she thought. What happened next shocked her. His face was pallid as he leant against the carriage.

'What's the matter?' she asked. 'Are you all right? You look ill.'

David's hand was pressing his chest. 'No . . . it's just a pain, that's all.'

'A pain? What sort of pain? Come inside and sit down.'

A half an hour later his colour had returned and David seemed rested.

'Do you feel better?' she asked.

'It was a bit of a turn. Probably something I ate last night.' He grimaced. 'Christine, let's not discuss John. He's a prominent businessman and there'll be those who'll resent his success. He's changed, yes, but I'm hopeful that it's just a phase. Things will settle down, you'll see.'

Christine busied herself with straightening the rug over his legs.

At her lack of response, David said firmly, 'I will not, repeat not, listen to gossip about any of my family and I suggest you do the same.'

She opened her mouth to reply but thought better of it. She'd sown the seed in David's mind and now it needed time to germinate.

The evening's formal proceedings had finished and Brian Atkins ushered his fellow Number Two Lodge Freemasons to the front door of the house. He gestured for two of these men to stand with him as the rest departed, after which he turned to the two men. 'Well, gentlemen, the evening's young. Would either of you or both care to finish off the night with a drink at the Club?' Atkins suspected Bill Thomas would accept.

'I'll share one with you, Atkins,' Thomas said.

'And I'll join you both,' Harry Shelby replied.

'Excellent,' Atkins responded. In the unseasonal mildness of a late August night they made their way to Macquarie Street. After they were seated with their drinks, Atkins wasted no time in getting to the point.

'I take both you gentlemen back to our May dinner party and a threat that I raised at the time.' Shelby looked at him as Thomas was lighting a cigar. 'I mentioned the rise and risk of the -developer–builder.'

'Leary, you mean,' Thomas said, blowing out his match.

Atkins was always surprised at Thomas's ability to remember. His drinking ought to have just about pickled his brain by now. 'Indeed.'

'Look here, Atkins,' Shelby said. 'Leary poses no threats to us. What say you, Thomas?'

The big contractor shook his head. 'Right, we're all builders only. We'll always get work.'

Atkins ordered them more drinks. 'Investors and business owners like myself, gentlemen, are simply driven in one special way. We want the cheapest cost to build our buildings.' He paused. 'When there's a tight squeeze on credit, projects dry up, supply dips and the cost of building goes down.'

'That's not good for us,' Thomas said.

'Agreed,' Atkins said and smiled. 'But good for the investor. With a person like our bog-raised Leary, he gets his development risk solved by having two advantages. The first is he makes sure he has a tenant to rent his building once he's constructed it or he has a guaranteed buyer lined up to purchase it.' Atkins sipped his whiskey.

'The second plus for him is that he can take a reduced profit on the construction cost, because he's getting both construction and development profit from the project.'

'All makes sense, Atkins,' Shelby said. 'But I still don't see him as trouble.'

Atkins felt frustrated, then knew that he'd have to really spell it out to these two. 'Look, when times are tight, the finance to build is tight as well, correct?'

'Yeah,' Thomas said. 'Otherwise, we have to use our own cash to start a project until the client pays us after a month or two. And if the client is slow in paying us our progress claims, we get stretched.'

'To bankruptcy, often,' Atkins said. 'So, banks hate risk. There's only so much money in the market that banks will lend for development and for building. The money the banks hold in tight times will only be given to low risk projects where the bank can be assured that they'll get their principal back with interest. That's why they favour the developer–builder. The banks know that they're getting a cheap building cost because men like Leary will discount his margin.'

'So, Atkins,' Shelby said, 'what you're saying is that if Leary and coves like him proliferate they'll suck up all the funds we builders need to finance the start of our jobs?'

'Couldn't have put it better, Harry,' Atkins said and smiled. He looked at Thomas, who was stroking his chin.

'So, how do we prevent this?' Thomas asked.

Right on cue, Atkins thought. 'Some builders are copying Leary already, not many, but they're growing. I want to stop Leary treading on my turf for a whole host of reasons. If we can squeeze him and force him back down the totem pole of builders, then the other upcoming builder–developers will be scared off. I'm sure of that.'

Shelby looked dubious. 'What are these other things that bother you about Leary, Atkins?' Shelby asked.

Atkins sat back and his mood darkened. He spluttered, 'I dislike Catholics by nature and I despise Irish Catholics who don't know their place.'

'So, your interest in Leary is personal?' Thomas said.

Atkins had overstepped. 'I'm not advocating violence, gentlemen, believe me. This is business only. We have to remove a threat to our livelihoods.'

'So, hit him in the pocket?' Shelby said.

Atkins was already taking steps to do just that but he wanted these two men in on it as well. 'That's what I'm asking you two to think about. Are we agreed that Leary is a threat?'

Shelby and Thomas looked at each other, then back to Atkins, whose breathing was becoming rapid. Both contractors nodded.

Atkins was relieved. 'Well then, gentlemen. Think hard and quickly on ways to hobble him. We'll talk again. Soon.'

Clarissa felt at home at McGuire Wire. She'd just completed five hours' work in her fourth week of employment and she wanted to keep going until five o'clock, surprised that the wall clock read three. Sighing, she put her quill down and knew she had to go home to Richard. The trimmed piles of paper and the ordered ledgers showed she was doing something, not only for her father's company, but for herself. She needed this job. Her son was an essential part of her life, but the satisfaction in working for her father filled a void in her.

It had been hard work getting to this point. Father was diligent in his business, knew a good deal when he saw one and could juggle cash. But his competitors had gained a march on him and Clarissa took the bookkeeping, staff rosters and general management duties seriously.

She straightened her blouse and tended to her hair in preparation for leaving. One thing left to do. Opening her drawer, she brought out her planning program for the next three weeks that listed her father's appointments and other meetings which she was required to attend. Confirming the date of the next appointment, she nodded. Her desk was in a large room overlooking the warehouse floor, and she shared it with two junior clerks and the manager of the business, Malcolm Robinson.

Mr Robinson was an expert in fencing wire, whom David had

enticed away from a competitor. He looked up at Clarissa as she walked to his desk to say goodbye. He was a man in his mid-thirties, tall and with a complexion Clarissa envied: one that tanned as soon as the clouds parted. From his heavy accent she knew he must have southern European blood.

'Finished for the day, Mrs Leary?' Mr Robinson said. 'Forgive me for keeping you this late.'

'That's quite all right, Mr Robinson. I've done the August reports for the stocktake. I'd appreciate you checking them for me this afternoon, if you have time?'

His full lips opened in a nice smile and his eyes lit up. He eschewed the fashion of having one's hair plastered down, and it grew dark and curly, which she thought attractive. 'Yes, of course I'll check them,' he said. 'I shall see you on Monday, then. Good afternoon, Mrs Leary.'

A pleasant frisson went through her as she left the room. He was looking at her; she felt it. It was good to know that another man noticed her, but then her vanity shamed her. People had told her she was attractive; it was just that she'd never believed them. Before she'd met John, a few Dublin beaux had caught her eye and she recognised the way some men looked at her. At times their attention made her uncomfortable, but at others it would send a pleasurable jolt through her.

Malcolm Robinson was her manager. She thanked her father that at least the man was reasonable. In fact, Clarissa thought, more than reasonable. But then, she was the daughter of the owner of the business and that probably explained why Mr Robinson treated her so graciously. As she left the building she wondered what it would be like to kiss him, a thought that surprised her. *Where did that come from?* Mr Robinson was certainly attractive, but he was married, or she suspected he was, and so was she. And John had been very attentive lately, making love more often than usual.

The driver clicked the horse and as the cab rode up from Darling Harbour in the late August chill, she looked out the window with a smile on her face, enjoying the feeling that another man found her attractive.

~

How inspiring the band sounded, John thought, with its brass section booming out a rousing fanfare at Sydney's Victoria Barracks. The music stopped and the Chairman of the Garrison Cricket Club stood on the rostrum.

'I welcome our visitors from Victoria,' he said, 'and hope that they give us a cracking game for this inaugural charity match on this day, the seventh of September, 1856.'

Loud cheers erupted from the populace, accompanying the more polite clapping from the colonial bourgeoisie in marquees, including John's, at the perimeter of the ground.

John took a glass of champagne from a servant and, as he surveyed his surroundings, he felt very pleased with himself. More than pleased: he was thrilled that he was on the way to becoming the biggest contractor in Sydney.

Liam and Maureen were in conversation with Clarissa, who was pushing Richard in a perambulator, a present from David and Christine. John's in-laws were chatting to the McCreadies. Near him were well-to-do merchants and importers, and in between them were sprinklings of red and blue: the uniforms of senior officers of the army and the navy—all enjoying his hospitality. John considered himself their equal. There were a few who owed him favours, and his chest expanded at the thought that he'd be calling in those favours to his own timetable. It wasn't knowledge or skills that made you powerful but the highly-placed people you knew and, more importantly, what they could do for you.

Two long-faced partners from the Bank of New South Wales stood with the Cricket Club's president, watching as the opening batsmen walked to the crease. John smiled to himself: bankers couldn't be lively, even on a day like today. Seeing the men reminded him of the letter he'd received from the bank and his good feeling waned.

The letter was couched in language that didn't threaten, admonish or exhort, but it was the sort of letter that could be tabled in a bankruptcy courtroom. It had warned John of the size of his overdraft. He had been going to throw the letter away when he'd first read it. But he'd thought better of it. Leary's cash flow was good and he was surprised at the bank's request.

Clarissa looked at him and he nodded to her but then Richard demanded her attention. Clarissa was a good mother and a good wife and he loved her, but there was also Beth, with whom he felt he could better share his troubles and his doubts. He couldn't understand why he didn't want to confide in Clarissa, who did understand business. Was it his old insecurity about their class difference rearing its head again? Despite the fact that he was stepping up the social ladder, due to his status as a top builder, the feeling still persisted that he wasn't good enough for Clarissa. With Beth it was different and he was more at ease. Was he in love with Beth? He didn't know, but she certainly excited him and he couldn't wait to see her in just over a week's time. Their last meeting in July at Randwick was too long ago.

And Beth had given him the means to finally have control of Leary's, well, almost. Beth's share was his, in all but name, and he felt secure that she'd always support him. What he hadn't asked her to do was put it in writing that he was to have first right of refusal to buy her share if she ever wanted to sell. That wasn't a problem, because she'd told him she'd always sell to him first, and he believed her. A feeling of exhilaration surged in him. He was his own man; he'd got what he'd always wanted since coming to the colony: enough power and money to be forever free of poverty, and respect from his fellows and the best members of society. He drained his glass and reached for another as the crowd applauded a good shot.

But there was no rest. He had to be free of the banks and their hands on his assets. Having the cash from his business to fund his new projects without the overdrafts was the way to go. Let him *demand* from the banks, not the other way around. Perhaps even doing proper development where he took all the margin, yes. And there was another hurdle to jump. Wexton still hadn't been able to uncover the shareholders of Maxton Constructions. He pondered that as he sipped his champagne and watched the game.

'I heard from John McCreadie,' Christine said coming to stand near him, 'that Henry Blackett's colts are high quality and doing very well. You know his wife, John, don't you?'

She held his gaze as he fought to control his surprise. 'Beth, yes. She was a barmaid before she was married.'

'And an attractive one, if I remember. You met her at the races in May.'

That was four months ago and he was going to avoid commenting further but there were too many people who would've probably seen them that day, so pointless not to tell the truth. 'I did and I had conversation with Blackett as well.'

'When you see the Blacketts next time, please give them my regards.'

'Come, Christine,' David said joining them. 'Let John watch the cricket. I've got a seat reserved for you. See you at the end of the game, John.'

Watching them leave, John was intrigued. Why bring up Beth after all this time? Was Christine suspicious that he was seeing Beth? She could just be protecting her daughter and he couldn't blame her for that. He felt guilty, just for a moment that he was embarking on an affair. How had Christine found out about Homebush? What else did she know?

John felt his elbow pressed.

'You seem to be lost in your thoughts, Mr Leary. Not interested in the game?'

John's nose tweaked at Bill Thomas's whiskey breath. 'I was a mile away, Mr Thomas, and you caught me. Are you enjoying yourself?'

The big contractor nodded and waved at the crowd, an act that sprinkled the grass with his drink. 'I'm having a good day in all things. Just speaking to Atkins over there.' He paused. 'You've met him?'

John remembered meeting him at the Australia Club. 'Fleetingly.'

'Right, so how are things with you? Are all your jobs making money?'

John smiled at his companion's frankness. 'I can't complain, but who knows? Materials and suppliers are getting tight and prices are rising.'

'Doing any developing yourself?'

An odd question John thought. He hadn't done any for eighteen months. Glebe was the last one. 'I don't buy the land myself, Mr Thomas, I just get an owner to act as developer.'

Thomas seemed confused and the drink wasn't helping him understand. 'But,' he said, 'there's still a development side to it, yes?'

'I guess,' John answered.

Thomas nodded. John had a thought and decided to ask a question, which had been needling him. 'How well do you know Harry Shelby?'

Thomas gripped the marquee pole and paused before speaking. 'Pretty well. Not the sort of man you'd have as a close friend, mind you, but he's useful in his own way.'

Some people had gathered near them, laughing and talking. 'Walk with me,' John said to Thomas. The two men left the marquee and stood under a camphor laurel. 'Do you know his family?' John asked Thomas.

'A little. What's on your mind?'

'Nothing. Just that I think he may have an interest in my welfare, or maybe he wants to see me fall?'

Thomas laughed, but it had a nervous sound to it. 'Why would he want to do that? You're a young man going places. Who'd want to nail you? That's too much to believe.'

John nodded, but he sensed a change in the big contractor. It was as if he'd caught Thomas out in a lie. It was puzzling but he feigned innocence. 'Perhaps you're right. I'll get you another drink and we can get drunk together.'

Sean's palm lay flat on the sandstone wall of the Park Street Memorial Hall, his fingers gritty from its warm grains, as if the stone had fire in it. The walls were a foot shy of full height and were braced at right angles by thinner internal walls of sandstone, forming the public spaces and offices. He knew, but the site's stonemason knew better, that the stone was top quality, and Sean had laughed when a long-haired, drab-dressed scientist had told him that the sandstone was millions of years old. Things that Sean couldn't see, feel or smell confused him—although he thought, grinning to himself, he accepted his faith, and that was full of mystery. The scientist fellow had also told him how the rock was formed, but Sean was more impressed that this stone had lain unused for so long and now would stand in this building as the evidence of what man could do with it.

Sean's foreman stood next to him. 'We're two weeks ahead of schedule.'

'I thought as much. I went to the Hunter myself to look at the timber you bought.'

'What did you think?'

'It's all good, Barry.' Sean had inspected the cedar for the internal doors and joinery. A steam clipper would bring the load from Morpeth to Darling Harbour next week. 'Let's get down,' he said. They climbed down the scaffolding to the ground and Sean turned to his foreman. 'I don't accept anyone's advice on timber. Only my eyes, fingers and nose are the true judges.' He smiled. He'd felt more timber than he'd palmed currency. Sean wanted the best, because he knew the Memorial Hall should stand a hundred years at least.

'What's got you in good humour, Sean Connaire, on this fine September day?' Gerry Gleeson's bulk appeared beside him.

'Just thinking. But I haven't got time for that. There's things to be done and I should be at Sydenham.'

'The stores job?'

'Aye. I'll leave you in Mr Watson's capable hands.'

'I'd like a word with you before you go,' Gerry said. 'If I could?' Gerry smiled at the foreman. 'No offence, Mr Watson.'

'None taken, Mr Gleeson. I'll check the drains, boss.'

Sean could delay his departure. He wanted to know something from the stonemason, too.

Gerry waited till the foreman was out of earshot. 'That's the last of the stone delivered. We'll be finished in two weeks.'

Sean nodded. In the shed, a billy was on the boil. 'Come with me,' Sean said. 'You've done a grand job. I haven't seen better stonework in my career. Learn that in the old country?'

'I had a hammer and chisel in my hand from as young as I can remember. I didn't play with marbles or jacks. We didn't have any. Ma was too poor.'

Sean closed the shed door behind them. It was crowded now with the big stonemason there. Busying himself with the billy, he pulled two tin mugs from their hooks and made the tea. 'Now tell me about the strike that's planned.'

Gerry sat on a stool and Sean smiled to himself, wondering if it would take the weight. 'On the eighteenth of August,' Gerry said, 'the Stonemasons' Society in Sydney issued an ultimatum to you builders and the bosses that in six months' time, stonemasons would only work an eight-hour day.'

'That much I know,' Sean said as he filled the two cups with the steaming brew.

'What you mightn't know is men working on the Garrison Church in Argyle Cut, and on the Mariners' Church in Lower George Street didn't want to wait. They're on strike now.'

'So, why didn't you strike?'

'I don't want to, Sean. We'll get our eight-hour day, and the scuttlebutt is, it could be as early as October.'

'Being prudent with time and cost is still the go,' Sean said. 'Just keep up your quality and don't charge too much. I'll not complain.'

They finished the rest of their tea talking about sandstone, then Gerry got up and stretched his back. 'You have to be elsewhere,' he said, 'and I've got stone to check. Thank Mr Watson for the extra sand. I was going to ask for another load but it was delivered to me sooner. Barry's a good man.'

'He is,' Sean said, grinning, as he and Gerry left the shed.

Harry Shelby moved out of sight behind his horse as the stonemason and another man left the site shed. In the next half hour

Shelby took in the site's progress and was impressed: the Memorial Hall would be a trophy project for Leary's Contracting. Shelby swore. He'd wanted the job for the same reason Leary had wanted it —exposure. It wasn't its size—Shelby had bigger jobs—but it was more important because of its location in the centre of town.

He thought he knew Clancy well enough. Shelby had looked after the fellow Freemason on the few projects he'd done for the City Council: the new carriage harness, presents for his children and such like. But he'd lost the Memorial Project. Lost it clean. Or had he? If Clancy had taken Shelby's money, would he take it from others?

Shelby would find out if Atkins was right. Leary was getting too big.

～

Jack Johnson, sitting beside his boss in a cab, glanced outside as it made its way along King Street, Newtown on a warm spring morning.

'Let me do the talking,' John said and grinned. 'I know these bastards. They'd knife someone in front of a priest, they would, and swear their innocence.'

'But what's the point of getting these coves angry? It's just them and Sydney that can give us bricks.'

'Jack, you have to be hard on these bastards, brutal.' He paused. 'Something that you don't do.'

'What do you mean?'

'It's not in your nature. I've been seeing how you're going these last months with the extra work and the bigger suppliers. You're not tough enough.'

'I know my business, John.'

John didn't seem to be listening. 'If you want proof, think about the way Baxterhouse blackmailed you. If you'd stood up to him, he'd have folded. You'd still be in Ireland and perhaps a commander now in your gold braid.' John smiled. 'No, Jack, you're weak.'

Jack's irritation rose to anger. John had never mentioned how

Baxterhouse had blackmailed him over a gambling debt, and at the same time had somehow hurt John's family. Now John was using that forgettable part of Jack's life to belittle him. Weak, was he? Bloody hell, no! He had been blackmailed and it hadn't been as easy to solve as John had said. 'You're wrong, John.'

His boss's eyes were hard. 'I don't think so. So, today, let me do the tough stuff.'

God spare me, Jack thought, the man's addled.

'I've got the ideas, Jack. Leave it to me.' The cab passed a church and John's confident smile faded. 'You know what today is?'

Jack was still angry. 'It's Thursday. Why?'

'It is, Jack and it's one year to the day since my men were killed. The eighteenth of September.' John looked out again, his face drawn, his eyes bright. 'I'll find their murderer if it's the last thing I do.'

'Miller killed them.'

'Miller caused the sabotage, Jack, but he had other monsters pay him to get at me. I'm certain of that.'

'He'll go to trial in November.'

'He didn't act alone,' John replied.

It could be true but Jack didn't think so. It was more likely a dispute between Miller and his bricklaying boss that had gone horribly wrong.

'We're here,' John said. 'Right on time.' They alighted from the cab.

Jack picked up his pace to keep up with his boss. 'We have to get our credit extended,' he said. 'Their last letter wasn't encouraging about the—'

'Don't worry about that. I want this brickmaker to beg for our order. Leave it to me. Say nothing, Jack.'

Jack Johnson wiped his forehead, wondering why John had brought him here. Just to gang up on the brickmaker? And perhaps to show Jack how tough John was, who knows? Jack sensed that John's ambitious drive fed on imaginary attackers and fantasy threats. In the cab, when John had talked about the murders, his face had had the look of a man who believed that hanging for the phantom men behind the killer would not be good enough.

They entered the St Peters Brick Company's offices for their nine o'clock meeting. Jack's eyesight adjusted to the dimness inside as a clerk showed them into the manager's office, where a smallish but well-built man sat at his desk with two chairs in front of it.

The manager stood up. 'Mr John Leary, it's been a while. It's good to see you.'

'Good morning, Mr Goldberg,' John said. 'This is Jack Johnson.'

The manager put his hand out to Jack. 'Pleased to meet you,' he said.

Jack took the proffered hand of the balding man. 'And you. I'm the Purchasing Manager of Leary's.'

'Please sit down, gentlemen,' Goldberg said.

A certificate on the wall behind the brickmaker was familiar to Jack. In his Navy days, he'd seen similar ones in China.

Goldberg followed Jack's glance and turned around. 'Do you know what that is?'

'It's a brown belt certificate in Judo.'

'It's a black belt, actually, Mr Johnson. I received it two months ago.'

Jack was impressed. The man was a skilled fighter in the martial arts.

'How's business?' John asked.

Jack suspected John had no idea what they were talking about.

'September's halfway through,' Goldberg said, 'but so far so good. I can't keep up to the demand. I've got a new quarry opening at Canterbury. Can I get you men anything to drink?'

'No, thank you,' John said.

Goldberg leaned forward. 'So, what can we do for Learys?'

John picked off a thread from his suit jacket. 'I want to place a big order and I want the right price.'

Goldberg smiled. 'Always here to please. Tell me about it.'

'We're terminating our current brick-supply contracts.' John glanced at Jack. 'They differ in conditions, price and deliveries.'

Thanks, John, Jack thought. His boss should have shared his strategy with him.

John continued, 'We want just one order with one supplier.'

'Excellent,' Goldberg said, clasping his hands. 'How many bricks do you need?'

John pursed his lips. 'Two million a year, minimum.'

Goldberg's eyes expanded. 'Are you serious?'

Jack swallowed. *They'd never want that many bricks.*

'You know the jobs we've got,' John said. 'We'll double that number in a year. Can you supply them?'

'All commons or a mix?'

'Just commons. What's your price?'

Goldberg spread his hands. 'That's a massive order, Mr Leary. The biggest I've heard. Can you take that many?'

'We can. Now, what's your price? And I want sixty days' credit.'

Goldberg paused. 'Let me get my production manager in here. Give me a moment.'

John pulled out his watch and looked at it. 'Please be prompt. I've got a meeting with Sydney Bricks at noon.'

'I won't be long,' Goldberg said.

The door closed and Jack leaned towards John. 'We don't want two million bricks! What's your game?'

'It's not a game, Jack. It's a battle. Now, shut up, listen and learn.'

Two minutes later, Goldberg walked back in with another man and they sat down. 'This is Max Dawson,' Goldberg said, 'my production manager.' Dawson was a giant, bull-headed and thick set.

John nodded at Dawson. 'Well, Mr Goldberg?'

Goldberg glanced at his manager. 'We can supply you, but we want some more information.'

'Such as?' John said

'Well, for a start,' Dawson said. 'How many bricks would you want per month, what's the mix of commons, select or ordinary?'

John brought out a notebook and referred to it. 'Average delivered to mostly town jobs, 155,000 per month, 60 per cent select commons, the rest ordinary.'

For half a minute, Dawson scribbled down some numbers. He showed these to Goldberg who nodded.

'We can help you.'

'Good,' John said. 'And the price delivered?'

Goldberg looked down at Dawson's figures. 'We can deliver the commons to you. The average price, between select and ordinary, is six shillings per thousand.'

That's cheap, thought Jack, very bloody cheap.

John stood up and pushed his chair in. 'Come on, Jack. Let's see what Sydney can offer.'

'Mr Leary?' Goldberg said, astonished. 'What are you doing?'

'I'll pay five shillings per thousand. No more,' John answered.

'Six is my best price on that volume.' Goldberg waved to a chair. 'Please sit. We can do business. We have in the past always agreed in the end. What do you say?'

'My price or I walk from here,' John said.

Jack blanched. This wasn't tough negotiating. This was nonsense. Sydney Bricks hadn't priced Leary's order yet and Jack doubted they would beat Goldberg's very low offer.

'Why the hurry?' Goldberg said. 'Sit down. We'll do a deal.'

'You're wasting my time, Mr Goldberg. Do you agree to my price or not?'

'You're not willing to discuss this? You used to.' Goldberg turned to Dawson. 'You can go, Max.'

After the office door closed, Goldberg cleared his throat. 'I won't be bullied, Mr Leary. Is that what you're doing? Because it's out of character for you.'

That's torn it, thought Jack and he waited for John's response.

John gripped the chair and leaned forward, his knuckles turning white at the effort. It was on, Jack thought and glanced at the certificate on the wall. John was set for a hiding, but suddenly his boss blinked then leaned back, his forehead wet with perspiration. 'Six shillings and seventy days' credit,' said John.

Goldberg paused for a moment. 'Done.'

John smiled. 'Very good, Mr Goldberg. We have a deal.'

Goldberg put out his hand and John and shook it. 'When would you like the first delivery?' Goldberg asked in a voice that lacked its previous warmth.

'I'll give you the dates with my order.'

Outside, John put on his hat and turned and smiled at Jack. 'I was willing to pay seven shillings for that number. Come on, Jack, there's a day's work still needed.'

Jack had nothing to say. His boss had ordered bricks in numbers that they'd never need and had nearly attacked the brickmaker after his character had been questioned. Yes, he had backed down, but what if he hadn't? It was all very weird and worrying.

The roses were recent and their smell sweet but some of their petals had fallen. John placed his own bunch of flowers and stood up. The graves were different and the work done on them was handsome: sandstone kerbing, marble headstones and pebbles covering each grave. It was the least Leary's could do for the eternal rest of his three men. But John had more to do.

'Well, one year on and I've got one of the bastards, but I want the lot.' He bowed his head and went into a deep, dark place. The sun was shining, the sky was blue and the breeze kind but John shivered. He knew he'd let these men down. One year on and their souls were still restless, still no resolution of the crime. 'I haven't given up and I never will.'

He walked away with heavy feet and his head lowered. As he got nearer his waiting cab, his load lightened to be bearable, just. He opened the cab door. 'Elizabeth Street, driver.'

A well-dressed man, on the other side of Elizabeth Street, looked up at Beth and she moved back from the window. She had mixed feelings. Part of her was excited, a small but dominant part, and her desire for John was palpable—had been since July and Randwick—but another part of her was guilt-ridden at what she was doing. They were committing adultery—a grievous sin. They were hurting their marriage partners and they were risking losing those marriages.

A cab stopped outside. It was four p.m. The door opened and John alighted. *Thank God, he's here.* She looked at his face and wondered what was troubling him. He pulled out his watch and looked at it, then he glanced up at the terrace. *Yes, he knows he's late.* Their time together would be short. Her guilt-ridden anxiety went, replaced by anticipation.

She only waited two knocks before opening the door and his smile made it worthwhile.

'I'm sorry I'm late,' he said. 'I nearly throttled a brickwork owner this morning.'

She closed the door, took his hat and turned towards him, wanting his arms around her. He took her and kissed her. Traces of tobacco stung her and the firmness of his lips bore down on her mouth. She responded and he filled her world. Somewhere along the way he broke away and looked around. 'So, what do you think of the place? Happy?'

She'd had a good look around before he arrived—one generous room with a large bed, chaise longue, two chairs and a wardrobe. The supplementary room held a counter with an enamel bath connected to the luxury of hot water. 'It's good,' she said. 'I think the bath is a treat, although I can't see us using it. Can you?'

He smiled. 'It depends.' He sat down on the chaise. His leg muscles stretched the fabric across his thighs, accentuating his slim waist and upper torso. He hadn't noticed her new dress that she'd bought just for him. But she didn't care.

'I got these rooms for a song,' he said. 'It's too small for a family and too large for one person. What's the best day for us to meet? Thursdays?'

She hadn't thought that far ahead and concentrated. 'Thursdays are going to be hard,' she said, 'Tuesdays would be better.'

'I'll try and make it each Tuesday.'

'Wonderful.' Her impatience at wanting him was making her irritable.

'But if I'm not here by half past three,' he said, 'it means I've been delayed on something. So don't wait.' John pulled his boots off. 'The bank's being a bastard. They want to cut back my overdraft, I can feel it. I'll see them soon and sort them out. The company's cash is sound.'

She smiled. 'Is my investment safe?'

'It is,' John said, as he loosened his tie while staring at the floor.

There's something else on his mind. She sat beside him and took his hand. 'What's wrong?'

'A year ago, my three men died. I've just come from the cemetery.'

'Oh.'

He forced a smile and shook his head. 'You were always the recipient of my bad news, weren't you? I told you of Maureen's attack, didn't I?'

'And that you'd fought that man, Baxterhouse,' she said. She leaned close and kissed him again. His lips didn't respond at first then they moved with hers. He put his arms around her. Now, changed from a listener to a demanding woman, her hands pressed him, her desire wanting her to be free of clothing, free of everything in between, just she and him. He removed her upper garments and kissed her breasts.

She took off the rest of her clothes and led him to the bed. He undressed and she caressed his broad shoulders and traced a hand down a bicep onto his forearm. Her other hand glided across his chest, down the slope of his muscled stomach then stopped. Naked, she pushed up against him and he leant down, kissed her again and pressed her back onto the bed.

Later, he brought himself up beside her and pulled the sheet to cover them. They remained silent for some time. 'How is it at home?' he asked.

'As always. And Clarissa? Do you still make love to her?'

John's silence gave Beth her answer. She should be angry or at the very least troubled that he was being intimate with them both.

But she wasn't, and that worried her somewhat. John might have another child with Clarissa. She herself might have a child with him. That would be wonderful! She would raise it as her own, Henry none the wiser. *What was she thinking!* Though if her child were very tall, that might take some explaining, she thought smiling. She had other questions for John but before she could ask them, he said, 'All right, a deal, let's leave others out of here. Fair enough?'

Beth flung her thigh across him and hugged him. She loved him and if she could be with him every now and again, feel the peace of his love, his tenderness, his passion, then she'd be happy.

From September to November 1856, Sean split his time between supervising the foremen on the shoe factory in Newtown, the Sydenham Stores and the Memorial Hall. Blunt's warehouse in Market Street had finished on time in October with a modest profit.

It was now the first day of December and Sean and his foreman were finishing the day in the Memorial Hall site shed.

'Here are the as-builts,' Barry Watson said. 'They're all done.'

'Let's look at them,' Sean said. He carefully scanned the drawing plans that the foreman had marked up indicating the final layout of utility services in the Hall. The dimensions might be different in some areas from the original design drawings as a result of site conditions unknown or those found during construction. The architect would use these layouts and amend his own drawings for a permanent record of the building's construction and services 'as built'.

Who knew, in some future time a young man could pore over these plans with the same interest that Watson had in completing them. Would the same person admire the work of his forebears? Would he value the neatly written notes about the location of buried drains or the suppliers of ironmongery? After five minutes Sean was satisfied. 'They're good. Now get yourself home. You've been here since six this morning.'

'Thanks, boss.' Watson grabbed his bag and opened the shed door. 'Will you lock up?'

'I will.'

Watson handed him the key. 'Night,' the foreman said, then left.

Sean rolled up the plans. He hadn't seen John for two weeks and was glad. His partner was becoming a stranger to him and Sean was worried. When John strutted around winning jobs, Sean put up with it. Knowing him, he believed he'd grow out of it. But he hadn't. In fact, John's arrogance had worsened.

A major cause of concern was John's treatment of suppliers and contractors. Jack Johnson had told him about what happened at St Peters Brick Company and there were other instances as well. What was he going to do about him?

The site office door opened and there was John himself.

'What's the problem?' John said.

Sean was surprised to see his boss. 'Are you here to see me?'

John looked irritated. 'You're supposed to be at the office. We had a meeting to talk jobs. It was supposed to have happened half an hour ago.'

Sean remembered. 'You're right, you are.' Sean slapped his forehead. 'I forgot.'

John shook his head. 'What's wrong with you? I arranged that meeting for your benefit.'

'Aye,' Sean said. 'I'm sorry. Well, we can talk now, if you'd like.'

'It's too late now,' John said. 'I'm off to a client's. It's always too bloody late. You want a nursemaid following you, tapping your shoulder, reminding you. Jesus, Sean, a simple meeting. Can't you manage that? I don't know what to do about you.'

In exasperation, Sean grabbed the rolled plans and flung them in the corner. 'No, not about *me*. This is about you, John. What the bloody hell is the matter with you?'

John seemed stunned. 'With me!'

'You!' Sean continued. 'You're angry, all the time. You're moody. You pick fights with people. People who have done nothing to you. What is all this?'

John closed his eyes for a second and clenched his fists. 'Don't make this about me, Sean.'

'But it is about you, mate.'

John frowned as sweat formed on his forehead. 'Too simple, Sean. You'll not get off that easy. You messed up.'

'I missed a bloody meeting, one meeting. All right. I'm sorry.' Sean paused and moved closer to his boss and partner. 'You tell me what else I've done wrong. Come on, I want to know.'

John paused then shook his head.

'See, you can't.'

John sat on a stool, still looking at him. 'I'm the one who is responsible for this company, its men and its money. I'm the one who has to protect it.'

'You can't fight everybody, for God's sake! It's anger you've got. Deep ugly anger and you're lashing out at everyone. You aren't even interested in getting the facts. That's what's changed you. You're acting from spite and fear.'

'That's rubbish, Sean.'

'Those men. Their deaths are eating at you, John. They eat at me, too, but I get on top of that. I don't let it beat me. I let people help me cope.' He pointed a finger at John. 'Do the same.' Sean looked at his boss and was about to speak when John got up, opened the door and left.

That's great, Sean thought, just great. Perhaps he should fight John? Blood and bruises might bring him around. But would it solve anything? No, but it sure would make him feel better. He picked up the plans from the floor. It was a shame, a bloody shame.

He shut up the site office. The hut would be removed at the end of the week and placed on another job. Setting off to check the rest of the building as he'd done each working day since he'd become a foreman, he thought about John.

Feeling in his pocket, he had enough to buy himself a non-alcoholic drink or two before going home to his family. He would've liked to have had John, the John he had so admired, join him. They would have shouted each other a drink and talked over the day's work, like they used to in the days gone by.

'Come with me to the drawing room,' Henry Blackett said to Beth after dinner.

She followed her husband into the drawing room, where he poured two glasses of sherry and handed one to her. 'I don't want you to see John Leary any more. Tongues are starting to wag.'

Beth took a tighter grip of her sherry glass. 'What's all this about?'

'You heard me.'

'I've met Mr Leary twice. Once in Bathurst and once at Homebush, both times by chance. You can't tell me that's enough for gossip—'

'And at Randwick?'

'No.'

He paused. 'I know you're keen on him, and I know your background and the hotel where you met him.'

She turned and faced him. 'I worked in a pub and I'm proud of it. Are you accusing me, dear, of having some feelings for this man?'

Henry put his empty glass down and walked up to her. She could leave the house now, grab the nearest cab, go straight to John's place and run off with him without even thinking about it. That's what she'd like to do. But she knew she couldn't. She would continue to defend herself in front of Henry.

'I don't know what you feel for Leary,' he said, 'and frankly I don't care. You're my wife and you'll do as you're told.' Henry pointed his finger at her. 'The only time you're to see Leary is when you're with me or at my invitation.' He walked to the door, stopped and turned. 'And if I hear that you've being seeing him, then you'll answer to me. Is that clear?'

She decided to lie, 'Very well Henry, if that's the way you feel.'

Gerry Gleeson forced his way through the evening throng, his eyes smarting from the smoke at the Hero's bar.

'Same again, Gerry?'

'Thanks, Colleen. Busy night for a Thursday. Only the two of you?'

'Yeah, and Christmas just three weeks away. Flo's off sick.'

Colleen Anderson poured half of Gerry's beers and while they were settling went to serve another customer. Watching her, Gerry noticed her eyes widening in surprise, but she quickly recovered herself. Gerry tried to see who'd made the barmaid so startled but the person was obscured by others. She smiled at the customer and returned to pulling the rest of Gerry's beers.

'Who did you see just then?' he said.

'Just go sit down, Gerry. I'll be over in a while.'

Gerry left her and, clutching his beers, squeezed through the crowd towards Sean and the others who were celebrating the end of the Memorial Hall job. They had finished the next round when Gerry felt his arm pressed and looked up at Colleen.

'It's him, Gerry,' she said as she sat next to him. 'It's him.'

'Who?'

'The toff. You know that night 'e was supposed to go to Skinners? 'E's in the corner. A well-dressed man. Don't look. He'll see you.'

'Are you sure?'

'What's happening,' Sean said as he moved closer to the pair, leaving his colleagues to their drinks.

'I'm sure,' Colleen said. 'I remember that night and his hand. He had a knob near his thumb. You gotta do something.'

'Do what?' Sean frowned. 'What's going on?'

'Sean,' Gerry said. 'Colleen reckons she saw the fellow who paid Miller.'

'Where?' Sean started to rise and Gerry stopped him.

'Look at me, Sean,' Gerry said.

'If he's here,' Sean said, 'I'll kill him. I will.'

'Steady, mate. What do you want to do, Coll?'

Colleen shook her head. 'I'm too scared to go back to the bar. He knows me for sure. He saw me look at him funny.'

'We can't do nothing here,' Gerry said. 'Best to follow him when he leaves.'

Sean nodded and exhaled. 'Yeah, Gerry, that's the way. I'll help you.'

'Good, Sean.'

~

At the police station, Inspector Neild looked dubious. 'It's an unusual request, Mr Gleeson and highly improper,' he said.

Gerry looked hard at the man. 'Too true, inspector. But it's the only way to get Miller to nail the person who paid him for the sabotage.'

Neild sat back and pursed his lips. 'I'll be back in a moment.'

With the inspector gone, Gerry thought again how they could arrange for the imprisoned Miller and the man with the strange hand to meet. Gerry had left the Hero the previous night with Sean and had tailed their man outside as he got into his carriage and took off. Sean had grabbed his horse and followed, leaving Gerry at the kerb side. The next day Sean had given Gerry the man's address. It was all they had.

The inspector returned. 'Mr Gleeson. I've just received permission, but it's under strict conditions.'

Gerry nodded. 'That's good. Now, how?'

'I don't want to scare this suspect by inviting him here.'

Gerry had thought the same. 'So, you'll bring the labourer James Miller to him as I suggested?'

'It seems the best way. We'll watch the house, determine its occupant and arrange a meeting between them. It may not be immediately but it'll be in the next few days. Miller's told us of this man and can identify him. Because of his wrist deformity, it should make a conviction easier.' Gerry smiled. 'But be warned,' Neild continued, 'if the suspect is a leading citizen, then the case will be much harder to prove.'

Gerry got up. 'Thank you, Inspector. It's over to you now.'

'It is. Thank you for your assistance. I'll want your statement and that of Mr Connaire and the barmaid, of course.'

CHAPTER SIX

To avoid the summer heat, Brian Atkins had placed his chair just shy of the December sunlight streaming through the banking chamber's windows. Looking up, he admired the fretwork of plaster above him. He then glanced at the banker opposite him, who had picked up his quill. This man deserved nothing but contempt. It was shameful that he was a Freemason. 'Well, have you managed to convince Leary?' Atkins asked.

Andrew Brown looked at him. 'We have sent a more demanding letter, Mr Atkins, and we await Mr Leary's reply.'

'When was the letter sent?'

'A week ago, 28 November, I'm told.'

Atkins got up, stretched his polished boots and flexed his thighs in his Savile Row suit. He had had enough. 'It's not up to me to tell you what to do. It's your job to follow up Leary. Make sure his overdraft is cut. I don't want to remind you of our agreement. If you've forgotten the details, I can prod your memory.'

The bank director's face perspired, filming his glasses and accentuating the worry crease above his nose. It was fear. The look Atkins had seen on people who were in debt to him. It didn't matter who they were—a supplier, a labourer or a partner in the biggest bank in

New South Wales—they were all human, all flawed. Atkins loathed the man in front of him. Atkins had done some mean things in his life and things he wasn't proud of but in the end he always got what he wanted. On a night out, he'd caught the banker in the act with an eleven-year-old, a cowering and naked waif. Two days later Atkins had obtained sufficient damning statements from the victim and witnesses. When Atkins had presented the evidence to Brown, the banker had agreed to do anything for him. Molesting children was something Atkins couldn't stomach.

The banker dropped his eyes. 'No, Mr Atkins, you don't have to remind me. I'll do your bidding. I'm due to retire from the bank next year anyway, so it's not a bad time—'

'I don't care about your timetable. Just do what I tell you and make sure that Leary's ability to trade is compromised. Otherwise . . .'

'Otherwise,' the banker said, 'you'll go through with your letter to the newspapers.'

Atkins picked up his hat from the adjoining chair and walked from the room. On his way out, he stopped. 'That I'd do, gladly. Indeed, I feel like doing it, anyway.'

Brown got himself together. 'I'll make sure Leary's overdraft is cut.'

'What about the other partners? What's their view?'

'I'm the senior. It's my decision.'

Atkins walked through the marble foyer to the entrance. The banker would suit his need but he had an insurance policy, just in case. Tonight at the annual business dinner he would cement that option.

At the business dinner, held in the first week of December, the awards for construction in New South Wales were announced. The prime recipient for the 1856 commercial category was John Leary. Atkins had pulled strings to ensure his table was near the winner and that evening he joined in the applause while thinking about his own victory. He and his guests, Bill Thomas and Harry Shelby, had to bring Leary down. It was getting serious and worrying now. Thank God, Miller had been convicted of murder. He was sentenced to hang on the first of January and that couldn't come quickly enough.

As the evening drew to a close, only Atkins and the two builders were at his table. It was the time for Leary's demise and Atkins was remaining sober to test his strategy.

'I say, Atkins,' Shelby said next to him, 'I was telling Thomas, things are hectic. Supply prices are going through the roof and I can't get the right labour for love or money.'

'Don't you pay your men well?'

'I do, more than most, but it's not that. There's no skilful men to *get*. All the good 'uns are well paid and most of them are at Leary's.'

Atkins smiled. 'Pinch them from him.'

'I've tried, but they won't move. I'm risking quality on my jobs using under-skilled workers, especially carpenters and masons.'

'Dead right,' a smiling Thomas said. 'I had the same problem ten years ago in the last boom and I stuffed it up then, good and easy, and I swore I'd never do that again.'

Shelby offered cigars to his friends and lit one himself. He puffed away. 'I don't want to speak about him again, but I have to. Leary.'

Atkins couldn't have planned it better.

'Word's got around,' Shelby continued, 'that Leary's got the touch in finishing jobs before time. Better planning, I hear, but I don't understand it.'

'He's still cheap, too,' Thomas said.

Atkins was curious. 'How can that be?'

'He's taking a smaller profit on the simple jobs like warehouses and bigger margins on the complex projects like the stores building.'

'Can't you men do that?' Atkins asked.

'I'm not winning the jobs, Atkins,' Shelby said. 'Like I said, it's a vicious circle. And here's the clincher. The more jobs Leary performs well on, the bigger his order book grows and, because he's in demand, clients will pay what he wants. Suppliers are fawning over him for business.'

'He had a run in with St Peters Brick Company,' Thomas said.

Shelby waved his hand away in dismissal. 'That's all squared away now, but timber merchants, iron suppliers and cement manufacturers know he's the golden boy of construction and are offering big discounts. We can't compete.'

Atkins decided now was the time. 'You aren't happy with Leary snapping at your heels, taking more of your market?'

Shelby looked at Thomas and back to Atkins. He said, 'Aren't you listening to us? I can't speak for my friend, but Leary is becoming a pest. More than that, he's a threat.' Shelby didn't take his eyes from Atkins. 'Forget about the builder–developer, Atkins, Leary is pushing us out as a bloody *builder*.'

'He's got eight jobs on,' Thomas said, 'including a stores building at Sydenham with me, plus warehouses in Balmain, Stanmore and Marrickville—'

'Plus three lots of terraces,' Shelby added. 'And he's just finished a shoe factory in Newtown. Yes, I'd like to do something about it.'

Atkins thought an understanding was growing between them.

'I suppose you've got something in mind, Brian?' Shelby said and smiled. 'You always seem to be the one to come up with smart ideas.'

Atkins nodded. 'I might have a plan to rid us of Leary. But I need your help.'

Bill Thomas pulled his chair closer to them. 'What sort of help? Dodgy?'

Atkins thought of Miller and the mess that that labourer had left behind. 'If you men want to do something, that's out of my hands, no—'

Atkins looked over Shelby's shoulder and smiled as the man himself passed an adjoining table. Leary moved closer to Atkins and caught his eye.

The award winner hesitated before speaking. 'Good evening, gentlemen. I trust that the night has been enjoyable for you?'

Shelby and Thomas looked up at him.

'Congratulations, Mr Leary,' Shelby said as he stood up, took John's hand and shook it. 'It's well deserved.'

'Thank you, Mr Shelby. I hope there's more to come. Excuse me, but I must go. People to see.'

Shelby nodded and sat down as Leary passed out of earshot. 'Arrogant man,' Shelby said. 'Looking down his nose at us.'

Atkins smiled to himself. Perfect. He caught the eyes of his guests and spoke in such a quiet voice they had to lean over to hear him, which he intended them to do. 'I want Leary out as well.'

Both contractors looked at him for some time. Their faces showed no emotion.

'So, my friends,' Shelby said, 'what do we do?'

Thomas tapped his finger on the table. 'Weren't you telling me the last time we met that you're doing something else to nail Leary? Something about money and drying up his finances?'

Atkins smiled. 'I am, but I need another weapon to rid us of him. What about buying him out?'

Shelby sat back and looked at him. 'That's giving in.'

'Not if he's willing to sell. We'll take over his jobs and make him an offer he can't refuse. We'll have as a condition that he can't carry on as a builder for say, five years. In that time we can get back to where we were.'

'It's possible,' Thomas said. 'Does he have full control of his company?'

'I suspect he does,' Atkins said, 'but I'll find out. If we can dry up his cash and force him to default we might not have to buy him out.'

Thomas smiled. 'You'd want to be a shareholder, Atkins?'

'I would.'

'We have no choice then,' Shelby said. 'Let's do it, but,' he pressed Atkins's forearm, 'first, drain him of his cash, my friend. If that doesn't work then . . .'

'I want nothing criminal,' Atkins said in a feigned innocent voice.

Shelby paused. 'No, but accidents happen.'

Thomas laughed and Atkins was heartened by what he had heard.

～

Next evening, Brian Atkins had finished his dinner and was relaxing on his back veranda in the warm twilight. Tomorrow, Sunday, he'd be having dinner with Thomas Higgins and his daughter, the delightful Elizabeth. He was happy also that Thomas and Shelby had agreed to his strategy and, more explicitly, Shelby seemed to want to physically harm Leary. All the better. Life would be simpler with the damned Irish contractor out of contention and removed as a threat. Atkins was convinced that Leary's cash was thinly stretched and that once half the overdraft was paid, Leary would break.

There was a knock on the front door. His manservant answered it and this was followed by a murmur of conversation. Footsteps came down the hall. Curious, Atkins stood up and when the door opened, there standing between two policemen was the labourer, Miller. Though shocked, Atkins managed to control himself. Hiding his left hand behind him, he looked only at the policemen and said, 'Good evening, constables, what seems to be the problem?'

'I'm Inspector Neild, sir. This is Constable Stevens and this is James Miller. Have you ever met Miller before, sir?'

'That's him,' Miller said. 'He gave me the money; he paid me to have the accident. Check the knob I told you about.'

Atkins took what seemed an eternity to gaze at Miller. 'I've not seen this man before, Inspector.'

'Liar,' the labourer said.

'Quiet, Miller,' Neild said. 'Miller's been convicted of the murder of three men on a Clarence Street building site in September last year—'

'Yes,' Atkins said, 'I read something about that in the news-papers.'

'You are sure this is the man you met with, Miller?' Neild said.

'It is,' Miller said with triumph.

'Sir,' Neild said looking at Atkins, 'we are here to arrest you in the complicity of those murders. If we can examine your left hand?'

Atkins was going to refuse but thought better of it. 'Of course.'

'See,' Miller said looking at the knob. 'I told you so.'

'You are sure of that?' Neild said. 'You are absolutely sure?'

'This is preposterous, Inspector,' Atkins said. 'I injured my hand last week and it's swollen. Moreover, I've never seen this man in my life. I protest this whole situation.'

'Please come along with us, sir,' Neild said. 'It will be better for you if you do.'

Atkins was about to plead his innocence and demand that the police leave but then he checked himself. It was his word against Miller—the word of a gentleman of note around town against that of a labourer. There was no need to panic. He had to give the impression of shock and irritation rather than guilt. 'I will come with you gentlemen, but I need to instruct my manservant, Albert, to inform my legal counsel to represent me. Where will you be taking me?'

'The main Sydney station, sir, in George Street, near Circular Quay.'

Atkins forced himself to smile and looked at his manservant. 'Please let Mr Hubert Travers know the situation, Albert.' He turned to the policeman. 'Let us go.' Walking towards the hall, he did not look at Miller, and hoped his own face bore the look of an innocent and untroubled man.

Rather than walk, John indulged himself and used his new carriage for the short ride to the bank. It was one of the latest Landau sprung type, robustly built and comfortable, given the state of the George Street potholes. He was irritated. The bank's first letter had been a polite reminder but the second, which John had a copy of in his pocket, was downright demanding.

He'd spent the morning with his accountant, Dan Reynolds, reviewing the figures and Leary's current money position. They had a fair cash flow. Most clients paid on time, but this month, two big clients hadn't paid—they didn't have Blunt's final payment on the Market Street warehouse or the one from the shoe factory job. Now the bank's second letter demanded Leary's pay 50 per cent of its overdraft within thirty days. It seemed a deliberate act to force his hand and he was going to find out the reason why.

He alighted in George Street and instructed his driver to wait. It was 2:30 p.m., and he'd give himself one hour with the banker before going to Elizabeth Street for some respite.

The bank's marble foyer settled him somewhat and a clerk looked up as John approached.

'Can I help you sir?'

'I'm John Leary, here to see Mr Andrew Brown.'

The clerk leapt to his feet as if John were His Excellency, Governor Denison coming to visit. 'Yes, sir, of course, sir. Please come this way.'

The man led him up two staircases and John's craftsman's eye noted the mahogany balustrading. It was fine work and he wondered who'd built it. He hadn't built any bank or major institution, as they had tight rules on payment and supervision. John was impatient and eschewed the form of control they'd demand.

The clerk stopped at a panelled door and knocked. John followed him into a room where, in one corner, behind a desk as big as John's new dining-room table, sat the man John was to see.

'Mr John Leary to see you, Mr Brown,' the clerk said and left them alone.

Andrew Brown stood up. 'Good afternoon, Mr Leary. Won't you please sit down?'

'Thank you.' John took a seat, removed his hat and placed it on the nearby chair. He looked at Brown. Five parallel threads stretched across his skull connected grey patches of hair one above each ear. John smiled to himself. *Well, God hasn't given this banker a thick mane. Let's hope what lies underneath it is more enlightening.*

'I'll come right to the point, Mr Brown,' John said on the offensive. 'It's about your letter of demand regarding my overdraft.'

Brown dropped his eyes and John knew something was amiss. He understood body language, having had many altercations with clients, suppliers and tradesmen. If the man had held John's look, then Brown was backed by strong argument. But the banker wouldn't look at him. He might be acting to assuage the worries of one of the bank's credit managers, or there was some other reason that was not in John's interests.

'Mr Leary,' Brown said, 'the bank is concerned about your exposure. Your overdraft is large by our standards and the bank sees a risk in that.'

'I don't see where the bank is at risk. My account is the second largest of any contractor in town.'

'That's correct.' Andrew Brown removed his glasses and cleaned them. 'I'm curious to know where you got your information on our accounts.'

John smiled. 'That's privileged. However, my accounts with the bank of New South Wales are creditable; there is a significant fund on escrow, which the bank can access. So where is the bank exposed? And why the call for the overdraft to be paid?'

Brown pulled a pile of documents towards him, selected a journal and opened it. 'Please give me a moment,' he said.

John settled in his chair, feeling better. This issue could blow over. However, Leary's Contracting, being a large client, should have been given special treatment, not a demanding letter with no meeting beforehand to outline the bank's position. He would seek satisfaction, otherwise he'd change his banker. Though this wasn't as easy as it sounded: the Commercial Bank of Sydney was starting to build its business and had written to Leary's Contracting, inviting it to be part of its growth, but on the bank's terms—not John's.

'It's all here,' Brown said. 'Your deposit funds are reasonable. However, they don't stay long in the bank but are withdrawn.'

John used the bank as a clearing house. Their interest rates were abysmal and John had taken David's advice and invested in trusts, bonds and other better-producing returns. He said, 'That's so, but what is the bank's risk?'

Brown looked at the ledger. 'This escrow fund.'

'Yes?'

'We can't access it. It's a quarantined fund held for your stores building in Sydenham with Mr Thomas. It's in place of our guarantee on your performance. If you breach your contract with your client and your client is financially disadvantaged, then the client can claim against these funds so that they are not—'

'I know how the process works, Mr Brown.' He'd forgotten

about that guarantee, because Thomas was looking after that job. Thomas had agreed to do the project in partnership with John if Leary's put up the guarantee funds, which amounted to 10 per cent of the value of the stores building contract. Placing funds in escrow was better than the bank giving him a guarantee for the same amount. A guarantee was really the same as a loan from

the bank, on which they would charge him interest.

'We cannot access that money,' Brown went on, 'unless the client on that project claims against you. You agreed to that rather than accepting our guarantee. That fund can only be released to you when the project is completed. When is that?'

'July next year,' John said.

'Indeed. So according to our records you have no other funds on which to draw.' John said nothing, as he knew this was fact. 'The bank is concerned about the construction industry generally, Mr Leary. There is a large group of highly-indebted contractors and the bank—'

'You're not saying that Leary's Contracting is insolvent?'

'—is entitled,' continued the banker, 'to have its overdraft paid.'

'But why the urgency?'

'It's the bank's prerogative to call the overdraft in at any time.'

John's mouth became dry. If he had to repay the substantial overdraft, he'd have reduced funds to trade and so limit his expansion. 'So the bank will call in the overdraft?'

'A proportion of it only.'

'Fifty per cent is a large portion.'

'That is the reason we wrote the letter, Mr Leary. It is a letter of demand which has the backing of legal opinion.'

John bridled at this. 'I've given the bank good funds, Mr Brown, and paid your hefty fee each month for the overdraft. It's not good for the bank to call most of it in.' John leaned over the wide desk. 'Believe me, if you don't withdraw the letter I will take my business elsewhere.'

The banker nodded. 'That is your prerogative, of course.'

Brown seemed to have expected John's threat to withdraw his funds. What was going on? John controlled his emotions and looked at the banker. The bank wasn't telling the truth. He wanted the bank to cave in, to give him what he wanted, withdraw the letter, anything but to go through with its demand.

'Is there any difficulty repaying the overdraft, Mr Leary?'

John thought about that. There wasn't, but he was angry. He forced his lips into a smile and responded. 'There's no problem,' he said, 'but if I do pay half the overdraft, the next thing I'll do is close my facilities and go elsewhere.'

Mr Brown stood up. 'As I said, Mr Leary, that is your right. However, let me give you some advice, and please don't mind my saying this. You are a young man. There is a new bank in town that is vying for business. You will find though that our rates are competitive and that if you do transfer your funds you'll have to pay set-up costs with another bank which will have the same overdraft rules as we have.'

John clenched his fists and pressed them against the desk. Now wasn't the time for an argument and he didn't want to show anger. Standing up, he forced himself to extend his hand. 'Give me twenty-four hours and I will write with my response. Good day, sir.'

'Well, do we get it or don't we?' Dan Reynolds asked.

John nodded. 'I'm seeing Blunt this afternoon for the last progress payment on the Market Street store. If I get that in three days, that'll be good. Mr Rubens on the shoe factory come up with the cash?'

'He did.'

'Bloody bank,' John said. 'It's out of character for them. I'm sure someone's twisting their arm.'

The door to John's office opened and a clerk stood there fidgeting, holding a newspaper. 'Mr Leary, I'm sorry to disturb you. But I think you should see this.'

'What is it?' John asked taking the paper.

'See, at the bottom of the front page.'

John read the article, then sat down and, for the first time in a week, he smiled.

'What's up?' Reynolds asked.

'Brian Atkins ... Brian Atkins has been charged with the murders at Clarence Street. Excellent.' John's good humour dimmed somewhat as he had a vision of the Waverley headland and its three graves. 'I hope the bastard hangs.' He looked at the clerk. 'That will be all.'

Reynolds picked up his ledgers. 'That's justice, but it won't get us our money. I'm giving you warning, Mr Leary, if we don't get payment in ten days, by the twentieth of December, the company's cash will be low. The bank has issued notices that if the fifty per cent of the overdraft isn't paid by then they'll liquidate us.'

'Dan, panic won't get us the money. Just leave it to me. I'll get it.'

Gregory Blunt stood up as John came into his office. 'Good day, Mr Leary. Please sit down.' John looked at Blunt's cluttered desk. 'Place is in chaos,' Blunt said. 'I'm trying to move into my new office and it's fifteen days to Christmas. I've got half my stuff here and the other half packed up. You've done a good job on my warehouse. I'm happy.'

This was going better than he thought. Now was the time to be frank. 'I've come for my money,' John said.

Blunt's good humour vanished. 'Money? I've paid your last progress claim.' He smirked. 'I took off a few extras I didn't think you're entitled to, but the bulk of it has been cleared. Any problems?'

John wasn't convinced. He'd heard much the same story from clients who'd said the money had been approved, or the cheque was in the mail or any other number of excuses when, in fact, they hadn't paid at all. 'We will wrap up any disputed amounts,' John said, 'when we settle the final account. But, as far as I know the bank said this morning there were no funds from you in my account.'

'That's strange,' Blunt said.

'Maybe, but I'll ask you to check for me while I wait.'

'I pay my bills when they're due, Mr Leary.'

John's defiance matched Blunt's stare. 'Perhaps, but I'd still like you to check.'

'I'll do that now. Once I pay a cheque, it's gone.'

John sat down after Blunt left and the tension eased from his shoulders. His client could be telling the truth. He didn't look like a man who'd play games and his record of past payments had been prompt. If John could cash Blunt's cheque, then he'd have enough funds to pay the bank its 50 per cent overdraft. The bank's action had been too sharp. Was Shelby or Thomas sitting on the sidelines, attacking Leary's? He'd get Wexton to find out about them and their link to the bank. He knew that must be it.

'Good news,' Blunt said coming back. 'My accountant said the cheque was taken to your bank one hour ago. I apologise for the delay but his wife died suddenly and he's been away. Here is a receipt of the cheque number and warrant.' Blunt's big hand almost covered the paper. John took the note and read. Yes, Blunt was right, the money had been paid.

John stood up and put out his hand. 'Thank you.'

'It's been a good relationship, Leary. My wife wants a big house built, and I've got investments in Melbourne that will want a good builder. Are you interested?'

John smiled. 'I'm always interested in helping my paying clients.'

'Good. We may do business then. Good luck, Leary. Now, let me get back to some work and sorting out my move.'

John looked back at the big man scribbling at his desk. One part of his problem was solved, but he still wanted to find out who was behind the bank's actions.

On a hot December evening, John opened his front door for his visitor. 'Come in, Mr Wexton. I'd see you at my office but home here is more discreet. Let's go into the study; there's a breeze and a nice port that we can share. I've got a few letters to sign.'

Damien Wexton took off his hat. 'I'll look forward to the coolness, but as you know, I don't drink.' Wexton looked around. 'You have a fine place. I bet you're proud of it.'

It had slipped John's mind that Wexton didn't drink. Well, this was business and the investigator would have to go without an alternative. As Wexton followed him to the study, Clarissa came down the stairs. She looked down at the visitor and smiled at him.

'Good evening, Mrs Leary,' Wexton said. 'I'm sorry to come to your house for business—'

'That's quite all right, Mr Wexton. If it has to be, it has to be. I'm used to my husband meeting people at all times, even the week before Christmas. So you're no exception.'

'Thank you,' Wexton said. 'All the best for the season.'

'Come, Wexton,' John said, looking at Clarissa.

The investigator followed John into his study. John left the door ajar to get the cross breeze and he sat at his desk. A table beside an armchair held a bottle of port and two glasses.

'Pour a drink for me will you? I shan't be a minute.' John became absorbed in his work as Wexton filled the glass for him.

Clarissa was curious about this meeting. She prided herself on being in control and, before she was married, she'd lived her life with confidence, completing tasks efficiently. Now, working for her father, she undertook each challenge with the same diligence. But her family was another matter. Something was wrong in her marriage, something she couldn't put her finger on, but it was worrying.

Wexton was an investigator; she'd learned that from her father and she was curious to know why John needed one now. The police had the perpetrators of the sabotage.

Richard was asleep and Stella was mending clothing, so Clarissa crossed the foyer towards the study and stopped beside its open door, a position she could leave on short notice, if the need arose. She heard the tinkling of a glass and then John's voice.

'Brian Atkins must hang,' John said. 'The *Herald* reported Miller identified him. He was right all along.'

Wexton cleared his throat. 'Miller said he had an accomplice.'

'Never suspected Atkins, though. I've got something for you to do. The labourer will hang but Atkins will get off, I just know it. He'll hire some fancy silk. All they've got is Miller's word and that of a barmaid. That's not enough. I want to get more proof. Also I'm convinced Atkins and the bank are thick as thieves.'

'I can try and find out about the bank's connection, if there is one.'

John took his glass to the mantelpiece and leaned against it. Dublin flashed before him, memories of another mongrel. He stuck his boot on the hearth and turned to Wexton. 'I want him fixed for good. He'll win in court on this latest evidence. I want him watched, around the clock. I want to find out if he's in with those two contractors, Shelby and Thomas. Do that, and I'll have the reason why the sabotage happened.'

'That surveillance will be costly.'

'I don't care. Do it. Leary's owes those three men justice. They died in innocence.'

Damien reached for his satchel and knocked the glass on the table to the floor. 'I'm sorry, Mr Leary.'

John heard a sound outside and went and looked. The hall was empty and he came back inside.

'I can do the watching,' Wexton said picking up the glass.

'Good. Then start right away.'

Wexton did up his jacket and John followed him in silence as they walked to the front door.

John opened it and said, 'Get the real gold on Atkins, Wexton, and get it fast.'

The fallen glass had startled Clarissa, causing her to hit the skirting board with her shoe. John would have heard that sound for sure. She fled upstairs.

She wished she hadn't been near the study, but it was better now to know, despite the added worry. John was more than still interested in the sabotage. He had a pathological obsession with it. That might well be the reason why he was a changed man, though she couldn't quite believe it. But then, her husband was an honourable man and with a half-smile she remembered how, a year before they were married, she'd told him to keep away from her. At the time, her love for him had been strong but he was prejudiced against her. The only way to solve that was to challenge him. So, she'd given him an ultimatum to stay away, never thinking he would. But he had.

That discipline he possessed was a blessing, but now it was a weakness, as he tried to solve the murders. John seemed to want to be the police, the judge and the jailer. Impossible. Footsteps came down the hall to their bedroom and she grabbed a book as he stopped, then the door opened. Her fingers pressed against the pages.

He sat down on the lounge next to her, loosened his tie and stretched his neck in relief. 'Why did you speak to Wexton like that? It was rude.'

Clarissa put down the book. 'It wasn't rude, dear.'

'It was rude and I want to know why. Is your job affecting you?'

Clarissa's concern for him was replaced by irritation. 'It's not my work. I like what I do. It gives me a respite from my worries about us.'

'About us? I don't understand.'

Clarissa went and closed the door, hoping to trap the restless spirits circling in the room. It was as if she and John had climbed a mountain from different sides and tonight they'd reached the summit and met; a confrontation was well overdue. She wanted a clear understanding of where they stood and where they were heading. 'Yes, I'm worried about us,' she said. 'We seem to be drifting apart.'

He looked at her in curiosity. 'I still don't understand.'

'It's about you and me.' John dropped his eyes. They seemed filled with guilt. So, he'd also sensed something wasn't right, or had he? She decided to push further. 'It's about us, our marriage and that part of you that I once knew and loved.' He was looking at her now. 'That part of you which you were willing to give me,' she said.

185

'That was the John Leary I loved, but it's not there any more. Where is it?'

'Clarissa, you're talking nonsense.'

She flushed in anger. 'Nonsense, is it? It's not.' She sat down again and tried to be objective. 'There is something missing. Can't you feel it? I can.'

John looked at her. 'I can't. Look, there's a ruckus with work at the moment. I'm up to my ears in problems—'

'Dear, this is me you're speaking to. Me. I know the condition of the company. I know you have problems with staff and clients and suppliers. I know all that. But that's part and parcel of the business world. You can't use that as an excuse. No, my intuition is that you're trying to personally solve the murders of your men.'

His eyes expanded. 'I have to, Clarissa. That's why I had Wexton here. I have to have certainty that the real murderers will hang.'

'I know you want justice. We all do, and the police will do their job.'

'It isn't enough.'

She was right. 'You see. This drive to get this settled, it's affecting you—badly.'

John composed himself. 'No, Clarissa. It's not.'

'I disagree. You were a different person before all this happened. Don't let all this lock me out.' It was time to beard the lion. 'You have to get over the deaths of those men.'

'I am over that.'

'Are you?' she said.

'I'm not locking you out, for goodness' sake. You may feel this but I don't. But since you've had the baby and with this new job, you're a different woman.'

Clarissa stood up, angry again. 'I haven't changed! *You* have. Rid yourself of this guilt and get back to being the man I used to know.'

John opened his hands to her. 'I'm the same man, but if I'm not, help me, because I'm dumbfounded. And that reminds me. I'd like to think that you weren't outside the study tonight.'

She couldn't lie, confident that she was right in her mind. 'I was there and I had a reason. I wanted to find out more about why you've changed. That conversation you had with Mr Wexton proves me correct.'

John seemed puzzled. 'You don't understand.'

She took his hand and squeezed it. 'Then help me to. Talk to me.'

He paused and shook his head. 'Not now. I have to prepare for a business trip. I have to go to the Hunter. I'll be back -Christmas Eve.'

'But soon, John, please. We have to sort this out.'

'Very well.' His eyes lit up just for a second, but they faded just as quickly.

Clarissa's stomach tightened into a knot. *A business trip?* 'Is there a problem up there?'

'Just a supplier who's causing us some grief. I'll say goodnight. There's some more work to do. I have an early start in the morning.' He left the room.

She walked to her dressing room and got ready for bed. She felt drained. Tonight hadn't sorted any problems but she would persist in trying to get him to talk. In an effort to take her mind off the situation, she thought about her job, and her spirits lifted a little. Tomorrow she'd be working with Malcolm Robinson on next year's budget. She liked him and enjoyed working with him. There was definitely an attraction between them but Clarissa had no intention of doing anything about it and she suspected neither did Malcolm Robinson. But that didn't mean that they couldn't flirt with each other.

Clarissa opened the window of the McGuire Wire's town office and called down, 'I'll be there in a moment, Mr Robinson.'

Malcolm Robinson, seated in the carriage below her, grinned back at her. 'Good, we want to get to Annandale by midday.'

After adjusting her hair in the mirror, she grabbed her files and went down the stairs, each step raising her heart rate. The previous night's encounter with John had been forgotten. That was home. This was work, and getting out to the warehouse with Mr Robinson for the day excited her.

A brisk nor 'easterly hit her as she exited the warehouse. Putting down her bag and out of sight of her manager, she did up the top three buttons of her jacket, dismayed that she wouldn't look her best. This wind would do more damage to her than a wheat thresher. Holding her hat on to her head, she walked towards the carriage.

'There you are,' Malcolm Robinson smiled again. 'I put the top of the carriage up to give us a little protection from the wind.'

'Oh, thank you. I didn't fancy being blown about all the way to Annandale.'

Malcolm Robinson laughed. 'Come on, hop on board.' He took her hand and helped her in. Settling on the seat beside him, Clarissa gave herself over to enjoying being close to him.

One click to the horses and they were off. As the carriage gripped the cobblestones and proceeded up to George Street, Clarissa felt an excitement she hadn't felt in a long time. She felt young and carefree; all her responsibilities seemed to slip away as she sat beside this attractive man who made her laugh and obviously admired her. She wished the journey to Annandale were longer.

Her thoughts must have been visible on her face because Malcolm Robinson was looking at her with an indulgent smile on his face. She blushed and blurted out, 'The gold fever's still with us and labour shortages in the warehouse aren't being filled. These new strikes in Victoria—more poor souls trying to get rich quick.'

He nodded. 'I know that tempts them, but I do feel sorry for them having to leave their loved ones, as I had to do.'

'Is your family here in New South Wales?'

'No, no, Mrs Leary. My family is in England. We had a good income in Italy from selling garment fabrics but the revolutions of 1848 imposed heavy taxes on us so we pulled up sticks and went to England. I studied there.'

'Where?'

'The Mechanics Institute of Bradford,' he replied.

'Really. So after your studies, you came here?'

'Yes, to see what opportunities were available, Mrs Leary. I've been fortunate.'

'Your name doesn't sound Italian.'

Malcolm flashed a dazzling smile, showing off his white teeth. 'I have a little secret. My family's name is Robini and I should be called Mario but my parents decided to change the name when we got to England.'

The carriage proceeded along George Street and passed Brick-field Hill. Sydney railway station came up and Clarissa looked at the steam train moving out on its way to Parramatta. She'd love to be able to go for a ride on it. Maybe she and John could do that. It saddened her that they hadn't done things together like that for some time.

'Whereabouts in Italy does your family come from, Mr Robin-son?' Clarissa asked.

'From Milano, in the north, though my mother is from the south. I come from a big family,' Malcolm said, smiling again.

'You must miss them,' Clarissa said.

'I do,' Malcolm said. 'My wife is back in England. She writes to me from time to time. I miss her. I miss my family.'

They had cleared the city confines on their way down to Black-wattle Creek where Clarissa's nose tweaked at the stench of the abattoirs. 'You have children?' Clarissa asked with a hand to her nose.

'Yes I do. Oh, that smell. *Madre mia!* Quick, get going, you hors-es.' He tapped the reins and within the next hundred yards the air was cleaner. 'I have two little boys and one girl. I got a letter last week and they are all well. But I do miss them. But what about you? You have a *bambino?*'

Clarissa smiled. 'A little boy, yes, his name is Richard. He's quite a handful and I'm fortunate that I have a maid.'

'It is good to have some help and very good for you as a young mother. It's Christmas just days away,' he said. 'You'll have to buy him a present.'

'I have.'

'That's good. We're not far from the warehouse now; let's talk about what we must do there.'

For the rest of the journey to Annandale, Clarissa enjoyed their discussion. Malcolm Robinson was easy to talk to. She liked the way he treated her as an equal, asking her opinion on many things to do with the business. And she didn't mind the odd look and gesture of frank admiration thrown her way either.

On reaching the warehouse, he stopped the horses and assisted her down. His closeness overwhelmed her and she concentrated on his silk tie and white collar. She nearly stumbled reaching for her bag of files.

'Here, let me get that, Mrs Leary.'

'Thank you. Now, let's get down to work,' Clarissa said, hiding her regret that the pleasant journey had come to an end. She would have liked to talk to him about his home in Italy, his children and his wife. As they walked together to the warehouse gate a thought struck her. His wife wasn't in Sydney and she wondered what he did away from work.

The clang of the closing warehouse gate pushed these thoughts from her mind and back to those of her father's business.

John closed the ledger with a bang as the clock in his office struck 9.00 a.m. He looked at Reynolds. 'I've paid the bank half their bloody overdraft, and that's all the money they'll get from me.'

He pressed his hands together. Some of the payments Leary's had to make to contractors and suppliers were now due. 'Let's wrap it up. I'm due at Sydney station at ten o'clock.'

Reynolds's eyebrows shot up. 'Why?'

John bridled at the directness. 'That's my business.'

His accountant seemed surprised, then smiled. 'To get out of town?'

John was insulted. Just because he was under the pump didn't mean he was giving up. 'I'm not running away, Dan.'

Reynolds was shocked at this statement. 'No . . . of course you're not.'

'I stand and fight. You hear me.'

'I do, Mr Leary. I do.'

He had been fortunate in locating the Gaden brothers. John McCreadie was a client for whom Mr Jenkins had built a wool store in Market Street. McCreadie knew the secretive shareholders of Maxton Constructions and had made the introductions. Looking at Reynolds now, he wasn't going to say he was going to make an offer for the equity share of the largest contractor in Sydney. It was pointless to try and convince a man who counted beans that it was good business. Reynolds would measure it in cash and trial balance, which John knew were essential parts to business, but they didn't build it.

John's temper had settled. He said. 'I'm meeting the Gaden brothers for a train ride. They invited me to join them after our introduction last week. Always good to know what your opposition is thinking about.'

'Good luck with that,' Reynolds replied. 'Oh, and by the way, happy birthday for this Sunday.'

John grinned and chastised himself for his sensitivity just now. On 25 January he'd be twenty-seven. 'Thank you.'

Outside his office, John hailed a cab. 'Sydney Railway Station, please,' he said to the driver.

Settling back, he thought about Sydney's new transport. Leary's was building a stores warehouse at Sydenham for the railways, in partnership with Thomas Constructions. They would not build another in a hurry. The railway company was pedantic in its inspections and tardy in its payments. The Great Southern and Western Railway Company had had a short life. It had failed with huge losses and the New South Wales government had bought the company out.

Paying the driver, he made his way through the station, showed his ticket and got on board. Being a little early for his appointment, he stood on the open platform at the rear of the fourth first-class carriage and waited for the steam locomotive to move off. A shunt alerted him and the train started forward. He waited for the gust of wind to clear the smoke, and then stuck his head out to look at the iron beast pulling him towards the western capital, Parramatta. The engine's strength infused the carriages with a force that thrust through him. He was impressed.

Closing the door behind him he stepped into opulence. The polished cedar panelling was top-flight, not a blemish there. All mitres and joints were square and flush and the lacquered paintwork reflected the late January sunshine coming through the carriage's windows.

Compartment numbers were annotated by gold lettering on mother-of-pearl oval panels over each doorway. Compartment number seven should contain the two men he wanted to see.

James and Brian Gaden were the principal shareholders of Maxton Constructions Limited, the biggest contractor in Sydney. Wexton had not found them and John wondered how his investigator was going, watching Atkins and his ilk. John stopped and knocked at the compartment he needed.

A man's voice called out, 'Enter.'

John opened the door and walked in. Seated in opposite corners against the windows were two men of equal height and appearance.

James Gaden stepped up to greet him. 'Welcome, Mr Leary.'

'Thank you, Mr Gaden.'

He gestured to the other man. 'You've met my brother, Brian.'

Brian didn't stand but nodded and John let his own hand drop to his side.

'Thank you for coming to meet us,' James said. 'Would you like some refreshments before the main course?'

John looked down at a silver tray crammed with oysters, slices of fine bread and caviar. It was just after ten in the morning and he wasn't hungry, but politeness forced his hand. 'Thank you.' John took a plate from beside the tray and helped himself.

'They say the weather on Foundation Day should be like this,' James said. 'Fine with a gentle breeze. How will you spend it?'

'With my family, in the Botanic Gardens.'

'Excellent.' James glanced out the window. 'This is our fourth train trip to Parramatta, but the first for 1857. I think it's - marvellous.'

John looked at the silent brother as the train approached Newtown station.

'I've been keeping track of you, Mr Leary. Your company has grown remarkably. I'm impressed. I suppose I should keep an eye on you,' James said smiling. 'You're taking a great deal of my work.'

John smiled in return. At least the man had done his home-work. This might make it easier in negotiating. John swallowed an oyster and placed the shell on his plate. 'It's been a struggle, but I'm proud of where I am. I've got a large staff, good people and quite a few projects.'

'Seven I believe and, if I understand, correctly, you've been awarded a contract for the new twenty-thousand-square-feet ware-houses for the military at Parramatta?'

That jolted him. He'd only heard yesterday via a leaked govern-ment memorandum that he was the preferred contractor. The Gadens *were* well informed. 'I don't know about that. I know that I'm the preferred tenderer.'

'You've got it all right, I have been told. More profit to you and yours.'

John glanced to the corner again. No word from the silent brother. 'If that's the case, then good luck to me. Look, Mr Gaden. I've come to put to you a business proposition.'

'A business proposition?' James asked surprised. 'Now, that sounds interesting, doesn't it, brother? What do you have in mind?'

John put down his plate and decided attack was best. 'I'd like to buy out your shareholding of Maxton Constructions, for the right price.'

James pursed his lips. 'I admire your candour. So, you think we would sell, do you? What do you think, Brian?'

John was curious as to what the silent man would say. 'Ashfield station is the next one.' Brian said and turned to look outside. 'Such a delightful area, Ashfield. Don't you think so, Mr Leary?'

One brother plays one role, the other brother counters that. A game, thought John? Well, let's play. 'I know a little about it, Mr

Gaden. I have a colleague who's built a fine townhouse not far from the station. He thinks it combines both the city
and country.'

'My point exactly,' Brian said. 'I've been trying to persuade James to build our next home in Ashfield or even at Burwood. There are some beautiful land sites just south of the station between the road to Liverpool and the railway line. It would make a fine house with a view north to the river.'

'All in good time my brother,' James said. 'So, what do you think about our fine railway John?'

'It will be excellent for commerce. For real estate values, it will be a goldmine.'

'A goldmine?' James said and tapped his mouth with a napkin. 'Don't tell me you're a fan of these foolish souls chasing the yellow dust? What do they call it now, mustard?'

'I mean in the longer term,' John said, 'because as each station develops, the property around it will go up in value.'

'Now, that's a good idea,' Brian said as he reached for more food. 'I think James and I should do the same. Would you have any recommendations?'

'I have ideas on some good sites but I'd like to return to our main topic, if you don't mind.'

James sat down and nodded. 'I think that would be appropriate. I don't wish to offend, but my brother and I don't wish to sell our share.'

John looked at both men. Was this still a game? He wondered. 'You're not prepared to sell, at any price?'

'Come now,' James replied. 'You're not going to pay just anything to buy our share, are you?'

Fair comment. James motioned John to sit as the train picked up speed. John then felt the blood rush to his face. Just like them and their class, to hang on for dear life to something they probably considered a plaything. To John, Leary's was his life, his blood.

James sipped his wine and said. 'My brother and I aren't builders. But we have a long association with Maxtons. It's a profitable company and we leave it to the managers to get on with its business. We have no debt.' That surprised John. No debt. That was something. And yet if they had spare cash, maybe it wasn't being used properly—lazy money, he thought, sitting around getting a pittance of interest. As if to read his thoughts James continued, 'Don't get me wrong. We keep the company working properly, and profitable but we're just not prepared to consider selling. Right Brian?'

Brian opened his arms like a priest giving a blessing. 'Indeed. We're of a single mind on this. We have enough income to live on but the company to us is like . . . a living person, part of the family, so to speak.'

There was a knock at the door and a servant entered with a tray holding sliced pieces of hot lamb, turkey and pork.

'Please help yourself,' James said.

John took a plate from the tray, determined not to let his irritation show.

'Ah, here's Ashfield now,' Brian said.

'Mr Leary,' James said, 'don't be too disappointed.'

'I'm not, believe me,' John lied, 'but if you change your mind, please let me know.'

'I'll do that and thank you for your interest. It does Brian and me proud to know our company is highly valued.'

John addressed his food and they discussed the market conditions and their effect on the costs of construction. Homebush Station came into view with its racecourse behind. It reminded him of Beth. He was due to meet her next week. As the Gadens continued eating, John thought about her and their next rendezvous, rather than ruminating over a lost opportunity. If the Gadens wouldn't sell he'd keep striving to be the biggest contractor in Sydney.

John looked at his wife over their breakfast table, wanting to keep this conversation friendly. Clarissa was now working three afternoons and one full day each week at McGuire Wire.

'I'm concerned about your working hours,' he said. 'You're looking tired. David has told me that his companies are all in sound shape. You can cut down your time there now.'

'I can manage the family and my father's business, John.'

Poised with his knife and fork over his plate, John was not to be put off. 'That's the last I'll say of it. I'll give it another two months, say at the end of March, and if I find it isn't working you may have to leave.'

'Don't put limits on my work, John. I'm coping quite well, so let's have no more talk of it.' Pushing her chair back, Clarissa stood up from the table and left the room.

Well, that solved nothing and he chastised himself for his abruptness. Where were his manners, let alone gentleness? Clarissa deserved better. From now on, he'd try to be more conciliatory. He continued with his breakfast and concentrated on the newspaper.

An hour and a half later, he was in his George Street office and a clerk knocked on the door. 'Excuse me, sir. Mr Gleeson's here to see you. He said it wouldn't take long, and I don't know if you have time—'

'I've got time. I'll meet with him.' John left his office, curious as to why his uncle had come to visit. It had been a while since they'd been together.

He went into the adjoining room where the big mason stood with his hands together. 'Uncle, how are you?'

Gerry smiled. 'I'm well, as far as my limbs will let me.' He eyeballed John. 'Have you a moment to spare?'

'Absolutely, come to my office.'

Gerry settled in a chair opposite John and said, 'This place is busy. I wanted to see for myself how busy. How are you faring?'

John was a little puzzled at the question. 'Good, Uncle, good.'

Gerry nodded. 'You know, John, I've been around men under stress, in the gangs.' He shook his head. 'God almighty, I've had enough worry of my own, but I saw what it did to them.' He paused, 'I see you going the same way.'

John smiled. 'It's all part of the deal, Uncle. That's all.'

'Maureen has talked to me about you, Clarissa as well. They're worried about you.'

This was surprising. 'There's nothing wrong with me, Uncle. Business is tough and hard. Maureen doesn't understand that, Clarissa perhaps, but not—'

'It's more than that. I've only known you for a short time so I'll wait and see, but your sister and wife have seen a change in you. Not one for the good.'

John felt he had to defend himself. 'Building up Leary's comes with costs, Uncle, personal and financial. It'll settle down, believe me.'

Gerry seemed not to believe him. 'Is that all it is? The company's growth?'

John couldn't see any other reason but there might be one that he couldn't quite name. 'Yes, that's all.'

Gerry smiled. 'If that's the case, then let me share the load. Not doing the heavy lifting, mind, but talk to me more. Share your misgivings. What say you?'

No harm in that, John thought. 'Let's give it a go.'

'We'll meet each week and chat,' Gerry volunteered.

'Surely.'

Gerry stood up. 'Good, now I'll let you get back to the grind. Take care, nephew. I'll see my way out.'

John watched him go and had mixed feelings. He wasn't stressed in his job. The women were over-fussing. What he didn't want either was to have his Uncle, pleasant as he was, to be a sounding board for Leary's problems. He reached for a contract to review and soon forgot his relative.

CHAPTER SEVEN

On a Friday night in late February, Gerry Gleeson glanced around at the Hero's thickening crowd. He was angry. Colleen Anderson had been so sure about Atkins. 'There seemed no doubt, Colleen,' Gerry said. 'Now, you want me to believe he wasn't the same man?'

'But the knob, Coll,' Bob Jones said. 'You know, on his hand? It all fits.'

The Hero's barmaid looked down and she was nervous, Gerry knew. 'I'm telling you both,' she said, 'I got the wrong bloke, I got the wrong bloke.'

Gerry sat back and looked at her. 'Who's got to you?'

Colleen rounded on him, 'No one's got to me!'

'I don't believe you,' Bob said.

She reached out and squeezed Gerry's hand. 'I want the murderer of those men. I do.'

'Have you told the police you made a mistake?' Gerry asked.

'I did, this morning.'

'What did they say?'

'What do ya think?' she said. 'They were as mad as hell. But

I know what I saw and he wasn't the man.' She glanced at the bar. 'I have to go. My break's ended. I'm sorry, fellas.'

So am I, Gerry thought.

'Something smells,' Bob said as he watched her go. 'She was so sure. Shit, without her word, Atkins goes free.'

'There's Miller.'

'They don't believe that labourer, Gerry,' Bob said. 'Atkins had a doctor say that his lump had only come up in the last month. No, that spiv mongrel's going to walk our streets again.' Bob's eyes glowered in the dim light. 'He's guilty, Gerry. He's as guilty as Pilate.'

'I know he is, but what can we do? Sean will be pissed off, and John.'

But the bricklayer foreman didn't seem to be listening

Clarissa linked her arm with her father's as she and her parents walked up the steps to the ten o'clock Mass at St Mary's. She felt loved and safe with him. She hadn't felt warmth and security like this with John for some time. He was in Newcastle on business just now, but it was always business. She nearly slipped as a chill March southerly wind forced her dress against her legs.

'Steady dear,' her father said. 'Let's get inside out of this maelstrom.'

David leaned against the entrance door to keep it open for Christine and Clarissa to make their way inside, the wind causing the candles in the vestibule to flicker. They then headed for their usual pew on the left-hand side.

As Clarissa sat there, one half of her, the stronger half, wanted to pray for John. This was the place to ask God to help them through their troubles. But somehow it was Malcolm Robinson who occupied her thoughts and this only made her squirm with guilt on the cold seat. After coming back from receiving the Blessed Sacrament, Clarissa knelt and focused on the Host in her mouth, saying the Our Father then a Hail Mary in an attempt to push tempting thoughts from her mind. But they remained.

Malcolm Robinson's warm smile, his European manners and his affection had become more obvious in the past months. She knew she shouldn't enjoy the attention, but she did. She closed her eyes. Should she have these thoughts? John was her husband. He was the one she loved.

'Come, Clarissa,' her mother nudged her, 'the blessing's completed and we have to go.'

Clarissa genuflected and turned to leave. At the entrance to the church, a man with shoulders as wide as a pick-handle looked familiar. It was Uncle Gerry. His hand was stretched out to the holy water font and Clarissa smiled as the waiting faithful gave him a wide berth. Clarissa blessed herself and, seeing her, Gerry smiled.

Wrapping herself up, she prepared to battle the winds. But as she stepped outside, the trees were quiet, though the early autumn chill numbed her face.

'Good morning, Clarissa,' Gerry said, 'and you, Mr and Mrs McGuire.'

'Good morning to you, Uncle Gerry,' Clarissa replied. Her parents nodded to Gerry.

Gleeson's companion stood beside him, clasping her hands as though she were holding a bouquet. Gleeson introduced her. 'This is Mrs Brophy.'

Gleeson's companion stepped forward. 'How do you do?' Her clear eyes softened her high brow and strong face. She was dressed simply, but her clothes were tailored and highlighted by an elegant brooch.

Clarissa opened the conversation, 'How do you do, Mrs Brophy? Well, Uncle, St Mary's is your church of choice today?'

'Clarissa, sometimes it's good to make a change, but Mrs Brophy comes here all the time. It's her parish.'

'Well, I hope to see you again soon, Uncle, and you too, Mrs Brophy,' Clarissa said, smiling at them.

'Indeed, Clarissa,' he said. 'Please give my regards to John, and tell him I'm thinking of him. Goodbye, Mr and Mrs McGuire.'

'Goodbye, Mr Gleeson,' Christine McGuire said, and David raised his hat.

'You're thinking of John?' Clarissa asked her departing uncle.

Gerry looked back over his shoulder. 'That's right. He'll understand.'

Clarissa turned to her parents with her eyebrows raised and a questioning look on her face, but seeing the grey colour of her father's face, it was soon replaced by shock. 'Father, are you feeling all right?'

'Just a little tired,' David said. 'Come on, we'll get home to a warm fire and a nice roast.'

They walked to the carriage but Clarissa was worried. Her father did not look well and this was not the first time. He'd had a few instances of suddenly looking very grey over the last two months. It was high time he saw a doctor. But he seemed reluctant to do so. She would make him go and see someone, she decided.

'Mrs Leary seems nice,' Mrs Brophy said as Gerry helped her onto the omnibus at Elizabeth Street. 'The mother's all class and her father's a handsome man, although a little off colour, I thought.'

They found a double seat away from the wind, which had picked up again. Gerry enjoyed being close to her, and she didn't seem to mind his bulk beside her.

She pulled her scarf closer around her neck. 'What was that all about? You know, the business about thinking of your nephew.'

'He and I meet weekly and have a chat, about the business mostly. We've had four so far and,' Gerry rubbed his jaw, 'I don't know, but the man's holding back something from me. I just

feel it.'

'You might try and ask his work colleagues what it is, but not straight out, I mean.'

'Good idea.'

While Mrs Brophy rummaged in her handbag, Gerry thought about what she'd said. He had a number of work sites coming up and one was for Leary's Contracting: a stone magazine for the military in Parramatta, part of their stores project. He'd ask around on those sites and perhaps talk to Sean to see if he could find out what was really worrying his nephew.

'I've got the fare here,' she said as the conductor came down the aisle.

'No, I'll look after it.'

'Thank you. What I thought we'd do this afternoon, after our roast dinner, if this wind behaves itself, is go down to the Botanic Gardens. There will be a band down there, for sure.'

Gerry paid the fares. 'That'll do me just fine.' She wasn't a handsome woman, but her beauty shone through everything she did. When she smiled at you and asked after you, you knew she was genuinely interested. To Gerry that was worth more than good looks.

The shadows flickering from the gaslights cast spiral patterns on the pavement as Brian Atkins walked along Macquarie Street to King Street where his carriage waited. After a late night at the lodge he was keen to get home.

James Miller's execution had been put back until after Atkins's trial in May. But the cursed labourer would die in jail before then. It had cost Atkins plenty but it would be done. Miller would have a simple accident, then the case against himself would collapse. It was already leaking like a rusty roof in a storm. The magistrate had said as much at the hearing, enabling Atkins to post bail. His trial in May would see him a free man; of that, he was certain. One end was still loose but he thought he'd tightened it—the barmaid. She had turned. Not right away, because forcing her to tell a lie hadn't worked, but when he'd given her the money for her mother's expensive medical operation, she'd agreed to vary her story. He might have to fix her for good, too, because she could change her mind back.

At the club the previous night, Shelby and Thomas had asked him how he was progressing on buying Leary out. He had told them he was working on it but he knew he could do naught until this

Miller thing had been settled. Atkins kicked a loose stone in frustration.

He leaned forward as a gust of wind flung itself against him. Two gaslights ahead were unlit and he was forced to peer through the darkness to find his way. Footsteps pounded behind him and, without warning, crippling pain seared his left side. His left knee collapsed and he fell. Hearing grunts behind him, he tried to get up, but more pain exploded in his head before blackness overtook him.

They had been in their Elizabeth Street rooms for the last hour and they'd just made love for the second time. Beth relished her time with John. It was her way of claiming a place in his consciousness, at least during the time they were together. It was wrong on so many levels, she knew, but not on one: her need for a child. Maybe this time she had conceived. She looked down at him, his face damp with perspiration. 'I love you,' she said. 'Just like this. I love you, John.' She settled back on the bed, pulling the sheet to cover herself.

'I know you do. I'm the same.' His eyes closed and she let him rest.

When he'd come to her this afternoon, there were no preliminaries. He'd kissed her and she'd gasped in surprise and allowed him to strip off her clothes and not make love to her ... but to take her. She withstood his force, knowing she was the reason for his lust.

After five minutes, he stirred. 'Will it be like this in years to come?' he asked.

Years? Dear God, she'd never thought that far ahead—but then, why not? 'I hope so. I think you and I understand each other.' His hand was caressing her and she closed her eyes, giving herself over to pleasure. 'Do you have to go back to the office this afternoon?' she murmured.

John withdrew his hand. She shouldn't have mentioned work. Doing so was like opening a window and letting foul air into their special place.

'I'm afraid I must. There's a lot to do.'

He sat up and turned, putting his legs over the side of the bed. She liked the way his back muscles moved as he retrieved his clothes.

'You know, it's strange,' he said.

She leant up on her elbow. 'What's strange?'

'The business. I mean, I wanted to be the best and the biggest, and now I am. Done in six years and I'm proud. I've got everything I've ever wanted. And yet, I just don't seem to be content. Does that make sense?'

She smiled. 'You certainly have more than most men in Sydney. A good income, prestige, a successful marriage.'

'On the surface,' John said as he stood up to pull up his pants.

'Maybe it's not a successful marriage,' she said as she got out of bed, 'but a proper social marriage.' As she started to dress, John's eyes moved over her, but she'd lost the mood. 'Nothing's perfect,' she continued. 'You've made your place, your mark on Sydney. Learn to enjoy it for what it is.' He looked down as she stood in front of him and she took his head in her hands and brought his lips to hers. 'And you'll always have me.'

John kissed her and smiled. 'I know. How are the horses going?'

Beth brushed her hair in front of the mirror. 'Improving. I've got new colts which I'm racing and then I'll sire them.' She fastened her boots and stood by the window, enjoying the sun coming in. As she put on her jacket, John put his hands on her shoulders then caressed the back of her neck.

'Until next time, my dear,' he said.

Beth kissed him. 'Until next time, my love. I'll leave now.'

'I'll follow you.'

≈

'Stop here, Herbert,' Lady Dalkeith said to her coachman.

The carriage came to a halt in Elizabeth Street and Lady Dalkeith turned the ring on her finger to catch the March sunlight coming through her carriage window. When it shone on the stone, she sighed with pleasure. She'd just collected the ring from the jewellers and she wanted to examine the stone in detail, again. It was a fine stone indeed. A horse's whinny took her attention away, and she glanced towards the buildings on the other side of the street. A curtain moved at an upper floor window, revealing a woman standing there with her back to the street. A hand then appeared at the base of the woman's neck.

The woman was clothed, but the gesture was intimate. Intrigued, Lady Dalkeith reached for a pair of field glasses she kept in a compartment of the carriage and trained them on the window. The hand caressing the woman's neck looked like a man's. Suddenly embarrassed, and afraid to be caught out spying, Lady Dalkeith quickly put the glasses away and concentrated on admiring her ring.

Just as she was about to order her coachman to proceed, the front door of the terrace opened and a woman of quality walked towards a cab outside. She must have been the one at the window, because the lace collar of her blouse matched the suede jacket that Lady Dalkeith had glimpsed through the window. The jacket covered a fine, full-length wool dress with little gold buttons down its centre. Before Lady Dalkeith could examine the woman's face, she stepped into her cab. Then a tall, well-built young man exited from the same front door, walked a few paces and bought a late-edition newspaper from a street seller. The man was John Leary.

The woman's cab drove by Lady Dalkeith's carriage and she saw the woman's face outlined in the window frame.

It was Beth Blackett.

John Leary must have been the man in the upper room with Mrs Blackett. They had then contrived a rather sloppy attempt to exit separately, so that no one would see them together. Lady Dalkeith smiled. Unfortunately for them, they had been seen. 'Get along there, Herbert,' she said to the driver. 'I want to get back to Glebe, immediately.'

She grabbed onto the handholds as the wheels sped over the cobblestones. On the way home she worked out a strategy for how she would tell Mrs Christine McGuire about her son-in-law. There was no doubt that Beth Blackett and John Leary were having an affair. It was becoming tiresome, hearing about Mr John Leary's sudden and illustrious rise in the construction industry. Time his family knew the truth.

Lady Dalkeith felt an excitement she hadn't felt for years. The feeling continued until her carriage stopped at her town home.

∽

At Leary's, John scanned the afternoon edition of the newspaper. He was about to fold it up when an article caught his eye.

A leading businessman, Mr Brian Atkins, was bashed and knifed in Macquarie Street on the 9th of the month and is in a critical condition in Sydney Hospital.

John's pulse raced. So, someone had acted on Atkins. Had it been Wexton? If it had been, John had mixed feelings. He'd said that Atkins was to be watched only, not attacked. And yet John felt a certain satisfaction at the assault. 'It's a start, men,' he said to his skilled employees. 'Atkins is out of action. Critical ... good. Hope the bastard dies.'

∽

Brian Atkins screamed and he opened his eyes.

'Steady there,' a voice sounded nearby. Shapes appeared in the light of the wall lamp. 'You're in a hospital, friend.' the voice said. 'A hospital. Now, for goodness' sake, go to sleep and let us have some rest.'

Atkins closed his eyes again as an invisible hammer crashed on its anvil, sending pain tearing through him. Each time the hammer hit, the pain ripped deeper, sharper now as the laudanum was wearing off. In between he saw a faint moon through a window and sensed the heaviness of his left side and back. He felt as though he'd been strapped to a sack of burning coal. The sack was nothing but bandages; the smell of its dressing wafted to his nostrils, joining other smells of the ward.

It might've been yesterday, or perhaps it was several days ago, that a white-gowned man had stood in front of him. Through the pain he had just been able to make out the words: 'It was close, Mr Atkins. Another inch and you would've been dead. We're still not out of the woods. You need to rest until the swelling goes down. We will give you something for the pain.'

Now Atkins focused on thinking about his home, anything to fight the pain of this pounding hammer. He wanted out of this place and out of this agony. Leary was behind this, he was certain. Getting back at that bastard could wait, but not for long, only until he could get the hammer to stop.

Atkins prayed for vengeance on Leary, clear in his piety that his cause was just. He hadn't had religious thoughts for years but still he prayed.

The hammer continued without respite. Sweat dripped from his forehead, down his nose and into his mouth. The fiery coals beneath him seemed to be steaming and yet somehow he knew he had to put up with it.

He tried to think of another time, another place, and he saw two boys playing, rolling in the autumn leaves, yelling and wrestling each other. His brother had laughed at an old joke and he remembered it and recited it, before the hammer dropped again.

Lady Dalkeith was visiting Christine McGuire.

'Lady Dalkeith,' the maid said as she took her hat and muff. 'Mrs McGuire is in the drawing room, where there's a nice fire to warm you.'

Lady Dalkeith followed her. Ever since she'd seen the lovers, she'd looked for the right moment to tell Christine McGuire. This was it.

'Welcome, your ladyship,' her hostess said as she walked into the drawing room. 'What would you like by way of refreshment?'

'Thank you, Christine. A cup of tea, hot, please. How are you?'

'Quite well, thank you,' Christine said. She gestured to a plate of pastries. 'A cake?'

'Thank you.'

'It's my grandchild who's suffering,' Christine said. 'The croup, you know.'

'The poor thing. It's dreadful to endure, but they grow out of it.'

Christine sipped her tea, then turned to the maid. 'That will be all, thank you.' She waited till the maid left. 'We have been busy of late.'

'How so?'

For the next thirty minutes they exchanged news of their mutual friends. Lady Dalkeith was getting impatient to tell her friend of her discovery.

The moment came as Christine mentioned Clarissa's work. 'I'm sure you know how horrified I am that Clarissa is employed in one of David's factories.'

Lady Dalkeith nodded and said, 'I sympathise with you, my dear. I know how difficult it must be for you to accept that your own daughter is in trade, so to speak.'

'It's scandalous. I'm so fortunate that some of my friends still converse with me and invite me to functions. I could easily understand if they didn't.'

'Well, you'll always get that loyalty from me.'

'Thank you, that's much appreciated.'

Lady Dalkeith put her teacup and saucer down on the side table. 'There's something I have to tell you. It concerns your son-in-law.' She studied her friend.

Christine's head was turned to one side and she had an eyebrow raised. 'Yes?'

'He's the largest contractor in town, they say,' she said. 'Do you see him often?'

'Sadly, no,' Christine said. 'The maid brings Richard around most days, but we don't see John as much as we'd like. In fact, I rarely see my daughter these days as she gallivants between David's businesses.'

Now was the time. 'It is distressing news that I bring you, Christine, and I want to underscore this by saying that I only have your good interests and our friendship at heart. Further, I can tell you that my facts are correct.'

'Well, out with it.' Christine smiled. 'It's about John, yes?'

'I'm afraid so.'

'What has my handsome son-in-law done now?'

'I have seen him with that woman again.'

Christine was still smiling, though somewhat tightly. 'Beth Blackett?'

'Indeed. Their meeting was not what I would consider within the confines of normal business. In fact, I think it was quite the opposite.'

Christine rose from her seat and refilled her cup. 'Are you sure it was her? If it was, I'm certain it was innocent.'

Lady Dalkeith clasped her hands on her lap. 'I was no more than ten feet from her and I recognised her.'

Christine nodded. 'In what situation?'

'In Elizabeth Street. They were leaving a terrace house on a Tuesday afternoon, nine days ago. She left first and he not long after. I noticed them previously at the upper window—'

'You saw them?' Christine said surprised. 'Were you spying on them?'

'My dear, I'm offended. I do not spy on people.'

'I'm sorry, but you must have. A terrace house?'

'Yes,' Lady Dalkeith said, 'and they left by the same front door. A little earlier, in the room above, I saw Mrs Blackett from the back, and a man's hand, which I assume was your son-in-law's.'

'But you don't know for sure.'

'No, I don't. But who else could it have been?'

'Another man, obviously,' Christine said.

'Perhaps. But why would Blackett and your son-in-law choose a terrace house in which to meet?'

'I have no idea. But I'm sure there was no intrigue.'

'But what reason would they have, other than to be alone? If they were to meet on an issue of import, surely they would have selected a more public venue, where this sort of thing would not be misconstrued.'

'Perhaps,' Christine replied.

'I'm sorry to say this, but I think it's serious and I think your son-in-law is being unfaithful. If you remember, in last May we had a conversation in which I warned you this might occur again.'

'Frankly, what you saw is not proof of infidelity.'

'It isn't,' Lady Dalkeith said, 'but it is one more incident of their being together.'

Christine pressed her lips together. 'If what you say is true—'

'It is.'

'Then I must protect my daughter from scandal.'

That's better, Lady Dalkeith thought. No dirty laundry fluttering near Christine!

'I must go, if you don't mind.'

'So soon?' Christine said, but without conviction.

'I'm sorry, yes.' Lady Dalkeith got up and took her friend's hands. 'It's not the news to bring a friend, but I do think that you should be aware of the facts and take appropriate action. I'll say no more on this. Whatever you choose to do about it will be your decision.'

'Thank you.'

Christine closed the front door, turned and walked back through the foyer. She was shaking. Clarissa loved her husband and he was deceiving her! It must have been John's hand that her friend had seen. Could there be any doubt? Lady Dalkeith had not caught them in the act, after all. But this was ample for Clarissa to worry about. She sat down.

Poor Clarissa. *How will I tell her?* Anger rose in her. John was a fool. Clarissa was a good wife to him, loving and generous—and it looked as though he had debased those virtues.

'There you are,' David said walking down the stairs. 'Do you have a few minutes to discuss something before dinner? What's wrong? You look ill.'

Christine pressed her elbows against her side to settle her emotions and her thoughts. Should she tell her husband? Or, should she find out more and discover for herself what was really going on? 'I'm all right, and yes I have a few minutes to talk. Let's go into the drawing room.'

'I'm worried,' David said walking into the room.

'What about?'

He stood with his back to the fireplace. 'I can't put my finger on it but for the last eight months or so I've been concerned about our family, the unease in both houses.'

She knew now what the basis of this might be, but she'd have to appear ignorant until she was more certain. 'I'm unsure of what you mean. There is the issue of Clarissa and her so-called working habits, to which I'm strongly opposed, as you know.'

He raised his hands. 'That's an issue, admittedly. But there are other things. Clarissa's behaviour, not only at her work as you call it, but also her general demeanour. I think she's distracted about something other than work.'

David was always a softie when it came to his daughter. Christine didn't feel that depth of affection but she loved her daughter nevertheless and now she felt protective of her. 'I think if Clarissa gave up working and stayed home, like any other well-bred young mother, then she'd be much better for it.'

He rubbed his chest. 'It's not as simple as that. You and I have differences about her working. At times I don't think it's the right thing to do either, but it's Clarissa's decision, and she spends enough time with Richard. She's not ignoring him.'

'David, it's fruitless to argue, we've already discussed this. Is there something else that's worrying you?'

He filled and lit his pipe and she waited until a plume of smoke drifted up towards the chandelier. 'Clarissa and John don't seem to be as happy and as close as they were,' he said.

'Really? They're just adjusting to normal married life.'

'But you remember before they were married, and just after,' he said while flexing his left arm. 'They wanted to be with each other every day. I mean, it was wonderful to see.'

Christine agreed. She'd always wanted to have that feeling for a man, and while she was affectionate towards David, she'd never felt her passion stirred. But John, it seemed, was a wolf in sheep's clothing. A sudden thought came to her: *My God, was he being intimate with both women?* That made her wince. She would have to be sure before she told David. 'Well,' she said, 'you know how I feel.

211

Clarissa working is the biggest problem. That's all I've got to say about it.'

His eye twitched. His fingers jerked open, dropping his pipe. 'David?'

He collapsed to the floor, face down on the carpet. She bent down and pulled hard to turn him over. His face was the colour of grey marble marked with some burnt embers from his pipe. 'The pain,' he said, 'the pain ... my chest, it's ... God, please Christine, please.'

She opened his collar as pain doubled him up. Then he lost consciousness. 'Help!' she cried out. 'Please, someone ... Come quickly!'

∼

Clarissa thought about the newspaper article she'd read that morning. Mr Brian Atkins was lying critically ill in hospital. He was the man John and Mr Wexton had talked about in the study. She had a worrying feeling that the attack on Atkins might have had something to do with John. Richard's cry distracted her and she went to his room.

Picking him up, she cuddled him till he settled. He coughed deep and hollow and she strained to hear the raised conversation on the floor below. Now there was someone running up the stairs.

Stella burst into the room, her face pale and perspiring. 'Miss Clarissa, Miss Clarissa,' she said, shock causing her to revert to the more familiar form of address, 'your father, he's collapsed. They've taken him to Sydney Hospital. Your mother is with him.'

Clarissa placed Richard back in his cot. 'Dear God, I must go to him.'

'The carriage is ready, you can go there now.'

∼

A seagull screeched as it hovered overhead in the southerly that blew through Waverley Cemetery. Clarissa looked up at the bird that seemed free and untroubled. She closed her eyes and tried to listen to the priest.

'I am the resurrection and the life . . .'

Another tear slid down her cheek, one to join the many she'd shed over the four days since her father's death. She had lived and breathed as if by rote—washing, changing, eating, all done in a dreamlike state. A nightmare.

The seagull squawked.

'He that believes in me shall never die . . .'

The wind pressed against her and Clarissa placed a foot behind her to steady herself. Her family party was not fifty feet from the cliff edge. All she wanted to do was to run and fling herself over it, anything to escape the sharp jabs of memory.

'Ashes to ashes, dust to dust . . .'

John stood beside her. His face was as grey as the marble tombstone behind him, his eyes dull as he stared straight ahead. Her father had been like a parent to him these past six years and the two had had a strong bond of respect and closeness. Clarissa's hand reached for his. It felt cold and hard and she thought how appropriate for the day and the moment. There was no response at first, then the pressure was returned. Their united hands seemed to give strength to each. Perhaps this terrible loss could bring her and John closer together, as they used to be.

'May he rest in peace.' The priest's stole slapped in the wind and he tethered it and closed his missal.

Clarissa's mind was blank and fear bathed her. What had she to do now? Where was Mother? Yes, to the left of the priest. Clarissa looked at her and saw only black; everybody was dressed in black. A veil covered the widow's face but instead of a dropped head, the jaw jutted towards the priest, defiant in life.

As a smattering of rain began to fall, John edged her forward and they stood, alongside the gaping pit with its sheer clay sides, staring down towards the coffin's shining redwood. The pit's mustiness filled her nostrils, making her feel nauseous and light-headed. She swayed forward but John grabbed her.

The sight of the gold cross fixed to the coffin lid steadied her;

she understood the grave meant finality. The cross became blurred by her tears as she watched her mother throw soil into the void. Christine then walked away to the waiting coaches.

Clarissa picked up some soil and threw it into the grave. John followed suit, then he took her arm, 'Come, my dear,' he said, 'let's get out of the rain.'

Clarissa allowed herself to be ushered away from the pit's edge. She wanted to stay but knew she had to leave. She would return another time. She made her way through the graves surrounding her father's, including those of the three dead Leary's workers. At the coach she looked back at the gathering for the first time. Who had come to see her father's final farewell?

There were many friends, some of her father's business colleagues and the family doctor who had pronounced David dead from a massive heart attack. And there, standing by himself, was Malcolm Robinson, his morning suit fitting him like a second skin. He looked at her with a sympathetic smile, which lessened her grief. She was glad he was there.

As she mounted the coach step, she felt another hand, a big firm one, on her elbow.

Gerry Gleeson stood bareheaded, dressed in a plain suit. 'Please accept my condolences, Clarissa. I didn't get to know your father well, but he was a good man.'

'Thank you, Uncle,' John said, his voice breaking. 'Come Clarissa, we must go.'

Something in the stonemason's blue eyes struck a chord with Clarissa. 'Wait, please, John. Thank you for coming, Uncle, and for your kind words.'

Gleeson looked at John as he spoke, 'If you want anything at all, John, please let me know.'

'Thank you, I shall.'

Clarissa nodded to Sean Connaire, who doffed his hat to her. Getting onto the coach she allowed John to put the woollen comforter over her knees, then looked out the rain-smeared window. None of it seemed real and she longed to wake up from this horrible nightmare. But she knew it was real: her beloved father was dead and she didn't know how she would cope without him.

On the ride back to Point Piper she could hear John speaking. At times she nodded when she thought she should, but nothing registered. It was as though someone had wrapped her head in a turban of pain that forced all things from her other than the memories of her father.

The comforter was removed and she looked up to find they had arrived at the house. She made it into the parlour where she shook hands with strangers and nodded out of politeness to their murmurs of sympathy. Hopefully, she thought, she wasn't rude to any of the guests but recognition wasn't there. Someone gave her a cup of tea and she sat down on a sofa.

'Mrs Leary, I said I'm very sorry for you.'

Clarissa looked up from her teacup to Malcolm Robinson. 'I'm sorry, Mr Robinson. Were you speaking to me?'

'I was, but I could see you were not here with us. You were somewhere else with your father.'

That he understood her so well touched her, bringing her undone and causing her to drop her teacup. It bounced on the floor, its contents scalding her ankles.

'Are you all right?' he asked with a concerned look on his face. He bent down to pick up the cup and saucer, which Stella quickly came over and relieved him of.

His clear skin, bright eyes and his concern pushed her pain to the side and she smiled for the first time in days. 'It seems so,' she said. 'I'm sorry I've made this mess.'

'That's all right, ma'am,' Stella said. 'But you'll want to change your stockings or you'll get a chill.'

'No. Leave them Stella, please. They remind me I can still feel something.'

'But, ma'am!'

'It's all right, Stella, thank you.'

The maid retreated as John came over.

Robinson stood up and looked from Clarissa to John. 'I'm

Malcolm Robinson, Mr Leary. I'm your father-in-law's ... sorry,
I was your father-in-law's manager at McGuire Wire.'

'Yes, I know of you and thank you for coming. Clarissa, are you
all right?'

Clarissa closed her eyes for a moment and nodded.
'Mr Robinson is looking after me.'

'I'm grateful to you, Mr Robinson,' John said. 'If you're all
right, Clarissa, I must get back to our guests.'

'I'm fine, John, thank you,' Clarissa said.

As John headed over to join a group of mourners, Malcolm
Robinson said, 'I'm glad I met your husband. I admire his ambition.
In Italy, such devotion to one's chosen profession is highly regarded.'

Clarissa looked up at him. 'Please sit beside me.'

He paused. 'Everyone else is standing. Do you think I should?'

Clarissa patted the seat beside her on the sofa. She couldn't care
less, today of all days, what people thought, especially about her. If
she wanted to sit close to Malcolm Robinson and talk to him, she
would do so.

He sat down, trying to keep a space between them; his sense of
propriety had been challenged. She found a little amusement in this,
which might keep back the tide of misery, if only for a short time.
'There now, isn't that better?'

His olive complexion coloured as his eyes darted around the
room. 'I suppose it is.'

'Please tell me about Italy. I want to know all about it: your
village, your family, everything.'

He started speaking and Clarissa listened. It reminded her of
the fairy tales her father had read to her when she was young. Then
the pain threatened to deluge her again with despair and she had to
force herself to listen. Malcolm told stories that were full of life and
love. His eyes lit up and his teeth flashed as he spoke with pride
about his birthplace, and she found herself caught up in his tales,
because of his joy in the telling. She was grateful to him for the
distraction from grief.

Through the crowd of mourners, Christine watched the man
sitting beside Clarissa—that foreigner whom David had put in

charge of his warehouse. What was his name? Robertson, or something like that.

David was dead, and sorrow at his loss had hit her hard. She had kept herself together at the graveside and had been proud of doing so, but now she felt vulnerable. Struggling to control her feelings, she turned and walked over to the French doors and looked at the March winds and lashing rain stirring white caps on Blackburn Cove. How appropriate today was for a funeral! Tears filled her eyes as she felt the absence of her companion in life. David was that to her and more, a kind, caring and generous man. He would leave a big gap in their lives, a thought that caused Christine to suddenly be gripped by anxiety. David had handled all their financial dealings and now she would need to turn to John for that. Bitterness now partnered her apprehension. She had to be dependent on a man who she had never completely trusted, and who didn't seem to love Clarissa any more.

Sean Connaire tucked his chin into his oilskin. It was foul weather for riding but he wanted to release his frustration. He had gone to the cemetery and paid his respects to a man he'd admired. But he wouldn't go to Point Piper, even though his conscience told him he should for Clarissa's sake.

His horse galloped up the hill from Bondi Bay. It was useless trying to keep dry. The southwesterly dumped icy rain on him, some finding its way down his back, but his temper was worse than the dirty gale. He wished that it were John under six feet of clay and not David McGuire. A horrid thought, he admitted. Faster and faster he rode, passing a hotel he'd frequented as a drunkard in another life. His fingers sweated on the reins and he beat the horse harder, sprinting away from the public bar and its tempting call. He had had no relapses this year but he knew he was always vulnerable.

Anger spurred Sean on. He wanted someone to knock sense into John. Perhaps his uncle might. Words said to Gerry Gleeson might stir the big stonemason to get his nephew into line. He hoped so. A hunk of mud stung Sean's cheek, bringing tears to his eyes. If his shareholding in Leary's Contracting hadn't provided him with extra cash, he'd get out now, especially with David McGuire dead. He kept riding, oblivious to the passers-by who cursed the mad horseman tearing down Oxford Street.

He decided not to ride back to the office but to go home. His wife was laid up with influenza and hadn't come to the funeral. This weather wouldn't be helping her. Heading his horse into the stable behind his house, he removed the saddle and bridle. A shiver rippled through the horse's flanks, making Sean feel guilty. 'There, there boy. I've given you a hard time. Here, have some hay.'

Grabbing two old towels, he gave the horse a good drying. He started with the head and worked along the body, administering care to his four-legged friend. He was gentle, to make up for taking out his frustration on the animal. He placed a blanket over the horse, checked its water and gave it another pat before closing the stable door behind him.

Sprinting through the slashing rain he went in the back door of the house, stripped off the wet clothes and put on the dry clothes he'd kept nearby. The room was warm and he was thankful that Vonnie had lit the wood stove.

'Is that you, dear?' a weak voice called from upstairs.

'It is. I'll be up in a tick. You want a cup of tea?'

'No, thank you. I just had one, but you help yourself. The pot's still hot. There's some cold beef in the larder if you're hungry.'

Sean shook his head. Even on her sick bed Vonnie still looked after him. Thank you, God, for a wonderful woman. Indeed, did he ever really know how lucky he was? Probably not. 'Thank you, I'll make a sandwich,' he called up to Vonnie.

With tea and sandwich in hand he went upstairs and opened the bedroom door. Vonnie was in bed, propped up by pillows, with inflamed nose and sunken eyes. But her smile warmed Sean's heart. He moved to sit on the bed beside her.

'Don't get too close, dear. The doctor told me that the influenza might affect the children. When they come home from school, they are not to come in here. Anyway, tell me, how was it?'

Sean pulled up a chair. 'As funerals go, sad, real sad. Clarissa looked knocked about, and John yes, he looked upset.'

'Well, he should be. After all he liked the man a lot, didn't he?'

Sean nodded. 'I suppose he did, but who knows what's in his mind these days. He's got no idea what's happening to his loved ones.' Vonnie tried to sit up. Sean stood to help her and noticed how much his wife was perspiring. 'You're still not well,' he said. 'I'll let you sleep.'

Vonnie sank back into the pillows. 'Thank you, dear. I'd like to hear more about it but I do need to rest.'

Going back down to the parlour, Sean looked around and was satisfied. He could afford a bigger house in a wealthier area but his needs were simple and he was settled here at Woolloomooloo. Seated in an armchair he continued his meal and considered himself fortunate that if it hadn't been for John Leary, he'd still be a carpenter. But, he'd been happy as a chippy.

David's death sent a depressing shiver through him. He had liked the straight way he'd lived and the man's keen mind. He was head and shoulders above any man Sean knew and yet David had been humble, despite his gifts.

Clarissa pressed her hands to her stomach as Stella removed the plates from the breakfast table. It wasn't the bacon and eggs that had made her sick. It was her body undergoing a change all too familiar. She knew she was expecting—she'd missed her second menses—but she wasn't happy. Her new baby would be born into a relationship that was in trouble.

John sat across from her reading the newspaper. 'It says here that Atkins is alive,' he said to her, 'although he's still critical, but the labourer Miller has died in jail. An accident, they say. It also says that because of Miller's death, Atkins likely won't face trial in May because of the lack of evidence. The man will go free.' John had looked angry as he read out the paper's report to her, but when he looked up at her, his expression changed. 'Is there anything wrong?'

'You had Mr Wexton keep tabs on Mr Atkins, didn't you?'

'I did, and at first I thought that Wexton might have attacked him, but the investigator was with another client at the time.'

Clarissa was relieved that John wasn't involved. 'I'm glad to hear that,' she said. 'I'm feeling a little queasy; it was probably the bacon. I might have a lie-down.'

'I hope you feel better soon,' John said, reaching over to press her hand. 'We're due at the solicitor's later this morning. Are you up to going?'

'Thank you, dear,' she said, covering his hand with her own. 'I'll be all right, once I've rested for a bit.'

Later, at the solicitor's, Christine sat opposite the desk with John on one side of her and Clarissa on the other. Even in mourning clothes, Christine thought, her daughter looked fashionable. Christine's own new dress was warm and comfortable. The colder weather was so much easier to dress for. There'd be another six months of it before the heat and humidity returned.

The document on the desk was David's final will and testament. David had told Christine many times that she'd be looked after, and she believed him.

The solicitor lifted the purple ribbon from the will, opened it then pressed his palms against the folds to straighten it. He cleared his throat and began. 'This is the last will and testament of David Alan McGuire. I hereby revoke all former wills and testamentary dispositions, heretofore made by me . . .'

Christine looked at John as Mr Wilson continued the legal preamble. She couldn't get it out of her head that her daughter was a victim of John's infidelity and that made her want to be vengeful —but she then felt guilty. Vengeance was a sin and as yet she had no proof of his cheating. Poor Clarissa.

'To my servants . . .'

She settled back to hear how the least of her husband's benefactors would enjoy David's largesse.

'To my son-in-law John Leary, I leave a ten per cent share of my McGuire Wire and Superior Sheeting shareholdings together with my gold watch noted in Appendix Two hereto.'

Christine was expecting she would get the remainder of the shareholdings.

'To my daughter, Clarissa,' intoned the solicitor, 'I hereby leave the ownership of the properties at 79 Wolseley Road, Point Piper and *Clontarf*, the Bathurst property.'

That was generous of David.

'To my wife, I hereby bequeath our own Point Piper home and all the remaining shareholdings in those companies named in Appendix One hereto.' Christine felt thrilled. 'With the condition,' the solicitor continued, 'that my daughter Clarissa remains in a management capacity in all such firms for a period of five years.'

That didn't please Christine, but at least she'd got the majority of the shares, and that was the most important.

'Thank you,' Clarissa said. 'Is that all?'

'Just a small matter to conclude: your father stipulated that in the event of his death the name of the silent partner in Leary's Contracting would be disclosed.' He turned his attention to John, who had been dreading this question. 'Mr Leary, would you please name the major shareholder in your company?'

'Phoenix Investment Group,' John said firmly. He watched the solicitor make a note of this and avoided looking at Clarissa or Christine. He prayed that neither would ever find out that Beth Blackett was sole party in the Phoenix Investment Group.

Wilson finished writing. 'That concludes the reading, Mrs Leary. I can make a copy of the will if you wish. I have one for your mother.'

'I would like a copy please,' Clarissa said. 'What's the procedure now?'

'There will be a period of time before all this can be put into place for the will to be probated; about two months.'

During that time, John wondered, should he make Beth an offer for her share of Leary's? He could now afford to buy it from her.

Jack Johnson came into Leary's George Street meeting room and sat opposite Sean. The Purchasing Manager looked worried.

'Now, what seems to be your problem?' Sean asked him.

'Do you have a few minutes?'

Sean glanced at the wall clock; he had to leave for Chippendale in twenty minutes to meet John. 'Sure. What's on your mind?'

'I'm thinking of leaving.'

'Leaving . . . Leary's?'

Jack nodded.

Sean put his pencil down and folded his arms. This was serious. Jack Johnson was a capable man and knew the business better than anyone. Leary's Contracting couldn't afford to lose him. 'Come on. Let's go outside,' he said.

Out in the storage yard, Sean leant against a stack of ladders and gestured to a sawhorse for Jack to sit on. The weather was warm for the middle of April. 'That's a big move, Jack,' Sean said. 'The reason?'

'I'm keen to head back to sea.'

'Oh, aye.'

'It's not sudden, Sean. I've been considering it for a while.'

Sean wasn't surprised but he suspected there was more to this and wanted to dig. 'Is it just the blue water that's pulling you hard or is it this place?'

Jack nodded. 'It's a bit of both. I can put up with a lot, the way we make money, and so forth. But when I see a man change for the worse and take licence with others around him, I have to take a stand.'

They both had the same thoughts. 'You're speaking about your boss, aren't you?' Sean said.

Jack said nothing for a while. 'Sean, I just can't work for an employer who uses people the way he does. I know he's your partner and friend. But let me ask you frankly, do you think the same as me?'

Sean had a responsibility as a shareholder. Whatever he thought of John, he couldn't discuss it with Jack, who although a senior man was still an employee. But he would say something. 'John worries me, too. The site deaths and how he's made the company big have affected him. I'm going to talk to him about it.'

Jack seemed to understand that Sean was on his side. 'Do you think there's a chance he'll change?'

Sean shrugged. 'I hope so. I do.'

Jack looked relieved. 'The trouble is, I admire him. His ambition and drive have always impressed me but he's using those now for all the wrong reasons.'

Sean held his palm outwards to Jack. 'Don't talk any more. I know your views. Do you have another job?'

'I don't. I wanted to air my grievances and to see what you thought.'

Sean got up. He loved the company, but he and John needed a showdown, on a lot of things. 'Let me speak to the man,' he said. 'I won't tell him how you feel in the meantime. Give it two months and then we'll talk again, say middle of June.'

Jack stood up. 'I'll agree to that, and good luck with him.'

'I'll need it, but now I've got a site inspection and you've got work as well.'

Clarissa was grateful that she had her work at McGuire Wire and tasks that forced her to concentrate. They helped mask the grief of her father's death only four short weeks ago. Now, she was filing correspondence from the pile on her table.

An hour ago, Malcolm Robinson had come in from a visit to the Annandale warehouse. She'd relied on him enormously over the last month and now he sat twenty feet away, concentrating on the monthly figures. His presence was like the air she breathed: constant and life-giving. Her thoughts were jumbled as she forced the metal punch to penetrate the paper. He had been a great comfort to her these last weeks, but she knew he was more than that to her. She had always been attracted to him, but now she felt her feelings for him were deeper; he was everything John wasn't. Yet she still loved John, and what's more she was probably carrying their second child.

She felt a jumble of emotions, frustration becoming the overriding one as she tried to get the metal punch to work properly. She slammed it down on the desk in disgust.

'Is something wrong, Mrs Leary?'

Her emotions settled. Connection had been made and that's what she'd wanted, for him to say something. 'Oh, that stupid punch refuses to do its job,' Clarissa said as she looked up and saw his animated eyes, which, with his grin, forced her to grin too. 'I shouldn't let it annoy me,' she said, feeling a little foolish.

'I'll have a look at it,' he said. 'It's good to see you smile, whatever the reason. The funeral hasn't been so long ago, and you haven't had much to smile about.'

Her sadness returned. Graveyard visions flashed before her, the foul weather and a damp coach. She looked at him.

'I'm sorry,' he said, the grin now replaced by a look of concern. 'I've made you think about that day again, haven't I?'

Clarissa closed the file. 'Only for a moment. It's passed now.' And it had. She picked up the punch and put it at the end of her desk. 'I want to thank you again for your support since the funeral. It has meant a lot to me.'

He shrugged his shoulders. 'Friends should help each other. Well, that's all I can do today.' He closed the ledger, squinted and pinched the bridge of his nose. 'I would like to ask you something.'

'What?'

She watched him stand up and put his jacket on: simple movements without effort.

'I'd like to take you to supper for some Italian food. Just something light and quick.'

Clarissa tilted her head. The wall clock showed four. She wasn't expected to leave work until five and Richard would be fed, bathed and put to bed before then. Why not? It sounded interesting.

'You're thinking too much,' Malcolm said. 'Come on, the spaghetti will be getting cold.'

Clarissa smiled. 'I'd like that, thank you. Is it far?'

'It's very close. Just down off Goulburn Street, in a little back lane behind one of the shops.'

Once outside, nausea niggled at her, the second bout of the day, and she wondered when it would abate. By the time they'd walked for a while she felt better and looked forward to the mysterious dinner. She felt relaxed in Malcolm's company and for a while her grief for her father and her worries about John's moods were put aside. Her father's legacy meant little to her now. In fact she'd been loath to read the will and she'd have exchanged her inheritance to see John smile at her again.

'Have you ever eaten Italian food?' Malcolm asked. 'The first course is usually pasta which is—'

'A mixture of flour and water, I understand.'

He stepped around a lamp post and said. 'Yes, essentially. Then we add a sauce.'

'It sounds deliciously light. You know the meals we have, stews and hot roasts, don't go well in our hot climate.'

Holding onto her elbow, he guided her around some pavement works. His touch pulsated through her and she was disappointed when he let go. 'Back in Italy,' he said, 'that is, in the south part of the country, where the weather is very hot in summer, a lot of people eat outside. It's called al fresco.'

'A grand idea,' she agreed. 'In my father's house, my husband included a veranda in the design for just such an occasion.' The mention of John pricked Clarissa's conscience, but just for a moment. She was simply having dinner with her manager, she reminded herself, just as John would do with his, so she was going to enjoy herself.

'Here it is,' Malcolm said, 'through here.'

Clarissa turned and saw nothing, not an inn or eating house, but she followed him as he went to a door in the wall and opened it. Clarissa gasped in surprise. On the other side was a wonderland.

A courtyard was covered with bright canvas awnings, and potted plants complemented the flagstones on which stood tables with chequered cloths. Vases of flowers completed the picture. Aromas filled Clarissa's nostrils: fried onions were familiar; others were foreign but attractive.

'I see it's surprised you,' he said, smiling.

'It's truly beautiful. Like a magic kingdom where there's a world beyond the world. And so near to Goulburn Street. A wonderful place.'

'Mario, welcome, welcome.' A man in a black apron and white shirt came up to them. He was of average height but wide in girth and with a smile that stretched from Circular Quay to Central Station.

'*Buonasera, mio amico,*' Malcolm said. 'It's good to see you.'

The two men hugged each other and the man kissed Malcolm on both cheeks, causing Clarissa to smile.

'And who is this *bella donna* you have brought here this evening, eh, Mario?'

Clarissa understood the compliment and smiled.

'Giovanni, let me introduce my friend, Mrs Clarissa Leary.'

Clarissa looked to see if the big man would bow, and he did.

'It's a pleasure, signora, to meet you. Welcome to our humble restaurant.'

'It's a lovely place, sir,' she said. 'And to think that it is camouflaged from the street.'

Giovanni put his head to one side like a puppy hearing a strange sound. 'Can of barge? What is that?'

'It means it is hidden and nobody can find it,' Malcolm said and smiled. 'She means, Giovanni, that she likes the place. Come, do you have a table for us?'

Giovanni threw up his hands and the grin returned. 'For you, Mario, I always have a table. Come this away, *per favore.*'

Clarissa felt no guilt as she accompanied her manager, going deeper into the dream of these enchanted surroundings. The British could learn from the Mediterranean, she thought. Giovanni stopped at a table in the corner, drew out Clarissa's chair and, after settling her, hurried off. Sitting down, she glanced at a nearby table where a thin man and his companion were eating pasta with skill.

'Now, Mrs Leary—'

'Malcolm,' she said, 'please call me Clarissa.'

He nodded once. 'Clarissa, what would you like to eat?'

She stared at the menu, which was in Italian, then looked up with a helpless look on her face.

Malcolm grinned at her. 'Would you like me to order for you?'

'Yes, please,' she said, grinning back at him.

Out of nowhere Giovanni appeared again with a jug of water, a basket of bread and two small bowls. Malcolm conversed with him in Italian.

After Giovanni left, Clarissa asked, 'So, what are we going to eat?'

'We shall start with something from the sea,' Malcolm replied. 'Some scampi, I think you call them prawns, and other seafood that will be cooked in a tomato sauce on some spaghetti.'

'I've not eaten prawns before.'

Malcolm grinned again. 'You'll love the dish. The taste of the seafood, the way it melts against the tomato sauce and the way the flavour of the pasta is all wrapped up—'

Clarissa laughed. 'You've convinced me. I'm sure I'll enjoy it.'

Malcolm poured a pale red wine from a bottle in a straw basket and lifted one of the glasses to her and she followed suit. '*Buon appetito.*' His eyes locked onto hers. 'And to our friendship.'

She touched his glass with hers. The horses' whinnying and the grind of wheels beyond the walls had quietened. Even the laughter around them seemed muffled. 'Yes ... our friendship,' she said, holding his stare. 'What are these?' She pointed to the bowls on the table, breaking the spell.

'Types of oils, which you dip your bread into. Here, I will show you.' He tore off a piece of bread, dipped it in the nearest oil and put it into his mouth. 'It's tasty. Giovanni makes the best bread in Goulburn Street.'

Clarissa copied him. He watched her to see her reaction. She liked the flavour. Oily, as she expected, but pleasantly tangy.

Malcolm smiled. 'You know, eating in the old country is a very important pastime. It is not just the act of satisfying one's hunger, but it is sharing something with the people you love.' He sipped his wine without taking his eyes from her. At his words, Clarissa's stomach did a little flip, but in a pleasant way. She knew she shouldn't encourage him, but this was just what she needed after the terrible loss of her father. She took a sip of her own wine.

The pasta arrived in two steaming bowls. Clarissa's bewildered look made Malcolm laugh.

'Shall I show you what to do with this?'

'Yes, please help me, Malcolm.'

Picking up his spoon and fork, he fed the spaghetti on to his fork, then into his mouth. Clarissa followed suit while Malcolm looked on.

The sauce and tangy spices of the seafood were different from anything she'd eaten and she liked it. Malcolm poured another glass of wine for her and she felt its glow infusing her, elevating her pleasure.

'Was it up to your standard, Mario?' Giovanni asked, appearing beside them with a large tray.

'It was, my friend. Ah, *secondi piatti*. The veal!'

Clarissa watched as a plate was placed in front of her. It held slices of meat with a textured coating, and potatoes and salad. 'I don't know if I can eat all this,' she said.

'Signora!' Giovanni said. 'It's a small serving. You'll love it.'

'Thank you, my friend,' Malcolm said before Giovanni left to welcome some new arrivals. 'The veal is *fritti*,' Malcolm said. 'Ah yes, fried in *impanata* . . . you know, when you crush bread.'

'Breadcrumbs.'

'Yes! It's very tasty.'

Clarissa cut a piece and ate it. It was very good and she watched him eat. They ate in silence but she experienced a contentment she hadn't felt in a long time.

'Thank you for another wonderful meal,' Malcolm said to Giovanni when he returned. 'Delicious.'

'I'm happy that you enjoyed it,' their host said clasping his hands. 'Please don't be too long before you come back, eh?'

Malcolm held her stare as Giovanni left them. His hand reached for hers and she clasped it.

'Clarissa, I've enjoyed this, very much. But we should go now. It's getting late and you want to see your son.'

He stood up and Clarissa did the same, though reluctantly. She wasn't ready to leave this magical place.

All too quickly, Malcolm had led her to the door, hailed a cab, handed her into it and said goodbye. As Clarissa headed home, her stomach full and her heart pleasantly warm, she knew she had opened a Pandora's Box in relation to Malcolm, but for now, she was just going to sit back and relive the evening.

CHAPTER EIGHT

CLARISSA DID UP THE BUTTONS OF HER BLOUSE AND SWUNG HER LEGS off her bed. 'So doctor, what do you think?' she said.

'Well, Mrs Leary, all the signs demonstrate that you are indeed at least three months' pregnant.'

Clarissa should be excited at the news, but she felt neutral about it. 'Thank you. I'll see you to the door.'

In the autumn sunshine, she said goodbye to the doctor, then closed the door and walked into the drawing room, where John was on the settee reading the Saturday edition of the *Sydney Morning Herald*. Her pregnancy was confirmed. Strangely, it made her think of Malcolm. Their dinner, two days previous, was still very much on her mind. She was expecting a baby, so her flirtation with him should come to an end. He was an honourable man: once he found out, he would withdraw from her life. But she wasn't ready for that. She just wouldn't tell him for a while, she decided.

'What did the doctor say?' John said looking up from the paper. 'Are you all right?'

'He confirmed that I'm expecting.'

He placed the paper down. 'That's great news.' He stood up and hugged her. 'Aren't you happy?'

His shining eyes reminded her of better times and his smile was genuine.

'Of course, dear, another child is what we've been planning, isn't it?'

'Another heir for the Leary family,' he said.

'An heir, John? Is that all it means to you?'

'No, of course not. He or she will be a child to love and raise in security.'

She walked over to the double doors of the drawing room, closed them and faced him. 'To tell you the truth, John, I'm unhappy about this baby because we aren't what we used to be, and a great deal of that is because of you.'

'Clarissa, we've talked about this. You know my view.'

'That my working for father has changed me?'

'Yes.'

'No, John. *You're* a different man. There's no doubt about that and I don't know whether you still feel the same way about me.'

His eyes told her everything. They had that look from their early days when she knew he loved her. 'Oh my dear,' he said, 'I still love you. I do.'

She held his look for a long time, wanting to be convinced. 'Do you?'

'Yes.'

She took hold of his hands. 'Then, if you do, I want you to start showing that to me.' He blinked and Clarissa guessed he was trying to think of something good to say. 'Not just words,' she continued, 'but actions. Listen, John, you can prove your love to me by being the person you once were, to—'

'You do go on about me changing!'

'You have changed. I don't know why but I can guess. Your ambition and those murders probably changed you, but what I'm asking is that you be more attentive to me, to my needs, and give time to your son, your uncle and your sister's family, and be -interested in your servants. If you do all that, you will be -demonstrating that you love *me*. Do you understand?'

He didn't respond for some time, then said, 'I think so.'

She persisted. 'You know I'm not a demanding woman, dear, and I'm still not, but I do expect that the man I love proves that he does love me.'

John paused and said. 'Well, I do love you and I'll do what you say.' He smiled at her. 'Because I don't want to lose you.'

That was what she wanted to hear, but it was now up to him to confirm his love. 'Good,' she said, embracing him. 'Now, off to work. That's a good place to start.' She kissed him and he responded. 'See you tonight,' she said.

John set off for town, happier than he'd been for a while, and, especially happy that he would be a father again. Clarissa had set him tasks to reassure her of his affections and although he didn't really think he had to do all the things she wanted, he would certainly try to accomplish most of them.

She was worth it and he was still in love with her. So what was he going to do about Beth? He loved Beth as well and she satisfied things in him that Clarissa couldn't. It wasn't about making love; Clarissa was as passionate with him as Beth was. At times, though, he still felt that old insecurity that he had in relation to Clarissa: that she was more intelligent, had come from better stock and that she judged his weaknesses. With Beth, he felt none of that. Yet, feeling secure in Beth's company was one thing, continuing to make love to her was another matter. In all things to do with Beth, be they physical or emotional, he was hurting his wife and that hurt him.

Perhaps he was beginning to understand what marriage was all about. His Uncle Gerry wasn't married, although last week he'd confided in John that he'd been in love with a girl many years ago. When John had prompted him to tell more he'd hesitated but went on to say that he now had feelings for Mrs Brophy. Gerry had mentioned to John that marriages were a compromise in many things. You couldn't expect your spouse to be *everything* to you, Gerry had told him, or that you had to the perfect person.

John had been surprised by his words, then laughed at himself. He wasn't the perfect man, yet Clarissa loved him and overlooked his faults. So for goodness sake, why couldn't he live with a loving wife who *perhaps* could not give him certain things? In the end, did those things really matter? It was *his* insecurity that was the issue, nothing to do with Clarissa. It was up to him to change, and not just do the things Clarissa mentioned. It also meant cutting ties with Beth altogether.

As he approached his office, his good intentions took a hit; he'd miss the former barmaid and all she was giving him. But he made up his mind nonetheless: he'd cancel their next Tuesday's encounter. That meant he couldn't talk to Beth about perhaps buying her share —but did he really need to do that? Neither Clarissa nor Christine seemed interested in Phoenix Investment Group, so the secret of Beth's ownership need never come up.

Two hours later, John was working in his George Street office and Sean was due to see him.

There was a knock on the door.

'Come in,' John said.

Sean entered and stood in front of John's desk.

'So,' John smiled, 'what's the problem?'

Sean withdrew a paper from his pocket, covered it with his other hand and looked at his boss. 'I'm leaving, John. I'm leaving Leary's.' The relief seemed to slip from Sean's shoulders as if he'd offloaded an eight-by-four beam. 'I want to be a carpenter again. Work with timber. It's what I'm happy doing.'

John was shocked to his boot heels. 'You're leaving?'

'Yes.'

Surely Sean was joking. 'A carpenter . . . but . . .'

'I've got a few years left in me for hard work and I want to make the most of it.'

John pressed his hands down on his desk. 'But why, Sean?'

'It's not sudden, John. I've been thinking about it for some months.'

'Is it money?'

Sean shook his head. 'No, it's not.'

'A carpenter?' John said. 'You're mad. A carpenter. You'll take a big cut in wages and have to be ordered about like a servant. Do you want that?'

Sean smiled.

'It's not funny, Sean,' John said.

Sean put his hand up. 'Oh I know, John, I know. But there it is. It did me proud in the past and it won't be hard, getting into the swing, like.'

John shook his head. 'You're serious, aren't you? But you're a general foreman. You run and train ten other foremen. All the men respect you. Don't I pay you handsomely?'

Sean pocketed his paper and looked out the window and pointed down. 'The Day Street pub where you and me first met and worked. It's still in good shape and I'm proud of it.'

'So am I, Sean.'

'Yeah,' Sean looked at him and continued, 'I remember how my arm moved to the rhythm of the plane as it sculpted the Hunter cedar into architraves and skirting. I'm itching to be back at my trade, just me and the material I'm working, knowing I can again be proud of the things I've built with my own hands.'

That was the longest speech John had ever heard from his partner. And it seemed that Sean wasn't finished.

'John, your view of life saddens me: a life where money means everything. It's not the wages I'm paid that matter, it's being happy in the job. I'm a carpenter. I'm not a boss, nor ever will be.'

'That's daft,' John said, still in a state of shock. 'The pay will be lousy. And another thing,' he said, leaning forward and pointing at Sean, 'won't you feel like you're not fully achieving, working as a tradesman again, rather than running a big team?'

'You miss the point, again,' Sean said. 'I want to get away, to a small company with a gang of blokes and simple tasks to do.'

John sat back, surprised at what he was hearing. 'There's something else; there has to be. I can't believe you'd just walk.' Sean kept John's stare. 'You've given no hint to me that you're unhappy. Are you going to a competitor?'

'I'm not.'

'Are you sure?'

'I just want to leave, John. I've made up my mind and I'll give you a month's notice.'

The man was determined and John's surprise turned to worry.

Sean was needed in the company and his loss would be felt. John would have to get him back, somehow.

'Now,' Sean said, 'I'm going to say something and I want you to listen.'

John smiled and was curious. 'Why? Is it so bad?'

Sean looked at him. 'No, but it'll be hard. I think you need shaking up.'

John tilted his head to one side. Well, it had been an interesting day. *First, Clarissa gives me a serve, now my partner.* 'What do you mean?'

Sean leaned forward. 'You're not the man you were. You've become a man with no conscience and not the person I knew and got to like.' Sean paused as if to consider what to say next. 'You've got everything a man could need and more, and yet you act like you're down to your last copper and drawing your last breath.' Sean ran a hand though his hair. 'God spare me, John, there's no consideration for others and what they've done for you. Your father-in-law, for instance. John, the man had no son. Saints be praised, you coming along gave him the means to at least have a son in his family. Yet you treated him like an associate, not the father of your dear one.'

John was taken aback again. What Sean said was true. John had used David for his own advantage. 'Go on.'

Sean paused, then took courage. 'I'm the only one who can say this to you.'

Yes, John thought, as a Leary's man, he was.

Sean took out his piece of paper again and held it out.

John glanced at it and knew it was Sean's resignation. He took it and said, 'What if I tell you that I've been listening to others? What if they're also telling me to change?'

Sean said nothing.

'And,' John said, 'what would you say if I told you I'm going to have a go at being a better man?'

'It won't change my mind.'

John was irritated now, but kept it in check. It would be best if he at least made Sean aware that he was being genuine. 'I mean it, Sean. I'm going to do it.'

Sean nodded. 'I hope you do, for your sake.'

John placed the resignation on his desk. Something that Clarissa had said resonated. You had to *show* you'd changed. That would take time. 'I think you shouldn't go, but I'll respect your decision.' He felt a sudden fear. 'What about your share of the business? Are you selling that, or what?'

Sean seemed surprised at John's nervousness. 'I'm still your part-ner; I just don't think I can work with you anymore. I might come back,' he added quietly, 'when enough of your friends tell me you've changed for the better.'

Fair enough, John thought. It was something to work on, and Sean would still be earning a dividend from his share in Leary's. He held out his hand and Sean shook it. 'Good luck, mate,' he said. 'My thanks to you for all your efforts over these years.'

Sean paused, then nodded and left.

Brian Atkins pressed his right hand against the side of his bath chair and eased his legs to the left. The sunshine warmed his lower limbs, but otherwise he was shaded on his Annandale veranda.

'Leary doesn't give up, I tell you,' Harry Shelby said. 'He's still poaching my staff and tradesmen.'

'Mine too,' Thomas interjected.

'But he can be stopped,' Shelby continued.

Brian Atkins smiled at Shelby's words. 'He's survived my squeeze on his cash.' The banker Brown had failed him and would now pay a high price. 'But what sort of things has Leary done to both of you?' Atkins had heard the scuttlebutt but wanted these two contractors to spell it out.

'Shelby?' Thomas said inviting his fellow builder to talk.

'Suppliers give Leary's a better deal than us,' Harry Shelby said. 'They see him as a bigger customer, able to buy more from them. Brickworks, iron suppliers, cement manufacturers are all giving Leary better prices.'

'We can't quote the same price to clients on jobs,' Thomas said, 'because we don't get the lower material prices that Leary gets. We'll both go out of business if that continues.'

'What are you going to do to him, then?' Atkins asked.

Shelby smiled this time. 'I'll think of something. Don't worry, Brian. It might be easier to do now that Connaire's going to leave him.'

'I heard that too,' Thomas said. 'Is it true?'

'A man I trust says that he gave his notice last Saturday,' Shelby said. 'Losing a valuable employee and partner like that will damage Leary's.'

'But not fatally,' Bill Thomas said.

'Nobody is invincible, Bill,' Shelby said, 'but I'll admit he's got nine lives and then some.'

'What are we going to do about the bastard, then?' Thomas sniffed as he helped himself to another generous glass of whiskey. 'It wasn't you who paid that labourer, was it, Atkins?'

'Not on your life,' Atkins said. 'Sabotage and murder are not my line.'

Thomas's nose reddened. 'Pity.'

Atkins thanked his own poker face. His colleagues were tough, but even they'd be jolted if they knew he'd sanctioned murder. Yet, he suspected Leary was behind his assault, and that had to be proven. A cab driver waiting for a fare had seen a medium-height man attack him in Macquarie Street that night. Leary was very tall. But Leary could have paid the attacker.

'What are your thoughts, Brian?' Shelby said.

Atkins ached for a drink but the doctors had said alcohol would kill him. Now and again his pain would return like the pain he'd felt in hospital: the pain of the trip hammer again reminding him of his attack. He'd come close to dying, causing him to reflect on his life, and life was precious, bloody precious. He had more than most. But Atkins's hatred of John Leary was still strong; the man had to be put down. So if he couldn't nail him, he'd influence one of these two men here to do so. 'If you two wish to pursue him,' he said, 'good luck. As for me, I'm backing off.'

'What about buying him out?' Shelby said.

'You know that he's not the biggest shareholder?' Atkins said. 'I'm still trying to find out who is. Until I do, Leary stays immune.'

Thomas tried to stand but fell back in his chair. 'So, you've become gutless, have you Atkins?'

'Steady, Bill,' Shelby said. 'There's no need to get personal. Brian's got his views. Leave it at that.'

Thomas put his glass down. 'I'm sorry, Atkins, if I've given offence. But to give up this easily, it's not like you.'

Atkins looked at Thomas. He could wound the man about his drinking but what benefit would that be to anyone? 'Bill, we all have a limit. Leary will get his comeuppance in due course. If it's not from us, it's going to be from someone close to him or someone who hates him.'

'So, you're out of the vendetta?' Shelby questioned him. 'It looks like you are.'

'I am,' Atkins said with conviction.

Thomas nodded and picked up his glass again. 'I think we all are.'

Atkins looked at Shelby, who said nothing. Atkins would bet all his assets that Shelby still had a mind to bring down the biggest contractor in Sydney. Atkins was encouraged by that thought, and who knew, when he was fully recovered, if Shelby failed, he might revisit the problem of the Irishman's demise himself.

The bushman's clock woke Clarissa and she smiled at the kookaburra's raucous call. She breathed in the scents of the lemon gums and acacias wafting through her bedroom window. The space beside her was empty. John was in the Hunter for business and she missed him.

Her good feeling heightened. Since their talk two weeks ago, John had shown signs of his old self and their intimate times had been more loving as well. It was early days but she was encouraged. Throwing off the bedclothes, she donned her dressing gown, went over and opened the French windows and looked out onto the harbour. It was going to be a beautiful day. Over the last week her nausea had subsided and, as it was the end of April, she was reconciled to her pregnancy. After brushing her hair she went downstairs to breakfast, hearing a rattle of crockery outside the dining room.

'No thank you, Stella,' she heard her mother say. 'I won't have a full breakfast this morning.'

Clarissa sighed. She'd forgotten her mother had stayed over the previous night; Christine was frightened living in her own house by herself. Clarissa was sympathetic but hoped that it wouldn't become a habit. Taking a deep breath she entered the dining room. 'Good morning, Mother,' she said, smiling. 'Did you sleep well?'

'I slept tolerably, thank you, and it was better than sleeping in an empty house.'

Addressing herself to the tureens, Clarissa selected two fried eggs and some rashers of bacon and was happy that a full breakfast didn't make her sick any more. Her mother's habit of always eating oatmeal, irrespective of the season, made Clarissa's smile widen. They ate in silence for the next few minutes, the only sounds coming from the kitchen as Cook fought with the saucepans and the crockery. Clarissa looked up as her mother spoke.

'I have to tell you something,' her mother said, 'and it saddens me.' Clarissa put her teacup down and prepared herself for one of her mother's speeches on a moral stance on some issue or another. Her mother continued. 'John hasn't slept here for two nights. Is that right?'

Another opportunity to have a go at him. 'He had business in Morpeth'.

'On both nights?' her mother replied, her voice harsh. She clasped Clarissa's hand, surprising her and said, 'I'm sorry, dear. I really am, because this is going to hurt you.' She took a deep breath. 'I know you won't believe me, but I have it on good authority that John is being unfaithful.'

Clarissa opened and closed her mouth. 'What do you mean?'

Her mother's eyes became moist. 'It's true, dear. I know it's hard for you to accept.'

Clarissa was again surprised at her mother's reaction. This seemed to be painful for her. 'Tell me what you know.'

'To tell you more is going to upset you more.'

'Mother, please!'

'Very well. An eyewitness saw your husband with another woman. Dare I say it, in a semi-intimate embrace in public.'

Clarissa leaned back in her chair. Her heart felt heavy.

'It's shocking news,' her mother said, 'but you have to know. I didn't want you to hear it from anyone else, believe me. I'm reasonably certain that John is having an affair and I know with whom.'

Clarissa's face flamed with anger. 'Who told you this?'

'I cannot divulge that. Suffice to say it was a close friend.'

Clarissa took a reasoned guess. 'Lady Dalkeith, no doubt.'

'It was. Now, it has sickened me to tell you.'

Despite her mother's genuine sorrow, Clarissa was angry. 'You were always against him. You never liked him.'

'Dear, whatever I say now you'll misinterpret, but yes, I've always held that he wasn't for you. But I have respected his hard work and I adore your child. I love Richard and he's part of John. If I really loathed the man, do you think I could love his child, even with you as his mother?' Clarissa's anger ebbed a bit. 'You are hurt and I sympathise. It's up to you, but you need to speak to him about this. Men are led astray. It's their weakness and he still loves you, I'm sure. You cannot divorce him.'

'Do you know this other woman?'

'Talk to John, dear, and get the truth. Please.'

Her mother was prevaricating. Clarissa would talk to him. Was it true? She knew her mother's penchant for gossip and jealousy, but it still might be true. Her mother's anguished look in telling her seemed genuine.

For the first time Clarissa felt threatened. Her confidence was jolted. Was his recent change for the better because he thought he might have been found out? Up to two weeks ago, John's inattention towards her, his behaviour and his attitude had all pointed to something that he was keeping hidden. Was his recent change due to guilt?

Who was this other woman? Her mother knew and Lady

Dalkeith knew. Maybe she should see Lady Dalkeith herself? She was about to confront her mother to demand to know the woman's name, but she hesitated. 'Excuse me,' she said.

Going upstairs she found Richard in his bedroom playing on the floor with his toys. He looked at her as she came beside him and gave her a big smile and grabbed her ankle. Clarissa swooped down and picked him up and held him for precious seconds.

Richard squirmed. A choke escaped her as she put him down and some tears fell on his head as she gave way to her anguish. Yet, there might be hope. It might all be just gossip. But John had to tell her the truth.

Gerry Gleeson was nearing the end of his day. He placed his chisel down and looked at the young men. 'That's it for today,' he said. 'Next week we'll start on keystones.'

Each Thursday Gerry trained a team of stonemasons in the Kent Street quarry. There were now fewer than twenty gun masons in Sydney and most of them worked on the Cut in Argyle Street. Many of the rest thought they knew how to cut stone but didn't. Gerry could count on the fingers of his right hand the men who really knew stone. 'Remember,' he said, 'easy movements. The chisel and the mallet have to work together. Don't let them fight each other. It's the art of the swing and the force. I've told you before, the swing and the force. Feel the stone, lads, don't fight it. It has a life like you do.'

A chuckle broke the silence. Gerry shot the smart apprentice a look and the youngster looked down. The lad was one of his best and if he had a better attitude, he'd be a better mason. 'I want you here at six next week,' he said. A series of groans sparked Gerry up. 'I mean six, not a moment later, and I'll fine anyone who's late. If you want to be good stonemason, then watch me and learn.'

After having a scrub, Gerry mounted the quarry's ramp and headed up Liverpool Street. It was a climb and his tired limbs ached, but when he saw Moira Brophy at Elizabeth Street, he smiled and said, 'There's a sight to gladden a heart. What are you doing here? Hate to think you're standing here just waiting for me to walk you home?'

She smiled and Gerry's heart beat a little faster. 'It's warm for May, isn't it? No, I had to visit a friend, so I took the long way around and hoped to meet you.'

'I'm happy you did, because I've had a big day.'

'Glad that it's over?' she said and smiled again.

'Aye. I've got youngsters who want to be masons overnight. They don't understand it, takes years—'

She put her arm through his. 'Come on. You were young once. Don't take it out on the lads. I bet they respect you and just want to be like you.'

He patted her arm. 'I hope they won't be like me. I think I'm a good mason but whether I'm a good man, that's another thing.'

'You're all right,' she said.

Gerry felt content. These last months had been good, better than all the years before. He'd been wondering where life would take him after his years as a convict. Yes, there'd been women, but that was long ago and he'd just about given up on meeting someone special again, but Moira fitted the bill. They were seeing each other often, including Mass each Sunday, and she wouldn't take any lip from him and he respected her for that. She knew about his past and he had left nothing out. It'd taken weeks to be able to call her by her first name and late last month he plucked up the courage to kiss her. When he had, he felt it was the most natural thing.

Moira stepped around a pile of fresh manure. 'How long will it take to train the lads?'

'It depends. They've got different standards of skills, they have. Some are nearly there and could work well by themselves. Others are still green. And there's one or two who aren't much chop.'

She nodded. 'But you enjoy it, don't you? Training them, giving them hints and such?'

They were nearly at her house. 'I do.'

'Speaking of building,' she said. 'Leary's Contracting is starting the big warehouse in Kent Street.'

'I know.' The site was just down from the quarry he'd left. The Learys had been at Mass at St Patrick's Church Hill only three weeks ago and from their manner there seemed more affection between John and Clarissa. Gerry was glad.

Moira stopped outside her house. 'Will you come in for a sherry, Gerry? That sounds funny doesn't it?'

'Don't be cheeky. Yes, I will, thank you, dear. Just a quick one.'

Following her inside he thought about the relaxing time he'd have for the next half an hour or so in the company of someone of whom he was becoming increasingly fond.

In the McGuire Wire Darling Harbour yard, Jack Johnson made way as two Leary's labourers took away the empty hogshead and replaced it with a fresh one, the third for the afternoon. John Leary knew how to celebrate. There must be one hundred and fifty workers enjoying themselves, and Jack wasn't surprised. The Kent Street warehouse contract they'd won had plenty of profit in it. Clients were now coming to Leary's to quote, accepting its price because Leary's was the best and the biggest, with ten projects under way, including three massive warehouses.

Labourers mixed with tradesmen, always with good banter, as both competed to see who contributed more to a job's success. It was almost four-thirty and the mid-May sunshine partnered with the grog to get the young ones drunker and the old hands adding more glory to their site stories. Frank Cartwright, Dan Reynolds and Sean stood in their midst, taking in all the fun, and yet Jack felt none of it.

Jack Johnson had waited long enough after confiding Sean, and would now definitely leave Leary's. A meeting with a naval friend, now a post captain on one of Her Majesty's ships, had led Jack to a job on offer in the merchant marine. It was his for the asking, his friend had told him.

It was fate. The timing of the offer to go back to sea coincided with his disillusionment with his boss. Jack liked the industry and its people and he'd miss it. But he wouldn't miss John Leary. And yet last week when John had spoken to him he had at least been polite. Jack was surprised but considered it a one-off.

Sean sidled up to him. 'Fine party, Jack. When are the big nobs due?'

Jack noticed Sean's glass of lemonade. It must be hard for him with all this grog around. The rumours had circulated about Sean's struggle with drink but the man had it under control, it seemed. 'It's a good party. The clients are here already with the boss,' Jack pointed to the upstairs office. 'That's where you'll find the fancy wines and the good tucker.'

'Aye, couldn't have them mixing with the rabble, could we?'

Jack and Sean moved to a quieter corner. Jack spotted John and was surprised to see him close the office door and head down the stairs.

'Here's the man now,' Sean said as he noticed John. 'He's not happy with me leavin', no he's not.'

Jack wasn't sure why Sean was leaving, but it had disturbed him. The Leary's partners went back some years and he wondered if they'd had a falling out. He decided to prod. 'Why are you leaving? If you don't mind my asking.'

'Don't mind at all. It's a bit like yourself—the boss. These past months, I've tried to figure him out but I come up with a blank. Put up with it for as long as I can but it'd gone beyond the pale.'

'You didn't change him?'

Sean hesitated. 'I thought I hadn't. But on the day I resigned, John told me he'd try to be better.'

'And you believed him?'

'Well, we've spoken four times since then and he's been all right.'

'It won't last, Sean,' Jack said.

'Maybe, Jack, maybe not. Next week, I'll be back as a carpenter, taking a cut in wages. Vonnie's all square with it and, to use her words, there's more to life than money.'

Jack studied him. It wouldn't have been easy to leave his friend and a high-earning, respected job.

As if reading his thoughts Sean said, 'Don't get me wrong. I'll see him from time to time. That's what mates are for, right? You don't throw somebody aside just because he's going through a rough trot.'

'No, you don't. That's honourable, Sean.'

Ten feet away, John was in his element, patting the workers' backs and laughing at the odd comment. Jack wasn't jealous. John deserved admiration for his hard work.

Their boss moved closer to them and said to Jack, 'Mr Clancy wants to know when to expect that sand and cement I promised him. He should've had it last week.'

Not paid for, I'll bet, Jack thought. 'Should be there in a day or so.' He had forgotten the Council man's order.

'Make it happen, Jack,' John said. 'Clancy will pay for it, don't worry.'

Jack didn't believe him and decided to blow John out of the water. 'Sean and I were just chewing the fat, but coincidences happen, and Sean's not the only one to leave. I'll be close on his heels.'

John's eyes closed as if trying to avoid a glaring reflection. 'What's that?' he said. Sean seemed just as surprised.

'I said, I'm giving notice,' Jack said. 'A month's notice, then I'm gone. Be out of here by the twelfth of June.'

John stood back to let a couple of drunken labourers pass, but kept his eyes on Jack. His face was shocked. 'You picked a good time. When did all this come about?'

Jack held his glass behind him and stood as if on parade before the Admiral. 'When is the best time to tell your employer you're leaving him? If you're in your office tomorrow morning—'

'Is tomorrow morning going to be different from now? Anything to add?'

Jack saw an argument brewing and kicked himself. Frustration had made him tell John now, but he didn't care.

'Sean?' John asked.

'It's news to me too, John.'

'The building industry isn't for me, John,' Jack said. 'I've got an offer as a first mate on a steam clipper, and I'm going to take it.

Nothing against you personally, mind. Just the sea's tempting me back.'

John pursed his lips. 'Whoa, that's a big call. Is that final?'

'It is.'

John shot his hand out. 'Then I'm the first to wish you well.'

Jack took the proffered hand with mixed feelings. It might be a cynical gesture but John's face had an honest look that Jack hadn't seen for a long time.

'Thank you, John. Sean and I will sail different courses,' Jack continued. 'There are enough young guns here to take our place.'

John shook his head. 'There are, but it's not the same as having seasoned veterans.' He sighed, 'All the best then. Now, if you two will excuse me, I've got clients to host.'

'Polite isn't he?' Jack said as his boss moved away.

'He took it well,' Sean said. 'Better than I thought. He'll miss your contribution, Jack.'

'Yes, well. That's as maybe.' He turned to Sean. 'I'll be going now. See you tomorrow.'

Sean nodded and moved on to another group of celebrating workers.

Disappointed, John ploughed back through the happy drinkers and, with a forced smile, accepted their beery congratulations. Jack's departure would leave a huge hole in Leary's procurement functions and he'd have to scramble to fill it. He'd deal with that tomorrow—now he returned to the upstairs office to manage his guests. His best wines would have mellowed his clients by now, but he must be sober enough to act as the humble contractor among the men who had the money. It took twenty minutes to get through the throng of workers who wouldn't let him go, but at last he opened the office door and closed it to the noise outside.

Here he was back in the world of cigars and champagne. Ruddy-faced merchants, businessmen, bankers and members of the colonial bourgeoisie all pressed his aching hand, congratulating him on winning his most prestigious project to date. They knew he was one of them now.

Power. It was an incredible feeling. Men wanted to talk to him, wanted to slap his back and give him champagne, only because John knew they were in a club—the club of the wealthy, to which admittance was high and John had paid his dues.

He'd achieved success at an early age. This is what he'd planned for over the last year and it was almost with disbelief that he had realised his dream in a short time. He looked around at his clients: all intimate associates of the group who controlled Sydney society. If he wanted anything, in any field, for any reason, within these confines now he could get it with a word here or a request there. Nothing would be withheld from him.

He viewed his guests. There was Blunt, who'd given him his first tender after the sabotage, Clancy from the Council, Alan Wallace and six other clients—but no Atkins. The bastard still lived and John was going to front him. And Shelby and Thomas were still circling. Wexton had told him of their April meeting at Atkins's house.

John confronted Clancy. 'Your goods,' he smiled at the council man, 'will be there in two days. Prompt payment would be appreciated.'

Clancy gave a forced smile and John sensed the Council man thought he'd get a present. Not this time. 'Thank you, Mr Leary,' he said.

John nodded and moved on. If you strove to get to the top, you had to walk over somebody or bribe somebody—it didn't matter who it was—to get what you wanted. John was satisfied that he'd done right to get here, tonight. But this was where all that would stop. No free goods from now on, and all things above board.

For some reason he thought about Clarissa and a shadow clouded his conscience. He loved her but he'd weakened. After their April understanding, he'd wanted to end it with Beth and had cancelled their next scheduled Tuesday rendezvous. The Tuesday following that, Beth had cancelled and John understood that it was that time of the month for her. However, last Tuesday he'd succumbed and made love to her. That night he'd been sleepless with guilt. And today the party had been his excuse not to see her. But what of the future? He would have to end it, and soon.

John felt a hand take his and he shook it, looking into the bright eyes of a client who was telling him in detail about his future plans for a new housing development that he wanted John to build. It was getting easier and easier to pick up the sort of work where profits were high and risk low.

~

Clarissa entered her drawing room in Point Piper. 'Hello, Mother. Stella said you needed something from me?'

'Good afternoon, dear. I've come to collect those new deeds to this house that I gave you to sign. You remember we talked about them last Sunday at dinner?'

Clarissa was so skinny that her shoulder bones showed through her dress, and Christine wondered if she was eating correctly. It was worrying. Her face was thin, her cheeks had lost their plumpness and there were lines under her eyes. 'Dear, have you spoken to John about . . . about, you know?'

'Mother, I said I'd talk to him. Don't harass me. I feel that the whole thing is just gossip.'

Christine was going to fire back but her daughter's worried look and lack of vitality curbed her tongue. 'Very well, but I must say that these last few weeks, dare I say months, you haven't been looking yourself. How is your diet? Has the doctor prescribed a tonic?'

'I'm eating normally, Mother. My nausea has passed.' She looked at herself in the mirror over the fireplace. 'But I agree with you that I've lost weight.'

'What does the doctor think?'

'He says I'm probably run down. What with father's passing and other things . . .'

'Well, you know my attitude towards your work. You should leave and have a complete rest.' She placed her hand on her daughter's arm. 'Please consider that and please talk to John, soon.'

'I'll think about it. Lately I've been feeling more tired than usual and perhaps a break from work may do me some good.'

Christine felt relief. 'Precisely. Anyway, if you give me those papers now, I'll leave you.'

Clarissa went and opened the bureau drawer and paused. 'Oh, I've left them at the office. I'll get them tomorrow, sign them and give them to Mr Wilson.'

'Good, dear.' Christine took hold of her hands. 'Please think about not working, just for a while.'

'I shall, Mother. I shall.'

Rain pattered down and the May sky was grey from Dawes Point to the South Head Toll Road. Brian Atkins pressed his boots against the wall of the carriage as it stopped at his house; the resultant compression in his calves and thighs pushed pain to his left side, a reminder of what he'd been through. Sometimes the pain would go away for days, then the trip hammer would again visit.

He'd had no second thoughts about ending his vendetta against John Leary, certain that Shelby would make a move for him. And he felt better after he'd paid the fee, in crisp bank notes, that morning to the man who'd taken care of the labourer. Miller was no more and nobody had suspected a prison officer of foul play. Also, wheels were in motion to bring a banker down.

The door opened and he leaned on his driver's arm for support. A cheeky raindrop found the gap between his shirt and neck and he shivered, bringing back the pain and making him feel ten years older. His servant Albert, a bull of a man, nodded to him and helped him inside the house.

Gerry Gleeson wiped his brow, scratched his stomach and looked down with pride as an unused belt hole accepted the tension of his slimmer self. That was Moira's doing. She had him eating well. The Skinners Hotel sign welcomed him and he congratulated himself that he'd cut back on his drinking as well.

He went inside and squinted in the dim interior. It was just after three in the afternoon and there weren't many drinkers. He was early to meet Rupert Jenkins and his mate wasn't there, but Bob Jones was. He joined the bricklayer foreman, who had his elbow propped on the bar. 'Can I buy you a beer?' Gerry said.

'You can.'

Gerry did the honours. 'How's it going?'

Jones's face was expressionless. 'Been busy. You?'

'The same. I see our friend Atkins is out and about again.'

Jones scowled. 'The bastard survived.'

'It takes a lot to kill evil, Bob.'

'I know.' Bob took a drink and looked at Gerry. 'I didn't do the job right.'

'What job?'

'Atkins. It was me who knifed him. I had to have a go. Those three men deserved that.'

Gerry was shocked, but understood. On the road gangs, he'd seen life in all its horrors. But attempted murder was a big crime and Jones was a good man. Guilt must be riding him hard and Gerry wouldn't judge him.

'The bastard's guilty as sin and he's got away.' Jones exhaled. 'But I can live with trying to kill him, I think.'

'He'll get his,' Gerry said. 'I'm going to try to get Colleen to tell the truth. It's the only thing we have left.'

'Can I join you fellas?' Rupert Jenkins interrupted them. 'What'll you have?'

'I have to get home, Mr Jenkins, sorry,' Jones said and drank the rest of his beer. 'Another time.' He nodded to them and left.

'Was it something I said?' Jenkins asked as he watched the man leave.

Gerry would keep the confession to himself. 'Maybe,' he said, smiling. 'It's my shout. Go and grab a table.'

'Looks like you've lost weight! You're running around more or just drinking less?'

'Just go and sit down.'

Gerry got the beers, returned and planted his posterior on a chair opposite his friend. 'What you see is because of good living. I've found myself a decent lady who's looking after me and we're walking out together.'

Jenkins winked. 'Knew it would happen sooner or later. I bet she's a fine woman.'

'One of the best. As a matter of fact I'm going to ask her to marry me and I'd like you to be best man.'

Jenkins stopped drinking and looked at him. 'Me? Me, be your best man?'

'And why not? I'm planning to pop the question to Moira this Saturday. I'm going to take her for a night out and I wanted to know if you could do me the honour before I asked the question.'

'The answer is simple, my friend. I'd be proud to.' Gerry nodded and looked at his grinning mate. It was good to have friends like this and it was grand he was marrying Moira. 'Where are ya getting married?' Jenkins asked.

'Dunno, but I think St Patrick's would be the best shot. I know the priest there and I think he'd be happy to do the job.'

'Here, *you* sit down,' Jenkins said. 'I'm going to get the best bottle Skinners can supply and we'll get drunk together.'

His mate returned with a bottle of Jameson's and poured Gerry a generous glassful. 'Well here's to you and your intended.'

Gerry tipped his glass against his friend's. 'Thanks. Now, how have things been with you?'

Jenkins swallowed the whiskey, followed it with a swig of beer, wiped his mouth and sighed. 'A fine drop Gerry, a fine drop.'

'Too true, too true.'

'Life's quieter,' Jenkins said. 'I've got a few things to do around the house and have my capital invested. I can live comfortably. But I can't keep away from the building game, you know, and you'll find me wandering the streets looking at new construction.'

'Glutton for punishment?' Gerry smiled.

'Something like that. And all I seem to find is Leary's Contracting signs. Warehouses in Kent Street and one in Chippendale, stores buildings in Sussex Street and one in Sydenham.'

'Terraces in Darlinghurst,' Gerry chimed in.

'That's just half of them. You'd think he's the only contractor in Sydney, building the whole flaming lot himself. Everything he touches turns to gold.'

Gerry took another sip. Yes, he'd heard about the same sites his mate had seen. 'I haven't seen him much lately. Have you?'

'At Mass some weeks ago with his missus. Gerry, she seems poorly. Have you noticed?'

'I have.'

'Look, we've got three-quarters of this 1850 bottle to knock over. If you don't stop yakking and start drinking, we'll be here all night.'

Gerry smiled as Jenkins poured another dash of the Irish. It was going to be a long night but one didn't get engaged every day.

It was Saturday afternoon in the third week of May. Beth was away on some charity function and Henry Blackett was sitting under a banksia tree in his garden, sipping his drink. The gossip mill was grinding. From two people, he'd heard that Beth was being unfaithful. From the first rumour, he'd felt as if steel bands were being wrapped around him, squeezing the life from him.

A man was due soon who'd be able to prove or disprove the accusation. Blackett had hired a private investigator and it had taken time to find the right man. Several names had come into contention and the one he wanted had been too busy. He'd chosen the second-best.

His manservant walked out to him, his shoes crushing the fallen leaves. 'Excuse me, sir, there's a gentleman to see you. He said his name is Smith. Shall I bring him out here?'

Smith was the name the investigator had agreed to use. 'Please,' Blackett replied.

'Very good, sir.'

Blackett's doctor had told him he had to cut back on his drinking, as he was ruining his health with his overindulgence. To add to this, Beth and he hadn't been friendly for many months and they had shared the bedroom even less. He had to find out who his wife's lover was and then deal with him. His gut told him it was Leary. But he wanted proof.

'Mr Smith, sir,' his servant said, as he brought the man over to Blackett.

Blackett stood up and faced a heavyset man who had to duck under the canopy of the six-foot-high banksia. His visitor wore a simple jacket, white shirt and tailored trousers. Smith didn't smile as Blackett's servant placed a glass of water on the table.

'Mr Smith, won't you sit down?'

'Thank you, Mr Blackett,' Smith said, taking a seat at the table.

Blackett pushed the glass of water towards him. 'I like the late autumn freshness, but we can conduct our business inside if
you'd prefer.'

'Here is acceptable, thank you.'

Blackett sat down. 'As I said in my letter, I wish you to follow my wife in her daily activities and find out what she does and where she goes.' Blackett felt the steel bands returning. 'I believe she's being unfaithful and I want to know where this is taking place and with whom.'

Smith nodded. 'That's a straightforward job, Mr Blackett. I'll give you what you want.'

It was odd how easy a stranger accepted his wife's infidelity and Blackett felt sad. Their marriage was a shambles but now this man knew about it, making it embarrassing. He had a thought. Gossip travelled fast and Blackett might be the only one who *didn't* know. 'I want results soon,' he said. 'Within a fortnight. I am presuming my wife's activities are obvious and her lover should be able to be found quickly. Are there any questions?'

Smith took a drink and wiped his mouth. 'I've taken the liberty of getting your wife's appearance. When do you want me to start?'

'As soon as you finish your drink.'

Mr Smith nodded, drained his glass and stood up. 'I'll see you in a fortnight, Mr Blackett.'

After Smith had left, Blackett sat back and thought. Beth would stay with him even if he had to lock her in a room for the rest of her life. A wife's role was to please the man and to provide him with children. Anything else was just fruit on the sideboard. But that was the issue. Beth had not fallen pregnant. She mightn't be able to have children. If that was the case, forget about locking her up, he'd divorce her for her infidelity.

But she had an attraction that he couldn't live without and if another man was servicing her . . . Standing up he grabbed a branch and snapped it in two, the sharp ends jagging him. Nothing like the pain he'd give Beth's lover. Horses and business were his world. Did this man move in his wife's circles? Was it a man he knew? It *was* bloody Leary. He was certain.

Blackett walked back into his house and he ticked off other businessmen who knew Beth. No, let Smith work that out. Why bark when you could buy a dog?

He smiled. He would enjoy confronting Beth with her infidelity. He'd enjoy breaking her stallion even more.

~

On a Tuesday afternoon in late May, Beth opened the door to their Elizabeth Street rooms to John, who went inside. She closed the door after him.

'Hello,' she smiled.

'Hello, yourself,' he said.

She kissed him and he took her hand and went into the bedroom with her. She held him and whispered to him, 'We can't make love today, sorry.' She smiled and ran a hand down his thigh, 'But I can make love to you.'

John took her hand and led her to the bed, which was banded in sunlight. 'Let's just hold each other for a while,' he said.

She nodded, bemused and lay down. He took off his jacket and joined her. He bent and kissed her and she moved, sighed and lay still. Lying back, he looked at the ceiling. It needed a coat of paint but that wouldn't matter now because he'd decided to cancel the lease of these rooms. He would end it with Beth, and soon.

She stirred next to him. 'Penny for your thoughts?'

'It's about us.'

Her mouth firmed in a straight line. 'What about us?'

'Us. Here, doing this,' he said.

She turned on her side and leaned on her elbow. 'You've been strange, my darling. I can't place it but these last five weeks you seem different.'

He knew why and couldn't lie to her. 'We've only been together twice in that time.'

'I know. I sense a change in you.' She ran a finger down his cheek. 'One that worries me.'

'I think what we're doing is dishonest,' he said. 'Not in the normal way, but it's dishonest to us.'

'Dishonest?'

'You know. Snatching small pieces of a life that have no links with anything and can never have.'

'Why? Don't you want me? Isn't what we have special?'

'It is. And yet you must admit that it's false.'

'But that's *all* we have, John. I love these snatches as you call them. They're as honest as I know. But you feel different. Tell me.'

She seemed to really want to know, so he told her. 'You've made me the person I am, in these rooms. It's like another world, a world where I find peace. But it's like a fantasy.'

Beth sat up. 'What is this all about?' He was going to reply but she put her hand up. 'I have little excitement outside of here, John, other than my horses. I love my mother and my sisters, but you're the core of my life.' She ruffled his hair and he reached for her but she held his hand. 'John ... the core. I want this,' she gestured around, 'but I feel you don't.' Her face was serious. 'You're getting tired of this? Is this an excuse to end this?'

He sat up and held her hands. 'If it wasn't for you,' he said, 'I think I would've gone mad these last months, not having anyone to talk to about what really troubles me.' He didn't want to end it and yet he knew he had to. Here was a fantasy, a vibrant sexual thing, but still a fantasy. He let go her hands and said, 'But I owe it to Clarissa to end this.'

Beth's eyes widened. 'You want to stop seeing me?'

He weakened. 'Not yet.'

'But soon, yes,' she said, her eyes smarting.

He kept silent.

'I love you, John. I love being with you for any time you care to name, whether it's two minutes, an hour or a day. Time has no measure when I'm with you.'

John conceded that point and felt the same.

'Maybe you're thinking too hard,' she said getting up and standing by the bed. 'Maybe it's the business at the moment. I don't know. Or maybe it's just you want to be away from me for a while.' She looked down and when she looked at him again there was a hardness in her eyes. 'I don't want to be separated from you. But I feel you want to and, darling, if it helps you, I can accept a separation in the end.' She looked away.

She didn't mention her share in Leary's. She had acquired it to help him, because she loved him, and that love of hers eclipsed everything else. She wouldn't put him under an obligation about it —she was too unselfish in her love.

He still wanted her so, and yet Clarissa appeared in his thoughts, pregnant and offering herself to him in the full knowledge that she loved him. Then a different Clarissa appeared, the thin stranger this morning when he'd left for work, and he felt guilty. He got up from the bed and put his jacket on.

Beth's worried eyes looked at him. 'You were thinking of her, weren't you?'

John looked at the autumn sun casting shadows over the walls of the adjoining terraces. That vision saved him the embarrassment of acknowledging her suspicion. Beth walked to the door, grasped the handle, and turned to him. 'Will I see you next week?'

John nodded, but knew he'd find some excuse not to see her. Christ, he was weak. He should end it now and leave for good. But he couldn't, not yet. 'You'll see me next week,' he lied.

'Until then, won't you kiss me?'

Just as she'd finished speaking he took her into his arms and found her willing lips. He broke away and went out the door.

~

Harry Shelby sat waiting in a cab in Sussex Street at six-thirty in the morning. Opposite, and just ahead of him, was Leary's site, which was hoarded up at ground level with freshly painted plywood. An access door in the wall was prominent. There were few people around.

Shelby smiled. It was late May but there was enough light to see John Leary crossing King Street and walking towards his site. The wagon. Where was it? It should be here any moment. Its driver had been well paid. Leary would be taken care of and if that driver got caught, Shelby would be in the clear. It would be Atkins who would be charged. It was a small risk and one worth taking. Unknown to Atkins, all communication with the driver had been by letter, written by Shelby and signed by him as Brian Atkins. He thought of Atkins and how that labourer had accused him of the Clarence Street murders. Was Atkins guilty of that? Shelby didn't think so. The man was no criminal. Still, there was mud slung and look at the mess now circling Atkins. Shelby had a thought that what he was doing was bad too, and against all his Masonic doctrine. It was, but Leary might get lucky, he might just be injured and that was all right too. The bastard needed a lesson.

The big man himself was right on time for his regular Wednesday morning site meeting and was walking near to the hoarding. Then the wagon appeared, fully loaded and travelling fast. Shelby alighted from the cab, paid the cab driver, then slipped into a side lane. The wagon rumbled closer to the footpath and mounted it just before the site. Leary, walking right alongside his site, looked around in alarm as the wagon careered closer to the hoarding and cannoned into it. There was a mighty crash. Leary was gone, cleaned up. The wagon driver pulled up, jumped down and fled the scene.

Harry Shelby walked off with a smile and turned up into Erskine Street.

CHAPTER NINE

JOHN LEARY HAD HEARD THE WAGON AND SPUN AROUND. IT WAS aiming straight for him. He had no time to reach the site access door before he'd be crushed to death. Clasping both hands together, he pounded on the plywood panels in the space between the nails, once then twice. It gave way and he fell inwards, rolling in the dirt just as the wagon crashed into the hoarding. The impact splintered the sheeting, but fortunately the framing held. A startled carpenter on site stared at John as he struggled to his feet, his left hand dripping blood. Using his good hand, John reached for the access gate, pulled it open and saw the driver race down the street.

The carpenter ran up to him. 'Bloody hell,' he said, looking at John. 'You're bloody bleeding, boss.'

'I'll live,' John said. He removed his handkerchief and wrapped it around his hand. 'Get this hoarding repaired now and remove that wagon.'

'Right. But let's get you fixed up first.'

John thanked his luck. Coldness settled in him and he began to shake. Glancing back at the damage he realised that death had been close. It might have been an accident but that driver fleeing the scene made it suspicious.

Atkins again? Probably, and this time he'd fix the bastard.

~

The newspaper print glared back at Gerry Gleeson and he knocked his beer over. He grabbed the glass from falling to the floor and stared at the paper. James Miller had died in prison in April and here it was 4 June, and the prison superintendent had decided not to hold an investigation. Gerry thumped the table, startling two of Skinners' nearby patrons. Accident, be damned. Atkins had got to the man. There was no doubt about it.

'There's a mess you've made, Gerry,' Doreen said. 'Lift the paper up, and I'll clean up. There's a love.'

'Miller's dead and that's the end of it.'

'What's that, Gerry?' she said.

'I said, Miller died in prison, and I'll bet my boots that Atkins got to him.'

Doreen paused with the cloth and her shoulders sagged. 'That means the toff will get off, won't he?'

'He's free now, love and he's going to stay that way.' It was a pity Bob Jones had missed with that knife. Gerry chastised himself for that thought but at least there would've been justice. 'Tell me,' he said, 'how's Colleen these days?'

'Don't see much of her,' Doreen said as she straightened up. 'Ouch, my back. I have to give this game away. She's been frightened, Gerry, you know.'

'What about?'

Doreen glanced behind her. 'I have to get back to the bar. Why don't you go to the Hero and talk to her? She's not been the same since she changed her story.'

'I dunno why she did. She was dead certain it was Atkins that night. He stood two feet in front of her speaking with Miller.'

'Maybe you should see her again.' Doreen seemed evasive.

'You don't believe her changed story, do you?'

'Just see her, Gerry and talk to her. I ain't saying nothing more.'

'I'll pay her a visit,' he said as Doreen scurried back to the bar.

Colleen might be frightened, but she had to speak to the police. He bet London to a brick that Atkins would make sure there was no prison inquiry, and without Colleen to nail him, Atkins would be a free man—for good.

~

Samuel Smith watched as the door closed and he concentrated on the person leaving the terrace. He recognised the woman and checked the time on his watch. Yes, two hours as usual. From across Elizabeth Street he watched Mrs Blackett shut the front gate and turn to hail a cab.

Over the last two and a half weeks he had trailed her movements from when she left home in the morning to her various activities. She kept to duties consistent with horse breaking and Smith hadn't been optimistic about discovering her infidelity. He'd notified Blackett that he needed more time, which Blackett had agreed to. Smith had been to Randwick and the stable hands had told him who'd come and gone. There was nothing unusual in Blackett's visiting her friends. Today, 9 June, was the same. The last two Tuesdays she'd come here and she was here again at the same time. And last week there had been no sign of a man.

Smith waited until Mrs Blackett's cab passed him. Today, he might get lucky and find the mystery lover. The hotel where he'd waited last week was nearby and he went in, ordered a beer and camped by its window, not taking his eyes off the terrace house.

Halfway through his second beer, a big-framed youngish man exited the same terrace's front door. Smith put his drink down and went to the window to get a better view. The man, over six feet tall and probably in his late twenties, and with a bandaged hand, went to a horse, got on and rode away. Smith left the pub and followed on his own horse at a discreet distance.

Along Elizabeth Street, in the northwesterly wind, Smith kept about fifty yards between himself and his quarry. He found this part easy—there was enough pedestrian and horse-drawn traffic at that time not to make him stand out. When the young man got to Market Street, he turned left and Smith, delayed by a heavy wagon, stretched his neck to keep his target in sight. When the wagon passed he continued the pursuit.

The man turned right into George Street as far as King Street and stopped. Smith dismounted some way short and waited till his man disappeared into a building near the corner of King Street. Smith crossed to the opposite side of the street and looked at the building with its sign 'Leary's Contracting'. Well, he was in there and Smith wanted to find out more.

Smith decided on the simplest approach. Going inside, he went to the counter where a clerk was scribbling a list of figures. 'Excuse me, I want to build a house and wondered if I could speak to someone. This is a builder's office, I take it?'

The clerk looked up and smiled. 'It is. A new house, eh?'

'The best,' Smith said, leaning over the counter. 'I've sold some nuggets and I want to get cracking.'

'Your name sir, please?'

'Samuel Smith.'

'You might be lucky, Mr Smith; the owner of the business has just come in and I'll see if he can see you now. I can't promise anything but you're a customer and they're always important.'

'That's a good attitude. Keep that up and you'll reap rewards. But, did you say that the proprietor just came in here? Because I think he passed me in the street just now. His hand was bandaged?'

The clerk smiled. 'That was Mr John Leary of Leary's Contracting and if you wish to wait a few minutes, Mr Leary may see

you now.'

Smith was satisfied that Leary was the man in the terrace and likely to be Mrs Blackett's lover. Extracting a business card with a false address from his waistcoat, he gave it to the clerk. 'It's not necessary to disturb Mr Leary now, my friend, just give him this. I would be grateful if he could contact me by correspondence at the earliest opportunity.'

The clerk looked surprised. 'But sir, you can still see him if you wish.'

'Please, just give him my card and he can write to me. Again, thank you for your time, and I wish you success in the future,' Smith said, before turning and leaving the office.

He rode back to the Elizabeth Street terrace, dismounted at the hotel and purchased the best bottle of whiskey they had. The publican had told him last week the name of the landlady who looked after the lovers' terrace house and said that she was fond of a drop. Clasping his present, he crossed the road and knocked on the door of her basement room.

'Who is it?' a raspy sounding voice answered. 'If you're selling anything I'm not interested.'

Smith knocked again and the door opened a crack. A woman of perhaps fifty years of age with sunken eyes and a drunkard's breath greeted him.

'What do you want?' she asked.

'My name is Smith, Mrs Harrington, and I want information. I'm prepared to make it worth your while.'

The landlady looked him up and down and let him in. Mrs Harrington looked at the bottle wrapped in brown paper. 'What do you want to know?'

'It's about your tenants,' he said. 'In particular a young man and the young woman whom he entertains on a regular basis.'

'Are you the law? If you are, you can go now. I don't trust coppers and all.'

'I'm not the law. Tell me about the young couple.'

Mrs Harrington shuffled over to a well-worn armchair and sat down. Every window was closed in the stuffy room. 'You seem to know about them already. Hee, hee, love birds I tell you. That's what they are and they're both married, I'll lay odds on that. The way they carry on.' She turned red as she looked down, and stammered, 'The noises they make, every Tuesday.' She giggled at her own words.

Smith unwrapped the whiskey and her eyes rounded at the label.

'This is for you, Mrs Harrington,' he said, 'if you tell me the names of the couple.'

'Well you didn't hear it from me mister, but the man's named John Leary, and I think the filly's called Beth.'

Smith clenched his fist in his pocket. He'd got them. How arrogant of Leary to use his own name in leasing these rooms. Smith put the whiskey on a nearby counter and bowed to the woman. 'I bid you good day, Mrs Harrington. You'll hear no more from me. Enjoy your drink.'

As he closed the door, he heard the landlady cackle, 'The noises they make, my, my.'

Smith rode back to his rooms, drafting in his mind the letter he'd write to Mr Blackett.

The northwesterly wind peppered John's skin with dust as he rode towards home later that same Tuesday afternoon. Passing Wool-loomooloo, he thought about Beth. It had been a fortnight since they'd met, as he'd cancelled their 2 June rendezvous.

Beth had wanted to know all about his damaged hand. He'd told her it had happened on site and because of it he couldn't make love to her. That might have been for the best, because she was cool towards him—polite, yes, but different. Perhaps, he thought, she was preparing for his leaving her and that was good in a way. It made his decision easier. Now he had to act on it. But it was hard; he still wanted to be with her. They'd talked about small things and then he'd left. He hadn't mentioned his idea of buying Beth out of Leary's, because that would have felt too final.

Since promising Clarissa that he would change, he'd only made love to Beth on two occasions, but he was still being unfaithful. The wind picked up and the tendons in his bandaged hand strained to keep his horse's head straight. He jerked the reins to avoid a large pothole and the horse bucked in frustration.

A cab waiting outside his Point Piper house made him curious. He put the colt in the stable, went through the hall and heard a cry from his son, Richard. As he climbed the stairs he heard another, even louder. He entered his son's room. Clarissa stood there, holding Richard against her neck. The boy's face was scrunched up in pain and Clarissa looked worried. 'What's the matter?' he said.

She turned to him. 'He's been like this all day, dear. The doctor's called and says that he's got a shocking temperature, likely from influenza. He won't stop crying.'

'Hello, John.' His sister Maureen came into the room, carrying a towel and a water jug.

'Hello, Maureen!' John said.

'I was visiting, and decided to stay to help Clarissa. Your boy's got a bad fever and has to be cooled down.' Maureen filled the bowl from the jug and Richard's hand gripped Clarissa's shoulder. John felt his son's flushed cheek.

'You're home early,' Clarissa said, putting Richard down. He started crying again. She sighed and picked him up again. 'Are things quiet at the office?'

John took off his jacket and placed it on the end of Richard's bed. 'They are. Here, let me take him for a while.'

Clarissa tilted her head and half smiled. 'Gladly.'

Richard felt like a bag of hot embers. 'He's burning up!' John said.

'I need to go downstairs and get a hot lemon drink,' Clarissa said.

'Stella can bring that up,' Maureen said.

'No, I want to see that the mixture's right. I shan't be long.'

Maureen straightened the bed, plumped up the pillow and placed a fresh slip on it. 'So, how have you been? It's nearly the middle of June and it's been a long time since we had a visit.'

'I've been busy,' John replied. Richard settled and quietened in his arms. Whether it was John's size or the boy was too tired, John didn't care; he just enjoyed holding him. He paced with him up and down. Maureen went to the window and opened the fanlight, which fluttered the curtains and cleared some of the stuffiness from the room. John believed any breeze was good, harking back to the between decks of the *Emily* on his voyage to New South Wales. 'How are Liam, Michael and Irene?'

'We're all well but Clarissa isn't, and she's not talking about it. Do you know anything?'

'Anything about what?' Clarissa said, coming back in the room carrying a steaming glass.

'Liam and I are concerned about you.'

Clarissa put the glass down and took hold of Richard. Maureen blew on the liquid and spooned some into his mouth but Richard pushed it away and howled. But he soon settled. 'I'm all right, Maureen,' she said. 'I just feel a bit run down. A few weeks of good rest and good food will set me right, don't you worry.'

With her head tilted and an eyebrow raised, Maureen looked unconvinced. 'Well, at least your time at McGuire has ended. That should make a difference.'

'It has.'

Maureen looked at her sister-in-law with concern. 'So you say. I want to make sure you don't wear yourself out here.'

'Don't fret, Maureen,' John said. 'And thank you.'

'Very well. Do you think that cab's here yet?'

'There's one outside, waiting,' John said.

'Then I'll go. I want to be home before Liam.'

Clarissa sat Richard on her hip. 'John, could you give me that medicine bottle? I find it soothes him. He's about due for some.'

John got the medicine, then turned to his sister, 'Goodbye, Maureen. Please let us know when we can come and visit.'

'You're welcome any time. You don't need a formal invitation.' Maureen gave him a fixed smile.

John bridled at the implied criticism but he knew he'd neglected his sister and her family. 'We'll see you soon, I promise.' He leaned over and gave her a kiss, which surprised her. She smiled.

'You'll be all right, Clarissa?' Maureen asked.

'Thank you, Maureen, for your help. It's really appreciated,' Clarissa said. 'I'll see you out.'

'You stay and look after the baby. I can see myself out.'

Maureen gave Clarissa a kiss then went out the bedroom door, closing it behind her.

Clarissa put Richard back to bed and dampened his forehead with a cloth. 'There, there, baby, sleep now.'

She sat on the edge of the bed and looked at their child, her fingers fidgeting. John knew she was anxious. He was too. Influenza was a killer. He walked to the window and tethered the billowing curtain.

'I'll stay with you,' he said.

'Thank you, dear,' Clarissa said, looking at him through tired eyes.

Henry Blackett reached for a cigar from a box in his study, struck a match and waited. He warmed the tobacco with the flame, drew on it and smelled its fragrance. A small gesture but it tempered his savagery at the news he'd just got.

'I knew it was that damned upstart!' he said as he tapped the letter on his study desk. 'At Bathurst, then Homebush and in town. Well, I'm going to fix her and fix her for good.'

He had had his suspicions after that day at Randwick when his servant had told him that a big young man had come to visit. Well, so Leary serviced his mare! Blackett sweated as he fumed. If Leary stood in front of him now, Henry would have put a bullet in his brain and he'd have walked away smiling. Why hadn't he picked it sooner? Well, he was in the box seat now and he could orchestrate this revenge as much as it suited him. Bastard! Leary wouldn't get away with this, his money and connections notwithstanding.

He glanced at his wall clock. Getting up, he went to the corner cabinet, opened it and poured himself a scotch. His thoughts crystallised. It all seemed to fit. She'd told him that on Tuesday afternoons she attended a charity function, which seemed as regular as a heartbeat. She'd played him for a fool, but he knew now, and he would act.

His investigator had needed an extra week to get the goods on Beth. He looked again at Samuel Smith's letter. It gave chapter and verse about the rendezvous, the time of day and many more details. Smith was worth it and Blackett would've paid twice more for the knowledge. Now . . . how to play this? A face-to-face with her? Divorce her? Take all the wealth, which he could do. Or he could play games with her. Give her little hints that he was suspicious and make her a nervous wreck. Or, the third choice, and this is what tickled him the most, was to get Leary into a compromising position with Beth and maybe even have Leary's wife—what was her name? Ah yes, Clarissa—find the couple rutting.

Footsteps sounded in the hall and he made his decision. 'Is that you?' he said.

Beth stood at the doorway. 'It's me. Hot for the middle of June, isn't it?' She patted her partly opened blouse, her skin there glistening. At any other time that would have stirred him, but knowing Leary had seen her naked angered him more. 'How was your day?' she said.

Blackett placed the letter on his desk. 'Passable, passable,' he said. 'I got the two new horses for our stud. And they are beauties, I'll tell you. The filly's got fine quarters—'

'Good,' she replied. 'I want a cool drink. Would you like one?'

Blackett thought his head would explode. He must calm down. She used to be interested in his views on horses and everything about them. But now, not so, and he glanced at the letter. Anger jarred him again and he blurted out. 'No, I'm not interested in anything to drink.'

Beth stopped patting her neck, lowered her hand and said. 'What's wrong, Henry?'

He stepped up to her. Her eyes widened in surprise and he felt a tightness in his groin, something at last from her. Not her feigning interest or polite conversation but—attention. 'What's got *me* so hot and bothered? I'll tell you. I've got proof you're having an affair with John Leary.' Her eyes expanded and he knew that she couldn't respond. 'Get in here and close the door. I don't want the servants to hear the filth about you.'

Beth closed the door and sat in one of Henry's chairs. She raised her head and folded her arms. 'Harsh words, Henry.'

'They are true words.'

'You seem confident about this.'

Henry bent over her. 'Oh I'm confident. You see, I have proof.'

She glanced at the letter. 'Is that supposed to be my record of guilt? Because unless you have an eyewitness, you have nothing.'

Henry chuckled. This was getting good. He was warming to her fighting him, his anger on hold. If the young buck serviced her wants, good luck to him. It was the way she'd gone about it that angered him and he would make her pay. 'I don't need an eyewitness. I only have to make it known around town about you and Leary, and that's it. Everybody will believe it because I'll make sure that I'm seen as the doting husband who's been cuckolded by a young harlot of a wife.'

'May I see the damning report?' she said.

Still confident. *Well, let's see.* Henry went around the desk and threw the letter on her lap. She read it, folded it and said. 'All this says is that I left a terrace house and a Mr John Leary left it some time later. It does not show any association—'

'Bulldust. You have me believe that you and Mr Leary meet secretly every Tuesday for some sort of *business* arrangement?'

Beth stood and went towards the door where she turned around. 'You believe what you wish. If you think I'm adulterous, then take action.'

'I can prove adultery,' he said. 'I can take all your property, and you'll be penniless.'

Beth walked back towards him, her eyes flashing in anger and her chin thrust towards him, inviting a blow. 'You take one coin from me, Henry, one coin and I'll make your life hell. We lead separate lives and if I've been unfaithful, which I won't admit, then I would have been discreet.'

'That's as maybe, but be assured that there are other witnesses to your infidelity. Do you wish me to name them?' Henry knew he had the high ground. Beth would now back down and do exactly what he wanted, because she feared the scandal.

'No,' she said, 'I don't wish to know them. As I said, you do what you think is best.' The pressure in his head passed to his chest. She wasn't supposed to say that! 'So, you see,' she went on, 'you don't scare me. The way you prance around and carry yourself like you're some big man, it doesn't wash with me. I'll not embarrass you and I will not embarrass my mother or my sisters. But my life is my own.'

Henry moved towards her. He expected her to move back at the same pace but she stood her ground. 'How dare you speak to me like that! I'm your husband, and you and everything you have are my property.'

'You don't frighten me, but you attack my mother and my sisters and you'll see me like you've never seen me before. I'm a Catholic and I'm obliged to stay with you because our church doesn't recognise divorce. I've kept my personal dealings secret and I'll continue to do so. I advise you to do the same.'

His cheeks were on fire and sweat dropped from his nose.

'But that doesn't mean,' Beth continued, 'I have to be your chattel or your slave.'

She turned to leave and Henry stared at her back. He went to lunge towards her but a thought struck him in midstride and he stopped. Instead of being afraid of scandal, she was daring him to admit to the world that he was a cuckold. He realised he didn't want that. *There is another way. I'll see what I can do to young Leary. That's what I'll do.*

It was Thursday, just over a week since Richard's illness, and he was on the mend. John's hand was healing too and the bandages had come off. At breakfast Clarissa seemed distracted and out of sorts. She was fiddling with her serviette and moving her cutlery around. Finally, she looked straight at him and said, 'I couldn't sleep much last night. I've been thinking about us. John, are you being unfaithful?' Clarissa's eyes didn't leave his.

'What did you say, dear?'

'I'm not foolish and don't treat me like a child. Are you seeing another woman?'

John didn't blink and it took all his skill to stare her down. 'Have you been listening to gossip?'

Clarissa stood up. 'I don't care what you have on at work. I want to speak now, in the study.'

Once they were in the study, she closed the door, then went to the window, looked out and folded her arms. 'I won't tell you what I know. I want you to tell me. Be honest with me, please. Just tell me.'

Beth had written to him on Monday at the office, telling him that she would end their Tuesday meetings from now on. She'd given no reason. John was certain now that it was over and he could be honest. 'I'm not being unfaithful.'

She turned to him, her eyes shining. He held his breath and kept her look.

'Do you promise me you're telling the truth?' she said.

'I am.'

She continued to look at him but he held firm. 'I have to believe you,' she said, 'but I have my doubts and I won't share them with you. If you're telling me you're faithful, then you are.'

He took a step towards her but she moved away from him. 'Let's go away somewhere,' he said.

She looked surprised. 'What? Just drop everything and go?'

'Why not?' he said, warming to the idea. 'Things at work are pretty settled and I can get away. Maybe we can go up to Bathurst, to the property.'

She seemed to consider it and gave a half smile. 'That would be a nice change. When Richard is fully recovered we shall plan something. Maybe then, just the two of us, we could try and build on what we've started these last eight weeks. Now, I've got things to do and you have to be at work.'

John watched her leave and wondered why he hadn't thought of going away before. He was ashamed that he hadn't been totally honest with her, but at least he was trying. It seemed that Beth wanted to end the relationship, making it easier for him to be true to his spouse. He cheered up. A stay at *Clontarf* would be the go. He wouldn't leave there until he'd convinced Clarissa of his faithfulness and his love.

He gathered his briefcase and papers and left for work. In the carriage, he brought out his weekly financial report. Dan Reynolds had inserted a cutting out of the newspaper, marked for his attention. John read the article in surprise. Mr Andrew Brown, a partner of the Bank of New South Wales, had been found hanged in the stables of his house. There were no suspicious circumstances but found on his body had been a suicide note admitting to crimes of such a perfidious nature that the details could not be published. *Well that's a turn-up.* He hadn't liked the man but never suspected that he had a secret life. Then John remembered that Brown had a close relationship with Brian Atkins. Was he involved in this? John flexed his hand and remembered the wagon and his escape from death. He'd have to do something about that man.

Christine McGuire's lawyer gestured her to a chair in his office. He then sat at his desk opposite her. 'I have done my search on the shareholders of the Phoenix Investment Group, as you requested.'

'And?' she said.

The lawyer sat back in his chair. 'The owner of the Phoenix Investment Group, and therefore the fifty-one per cent owner of Leary's Contracting, is Mrs Beth Blackett, wife of Henry Blackett.'

Christine's head jerked back as if she'd been hit by a boxer. 'Are you sure?'

'I am.'

Beth Blackett, the major shareholder of Leary's Contracting! Christine's shock turned to sadness for Clarissa, then anger. That woman's shareholding was further corroboration of John's infidelity. 'Are you telling me that a woman can own property like this?'

The lawyer moved closer to his file and examined the papers again. He seemed to want to assure himself what he was saying was correct. 'I admit, Mrs McGuire, that it is unusual. However, it is not illegal or unlawful for a woman to own property and it would appear that Mrs Blackett has been well advised in the terms of her dealings, because these documents are well drafted. I admire the handiwork.'

'I'm not interested in their composition, Mr Wilson,' she said and started to think. Beth Blackett controlled Leary's Contracting and would continue to do so. But David was dead and John must have known that Beth's name would be disclosed. Had he been planning to buy her share? He could afford it. Otherwise everyone would eventually find out who the current main shareholder of Leary's was, including Clarissa. *I have to protect her.* She concentrated and tried to think what she could do. *What if I buy Blackett's share?* Yes. She must do it before John had a chance to. 'I'm interested in excising Mrs Blackett as a shareholder of Leary's,' she said. 'What is its stock's current value, do you think?'

Wilson stood up and walked to the blind, pulling it down over the window to shade his desk from the June sunlight. 'Just give me a minute, please.'

Scanning a bookcase running along one wall, the lawyer took a book and thumbed through it, stopping at a page to look at her. 'It's difficult to value. Shareholding worth in construction companies is volatile, especially private companies. But I would suggest that Mrs Blackett's share on a conservative value would be within the range of fifteen thousand pounds.'

Christine fanned her face. A considerable sum but not entirely indigestible, she thought. With a little belt-tightening and selling some stock in David's companies, she could buy out Beth Blackett and strengthen her own position—and at the same time protect her daughter from shame and put an end to Beth Blackett having any involvement with Leary emotionally, physically or financially. She said, 'Mr Wilson, I want you to draw up the necessary papers which will include a formal offer to Mrs Blackett of ten thousand pounds.'

'That is below the value, Mrs McGuire. How do you know she'll accept?'

Of course she'll accept. But then Christine had a second thought:

why should she pay her anything? She smiled. There might be another way to get that stock—for nothing.

'Is there something amusing, Mrs McGuire?'

'There isn't, and let me worry about the commercial details. You just prepare the transfer papers, but leave the amount for the offer blank at this stage.'

'Blank?' he said.

Christine got up. 'Good day to you, sir. I'll see you at the end of the week, when we can discuss things further and I will review the papers. Just send a letter to Mrs Blackett informing her that I'm prepared to offer her ten thousand pounds for her share. A letter, that's all.'

Brian Atkins opened his front door and stepped back to look at his guest. 'Please come in, Mr Leary. You have to excuse me but I'm still unsteady on my feet. Right out to the back, please, to the sun room.' Atkins favoured his left leg as he followed his guest. He suspected Leary's intentions and wanted some personal protection. 'My man Albert is in the yard collecting more wood for the fire. July has just started but it feels the coldest of any year I've known. But then it may be I'm just getting older. Please sit down.'

Leary sat in one of the armchairs and Atkins positioned himself in a straight-backed chair opposite him. Atkins smiled. 'Albert will join us shortly.' He forced himself to relax and tried to appear unruffled. 'Your correspondence requested a meeting with me.'

A muscle in Leary's neck twitched. 'That's right.'

'Would you like some refreshments? A glass of wine or perhaps a Scotch whisky?'

'No, thank you.'

'Very well, then. What would you like to talk about?'

'I'll be frank, Mr Atkins. I'd like to talk about the sabotage of the Clarence Street building site. There are things about it that puzzle me and you might be able to help.'

'Me?' Atkins forced a frown of puzzlement. 'I know nothing

about that, only what I've read in the papers. I'm sorry for the loss of your men.'

Deep creases appeared on Leary's forehead. 'Why would Miller identify you as the man who paid him to do the sabotage? He was certain it was you.'

'That man's a maniac, Mr Leary. I've got no idea why he picked me.'

'Miller had no personal reason to attack Leary's, none. He did it all on your say so.'

Atkins shook his head. 'He probably saw my name in the newspaper and thought I was as good as any to blame for that shocking crime.' Atkins kept still and held Leary's stare for seconds. This was the test. He'd have to assure Leary of his innocence.

'But, he was so convinced. Why would he name *you* of all the businessmen in town? Why you?'

Atkins repositioned his leg, giving himself time to think. 'I've no idea, really, I don't. Scum like that will do anything to get off, Mr Leary. They learn untruths in their cradle, and believe their own lies by the time they can walk. It's a load of rubbish!'

Leary leaned forward. 'No. It was you. You wanted to get at me and you used Miller to do it. Don't give me lies. That labourer's too dumb to organise sabotage on his own. You did it.'

Atkins started to perspire. 'I've told you the truth. I've—'

'The truth! You wouldn't know the truth if it gave you a black eye,' Leary said with a menacing look in his own.

Atkins felt a surge of strength. 'If you continue this line, Mr Leary, you can leave. All the police have is a statement from a homicidal labourer. That man would have done anything to save his neck. Unfortunately, I believe he died in prison from an accident.'

'Which you caused,' Leary said.

Atkins pushed himself upright, ignoring his pain and said, 'You had better leave. I accepted you here as a gentleman and have given you the courtesy and manners to which a gentleman is entitled. However, it's obvious your visit is to threaten me, and that's not acceptable.' Leary lunged and Atkins jumped clear, the pain jarring him again. Leary grabbed him by the throat as footsteps sounded in the adjoining room. 'Get your hands off me,' Atkins said.

Leary's fingers were tightening on him when they were forced away. Atkins's servant grabbed hold of Leary's shoulders and held onto him. Atkins rubbed his neck and leaned on the chair gasping. 'Get out,' he said. 'I suspect your grief has made you hate me. That's your problem, not mine.'

Albert attempted to manhandle Leary towards the door but Leary held his ground. 'Oh, you're guilty, you bastard,' he said, 'and I'm coming after you.'

'That's a threat, Mr Leary.'

'It is,' Leary said, as he exposed his wrist showing a nasty scar, 'and I'll get you for this too. You nearly killed me in the street.'

Atkins had read of the incident in the paper. At first he'd suspected Shelby might have had a go. 'Tread lightly, Mr Leary. I'll see the police about your behaviour today. If anything happens to me, you'll be their first suspect. Thank you Albert.'

Albert forced Leary out of the house.

The attack and his defence had drained him. When Albert returned, Atkins said, 'Take me up to bed and prepare my medicine. That was very tiring.'

As he leaned on his servant, Atkins pondered. Leary had nothing on him and the labourer was dead. Atkins had done the right thing, meeting the builder. He'd had doubts at first, but was glad it was over. He would rest, then write a statement about today's altercation and get Albert to take it to the police station.

He had another thought. Something had kept surfacing, ever since he was attacked in Macquarie Street. Had that been random? His cash had been stolen and his watch—but what if there had been another reason than theft? What if Leary had arranged the attack on him? Possible, he thought, and because Atkins had survived, Leary had attacked him today. Even more reason to alert the police.

Albert put him into bed and gave him his draught. He had enough income to make himself comfortable for the rest of his life. The doctor had said that within six months his injury would heal, and to Atkins that was worth more than all the gold in the Bank of

England. Pain started to fade from his side and he thought he'd write that letter to the police and get Leary out of his life. Even better, perhaps the devilish Irish contractor might still be charged with assaulting him.

Christine stood waiting in the foyer of John and Clarissa's house. She watched Clarissa, with Richard in tow, accompany the carriage driver as he carried the two cases down the stairs.

'Leave these here and see to the carriage, please,' Clarissa said to him.

'Yes, ma'am.'

'Goodbye, Mother,' Clarissa said, giving her mother a hug and a kiss. 'We shall be away for about ten days.'

Christine pressed her daughter's hands. Clarissa had colour in her cheeks and had put on weight and she was relieved to see this. 'Look after my grandson.'

'Don't worry, we shall.'

'Come and give your grandmother a kiss,' Christine said, leaning down with her arms open. Richard ran to her and she hugged him and gave him a kiss. 'I'll miss you. Be a good boy.'

He nodded.

'Thank you, Christine,' John said joining them. 'I think the break from Sydney will do us all good.'

She hoped so, for her daughter's sake. 'Well, goodbye you three. Have a restful time.'

John stood on the veranda that fronted the southern and eastern sides of the main homestead and looked towards the Macquarie River about a quarter of a mile away. It glittered in the midday July sunshine. The cool westerly fluttered through the trees that, rooted to the river's edge, appeared too shy to spread into the paddocks surrounding them. *Clontarf* was a pretty spot. He breathed in the air, sweet like champagne. Such a change from the city with its manure, dust and noise. It was good, too, to be free of collars and suits.

It had been over a week since the altercation with Atkins and John was still irritated by it. He knew the man was guilty of the murder of his labourers, but he couldn't make the man admit to his crime. It was frustrating, especially as the police had questioned and warned him over his attack on Atkins. A squeak in the veranda boards distracted him. He took two steps backwards, just to repeat the action, and grinned.

'Doing a jig?' Clarissa said and smiled.

'You caught me. Is Richard settled?'

'He is. Tired out, the poor thing.' She stood beside him looking at the view.

In the distance, well beyond the sheds and overseer's quarters that lay to the east of the homestead, skilful men on horseback were herding sheep. John admired the way the horses responded to their masters' commands and the sheepdogs worked with the same diligence.

'It's beautiful isn't it?' he said.

'It is.' Clarissa's hand touched his on the rail. It felt good. 'I could live here, you know,' she said. 'It's peaceful and the space just never ends, and the heat of summer is easier to bear now.'

She looked better than she had for a while, and he sensed it was because of this place. He, too, felt a peace he'd not known for a long time. As if somebody had lifted a great load from him. The strong smells of sap and bud were adding to his contentment. 'What do you want to do this afternoon?' he asked.

Clarissa sighed. 'I don't know. I might get a chair and sit here for an hour or two and soak up this scenery. Is there anything special you wish to do?'

John said 'No, I'd be happy to sit here too.' Was this place making him happy or was something else making him feel good? An image of Beth came into his mind. No, that could be no more.

A finger poked his side. 'You're miles away. What were you thinking about?'

'About work,' he lied. 'Look, I'm easy this afternoon, whatever you want to do, I'll join you. Do you want anything to eat?'

Clarissa folded her arms and John sensed she didn't believe him.

'I'm not hungry. I'll go and check on Richard, then lie down. Even though we stayed overnight at Parramatta, I'm still tired.' She turned and went inside.

John was disappointed in himself; it would take some effort to win Clarissa's trust back.

Needing distraction, he went inside. Down the hall he passed the drawing room on his right with its polished floorboards and large fireplace, and three bedrooms on his left. At the end of the hall was a kitchen big enough to contain a table and with windows that looked over their land to the north. The overseer's wife had left the icebox stuffed with sufficient food for an occupying army, and John fixed himself a meal and read the Bathurst newspaper, checking the gold prospects. Most of the miners were still only making wages, but a few of them had got lucky. He hoped they spent their money wisely.

After eating and cleaning up, he went back down the hallway and peeked around the bedroom door and saw Clarissa on the bed with her eyes closed. He checked that Richard was still sleeping and went out to the veranda, walked down its steps and headed over to the stable, where he mounted one of the homestead's horses. The midday sun had passed and the coolness of the afternoon had started to settle on everything. It would be a cold night and a fire in the drawing room would be welcomed. He rode a short distance, dismounted and entered the main storage shed and inspected his handiwork, curious to see if his carpentry had stood up to the past nineteen months of country weather.

The last time he was up this way he had met Beth. His thoughts again returned to her. One week ago, she'd sent him a note asking him to meet her at the General Post Office. He'd been intrigued to know why. She'd smiled when she'd spotted him but her stance had puzzled him—her left leg a little in front of her, her shoulders drawn back, her hands clasped together and her chin thrust outwards. Seeing her again had tested his resolve.

She'd ushered him to a quieter corner of the busy place. 'Henry knows about us. We had a confrontation.' Beth's clear eyes showed no fear, but defiance.

'He knows? What do you mean he knows? We've been discreet.'

'Apparently not enough, dear,' she said. 'He had a private investigator follow me and our regular Tuesdays were our undoing.'

He paused. 'Did he threaten you?'

'I'm not scared of Henry. He struts around, makes a lot of noise, but he's nothing underneath.' She looked at him. 'But I have my mother and my sisters to think about, and, after our last meeting—'

'I've thought about that.' John moved closer to her and made his decision. 'We shouldn't see each other any more.'

Beth looked at him. The tears in her eyes told him she was feeling as bad as he did. People near them seemed oblivious as Beth dabbed her eyes. 'I knew this would happen. That's why I chose this place because . . .' She took a breath. 'Now, I'm going. Please don't try to see me again.'

He wouldn't.

Beth took a step backwards. 'And don't write to me John, please. If you do, I won't reply. If we see each other in the street, I will nod, that's all.'

Before he could reply, she'd turned and left. All he remembered was how lovely her back looked as she disappeared into busy George Street. He'd followed her for a bit but then she was lost in the crowd. He'd stood staring at the place he'd last seen her for five minutes, realising what they'd done.

The loss of Beth hit him hard, but he had to give her up if he wanted to keep Clarissa's love and their marriage.

A crow squawked and John looked up at the bird sitting high on the tallest gum. He concentrated now on his workmanship in the shed. Satisfied it was all in good order he mounted his horse and rode to the river's edge. Sitting near a weeping willow he thought about Eire. In the stream on his family's Kildare farm he'd relaxed and cavorted in summer with his friends. Good times.

He looked back at the property's built form with a contractor's eye and gave it the thumbs up. Builders of country houses had responded to the climate with a lot of corrugated iron and wide verandas. The storage sheds were of little architectural merit but they were functional and sturdy. No sound was heard, save the wind through the trees and the gurgling river, and he mused that all the money he had would not buy the pleasure of sitting here. He sighed, stood up, mounted his horse and rode back to the homestead with the breeze ruffling his hair.

He was distracted during the evening meal thinking about the one loose end: Atkins. John had failed when he'd confronted him. But he'd not given up. He'd never give up till that man was behind bars. He had to pay for the murder of those three Leary's workers.

'Do you agree?' Clarissa's head was tilted with an eyebrow raised.

'I'm sorry?'

Clarissa shrugged. 'It doesn't matter.'

After dinner they sat beside the fire, its flames soporific.

'I would like to know something,' she said.

John tapped his cigar ash and looked at her. 'What would you like to know?'

'How your work is going. It's sad we have to come here to talk, because I used to be very interested in it.'

'The cash flow is good, my dear. I still want to be active with the sites. Losing Johnson and Sean was a king hit.'

'Where is Sean working?'

'I don't know,' he said.

'Vonnie says he's happy.'

John became irritated, not at what she'd said, but because John had no idea how to get Sean back into the company. 'It's his loss. Anyway, work's still demanding.'

'But you love your position and the power it gives you.'

Power? John bridled. Where was she going with this? To an argument maybe? He'd tread with care. 'It's not the power. The ones who lend the money are the powerful ones, the bankers. But I'm comfortable that we don't want for anything and I've reached my goal.'

'Yes. You have what you've always wanted. Now, what are you going to do?'

John relit his cigar. What would he do now? Make more money, of course. That would have been obvious to anyone, he would've thought. But he didn't say that to her, because there was something more important that needed to be said. 'The one thing I'm not going to do,' he said, 'is neglect you.'

She smiled and it was genuine. 'I'm glad,' she said.

'Besides that, there are many doors open to a person with money and position, and we certainly have that.' Clarissa's eyelids looked heavy. 'You are sleepy?'

'I am. I thought this afternoon's nap would satisfy me but I'm still tired. I think I'll go to bed, if that's all right. Goodnight, dear.'

When Clarissa stood up she seemed to lose her balance. John put his cigar down and jumped up to help her. 'Steady dear, are you all right?'

Clarissa held his arms and leant towards him, putting her head on his chest. 'I haven't hugged you for some time. It feels nice.' She broke away but held onto his hands. 'We have a few days together. I really want to . . . I want to understand the person who I used to know so well.'

'What about now?'

'Not tonight, darling. We have time, and I've challenged myself not to leave here until you and I are starting to get back to what we were.' Clarissa stretched and kissed him on the lips. Friendly, but good, John admitted. She released his hands and left the drawing room. John picked up another log and placed it on the fire.

He yawned and decided he might as well go to bed too.

Next morning he woke up and looked at the clock. Eight a.m. He'd slept in and was surprised. Perhaps it was the country air or that there was less tension between him and Clarissa. Whatever it was, it was pleasant, no, more—comforting. He got out of bed, slipped on a robe and went to the kitchen. Clarissa wasn't there.

'I'm on the veranda, dear,' she said.

She sat there rugged up with a cup of tea beside her and some papers. Richard was sitting beside her chewing on a biscuit and playing with a toy. 'It's just such a grand morning,' she said. 'I had to look at the view. There's tea in the pot if you'd like a cup.' She reached for the sheaf of papers. 'This is father's will and some supporting papers. It's the first time I've really wanted to read it. Do you mind?'

Her smile was genuine and John returned it. 'Not at all. I'll get a cup and join you. Do you want anything else?'

'No, thank you, dear.'

He looked at the mist still settled in the valley. It was enchanting. He went in to get his tea and decided to make some toast.

Returning with his tray five minutes later and eager to continue the good interaction with Clarissa, he pushed open the veranda door. Clarissa looked at him. Her face was flushed and her eyes were glassy.

'Beth Blackett owns the majority of Leary's shares!' she said.

John was shocked, then rallied. 'Those shares are owned by Phoenix Investment Group. You knew that.'

'Now I know the real truth. I misplaced my copy of the will and gathered up Mother's copy, which included this.' She held up a single piece of paper. 'Beth Blackett is the only party to the Phoenix Investment Group.'

John put his tray on the table. He had to appear calm. 'It was purely an investment to her, dear. She never wanted control.'

'And Beth Blackett is your lover. She is, isn't she?'

'No.'

Clarissa's lips trembled. 'No? Then who is?'

John paused. 'There is no one.'

'Dear God,' she said. 'More lies? It's Beth Blackett all right and she's not only your lover but she's been backing you since May last year when she bought father's share. John . . . How could you!' Tears filled her eyes. 'I know now why you didn't tell me who it was.'

Richard grabbed her dress and started to cry. Clarissa picked him up and cuddled him.

John was in a dilemma over which issue to answer first, his infidelity or the shareholding. He chose the latter. 'Clarissa, how could I tell you about her being the silent partner? You would never have understood.'

'This is what I mean.' She lowered her voice. 'No, I wouldn't have liked it. I would not have welcomed a former rival back into your life, even for business, but I *would* have understood—if you had just told me. All this points to subterfuge and lies. And worse, it makes me believe that you've been unfaithful—with her.'

'It was business only, dear. Just business. I'm actually thinking seriously of buying her out and being in full control again.'

She looked at him as if she wanted to understand. 'Would you really do that? Or is it because I've just found out about her?'

The thing was, he had given a lot of thought to buying Beth's share; he'd just never broached it with her. But if he said that to Clarissa it would seem implausible. 'I would probably have asked her to sell in the near future.'

Clarissa kept looking at him. 'And would you have told me, even then? I don't think so.' Richard had stopped crying and had become restless. She put him down and turned on John. 'In fact, I know you wouldn't have. And I want you to tell me straight. No lies. Have you been unfaithful to me with her?'

He had to convince her she was wrong. 'No.'

Her eyes narrowed. 'I don't believe you.' She closed them for a moment. 'Please get a message to town. I'm leaving by coach with Richard. You do what you want.' She picked up the boy, turned and opened the door.

'But Clarissa!'

'Just get the message to town,' she said.

Clarissa's discovery of Beth's shareholding was bad enough— but then he went even colder, from fear. Christine knew about it, too, and Christine would do all she could to protect Clarissa. She had the money to do that now.

He had to get to Beth. He had to get her to sell her share to him. What a bloody mess! His grip on Leary's was slipping from him. His wife didn't believe him about the affair. Why would she? He slammed his hand on the post.

John ignored his breakfast, got dressed, grabbed a jacket and oilskin from the hall cupboard and rode into Bathurst thinking about his letter to Beth. On the way, the wind knifed through him as if Clarissa was punishing him—and for good reason, he knew.

CHAPTER TEN

JOHN LEFT *CLONTARF* THE DAY AFTER CLARISSA. HE WAS IRRITATED
that Clarissa didn't believe him about Beth, and he felt guilty
because he'd lied to her. This mess was all his fault, he should never
have started the affair.

When he arrived home, he found that Clarissa had moved into
the second bedroom and he was embarrassed at what the servants
must think. When he returned to work, he cancelled all plans for
two days, waiting on an answer from Beth to his request. He'd tried
to couch his letter in as businesslike tones as possible, eschewing all
romance, presuming that it would be enough to get her to reply, but
still no answer. So he stalked by her house, hoping to catch her and
make good his offer to buy her out, but he didn't sight her. By the
afternoon of the second day, John was frustrated.

He got drunk at Cochrane's, poured out his misery to a stranger
who bought him more drinks and barely remembered staggering
home to the loneliness of his bedroom.

~

Sitting in her solicitor's office, Christine McGuire was waiting for her meeting with Beth Blackett. She was curious to know what Mrs Blackett's response to her offer would be, and determined that she herself would come out the winner from their meeting. Muffled voices came from the room adjoining her solicitor's office and her anticipation heightened.

The door to the office opened. 'Mrs Blackett is waiting in our anteroom, Mrs McGuire,' Wilson said.

'Thank you, Mr Wilson.'

'All I need,' he said, 'is the figure to place in the contract which is dated today, the twenty-third of July. We did discuss an amount of ten thousand pounds, was that correct?'

Christine McGuire looked at her solicitor. This transaction was to be clean and clinical. She derived no satisfaction from it other than the reassurance she needed to protect Clarissa. 'We did, Mr Wilson, but please leave the space for the amount blank, as before.'

'Blank? But—'

'Blank, sir and I want to meet Mrs Blackett in person—alone.'

'I need to be with you. You may want—'

'Please, Mr Wilson, just ask her to come in here. We'll call you when we've completed our business.'

'As you wish.'

As the lawyer left his office to fetch the visitor, Christine reviewed her strategy. Mrs Blackett would have to accede to her, as Christine held all the aces. She heard the door open and the lawyer speak.

'Mrs McGuire, Mrs Blackett.'

Christine stood up. Beth Blackett was as she remembered but there was a confidence in her bearing and her clothing was expensive and fashionable.

'It's a pleasure to see you again, Mrs McGuire.'

Still attractive, Christine thought, with just a hint of her past on show, though her perfume was French. No wonder Leary had fallen for her charms. The tucks of her blouse accentuated her bosom and her face powder was minimal, her natural beauty shining through.

'Mrs Blackett,' she said, 'I'd like to speak with you alone.' She expected surprise but her opponent's smile only widened.

'Of course. Here?'

'You can use my office,' the lawyer said. 'Let me know if I can be of assistance.'

'Thank you,' Christine said and closed the door after him. She faced Beth, who had sat down.

'I've reviewed your offer,' Beth said.

She's opened first. Well, I'll turn that around. 'And?'

Beth eyeballed her.

She's bold as well. She must have Leary on a string.

'It's below market . . .'

'That's not my advice.'

'. . . but I'll accept,' Beth said.

This was unexpected. Leary's was operating profitably and the dividends would be handsome, a lot to forego. Perhaps Mrs Blackett had lost interest in John. The young woman did seem at ease. 'I wrote to you,' Christine said, 'so we could meet. I was curious about your shareholding. I'm opposed to women in business—'

'Your daughter is demonstrating proficiency in hers.'

'Let's keep Clarissa out of this. She's been hurt enough already.'

Mrs Blackett looked away and for the first time seemed to have lost some of her confidence. 'I'm sorry to hear that.'

'This is about business, Mrs Blackett.'

'Very well. Now we've met, I'd like to conclude our arrangement. Shall we call the lawyer?'

'My letter stated ten thousand pounds,' Christine said, 'but I want your share for just one pound.' Christine enjoyed the look of confusion on her opponent's face.

'I beg your pardon?'

'You'll sell me your share for one pound.'

Beth shook her head. 'Why should I do that?'

'To save you the public humiliation of an adulterous scandal,' Christine said.

Beth's eyes widened and her bosom heaved. 'I don't know what you mean. I—'

'Please spare us,' Christine said. 'I've got the evidence I need, so agree to the offer or I'll act.'

Beth tapped her fingers on the desk. 'I'll deny it.'

'You could, but the mud will stick.' *Here it comes.* Christine felt triumphant but then her conscience paid a visit. Callousness was foreign to her and now she felt she was being cruel. She was about to agree to pay the full amount when Mrs Blackett stood up.

'Then my share is not for sale,' she said. 'You do what you must. You realise the scandal will ruin his marriage and mine, don't you? Then all we'll have is each other. That's enough for me. You might find that's enough for him, too.'

Christine was shocked. 'You'd let me tell the world, and risk all that? For *him?*'

Beth sat down again and looked away.

That was cruel, too. John had shown weakness in having an affair with this good-looking woman but it seemed as though Beth Blackett was in love with him. 'He's not worth it, you know,' Christine said.

Beth shook her head. 'Mrs McGuire, what happened between me and John is personal and I understand Clarissa's hurt. I would feel the same if I was in her shoes.'

Christine was starting to believe her.

'But let's stick to the point,' Beth continued. 'If you want my share, it's for sale for ten thousand pounds. If you don't agree to pay that, I'll bid you good day and you can spread as much scandal as you like.' Beth stood up and went for the door.

'Wait,' Christine said. Beth turned and faced her. 'Call the lawyer. You'll get your money.'

Beth's face remained passive. 'Very well, but he's your lawyer. You call him.'

Christine wanted one more shot and pressed Beth's arm. 'Men are weak. John has hurt Clarissa terribly and for that he deserves my loathing. *He isn't worth it.*'

Beth looked down at Christine's hand on her arm and said, 'Get your lawyer.'

~

In the cab back to Glebe, Beth looked at the contract she held in her hand. So, Christine had discovered their affair, well there you go. Beth felt numb. Separation from John had affected her deeply. She had difficulty sleeping and eating and if John appeared before her now, she wondered if she could resist him.

She shivered. What would she have done if Mrs McGuire hadn't paid up? Then Beth shook her head. A woman of breeding like that would have preferred a cartload of manure on her front doorstep rather than a public scandal.

The shareholding had been Beth's lifeline to John and she hadn't wanted to let it go. But now she had. The money meant nothing to her. What mattered was that she had cut the final link to the man she loved. She had decided that day at the post office not to have contact with him. She'd even destroyed the letters he'd written to her, without opening them. She'd seen him near her house once and had avoided him. Yes, she'd considered selling her share to him but she'd wanted no dealings with him.

Christine McGuire's offer had been a surprising and timely answer to her problem. But it hurt her as well. John would definitively lose control of the one thing that was more dear to him than herself or Clarissa: Leary Contracting. Well, that was his burden now.

Henry and she weren't speaking much to each other these days, and she was content with that, not willing to share anything with him. He had not yet carried out his threat to divorce her. Meanwhile, she was miserable about splitting with John. Her sisters filled some of the void and accepted her extra attention with gusto. Her mother had been curious at first at Beth's behaviour, confirming her own view that Beth's marriage wasn't working. But then her mother's attitude about men and relationships was that it was the wife's duty to grin and bear it. That was not for Beth.

The intimacy with John had been the core of her life. From the first, she'd only ever wanted to be with him. But she was determined, now, through all the pain, to stay away from John Leary.

Beth suspected he might weaken, change his mind and want her back.

She sighed as the cab arrived at her house. Even if John were a free man, would he make her his complete love or was she just another trophy to him, part of his glory cabinet? He already had a mistress—Leary Contracting.

Mounting the steps to the front door, she didn't know what her future would be but an extra ten thousand pounds wasn't to be sneezed at.

Gerry Gleeson smiled and took a breath, feeling his waistcoat tight on his shrinking but still acceptable middle. His tie itched and he wanted to stick a finger between his collar and his neck to get relief but there were too many people watching him in St Patrick's Church Hill.

A few of his own friends and family were present, but more were there for Moira, including her family, who'd come down from the country for her wedding day. He was very happy. He loved her and she loved him. As if to answer his thoughts, she leaned towards him as the priest asked her to recite her vows and Gerry looked into her eyes and reciprocated. He turned to Rupert Jenkins and received the ring and as he slipped it on her finger he heard the priest declare them man and wife.

'You may now kiss the bride, Gerry,' the priest said and smiled.

Gerry bent down, ignoring his restrictive clothing, and gave his wife a kiss. She responded, then broke away and blushed, and Gerry smiled again.

'Let me be the first to congratulate you, Mrs Gleeson,' Jenkins said and gave her a peck on the cheek.

The happy couple followed the priest into the sacristy where they recorded their union. Gerry hadn't known such contentment for twenty years and wondered why he'd left it so long to find a woman to love him. His prison term had punched the stuffing out of him and his stint on the roads had nearly killed him. But it was better late than never and with Moira gripping his arm, he seemed to float above the floor as they walked down the aisle, acknowledging the good wishes of friends and family.

She held her veil against the late-July wind and Gerry guided her down the steps to their carriage. They had argued about the extravagance of such a gesture but Gerry was adamant—nothing was too good for his Moira, especially on their wedding day.

The Skinners publican had closed the hotel to the public and it was Gerry and Moira's for the afternoon, all grog supplied at wholesale rates, the publican's present to them. During the carriage ride, Gerry thought about the future. He had some savings, enough to put a deposit on a terrace house at Redfern. They would rent out Moira's house, left to her by a wealthy aunt, so they were more than comfortable. Next week they were going by steam clipper to Melbourne for their one-week honeymoon, because Moira had never been there.

'The service was wonderful,' she said. 'He's a nice priest, that Father McCauley.'

'Too true, too true my dear. Well, we're hitched now, like the horses in front, and I'm going to be true to you, girl, for the rest of my life.'

Moira reached across and kissed him again. 'And I'll be the same to you, dear. I'm looking forward to Melbourne. Being on the clipper, what a treat!'

John waited in the foyer of their Point Piper home. 'Are you ready, dear?'

'Yes, I'm here,' Clarissa said as she walked down the stairs.

John helped her into the carriage. A month had passed since Bathurst and things were still tense between them. Going down the toll road, Clarissa's proximity increased his self-consciousness. It was as if he had the plague; when the carriage bumped out of a hole or went around the corner, he felt her thigh flex against him as she pushed herself away.

Their carriage stopped at St Mary's and Clarissa alighted, not waiting for him. John followed her into the coolness of the Cathedral for Sunday Mass. Despite their problems, she'd put on weight and John was pleased that she was looking better. If she could only believe that he now only loved her, they could be friends again. Yes, he had been moved by her tears when she'd found out about Beth's shareholding, which had also added to her suspicions that he was having an affair with Beth. He had hurt her terribly. But what was really troubling him now was that the majority shareholding in Leary's was still at risk of being bought by Christine.

During the service, that's all he could think about. After the Mass ended, Clarissa hesitated on top of the steps and looked around at the gathering. John sensed she wanted to stay and chat. He wanted to go home and drink. He was about to take her elbow, when she spoke.

'Hello, Malcolm,' Clarissa said.

A tallish man in his mid-thirties smiled at Clarissa. His dark complexion and black curly hair contrasted with those of a petite woman beside him. Who was this fellow? And why had Clarissa addressed him so informally? But he looked familiar and he remembered that the man had been at David's funeral.

'Good morning, Mrs Leary.' The man put his hand out to John. 'Malcolm Robinson, Mr Leary. Do you remember me?'

'I do,' John said, shaking his hand.

'I'd like both of you to meet my wife. She's just arrived from Italy.'

'I am pleased to meet you, Mrs Robinson,' Clarissa said.

Malcolm's wife nodded twice.

'I'm sorry,' Malcolm said, 'her English is not too good. She's still learning.' John was astonished at the way Robinson and Clarissa looked at each other. It was as if they shared a secret. 'Well, we bid you good day,' Robinson said. 'If we don't see you again soon, please know you have our regards.'

Clarissa continued smiling at Robinson. John sensed something here and was ready to belt this foreigner. 'Our sentiments also,' she said, 'and please explain to your wife that she is very welcome here.

If I can do anything to assist her in settling in, please do not hesitate to correspond with me.'

When they were back in the carriage, he couldn't restrain himself. 'You were very familiar with that man. He's more than a business associate, no doubt.'

Clarissa looked straight ahead. 'Malcolm is a dear friend. He understands me and my father's business and I intend to continue to enjoy his friendship.'

The carriage picked up speed and went down College Street. 'As long as it's just friendship.'

She faced him and he sensed he'd pricked something deep within her. 'Are you accusing me of anything? Because, if you are, I find that rather comical coming from you. I don't want to discuss it any further. But I'll say this, I'm thinking of going back to work.'

He was about to reply but kept silent. An argument now would push her further from him. He sat back in the carriage. Now, he had something else to worry about—his wife's attention towards another man. What was so special about that Italian?

After their midday meal, John was in the drawing room, reading, when Clarissa came in. He looked up and saw that her face was pale.

'Yes, dear?' he said.

'I'm not feeling myself,' she said. 'I think I'll . . . just go upstairs.' She brought a hand to her forehead, closed her eyes and slipped to the floor.

John rushed to her side. 'Clarissa, Clarissa?' he cried. But there was no reaction from her. He picked her up and carried her towards the stairs. On the way he called out, 'Stella, Stella get the doctor for your mistress, hurry.'

Stella rushed off. John, now distressed, carried Clarissa up to their bedroom and laid her on their bed. A bed he hadn't slept in for a month. She was still unconscious and now John was really worried. He rubbed her hands and moved her head gently from side to side. Her chest was rising and falling and that was a good sign, but he was still cold with fear. She looked too serene, lying there, and his heart went out to her. *Dear Lord, please, make her wake up.*

There was eye movement and she opened them and looked at him. *Thank God.* 'Darling, you fainted,' he said.

She seemed not to know where she was at first. 'Did I?'

'You did. How are you feeling now?'

'All right, I suppose,' she said and touched her temple.

Stella came in with a towel, water jug and bowl, and a glass of water. 'Here, ma'am,' she said, 'drink this.'

Clarissa did and lay back. Stella wetted the towel and applied it to Clarissa's head.

'That feels better,' Clarissa said holding the towel in place. 'Thank you, Stella. That will be all.'

'The doctor's on his way, ma'am,' she said.

'It's not necessary. I just felt a little woozy.'

'Better to make sure,' John said. 'Thank you, Stella. You may go and keep an eye out for the doctor.'

John watched her leave and took hold of Clarissa's hand. 'Darling, I thought I'd lost you.'

Her eyes softened and she closed them for just a second. 'When I was asleep I had a dream. It was unreal. You were in it and we were at sea somewhere but it wasn't somewhere I knew.'

'It doesn't matter.'

'Yet it was nice,' she said. 'There was someone talking to me but I couldn't see their face, but I heard good things about you.' She pressed back on his hand. 'I love you, John. I always have and I believe that you are true to me.'

He was overcome. It was a magnificent thing for her to say and he loved her even more. Yes, he carried an anvil-filled collar of guilt at how he'd betrayed her, but they could move on now. 'Oh my love, my love,' he said and kissed her.

Colleen grasped Gerry's forearm as they walked up the steps to the police station. It was as if she was the one fronting the hangman and it had taken all Gerry's persuasive talents and two months of effort to get her here. And it was still not certain that she would go through with it. 'I can't do it, Gerry,' Colleen said. 'I can't.' She let go of him and went back down the steps.

'Colleen, come back, love.' Gerry followed her, took her hand and turned her around. 'This is the hardest bit, it is. Just give the policeman the truth.'

'But they'll think I'm mad! I've changed my story once; now I'm doing it again!'

She was right but he had to persist. Damn Atkins and his guile. The man had found out Colleen's weak spot and had used it well. They had been so close to getting him convicted and the barmaid was the key. He led her away from the entrance. 'Tell them that Atkins got to you, which he did. Tell them ... he threatened you. Don't tell them about the money he gave you. It isn't important.'

'But I did take his money, Gerry. I had to. Mum was so crook. I couldn't afford the doctor's bill, the medicines and the operation.' Tears filled the barmaid's eyes. 'I did it for her.'

'And a grand gesture it was,' he said. 'But that man killed three men. Those dead men and their families have to have justice.'

Colleen looked at him for a long time. She sighed. 'But you ain't gonna be the one sitting there in the court, Gerry,' she said. 'It's me. You're big and tough. I can't do this.'

'Come on! You, the Hero's best barmaid! Fought off more punters than I've had hot meals. Should be easy for you.'

Colleen nodded and put her hanky away. 'All right then, but you stay close and hold my hand. I hate coppers, I do.'

'Good girl,' he said but his enthusiasm wasn't matched by his thoughts. It wouldn't be easy. Colleen would have to attend a trial and sit in a box and be frightened and confused out of her wits by Atkins's lawyer. Gerry would work on Colleen in the meantime and build up her courage for that day.

They went up the stairs and into the lion's den.

'Thank you, miss,' Constable Stevens said after Colleen had told him everything. 'Now, is it the truth this time?'

'The last time I was frightened,' Colleen said looking at Gerry. 'That man threatened me.'

'As you say,' Stevens said. 'Very well. Please wait while I write out this statement.'

They went and sat down on a nearby bench. Gerry patted Colleen's hand. 'You did well, girl. Did well.'

'That's the easy bit, Gerry. The hard bit's to come.'

Five minutes passed and Stevens called them over. 'Please read and sign at the bottom of the sheet,' he said.

Colleen read her statement, dipped the quill and scratched her name. 'What's the date?'

'The nineteenth of August,' the policeman replied.

Colleen completed the form and asked, 'What happens now?'

Stevens blotted the statement and placed it in the file. Easy for him, Gerry thought. All he has to do is give the paperwork to the prosecutors and his job's finished. Worry lines creased Colleen's forehead, making him wonder if he was doing the right thing.

'I'll give this to Inspector Neild,' Stevens said. 'Two doctors have stated that Atkins's left wrist deformity was from birth and not recent. With your testimony, miss, we'll be able to arrest Mr Atkins, because you have reaffirmed your eyewitness account of that deformity. If you hadn't been at the Hero's bar that Easter Monday night and overheard Miller talking to him, Atkins would have got away with sabotage, manslaughter, and conspiracy to murder.'

'And the bit about me changing my story?'

'Did you see any of that in your statement?'

Colleen shook her head.

'Then that's settled,' he replied.

Gerry knew he'd done the right thing. A murderer was a murderer. Justice had to be done.

'It wasn't easy, Constable,' Colleen said. 'When will I have to go to court?'

Gerry caught the constable's eye before he could say anything. 'Let's leave these good men to do their job,' Gerry said. 'Come on, come with me and I'll shout you a meal.' At the front doors of the station, Gerry said. 'You go outside and get some air, love. I want to speak to the police about another matter.' Gerry went back to the front desk. 'She'll have to go to court, won't she?' he said.

Stevens nodded. 'It's a murder case, Mr Gleeson, serious, and she'll be put in the box for sure. I saw your look. It'll be rough for her but it'll be short. It's damaging evidence and the defence won't have much to throw at her.'

'Let's hope so. She's a good lass, doing the right thing.'

'We'll look after her, Mr Gleeson, don't worry.'

The dusk had started to darken Clarissa's bedroom when Stella came in.

She went to the window and drew the curtains closed. 'Here's a letter for you, ma'am,' she said. 'It was hand-delivered. Would you like to read it or shall I take it downstairs for tomorrow?'

'No, leave it,' Clarissa said. 'Could you help me sit up please, Stella?'

Stella helped her and plumped the pillows up before Clarissa leaned back on them. Clarissa tried to reach out to adjust her bedside light but could not. Her arms seemed weaker than yesterday and any energy she had seemed to ebb from her like a leak from a full bucket.

'Let me do that,' Stella said.

'Thank you.' Once the light was on, she took the letter and sank back to open it. 'That will be all, thank you, Stella. I'm not hungry. I don't feel like eating.'

'But you must have some dinner, ma'am. You haven't eaten for two days and only had water. It's not right. I'm worried about you.'

Stella, who'd been her maid and close companion ever since she'd arrived in the colony, had a worried look on her face. Clarissa felt a constriction in her throat from her feelings for her friend. 'I'll be all right, really. I'm just feeling a bit run down. Just leave me for the moment.' Stella still looked worried but she left.

Clarissa was exhausted. After her fainting attack a fortnight previously, which the doctor attributed to her pregnancy, she seemed better. Then about a week ago she'd felt awful again, but fortunately no dizziness this time. What could it be? No high temperatures, that ruled out influenza. But her body felt like a heavy sack. The only place was bed. The doctor had prescribed tonics and mumbled something that she was just having a turn and she would be all right in a week.

Her thoughts turned to John. During this time in bed, she had thought of little else, which had aggravated her weariness. He had seen her on a few occasions and his look concerned her.

Her mother told her that, yes, she knew about Beth Blackett and her shareholding but had wanted to keep it from her. Clarissa was at first angry, then understood and was grateful. The six weeks since Bathurst had been difficult, but then she'd had that dream, which seemed to assuage her concerns about John.

She wanted distraction and took the envelope, opened it with difficulty and started to read its contents by the gaslight.

The letter felt heavy, as if some invisible pressure was pushing it down. Its words appeared jumbled, and dizziness pressed her eyes. She concentrated. It was from Henry Blackett, and in two paragraphs he told Clarissa that Beth was John's mistress and that their affair had started in July the previous year. The single page slipped onto the bed sheet and a wave of nausea flooded Clarissa's stomach, the most violent yet, but she couldn't vomit. There was nothing in her.

This letter. This was the final evidence. Despite John's protestations, he'd been accused by the one man who could be certain of his guilt. She had fought all alone to convince herself of John's faithfulness, and now this.

John and Beth. Why hadn't she believed they were lovers?

The nauseous wave continued, forcing her fists to clench. It began to subside, and a dull ache trembled through her lower body. She closed her eyes and floated as the wave receded. Then she felt the pain lessen and she saw in front of her the smiling face of her father.

~

A little while later, Stella came into Clarissa's bedroom to check on her before she herself went to bed. Her mistress was lying awkwardly in the bed and she went over to make her more comfortable. When she got there she noticed that Clarissa lay as still as a statue and her eyes were open.

'Ma'am! Ma'am!' Stella cried, and shook her. But she knew her mistress and friend was lifeless. Stella's legs gave way and she knelt by the bed. 'On my God ... no, no.' A coldness filled her and she jumped up, terrified. Fleeing the bedroom she ran downstairs. 'Sir! Sir, come quickly.' John came out of the drawing room. 'It's Mrs Leary, sir. Please come.'

'What's wrong?'

The maid stood there clasping and unclasping her hands like a marionette. 'Please!'

She ran back up the stairs and John followed her. 'What's wrong?' he said. 'Please tell me.'

Going into the bedroom, Stella stopped. John came behind her, paused, then moved closer to the bed. 'Clarissa?' he said. He touched her, then shrank back, startled by the coldness of her skin.

He stared for several seconds, then pulled back the bedclothes to examine her. He ran his hands over her, pushing aside a piece of paper as he did so.

'There's no blood ... there is no blood.' Raising her head a little, he felt around it and then eased it back on the pillow. Rising, he walked around the room, going to the window and then back to the bed. 'How? Why?' He sat down on the bed and his shoulders sagged. He brought his hands to his face for a moment and then dropped them by his side. 'Get the doctor, Stella,' he said. 'I'll stay here till he comes.'

John didn't hear Stella leave as he reached over and closed Clarissa's eyes, her skin cold under his hands. She was there in the bed in front of him, and she was dead. She and her baby were dead. He looked at her but didn't see her clearly. It was as if he were looking through a thick glass, the vision obscured, like looking at something in a museum where you had to focus on the specimen in front of you. Picking up the piece of paper, he read it and dropped it to the floor. Invisible arms trapped and clasped him.

He was still like this when the doctor came. John moved out of the way, as if in a trance. Voices spoke to him, but he heard nothing. He was aware, however, of the bed being stripped and other men coming in, men in dark suits. The smell of carbolic was pungent. Then somebody pressed his elbow, steered him like a yard trolley out of the room and down the stairs. Faces, some he knew, some he didn't, drifted in front of him, then disappeared, and time had no meaning.

In the days following, he was still in a trance-like state, going through daily motions as if he was watching himself do these things from a distance. It reminded him of the time he'd employed a labourer, a simple man. The man would come to site, nod once or twice to his fellow workmates, then go about his tasks during the day until someone would come to take him home. Sometimes John had envied him, because he had no stress, no worries, no responsibilities. Sometimes the man had smiled at John, a smile full of love, genuine and meaningful.

He was like that labourer now, sitting in front of an official who was talking about Clarissa. Beside this man was another man, with a bald head and glasses, clothed in a white jacket, whom John remembered from somewhere. This man's voice opened the door to John's consciousness. As though he were seeing the sun illuminate the morning sky, he rejoined the real world.

'It was large, Mr Leary,' the doctor said. 'The size of an orange, the biggest tumour I have seen in that area.'

John concentrated. A tumour? 'I'm sorry doctor, did you say a growth? Where?'

The doctor glanced at the official beside him, who nodded. 'Mr Leary,' the doctor continued, 'we had to do an autopsy to determine the cause of your wife's death. It was necessary, under the circumstances.'

An autopsy, John thought. A vision exploded before him: his naked Clarissa lying on a slab, exposed to strangers and being cut up. Tension filled him and he forced his eyes shut, trying to expel the horror.

'Your wife had a massive growth on her child-bearing organs. It's something we find often and unfortunately there are no symptoms to indicate this illness.'

John opened his eyes. 'But the baby?'

'There was no foetus. It was the cancer.'

John tried to understand. 'But her symptoms? There were all . . . like she was going to have a baby?'

The doctor sat back and folded his hands on his lap. 'This is a sad fact, Mr Leary that the illness, in part, gives the impression of pregnancy and presents no outward signs of pain or loss of bodily functions. Sometimes there is a weight loss.'

'Yes,' John said and he nodded his head twice, the movement forcing muscles to act. He wasn't dreaming. 'My wife lost weight recently, but then she seemed to get better and she put it

back on.'

'That's just it,' the doctor said, looked again at the official, who nodded again. The doctor stood up, collected his papers and walked around and stood in front of John. 'I'm very sorry, Mr Leary. It's times like these we feel frustrated by not knowing more about this kind of cancer. Maybe in the future we will.' Reaching out, he placed a hand on John's shoulder. Clarissa was dead. His wife, his partner, his beloved, was no more. The doctor's pressure on his shoulder made him start to face that fact.

The day after the funeral, John started back at Leary's at a pace as if the liquidators were due by midday to close him down. Nothing was overlooked. He attacked every part of the business and in the first three days slept in snatches on a camp bed in his office. In sleep, people and events came together in no pattern, but Clarissa wasn't among them.

John faced each day as a single unit of his life left, to fill in as wanted. Another day followed that with the same approach. This effort was his contribution to both Leary's and his son, seeking no gain other than to provide for both, with no enthusiasm.

Wounded by the loss of Clarissa, he tried to heal his pain, but each day it reappeared. Clarissa's eyes, begging him to be honest with her, sharpened the pain. Richard's fingers pulling at his cheek or the gurgle of his laugh sometimes numbed it. There was no pattern to it. He lived with it but the wound called the tune.

Christine tried to help him but John ignored her.

He'd flung off the numbness of Clarissa's death, letting work take its place. He continued to drive everyone hard, demanding they keep to his hours, not theirs; arranging meetings, rescheduling building programs and exacting latest figures and cost reports.

On a warm September morning, in the course of one of these audits, he was sitting with Dan Reynolds when his eyes locked onto a name on the paper in front of him. 'The shareholder list is incorrect,' he said. 'Mrs McGuire has no shareholding in the company. She's a shareholder of—'

'No, Mr Leary,' Reynolds said. 'Phoenix, the trust that held the shareholding, sold the shares to Mrs McGuire.'

John baulked. He held forty per cent of Learys, Sean nine per cent. He knew Beth held the rest. 'When did this happen?' he said.

'We received papers from Mrs McGuire's solicitors last week. The transaction was done on the twenty-third of July.'

'That's not right,' John said in a quiet voice.

The accountant sighed. 'With your wife's death, I kept it from you and all, but yes, Mr Leary, Mrs McGuire has fifty-one per cent of the stock. She's—'

'Get out of here.'

Reynolds gathered his files and stood up. 'I'm sorry.'

'Get out,' John said and waited for his accountant to leave before grabbing his hat and racing out of his office and yelling at the bewildered clerk, 'I'm going to see Christine McGuire at Point Piper.'

His thighs burned as he pressed his horse onward, glad of the wind cooling his face. Beth had sold her share. Why? She didn't need the money. Why hadn't she told him she was going to sell? He would have bought her share! Christine McGuire now controlled everything.

John had to act. He worked through his strategy on the way. Throwing the reins to a servant, he bounded up the front steps of the McGuire house. 'Is Mrs McGuire in?' he said to the startled servant in the foyer.

'Yes, she is, sir. I'll tell her you're here.'

'I'll follow you.'

In her drawing room, Christine sat reading. She looked up. 'John! Can I help you?'

He stopped to get his breath. Christine's head thrust forward like a ship's bow and he saw challenge in her eyes. She put the book down and clasped her hands and he sensed she was prepared for confrontation.

Walking into the room he stood in front of her and said, 'So, you've got Beth's share.'

'I have. It cost me more than it should have but I wanted control. My daughter—' Christine's jaws clenched, but it seemed she didn't want to show any weakness, and continued. 'Clarissa couldn't see what you are, blind to your faults. I tried to tell her.'

'Yes, like that filthy letter Blackett wrote about me,' he said.

She seemed surprised. 'I told no one of your affair, other than my daughter.'

John kept her stare, as if to break that bond meant she'd won the first round. 'That was my business,' he said.

'Not when it affected Clarissa, it wasn't! Yes, I bought Blackett's share. I had to. Clarissa was too fine a woman. She believed everyone and only saw the good in people. You took that love and destroyed it. She needed a champion to save her.'

'But you haven't, have you?' John said with sadness. Grief was now replacing his anger.

Christine blinked and seemed to understand his distress. 'No, I haven't. But I have saved her estate and Richard's future. I've got carriage of everything that will be his.'

John reached back and felt the comfort of the nearby chair. It's true, he thought. He'd been remiss and now Christine controlled the lot.

'I feel no joy in taking what you prized more than anything,' she said. 'But I had to get Mrs Blackett out of all our lives. I wanted you and Clarissa to be the married couple you started out to be.'

'I don't believe you.'

'John, I saw your grief at the funeral and through this week. It seemed genuine.'

'It was.'

'You will have to live with that and I can't help you there.'

'Selling me back your share would be a start,' he said.

She paused. 'No. I've seen you change over these years and I'm convinced that if my daughter had not died you would have continued your life as it was.'

She was wrong in that.

'So I had to make a decision,' Christine said, standing up. 'Clarissa's needs came first. I wanted to control Leary's for one reason—to make you change for the better. To make you see the love Clarissa had for you and for you to repay that love by being trustworthy, sincere and faithful to her.'

The full impact of what she had tried to do hit him. 'But I can't, now!'

'No, you can't, but you can prove it to *me*,' she said. 'Over time.'

John's sadness vanished and he became angry. Christine would never give him back what was rightfully his. He pushed himself up from the chair and faced her, wanting to force her to change her mind. Her shoulders were squared and he admired her courage, not to move or call out.

'Can I get you some refreshments, sir?' said a voice behind him.

John turned to the servant and then back to Christine. His anger was now under control. Would he have attacked her? 'No, I'm leaving,' he said. 'Christine, you've started this on your terms, but be assured that I will end it on mine.'

John brushed past the servant, left and rode back to his office, where he was greeted by a scared clerk.

'There's a gentleman to see you, sir. A Mr Blackett.'

Blackett? Henry Blackett? About Beth no doubt, John thought as he went up the stairs. If Blackett wanted a confrontation, John was in the mood to give him one.

Blackett's forehead glistened with perspiration as John came towards him. 'I want to see you, Leary,' he said. 'It's about my wife.'

John nodded and said. 'Come in here.' He closed his office door after him.

'I'm thinking of divorcing her,' Blackett said.

'You're a low life,' John said, his voice shaking. 'Sending that stinking letter to my wife.'

The horse breaker seemed unmoved. 'I'm naming you as co-respondent in my wife's adultery.' Blackett ran his hands around the brim of his hat. 'I'm sorry that your wife has died, but don't think that gives you a free hand with mine.'

There's no chance of that.

'She's leaving Sydney.' Blackett stepped closer. 'It's queer the way life works. She's told me she doesn't want to see you again and will never marry you. That's what she says and you know something, Leary, I believe her. Her religion is too precious to her and she can't remarry.'

'Is that all?'

'It is. I bid you good day.'

John walked back to his desk. 'See your own way out, Mr Blackett,' he said. 'Just remember, if you lay a finger on Beth, you're gone.'

'Ah! That's a threat. Good, that makes it easy.'

'Get out.'

John watched Blackett leave. What a day, he thought and slumped in his chair. But there was a much more urgent challenge. Leary's Contracting was no longer his—no longer his! He reached for a pencil and started scribbling.

Christine might have the ownership of his company but he had the know-how and the contacts. Her position on top would be short, very short.

~

On a late-October afternoon, Gerry Gleeson followed the publican through an open door to a room next to Cochrane's public bar. 'Thank you,' he said.

'Would you like a drink?' the publican asked, smiling.

Gerry was choking for one but would wait. 'Not just now.'

The publican nodded, left and closed the door after him. It was four-thirty and John was late. He had agreed to meet Gerry here this afternoon but he might not come. Yes, Gerry had heard rumours of John's affair but wouldn't judge him. Gerry had kept close to John these last two months and had tried to console him, but his nephew was not opening up to him about his grief. John had not mourned, not right away, working hard instead. That was understandable—to a point. But about a month ago, something had happened. It was as if all the stuffing had come out of him. John had become soft-spoken, attentive to others' views, and had lost weight. All that might well have been due to Clarissa's death but it could be something else and Gerry was keen to find out. He did not want to see John fall sick. In the road gangs, Gerry had seen despair kill strong men.

The door opened and John came in. He'd lost more weight in the last two weeks. Gerry gestured a chair opposite him.

'How are you faring?' Gerry said.

His nephew looked at him as if he was being threatened. This was a worrying development and Gerry was disturbed.

'Middling,' John said. 'Was that all?'

'Would you like a drink?'

'Yes . . . I would.'

'I'll get them.' Gerry went into the public bar where Rupert Jenkins and Jack Johnson were deep in talk. Jenkins spotted Gerry and he waved. On his way back from the bar, Gerry went by their table. 'I'm having a chat with John,' he said.

'We saw him come in,' Jenkins said. 'Ask him to join us when you're done.'

'I'll tell him.'

Gerry went back into the room and closed the door. John was staring out the window. He kept this up even when Gerry put the drinks down. 'Still feeling the loss?' he said.

John's face was tense and wary, as if Gerry were a stranger. Then his face relaxed. 'I am, Uncle. I am.'

'Are you spending more time with your boy?'

'Not as much as I should. You see'—John's eyes filled—'I don't know what to tell him. I've struggled. When he asks for his mother, it tears at me. I've said she's gone to heaven. But how, dear God, can you explain to a near two-year-old what all that means? How?'

Gerry was going to reply but John continued. 'It's Stella who's been the strength for him, and his aunt and his grandmother.'

'John, they're family. It's what we do.'

'Christine has been good, I'll admit.' John exhaled. 'You know she owns most of the company now?'

This was startling news. 'I didn't know,' Gerry said.

'Yeah, well that's another matter.' His eyes looked despairing, 'I'm trying to change. I am.'

'I know,' Gerry said. 'How about I come to your house this weekend? Maybe I can help you and your boy. What do you say?'

John looked away. He sighed, then looked at Gerry. 'Would you like to bring Auntie Moira, too?'

'Let's just you and I spend some more time together for a while. We can then see what happens.'

John put his hand out. Gerry clasped it and squeezed. 'It'll be rough for a while, still.'

'I know. I've got a lot to do and some bridges to mend.'

Gerry believed him and released his hand. 'Your beer's gone flat. Leave it there and go and join some people you know in the pub.'

John looked on guard again. 'What people?'

'Rupert Jenkins and Jack Johnson.'

John shook his head. 'Not yet. They're some of those bridges I've got to mend!'

'Healing starts with people you know, and here is as good a place as any. Come on.'

As they walked over to join Jenkins and Jack, John was surprised by their warm welcome. He felt he didn't deserve it after the way he had treated them. These men had been loyal friends and he had not valued them, just as he hadn't valued Clarissa. He'd never be able to make it up to her, but he could to these men and to the others, especially Sean.

∼

John was in his drawing room at Point Piper, reading poetry and finding some comfort in it, when Maureen came in.

'I thought I'd see how you were.' She looked at his book. 'Byron?'

'No, too close to home. Coleridge.'

'A good choice. How are you?'

'Not bad, considering. How's Liam?'

Maureen took off her hat. 'Liam is well. Saturdays, he still tutors. It's warm, isn't it?'

'It's the middle of November, Maureen,' John said.

'I know and Christmas is nearly here.'

Stella came in and handed Maureen a cool drink.

'And Michael and Irene?' John asked.

'A handful, both of them.' She looked at the maid. 'Thank you, Stella. How is Richard?'

'He'll welcome your visit as always, Mrs Forde.'

'And you? Are you coping?'

Stella's lips trembled. 'Oh, Mrs Forde, I miss her, I do.' She glanced at John. 'It still feels like she's here and I call her sometimes, forgetting.' Stella reached for a handkerchief and Maureen went to her.

'There, there.' Maureen comforted the maid and John stood up and went to the window and looked out.

After a few minutes Stella settled herself. 'Thank you Mrs Forde, you've been very kind.'

Maureen said, smiling, 'I'll come and see Richard in a moment.' After Stella left, Maureen sat down near John. 'I hear you've been busy?'

He turned to her, his hands in his pockets. 'Things need doing and I'm it.'

'Come, sit down,' she said. John hesitated then sat beside her. He always knew Maureen could find the weak link in his armour. 'You're soft, you always were, and things got to you. Remember?' she said.

'That's a long time ago. I was a child then.'

'True, but our family back home went through tough times and we pulled through, together. This horrible time for you will pass, even though you think it mightn't. I'll be here for you, like you were for me in Dublin.'

John thought differently: when his sister was raped, he had done very little for her in the short time he'd had available before sailing for New South Wales.

'Just you being there,' she said, 'and seeing me in hospital, was sufficient for me to get strength, because you were family. I'll be here for you now.'

He pressed her hand and looked out to where the sea lapped at the cove. Ever since the deaths of his three men, one thing had kept him going—making sure he and Leary's survived. Keeping going had enabled him to get justice for his dead comrades. Soon the man who had ordered the fatal sabotage would come to trial. But the struggle had cost him. 'Clarissa never understood what I went through,' he said.

'She did, Johnny. You just didn't let her help you.'

Clarissa had loved him, accepted him, and he had failed her. In his arrogance he had built and then destroyed everything he lived for. He'd created a legacy, he thought . . . but what a joke that was. Despite all he'd achieved—the power and the wealth—he'd lost the one thing of real value.

Many seconds passed and then he concentrated on his sister, who was looking at him earnestly.

'Come,' she said. 'Let's play with Richard. That's where you'll get strength from, too.'

On the last day of November, a weekday, John left work just after his noon meal and went to a site in Clarence Street, a new two-storey bank. Its internal timberwork required the services of a specialist carpenter and joiner.

John wanted Sean back in the company. Maybe Sean didn't want to work with him again but he had to try to convince him. Sean was his mirror, the man who shone John's conscience back at him, and he needed it.

The foreman gave John directions and he climbed a ladder to the first floor. He walked onto the sweet-smelling pine floorboards to stand behind a man who was assembling the last of a series of single box-framed windows. John still considered this type of window a logical and practical invention. The timber frames of the window contained a track in which the sashes could slide vertically and a box in which the balance weights of each sash could operate. The carpenter was now plumbing up the pulley stile or frame that was fixed against the brick opening. The brass pulleys were set into the stiles at the head. He waited until the craftsman checked both stiles with a spirit level.

'It's looks easy enough,' John said. 'But only a man who knows what to do can do it without effort.'

Sean turned around at the sound of the voice. 'Aye, you can be sure of that,' he said as he rested his spirit level. John put out his hand, not knowing whether his old friend would take it. He prepared himself for rejection, but Sean's grip still hurt. 'Want a closer look?' Sean said.

John went to the unglazed window and took in the quality of its assembly. Leaning against the brickwork near him were two quadrant-shaped lengths of finished timber, the storm moulds. These were the same length as the height of the window and would be fixed to the outside of the frame to seal up the opening between the frame and the brickwork. John looked out at the building next door.

'The warehouse,' Sean said. 'Odd that, here I am working right alongside where the sabotage happened. See the brickwork? It's weathering nicely, can't see the join.'

John's stomach turned. Yes, so long ago . . . but was it? 'No, you can't tell,' he said.

Sean started sweeping up. 'That place knocked me, it did. Those men being killed. Atkins will hang, I'm sure. Not that it makes me feel better. You know, Bob Jones heard a prison guard talk about our murderer. The man said that Atkins was a big-ticket Freemason and he hated Catholics. He would pace his cell and curse us all. Maybe that's what drove him, who knows. But that's life.'

John agreed. All those deaths, for what? Death made him think of Clarissa. He shook his head and looked at the man in front of him. He said, 'How are things with you?'

'I could tell you about it over a beer,' Sean said. 'If you have the time.'

John held his breath and tried to control the relief he felt, then yielded to it. It beat his pain, any day. 'Your shout.'

At Mass in the week before Christmas, John stood in the cathedral, with his son Richard beside him and the maid, Stella. Stella's hair looked as though it was touched with powder, but John knew it was the grey of grief's stamp, which had also drawn down the skin each side of her mouth, making her look older than her years. Since Clarissa's death she'd brought Richard closer to her, not leaving his side. John thought she fussed over him too much, but understood her need to maintain the connection with Clarissa.

When the service had finished, John stood on St Mary's steps and spoke to worshippers that he and Clarissa had known. He was still receiving commiserations from people who hadn't been at the funeral or attended the house afterwards. Every time someone mentioned Clarissa, a knife seemed to stab his heart, tearing its rawness.

His uncle came up to him. He and John had spent the last three Sundays together and Gerry's continuing and supporting company was having a good effect.

'I thought of coming back home with you today,' Gerry said kindly. 'But not if I'm intruding.'

John said, 'You're always welcome, Uncle. Don't let me keep you standing—wait in the carriage if you like.' He glanced at his son. 'Richard will go along with you, won't you, son?'

'Come, Richard,' Stella said. 'Let's go to the carriage with your great-uncle Gerry.'

'Thank you, Stella,' John said as the three moved away.

John stayed on the steps, surprised by the number of people who wanted to speak to him. He knew there had been gossip about himself and Beth, but because Blackett had made no move to divorce her, it had remained rumour only. Now his wife had died, and people were prepared to express sympathy. John was still acceptable in society, as this sad day showed.

John had just said goodbye to the last gentleman who had come up to pay his respects when he saw Beth, a few paces away. His first reaction surprised him; it wasn't excitement or want, or even nervousness that she might be recognised, it was pleasure at seeing an old friend.

'Hello, John,' Beth said. 'I went to your wife's funeral, you know, but I stood at the back. I'm . . . very sorry for you.'

Her words soothed him. She hadn't been in his thoughts each day but had popped into his dreams like an uninvited guest. John looked around for Blackett. Was she alone?

She said, 'I'm going away. I'm leaving Sydney, for good.'

'Your husband told me he wanted a divorce. Is that what's happening?'

'No. In the eyes of the church Henry and I will always be man and wife. We've decided to separate instead. He stays here and I'm going to Melbourne. There'll be no talk about us there.'

John didn't know whether to be relieved or not. 'When do you leave?'

'In two days.' She paused. 'I wanted to see you before I go, for two reasons, both hard.'

She still looked lovely, but he was not tempted. 'Tell me,' he said.

'I wanted to test myself, and to give you my condolences in

person. You see, I feel guilty about what happened to Clarissa. Not her illness, but what she must have been through because of us.'

'So do I. What I could have done—no, *should* have done—is with me every hour of each day.'

Beth nodded. 'Walk with me, John.'

John moved down the steps with her. Her elbow touched his but he felt nothing.

'It feels like revenge to Henry, throwing me out. But I can do without him, and I'll make a new life in Melbourne.'

He said nothing and they walked on a little further. The lemon scent she wore was fragrant.

She stopped and turned to him. 'Melbourne was familiar to my father. I have people down there who can help me with my horses. Henry and I will cross paths, I'm sure, in that business.' Beth's eyes glistened and she gripped her purse. 'At least in that we can talk civilly.' She looked down. 'My sisters want to go, and my mum. I'll be all right.' Beth looked up at him and her hand reached out. 'You'd better join your son. He'll need you more than ever now.'

John took her hand. 'I want to say something to you.'

Beth brought her chin up. Her lips parted.

'I . . .'

'No need to say anything, John. We have'—Beth closed her eyes for a moment—'*had* something wonderful that we shared.'

He pressed her hand. 'I wish you all happiness, in whatever you do . . . wherever you are.' He felt the pressure returned by her slim fingers, only for an instant, and then she dropped his hand and walked away.

ACKNOWLEDGMENTS

Grateful thanks go to Bert Hingley, my mentor. His insightful, pragmatic and thoughtful contribution informed the work to a better level.

Cheryl Sawyer, herself a published and respected historical fiction author, managed the myriad sequences of production in a seamless way and deftly highlighted details in the work.

Final editing credit goes to Kathy Mossop, who helped me greatly in nuancing and deepening the protagonist's character in his struggles.

The builders of the colony get my thanks and admiration. Without their passion, sweat and contribution, their legacy and the world-class quality of today's built environment would not have been possible.

HISTORICAL NOTE

At the time when this novel begins, wealth was flowing from the goldfields into the economy and a builder like John Leary would certainly have attracted clients who needed his talents. According to JM Freeland in his *Architecture in Australia, a History*: 'The newly rich men of means wanting large and substantial warehouses and offices; town councils wanting magnificent city halls befitting their new-found place in the sun; the churches with coffers filled by affluent respectability-seeking parishioners wanting larger and proper Gothic edifices; the publicans wanting imposing palaces in which to milk a sybaritic clientele, and tens of thousands of people just wanting a home—all this created a splendiferous boom for the building fraternity.' The Park Street Hall Memorial project is fictional; however, it typifies the scale of buildings constructed and planned.

The prefabricated wall frames trucked to sites around Australia for modern project homes had their beginning in the 1850s. Borrowing from an American idea, the colonies' builders succeeded in '... joining the corners so that the whole length of wall frame could be cut and nailed together conveniently and quickly on the ground then levered upright into position. At first the frame was set on timber blocks fixed to a continuous timber bottom plate buried an inch or two below ground level but this practice later gave way to separate squared timber stumps with a timber sole nailed to the bottom to spread the weight and sunk 18 inches or more deep. Rot-resisting hardwoods such as red gum were used in these vulnerable positions and were often painted with creosote to increase the durability.'

David McGuire's fictional Superior Sheeting Company would have been equally busy. The sheet-metal product was made to be more durable and cheaper than before. The process of galvanising, in which the sheets of corrugated puddled-steel were protected by a skin of non-rusting zinc, had been patented in England in 1837. The sheets of iron that came to Australia in the 1850s were all galvanised.

Architectural styles during this period ran along the lines of Gothic for ecclesiastical work and schools, classical for public buildings and a 'frivolous impure dress of either for houses'. Flamboyance abounded as gold-rich people tried to outdo each other with their dwellings.

Another Australian contribution to world building techniques was the cavity wall. In order to prevent the ingress of moisture from the outside, paint used to be applied, but this was ineffective. By 1854 two methods had been imported from England and were in limited use. One was a partially constructed hollow wall of two skins of brickwork; the other was made by the London method. 'This was an 11 inch (230 mm) wall where the stretcher bricks on the inner face were corbelled two inches, leaving a gap between them and the outside neighbour. To enable the inside face of the wall to be plastered, batons were fixed to the corbelled bricks and onto those were nailed close-spaced, thin, oregon lathes to form a key for the plaster. There was no direct path for water

to pass between the outer face and the plaster but there was still an indirect connection.' This was at least a start and by the next 25 years a full cavity wall eventuated, where both skins of brickwork were separated and only connected by mild-steel wall ties.

A History of Australia by Manning Clark, Volume Four, has also been a rich resource. The following facts helped build the world of *Unshackled*.

By the beginning of 1854 Cobb & Co's coaches were acknowledged to be the easiest conveniences in the colonies, the drivers distinguished by their civility, and the horses by their perfection. Before Freeman Cobb returned to America in May 1856 he was given a dinner in Melbourne to honour the great benefits he had conferred on the colony by his energetic and successful efforts to establish communication with the interior.

On the 3 March 1854, there was the beginning of limited telegraphic capacity in Victoria.

At Sofala and the Turon at the end of 1854, three thousand diggers were furiously burrowing in the ground.

A worker might end up the owner of a mansion he had worked on as a builder's labourer.

On the 26 March 1856, it was resolved in Melbourne, by a meeting of workers including stonemasons, that an 8-hour day be introduced in April of that year.

In January 1856, Van Diemen's Land became the colony of Tasmania.

On polling day for the electorate of Sydney in March 1856, fights broke out between the ten to twelve thousand people at the racecourse as discussion between the supporters grew warm.

The New South Wales government did take over the Great Southern and Western Railway Co in September 1855. The journey from Sydney Station to Parramatta took 50 minutes and the No 1 Locomotive ran on 14 miles of Barlowe Rails. It stopped at four stations: Newtown with its few buildings, Ashfield and its market gardens, Burwood among its gentlemen's residences, and Homebush with its racecourse. The first-class fare was four shillings per passenger.

So, great wealth, magnificent buildings, railways, new forms of communication and a burgeoning new form of electoral government all happened in the background of the second novel in the Sandstone Trilogy.

THE AUTHOR

Michael Beashel is Sydney-born and his Irish forebears immigrated to New South Wales in the 1860s and settled in Millers Point. He spent his youth in Bondi, is married with adult children and lives in Sydney's inner-west.

Beashel was head of Asset Development for a global accommodation services company registered on the NYSE and has made his mark in some of Australia's iconic construction companies. In Sydney, he has restored government buildings such as the Customs House and the Town Hall, and completed commercial buildings in the private sector. In SE Asia, he managed a construction division that built apartments and hotels in Bangkok and Ho Chi Minh City.

This industry—its characters, clients, trades people, designers and bureaucrats—provides rich material for his writing. He has an eye for the emergence of Sydney's built form, from the early days of the colony to the present, and a love of construction. He says about his writing, 'It's a passion. I revel in using the building industry as a tapestry to weave a great tale seasoned with historic facts and memorable characters. Human shelter is an essential need and I suspect people have a fascination for understanding its context and construction within their societies. Australia still is a young country but there are many, many outstanding building stories.'

Beashel holds a B. App. Science (Building) from Sydney's UTS and is a member of the NSW Writers' Centre. *Unshackled* is his second novel, the first is *Unbound Justice*, and *Succession* completes the Sandstone Trilogy.

Connect with the author

Author Website: https://michaelbeashel.com.au
Facebook: https://www.facebook.com/MichaelBeashelAuthor

Printed in Great Britain
by Amazon

14431617R00192